TRIGGER WARNINGS

For the full list of 44 trigger warnings, pleas e scan this QR code, where you will be directed to my website –

www.JodieKingAuthor.com

Authors Note: These warnings are laid bare; it is now your choice to read this book or not. Please take every single warning with seriousness and beyond. Your mental health matters.

PLAYLIST

STRAITJACKETS & ROSES — DIGGY GRAVES

CIRCUS PSYCHO — DIGGY GRAVES

CRADLES — SUB URBAN

JAWS — SLEEP TOKEN

DEATHBEDS — BRING ME THE HORIZON

THE DEATH OF PEACE OF MIND — BAD OMENS

DON'T LET ME GO — RONItT

ALKALINE — SLEEP TOKEN

SECRETS — NOMYN AND ANGELICCA

HEATHENS — TWENTY-ONE PILOTS

JOKER — DAX

CONTROL — BRYCE SAVAGE

Ever wondered what it's like to fucked by a clown?

And no. I'm not talking about your ex.

Welcome to Oddity Carnival & Cirque

This twisted tale is for you..

Leave your morals at the gate, because if you don't, Hell

will strip them from you, and make you take it like his good

Little Dolly.

PROLOGUE

Running fast through the dark forest, trees, and thorned bushes whizz past me, slashing at my skin and nightdress. The rain pelts down on my hot flushed skin and my feet tear over the rough, muddy earth. My breathing is erratic, the cold air piercing my lungs. The sounds of gunshots and dogs barking in the distance get closer behind me. I run for my life, desperate to escape, because I know if I am captured, I won't make it out alive twice. This is my only hope for freedom.

When I don't hear her behind me, I stop abruptly, skidding along the mud. "Arabella?" I yell, getting to my feet, my eyes darting around frantically in the darkness.

"Just run, we need to split! It's the only way!" She shouts back, but I can't make out where her voice is coming from.

"No," I cry, squeezing my eyes shut, disorientated from lack of energy.

"Please!" She begs. "Just go and don't look back! I'll be right behind you, I promise!"

I whirl around, wanting to find her. "I can't leave you, Ara!" I sob.

"Yes, you can! Now go!"

I hear the men gaining on us and I run. As I look back over my shoulder, I see her shadowy figure drifting away in the distance, being swallowed by the darkness. A cry escapes me, but I continue to run as fast as I can, not stopping for a second. Hoping that somewhere, we will reunite once again.

CHAPTER ONE

Exiting a broken-down gas station, I feel the warm, gritty wind playfully tangle my long, blonde locks. As I scan the huge sandy landscape stretching out before me, the bright sun burns my skin, and I think about where we should head to next.

As Eli enters my line of sight after appearing from the male restroom to my right, he closes the gap between us, peering at me over the rims of his sunglasses. He is dressed in a white tank top paired with worn, tattered jeans and his blonde hair dances, mirroring the gusty chaos around us as he adjusts himself.

When he is within reach, I offer him one of the cold bottles of water I had just brought. He accepts it, but I catch him lifting his sunglasses fully, his gaze drifting up to the grimy window. Curious, I move closer, taking my sunglasses off my face to look at the weathered poster that has a circus on it, the faded letters drawing me in.

Oddity Carnival & Cirque. Seeking dancers and extraordinary talents.

When his green eyes meet mine once again, he arches an eyebrow, leaving me wondering what he is thinking.

"Write down the address, Noir."

My brows pinch in confusion as I respond, "What?"

"We should see if we can join."

Returning my focus to the poster, I notice his eyes following suit. "But why?" I ask, my curiosity piqued.

He shrugs his shoulders before turning his head to look down at me again. "It's a carnival, maybe I can work there, but you can dance, right? They could take you into the circus."

My mind drifts back to a time when life felt carefree, and the memory of my brief escape through dance resurfaces, reminding me of the unfulfilled promise I made to my mom. Dancing, gymnastics, and aerial silks once made me feel truly alive, but it's been so long since I've felt even an ounce of that buzz. It's been years, yet I can't help but wonder that those skills might still be woven into the fabric of who I am.

His hand sneaks around my waist, pulling me closer to his tall frame, yet I remain distant, my gaze fixed on the circus image, lost in thought.

"It could just be short-term, so we can make some money to get our own place. Aren't you sick of the motels? The truck?" he says, his words laced with temptation.

I lift my eyes cautiously to his, observing his features and contemplating whether it's smart for me to settle in one place given my circumstances, but he continues. "I really think you can get this job and I am pretty sure they will hire me as well once they see what you can do."

I let out a defeated sigh, my palm gliding down his chest as I shake my head in response. "I haven't danced in years, E, and I'm not sure if—"

He kisses my forehead, cutting me off, and my eyes lower as he murmurs against it, "Have faith in yourself, Noir. I've seen the way you can move."

When he pulls back, he has a smirk on his lips, an eyebrow lifted. I chuckle while shaking my head before facing aside, yet I cannot shake the unsettling feeling inside my gut.

"Come on, sweetheart, it could be fun."

I gaze at the poster once again before finally pushing past my reluctance and taking my bag from my shoulder. Unzipping it, I retrieve my small doodle pad and a pen and glance back and forth between the poster and pad, hastily jotting down the address. As soon as I cap my pen, E takes my hand and guides me back to the truck without hesitation.

HOLLOW HELLION

As we drive, I reach into the dash compartment and pull out a map, trying to pinpoint the carnival's location. The wind tousles my hair through the open window beside me, but I squint, scanning the map until something sinister catches my eye. A large, desolated area surrounded by woodland stands out, its clearing eerily resembling an odd shape.

With confusion, I turn the map toward Eli, pointing to the strange landmark. "Does that look like a skull to you?"

He briefly takes his eyes off the road to glance at the map, letting out a soft chuckle before refocusing on the path ahead. "Fuck yeah, it does," he replies with a grin. "Don't tell me this is one of those messed up circuses."

My brows pinch as I lay the map on my lap. "Messed up circuses?" I repeat, my tone sceptical.

"Yeah, you know?" he sighs, slumping further in his seat. "Where they do weird and horrific acts."

I laugh, peering out of the window beside me. "Babe, maybe you've been watching too much TV," I tease, shaking my head.

I know telling Eli that is a big fat lie. I've seen the dark underbelly of this world firsthand, felt its cruel sting repeatedly and absolutely nothing surprises me. In my youth, I was surrounded by one of the most malevolent men in the States, which drove me into hiding. From what I remember, for a year, I wandered alone, sleeping rough or hitchhiking from one place to another. That's how Eli found me four months ago—alone and broken on the side of a road. I still don't know the full story of what happened or why I was in that state. The memories of the day I fled, and eight months after are hazy at best.

Eli has been my anchor ever since, being there for me when I had no one else. He is the only person I've let in since I left and we both carry scars from our pasts; he is a recovering heroin addict, and I have battled with self-harm. In each other's company, we've found peace in a strange way, a refuge from our fucked-up pasts. But love? That's a concept I struggle to grasp. I'm not sure if I'm even capable of it.

Despite my appreciation for Eli being in my life, there's a barrier between us—a barrier built from my hesitation to talk about my past. It's difficult for me to fully open up and show the darkness that lurks within me. Maybe that's what stops me from feeling any romantic love for him or it might be the fact that he doesn't make me feel anything at all. Yeah, we're in a sexual relationship, even if it lacks, but to me, that's all it is: friendship. I suppose it's more like friends with benefits, two people finding some kind of calm in each other's company during their lonely lives.

I know Eli possibly loves me, although he has never said it, and that realization weighs heavy on my heart. He shouldn't be in love with someone as damaged as I am. The wounds that scar my soul run deep, hidden from prying eyes, never to be shared despite the desperate need for someone to rely on. Trust issues cling to me like shadows, making it nearly impossible for me to show my true self to anyone.

Revealing the truth about who I am would leave me vulnerable, exposed not just to judgment and rejection but to death. Nothing in my life has ever been simple, and I am anything but simple. So, I keep my horrifying secrets locked away, protecting myself from the pain of letting someone in too close. It's a lonely existence, but it's the only one I know how to control.

The ache for my sister, Arabella, claws at me like a relentless itch, a gaping wound that refuses to heal. The thought of her out there lost and alone, hurts me. She was the only family I had left, and she was the only person who was there for me when no one else was. We ran together, but somewhere along the way, we were torn apart. Since that day, I've just hoped that she is still alive, but the thought that she might not be drives me into madness. My secret search for her has consumed me, pushing me to the brink of insanity as I try to explore every corner of the United States, desperate to locate her and until I find out what happened to my sister, I don't think I will ever find closure.

Sitting here, just the thought of her sends my heart into a frantic rhythm, hammering against my chest. My palms grow clammy, my mind swirling with the memory of her long, dark hair blowing in the rainy wind and her piercing blue eyes that would see right through me. Desperate for calm, I instinctively reach for my pills, stored inside the dash compartment and with trembling hands, I tilt my head back, popping a couple into my mouth before swallowing them down in the hope of squashing the anxiety that is threatening to boil over.

As the medication takes effect, I lean back with a heavy sigh, the tension slowly subsiding. I catch Eli's gaze out of the corner of my eye, but I can't bring myself to meet it, instead, I focus on the warmth of his hand sliding into mine.

"You alright?" he asks, his voice gentle.

With my head rested back, I face him, offering a soft smile.

"I'm fine," I reassure him. "We're not too far away now and we should get there by the time it's dark."

His nod is filled with concern before he shifts his focus back to the road ahead, and my thoughts drift to the time when Eli first found me. He wasted no time in getting me the help I desperately needed, taking me to a doctor who prescribed medication that feels like a fucking lifeline. The pills make me numb, and offer a brief respite, allowing me to catch my breath. Yet, despite their efficacy, I still find myself fighting with the insatiable urge to inflict pain upon myself. It is a twisted compulsion that I struggle with, especially in moments of depression. Pain, for me, is not just a beautiful sensation—it's a distraction, a means of escape from the relentless suffering in my mind. It's a contradictory haven, offering both release and peace from the chaos that rages inside me, quieting the urges that claw at my sanity.

Since my early teenage years, I had harboured the craving for self-harm and while blocking out what I was going through, I made pain my main focus, and I became obsessed with the feeling. It began innocently enough, with habits like pulling my hair out or pinching my skin because I didn't have access to anything else, but it wasn't until I left Chicago behind that I somehow found comfort with the razor's edge.

As my eyes trace the patterns of scars along Eli's arm, I notice how different they are from mine. They aren't the jagged slashes that spoil my forearms and inner thighs; instead, they are red dots, remnants of the toxic needles that once punctured his veins. When I first met him, he was already on his prescribed methadone, a huge step in his journey toward recovery from addiction and although I've never seen him inject heroin, I have seen the toll of withdrawal and the effects of his medication. I have never judged him for it, Eli has always been open about his struggles and it has built a bond of understanding between us, even if I have not been completely truthful with him in return.

We made a pact to never harm ourselves again in such destructive ways and so far, we've both stayed true to our word.

CHAPTER TWO

After some time of driving, we find ourselves surrounded by woodland as I direct Eli along the route. The setting sun casts shadows through the dense forest, dimming the road ahead and he flicks on the headlights, illuminating our path.

"Take this next right turn, Eli," I instruct, knowing we're close and as he does, our eyes catch sight of a looming sign that reads: "*Welcome to Oddity Carnival & Cirque. May your time here be terrifying, if you make it out alive.*"

A shiver runs down my spine at the ominous message, and for a quick moment, our gazes meet until Eli lets out a low chuckle, shaking his head in amusement. "What the fuck."

He returns his attention to the narrow road ahead, steering us further toward the heart of the carnival. As we emerge from the overgrowth of trees and drive onward, the weather suddenly shifts and the sky darkens, becoming a shade of grey. Gloom settles over the landscape, the bright day disappearing into a sombre atmosphere.

I spot the grand entrance in the short distance, and we drive through an archway decorated with faded torn banners that flap in the breeze with flickering lights hanging over the tall, spiked fence. The pathways stretch out before us, lined with empty booths and neglected attractions, their exteriors peeling.

"It seems to be closed," Eli says beside me.

While looking around, he seems to be right; there is no sign of life, and my confusion grows. I point with my finger towards the side of the path, urging him to pull over. "There must be someone here, E. The gates are open, right?"

As soon as the car comes to a halt, I unbuckle my seatbelt and reach for the door handle, but his hand on my thigh stops me. I turn to face him, and he addresses me firmly. "Put a sweater on."

His eyes linger on the scars on my arms, and a surge of irritation courses through me at the judgment in his eyes. Though I know they may be disgusting to some, they are a part of me and a proof of the strength I have found within myself.

With a grit of my teeth, I reach for my hoodie on the back seat, pulling it on to hide the marks and beside me, Eli follows suit, slipping into his own as if mirroring my actions.

"Are you sure you want to do this?" I question, my tone full of hesitation.

"Come on, Noir. It's not that bad. Besides, it'll be fun once we get used to it."

I let out a defeated sigh and open the door beside me. Once I am out of the car, I close it with a soft click, and my eyes scan the eerie surroundings. Even though the huge carnival appears normal on the outside, despite the ageing amusements, there is a noticeable weight in the air, a sense of unease. It's as if something isn't right like sinister spirits lurk in the shadows.

"I wonder where the Circus is?"

When Eli's voice breaks through the silence behind me, it causes me to jump, and I slam a palm against my racing heart. His big hands find my shoulders, trying to calm me, but I shrug them off with a flick before turning around to face him.

I'm not usually this jumpy; nothing generally fazes me. Fear is an unfamiliar feeling, an emotion I've lost beneath layers of myself, and I haven't felt anything in such a long time whether it is excitement, fear, or even sexual arousal; the only thing that truly haunts me is depression. It's just this place, the unsettling atmosphere; it stirs something within me that I can't put my finger on. But if there's one thing I've learned, it's that facing your fears head-on is the only way to destroy them, and even with the red flags flapping in front of my eyes, I won't turn away.

As Eli's gaze lingers on my face, his lips part as if he is about to speak, but I seize his hand in a sudden burst of energy and pull him along behind me, not waiting for him to say a word. I take the lead, my pulse quickening with each step and my gaze follows the path of my feet, noticing the weeds poking through large cracks in the pavement, nature reclaiming the space that was once its own.

As I dodge large puddles, lost in my thoughts, I lift my head but come to a sudden stop as soon as I spot it. Eli bumps into my back, startled, but my focus becomes fixated on the towering circus in the far distance. Beneath the grey clouds, its huge silhouette creates darkness over the landscape around it. The chilly wind whispers through the surrounding trees, but instead of carrying what would be the usual scent of candy, it brings a bite that scatters over the surface of my skin.

The circus tent stands imposing and foreboding, its once vibrant red and white stripes now faint and tattered, the flags on top, flapping ominously. Around the edge of the tent and carnival, the twinkling lights that stretch from post to post should bring comfort, but instead, they flicker and dim.. There's an unsettling force urging me to run another way, but it's also fighting with a strange magnetic pull that is drawing me closer. I hold Eli's hand tighter and continue forward, my interest outweighing my tinge of fear.

As we approach the looming entrance of the tent, it seems to grow larger with each step, shrinking us, and just as we're about to reach the threshold, we hear a deep males voice from behind, causing us to come to a stop.

"Hey!"

We turn around to see him closing the distance between us. An older man, dressed in faded blue dungarees and a dirty white tank top. His gaze flickers between me and Eli, a scowl etched onto his old face. "We're closed to visitors right now, that means you're trespassing."

Both Eli and I raise an eyebrow in unison, sharing quick eye contact. Giving a touch of my fake bubbly attitude to break through the tension, I am the first to speak. "Sorry, Sir. We're not visitors. We are here for employment after seeing a poster."

Suddenly, he breaks into a wide, creepy grin, revealing an almost toothless yet brown smile. With a heavy hand, he slaps Eli's back a few times, the force almost enough to wind him. "Well, why didn't you say so? I will take you to Madame right away!"

As he latches onto the top of Eli's arm with his short, grubby fingers, he drags him away from me with surprising strength. My eyes widen, and without hesitation, I quickly follow them inside the circus.

HOLLOW HELLION

As we step through the entrance of the tent, goosebumps immediately scatter across my skin. The air inside is thick with a musty scent, like old wood and decaying fabric. The space is dimly lit, with the only light coming from flickering lanterns that cast a creepy glow across the worn red carpet.

Walking further inside, the darkness seems to press in around us, enveloping us in a suffocating embrace that leaves me feeling unsettled and on edge, as if the very air itself is alive with evil energy. As I trail behind Eli and the old man, the fabric above us grows thicker. The old man draws back a red, velvet curtain, revealing a hidden room behind it and his eyes gleam with a wicked glint as he looks between me and Eli.

Stepping back, he gestures for us to enter the room and Eli takes a hesitant step forward first, his movements cautious as I follow closely behind him.

As soon as we walk into the smallish room, my eyes dart around, taking in the surroundings draped in fabrics of black, royal red and gold. Potent incense and candles assault my senses, reminding me of some kind of witch's cove.

My gaze is drawn to an oak chest of drawers that line the walls, decorated with sparkling crystals and mysterious ornaments. It's as if we have entered a hidden realm, a place where magic and mystery collide.

"Madame, we have visitors!"

As the old man's voice raises behind me, I step around Eli when he comes to a stop to see a large desk in the centre of the room. Behind it is a shimmering curtain that catches my eye, leading to another chamber.

Before I can fully grasp what is inside, a figure comes into view, only to be swiftly pulled back. An older woman steps through the curtain, her presence commanding attention.

Although she is a mature woman, which I estimate her to be in her fifties, she exudes an undeniable beauty. Her long black hair, streaked with grey, cascades down her back, framing her elegant features. She is dressed in a vintage-looking, long red dress with swirling patterns of gold.

Her dark eyes dart between Eli and me, her expression unreadable as she reaches for an unlit cigarette resting in the ashtray on the desk. She tucks the black cigarette holder between her lips, igniting the end with a match before extinguishing it with a flick of her wrist.

Taking a deep drag, she exhales a cloud of smoke into the air, the scent of tobacco mingling with the heady aroma of incense. As she circles around the desk, her gaze locks with mine, a silent intensity in her eyes. Stopping in front of me, she scans my face as if searching for something hidden beneath the surface before reaching out with a delicate touch, her fingers tangling in a few strands of my hair.

"What do you want?" she asks, her voice calm.

Holding her stare steadily, I fight the urge to look away. There is a flicker of curiosity in her orbs or perhaps something darker. As she cocks her head to the side, her eyes narrow ever so slightly. "Please don't waste my time, I am a very busy woman."

Raising an eyebrow in response, I inhale deeply before giving her a small nod. "We're here for employment."

She raises her chin suspiciously, her eyes shifting to Eli beside me, her scrutiny lingering on him. "You both have talents?"

Before Eli answers, I respond, taking charge of the situation.

"I do." I say with confidence.

Her deep brown eyes meet mine before trailing down my body while she takes a small step back. She draws another pull from her cigarette, the smoke curling around her.

"You dance?" she inquires with a lifted brow and raised chin.

I give a small nod and then she glances at Eli and my gut twists. "And what about you? What talents can you offer?"

I side-eye and watch Eli give a small head shake so, I try to explain. "We thought that maybe if you employ me into the circus, he can work in the carnival or at least learn how to do something. We need somewhere to stay and work."

She lets out a scoff, her eyes moving to mine. "Oh sweetheart, that is not how it works. I do not house people who cannot bring anything to my insane world. Anyone who lives here must work at the Cirque and I don't house outsiders."

I remain silent, my jaw tense with suppressed emotion as she waves me off dismissively. But, instead of obeying her gesture for some reason, I hold my ground, refusing to leave so easily as she attempts to walk away.

"You're missing out, lady," I declare boldly.

In an instant, she comes to a stop, and she gives me a sidelong glance over her shoulder. Sensing the tension in the air, I straighten my back. "I can out dance any fucking chick you have here."

A wide smile spreads across her lips before she turns around to face me fully. "Is that a challenge I hear?" she responds with amusement.

Her dark eyes twinkle with mischief as she takes another step forward, her movements graceful. "The thing is this is not just any Cirque. It's not just dancing. It's not having the time of your life. It's extreme horror. It has no place for fear."

When she halts in her tracks, her eyes flash with disdain as they fix on Eli, a silent judgment radiating from her as she continues. "You may have none and I can sense your bravery which I admire, but I can smell it from your pretty puppy here," she looks at me again as she continues. "This place and the Hollow's will eat him alive. We have no room for weaknesses."

Eli speaks up beside me, trying to prove he is worthy. "You're wrong. It was my suggestion to come here. I am not scared of this place."

She stares at him, ready to respond with a condescending smile, but I cut her off. "Just let me show you what I can do and then you can decide."

Her lips press into a thin line, her eyes scanning mine in silence. Suddenly, E's grip tightens on my upper arm, his knuckles paling as he shifts uncomfortably under Madame's scrutiny.

"Maybe we should just leave; we're clearly not welcome here," he murmurs, his voice barely above a whisper, betraying his anxiety.

My brows furrow in confusion, an argument forming on the tip of my tongue. Now more than ever, I want to prove myself, to show what I am capable of, but before I can protest, the lady's soft chuckle interrupts, drawing our attention back to her.

"Yes, go. You two do not belong here," she says with a wave of her hand, her tone final.

"Are you sure about that?" I say with darkness in my eyes.

After a moment of silent, intense staring between us, she finally responds with a knowing smirk. "Fine. You have five minutes of my time to convince me that I want you here."

HOLLOW HELLION

With a deep breath, I steal a glance at Eli beside me who gives a small grin. Once the lady strides past us toward the door, I ready myself and follow, determined to confront whatever lies ahead, despite the anxiety churning in my gut.

As we step into the huge expanse of the empty circus tent, it's silent, except for the soft rustle of fabric and the creaking of wooden beams above. I glance around, noticing high above, the aerial silks hang still, their vibrant colours bright. Without the presence of performers, they appear like forgotten ribbons, waiting patiently for someone to breathe life back into them.

"Billy, you know what to do," Madame instructs, her eyes shifting between me and the departing old man before finally settling on me. "You need to get undressed," she adds.

As I meet Eli's wide-eyed gaze briefly, he gives a shake of his head, a wordless plea for me not to, which again, confuses me since this was his idea in the first place.

Ignoring him, I turn my attention back to the lady and nod in agreement because I know dancing in a hoodie and jeans will not do me justice. I begin to strip down, shedding layers until I am only in just my black panties and sports bra. I raise my head and arms, tying my long blonde locks into a scruffy bun atop my head.

Standing before her, I boldly reveal my scar-ridden body despite the potential judgment. Her gaze lingers on the blemishes, yet instead of scrutiny, I sense approval in her eyes.

When our gazes finally meet, she gives me a smile. "You are perfect," she assures. "Now, let's see what you can do."

I look over at the silks dangling above the stage, while Billy lowers a large silver hoop nearby, but confusion clouds my thoughts and I turn to Madame, "What about the safety net?"

She gives me a wicked smirk before responding. "Darling, we don't practice safety here."

Her expression changes to seriousness before she turns around and strides toward a nearby seat. I glance at Eli, who still appears stunned before I draw my eyes away from him and I mentally prepare myself as I ascend the steep steps leading up to the stage.

Nerves and anticipation course through me while I reach the platform, the familiar rush of adrenaline hinted with doubt. It's been so many years since I last danced like this, and I can only hope that I still have the same rhythm and grace that I once had. I take a deep breath, pushing aside my worry and focusing on the task at hand. It's time to show her what I am made of.

As the hoop comes within reach, I grasp it firmly in my hand, the familiar texture smooth beneath my fingertips. I perch on it, crossing my legs before taking hold of the other side. I straighten my shoulders and look over at Billy, who waits patiently for my signal. Giving a small nod to indicate I am ready, the music comes to life, its pulsating bass filling the air and echoing through the huge area of the circus tent.

With a gentle tug, Billy begins to reel in the rope, propelling me upward into the air. I feel a rush coursing through me, the sensation washing over me like a long-lost friend. This is where I belong, high above the ground, free from the chains of gravity and reality.

As soon as I am at the highest point and the bass dips, I release my grip on the hoop without hesitation, allowing myself to drop backwards, surrendering to the free fall. The hoop latches behind my knees, and I twist my body, my arms dangling gracefully as I spin fast. With an outburst of power, I push my body upward, reaching for the hoop once more and I repeatedly propel myself through the hoop, holding on to it by my knees, the tempo of the music guiding me.

I drop again, but this time, catching the hoop with my hands, hanging beneath it, my body whirling, and I split my legs. I twist them with effortless skill and with each rotation, I feel a sense of freedom wash over me, the baggage of the world fading away as I lose myself in the dance.

I slow down, swinging myself beneath the hoop above me, my eyes fixed on the silk dangling from the beam above at a distance and as I push my body back and forth, the speed carries me higher and higher. As soon as I reach the peak of my swing, I draw a deep breath, readying myself for the moment of release. Then, with a burst of fearlessness, I let go of the hoop, flying through the air like a bird.

With perfect timing, I reach out and catch the silk, the fabric wrapping around my hands as I come to a stop.

While I hang, I wrap it securely around my legs, feeling the smooth material enveloping me. Twisting and turning, I create complex patterns, weaving a web of beauty around me. Once the silk is firmly in place, I begin to dance, my movements effortlessly beautiful as I twirl and spin in mid-air. The fabric supports my weight, allowing me to execute each movement with ease.

As soon as I hear the music reaches its end, I seize the moment, wrapping the silk tightly around my body for the final act. I can feel a sense of excitement building inside of me, fuelling my will power to make this performance one to remember. When the music fades into silence, I release my grip on the silk, allowing my body to turn sideways and unravel. I spin rapidly, my arms stretched out above me as I descend, the fabric spiralling me like a tornado, until finally, I land on my feet at the bottom.

My chest heaves, each breath a struggle as I fight to regain my composure. Slowly, my eyes focus on Madame and Eli, their expressions a mirror of my own dizziness.

The silence hangs between us, but then, they both suddenly stand in unison, their hands clapping together in a loud applause. Relief floods through me, my shoulders relaxing as I realize that I have clearly won Madame over. She climbs the short steps, approaching while still clapping, and when she reaches me, she firmly squeezes the tops of my arms.

"You are magnificent." She says with a big smile.

I cling to the silk, feeling its soft texture wrapped around my hand. "I haven't danced in years, so I may need to train more," I admit through heavy breaths.

My gaze meets her, and I swallow before asking the question that is on the tip of my tongue. "So, does this mean I am hired?"

Her face falls as she glances over at Eli, who is still seated, before returning to me. "You are, yes, but unfortunately, I cannot employ your—"

"If he is not with me, then I will not perform here. Maybe another circus will take us both." I cut her off firmly.

She raises an eyebrow at my brazenness, watching me as I continue past her. "Thank you for taking the time to watch me, Madame."

"Wait." She snaps out the word.

A sinister smirk spreads across my lips while I have my back turned to her. As my expression turns serious, I face her and she closes the small gap between us, her jaw fixed tight.

She scans my features before finally giving me a small nod in approval. "Okay, but—" Her eyes shift to Eli at a distance, her tone adamant as she continues. "I will not be held responsible for how he is treated here. He will have to prove himself and quickly adapt to how we operate."

As I ponder her words, a sense of confusion washes over me. I may not fully grasp their meaning, but one thing is clear: I will not stand by and let anyone bully Eli, no matter who it is. Even though I do not feel romantic love for him, I still owe him a debt of thankfulness for showing me kindness when he didn't need to and when no one else did.

Suddenly, Madame turns, shouting toward Billy. "Billy, take them to one of the empty double-trailers."

Her gaze locks onto mine, and a bead of sweat forms on my brow as she addresses me again. "Come and see me in a few days; I will explain the dates we open the circus. Settle in for now. The next show is this weekend, so your training will start at once. As for pretty boy, I will find something for him to do to earn his keep."

I give a small nod and smile. "Thank you, Madame."

"What is your name?" She tilts her head to the side in question.

"Noir." I answer with my chin raised.

A big grin spreads across her aging face. "Absolutely perfect. You are going to fit in just fine here, Noir."

She averts her gaze from mine, striding past me, and I watch her movements until she exits the tent.

I turn my attention to Eli to find him standing beside Billy, holding my clothes in his arms, waiting for me. While feeling a sense of satisfaction, I release the silk from my hand before making my way toward them, eager to get dressed and see where we will be staying.

HOLLOW HELLION

When we step outside, it is dark, the stars are twinkling above us in the clear night sky. I take in the scene before me as we find ourselves at the back of the circus, surrounded by a sprawling landscape of trailers scattered as far as the eye can see. It shows the sheer number of people who must work and live within this community.

Lights hang like little bulbs from trailer to trailer as we navigate through and we get suspicious glances from the few people we see as we pass them, as if we're intruders.

Suddenly, Billy comes to a stop, his hand gripping the door of a large white trailer and after giving a silent gesture, he steps aside, allowing us to enter. Eli casts a brief glance at me before taking the lead, crossing the threshold and I follow behind him while he flicks on the lights, filling the space with a soft, welcoming glow.

I look around the cozy living room, admiring the white and cream interior with its small kitchen to the left. As Billy closes the door behind us I continue to scan our new home, excitement building inside of me. It may not be perfect, but it is a huge improvement from the truck and motels we have had to deal with. As a thrill courses through me, I spin around, eager to see more. I quickly make my way down a narrow corridor, flinging open doors as I go and when I reach the one at the far end, I swing it open.

I flip on the light switch, noticing it's the bedroom complete with a double bed that sits in the centre, two matching bedside cabinets and a double wardrobe. A grin spreads across my face as I leap into the air, sprinting forward to bounce onto the bed like a child. As Eli enters the room, I fall back onto the springy mattress, bouncing lightly as I inhale deeply, relishing the comfort of the softness beneath me.

"Can you believe we finally have somewhere to stay, E?"

When he stays silent, a crease forms between my brows and I prop myself up on my elbows, meeting his intense gaze with a questioning look.

His jaw tightens slightly before he starts to pace around the room. "It's okay I suppose, but why didn't you listen to me, Noir?"

I sit up fully, watching him closely. "What?" I ask, my tone full of confusion.

"You were practically fucking naked in that Circus. Your scars—"

Defensiveness surges within and I spring to my feet from the bed.

"Ex-fucking-cuse me? Have you forgotten about your own scars? When the hell did you start passing judgment? What the fuck, E?" I seethe with fury.

He releases a defeated sigh before turning to face me, his expression remaining neutral as our eyes lock in a silent battle. In that moment, it dawns on me, and I cross my arms over my chest, knowing the reason behind his behaviour.

"Is this about other men? You do realize what a circus dancer dresses like, right? This is not the time to get jealous now, E, it was your idea to come here!"

His eyes ease, taking a step forward until his hands find my shoulders. "Of course not. I just worry about you that's all." He says softly.

I analyse his features, still irritated because I know I am right.

He stands straight, releasing my shoulders with a sluggish movement before his rubs his eyes with his finger and thumb.

"Look, it's just been a long fucking day. I am going to get the truck, take my meds and get some sleep."

I remain silent as he walks away, my gaze following him until he exits the room. The sound of the trailer door opening and closing echoes through, and I release a tense breath, feeling a mix of frustration and confusion within me.

What the hell? I secured us a place to stay, made sure we'd be fed, and found an opportunity to make money just as he wanted, and he is being like this? I hope he is just tired, because this is not like him at all. Never has Eli had a problem with my scars being on show, so why the sudden change?

CHAPTER THREE

NOIR Alone in the living room, I pass the time watching the small TV mounted on the wall. Eli has gone to bed as he said he would, without saying a single word to me when he returned from getting the truck.

Despite it being past midnight, my restless energy refuses to let me sleep. Starting to crave fresh air to clear my mind, I rise from the couch, throwing on my black hoodie, and slip into my black, high-top Converse. As soon as I am ready, I approach the door and gently pull it open, stepping out into the crisp night air, the coolness hitting the exposed skin on my legs.

After closing the door softly behind me, trying not to make a sound, I adjust my tattered, blue shorts, tugging them downward. I glance around, ready to explore the trailer park, then I start taking steps forward. As I weave through the narrow spaces between the small homes, my eyes scan the dark surroundings for any signs of life, until I suddenly spot a young woman appearing from one of the trailers.

My steps slow as our gazes meet, and there is a silent exchange between us. She is striking, with long, black hair with bright pink tips, and her curvaceous figure is outlined by her tight, all-in-one black jumpsuit.

After some time of staring, her expression transforms into a wide, cheerful smile, and she begins to skip toward me with a playfulness. As she comes closer, a sense of curiosity mingled with caution runs through me. When she stops in front of me with a leap, my gaze widens slightly, realizing she has pink eye contacts in.

"Hey! What are you doing here, beautiful? You shouldn't be here." She asks with a big grin.

I pull my hood over my head, letting my long blonde hair spill out in front of me as I respond. "I'm new here."

Her gasp is loud, filled with excitement as her smile spreads even more. "Holy fucking shit! Are you a new dancer?"

As soon as I nod, she snatches my arm, intertwining hers with mine, and I feel her vibrant energy pulsating through her touch. She pulls me forward, then she skips beside me merrily.

"You MUST meet everyone!"

I stumble, attempting to keep up with her long strides, "Everyone?" I respond.

"Yes! We all meet up at the campfire in the woods any time after midnight most nights." She leans in, suddenly being quiet but keeping her smile. "Well, the younger group. The elders are fucking boring."

As we start entering the dense woods that encircle the circus and carnival, I can't help but think about Eli back at the trailer, fast asleep and missing out on the opportunity to meet everyone, but I tell myself that there will be more chances for him to join us if this is a regular thing.

As we trek deeper into the darkness, the glow of a distant light catches my eye, drawing us closer and the girl beside me peppers me with questions. "So, what's your name and what dance do you do?"

"My name is Noir and I do just about everything dance wise." I reply.

I turn to look at her, and her curious gaze is already fixed on me, close to my face, a creepy wide smile still stretched across her lips. As we continue our conversation, I can't shake the feeling that there is something more to her demeanor and I begin to wonder if she might be fucking high, or if this could just be her bizarre personality.

"What's your name and what do you do?" I ask.

She appears ecstatic when I say the words and we both look forward, the campfire becoming closer. "I'm Blush. I am a fire breather and dancer." She answers with proudness.

I look at her with wide eyes, instantly admiring what she does. "Wow, I can't wait to see you at work. I would love to know how to do that."

She squeezes my arm a little tighter into her side. "Well, maybe I will teach you one day, Noir."

As we step into the clearing, the chatter among the group gradually fades to silence, all eyes turning towards us. The campfire casts a flickering glow across the faces of the young men and women, some still decorated with face paint, others bare like myself. Each one has a unique personality in their styles of outfits and their dark gazes lock on me, expressions ranging from confusion to intrigued.

Blush is seemingly unfazed by the sudden shift in the atmosphere and decides to announce my arrival to the group with a cheery attitude.

"Everyone, this is Noir. She's a new dancer here."

Just as I am about to speak, the distant sound of motorbikes cuts through the moment. Blush suddenly grabs my arm, yanking me around the campfire, where she pulls me down to sit beside her on a nearby tree trunk and the quickness in her actions leaves me feeling on edge about the approaching noise.

The thunderous roar grows louder as they get nearer, sending vibrations through the ground beneath us. I gaze ahead until all three dirt bikes soar through the air. When they land dangerously close to the campfire, I flinch but the riders rev their engines aggressively, their evil laughter echoing through the forest as they circle us at rapid speed. Mud and leaves are flung into the air, swirling around us in a chaotic dance. I attempt to see their faces, but their speed makes them into blurs, leaving their identities shrouded and my mind dizzy.

As the bikes finally come to a sudden stop with a skid of their tires, I take in the sight of them as soon as their engine's cut out, each bike a different colour. One gleams in vibrant red, another in a neon green, while the third is black and white. The riders remain hidden; their features concealed by shadows, but their presence looms heavy around us, radiating an aura of darkness, danger and unpredictability that sends a shiver down my spine. I keep my gaze on the trio until one of them steps off his bike and turns around.

"The Hollow's" Blush murmurs into my ear from behind.

With tousled blonde locks atop his head, his piercing green spiral contacts draw my attention, and he has a big mischievous smile on his lips. Colourful tattoos scatter across his exposed skin and since he is only wearing a black tank paired with sweatpants, I can easily see his toned physique. The eerie swirls that are on the sides of his face only add to his unsettling vibes.

"Hollow Soul has green eyes." Blush whispers.

The second biker turns around, lighting a cigarette. His spiral eyes are a bright red matched with his deep brown, wavy hair, partially hidden beneath his black hoodie. His face paint blackens around his eyes, and I notice the stitches criss-crossing over his lips and across his cheeks. A nose ring glints in the dim light, and his tattoos seem to cover his body from head to toe. He is nothing like Soul; there is something much darker about him, but they are both still oddly handsome in a strange way.

"Hollow Wrath has red eyes."

I observe the third figure between them, feeling drawn to his presence amongst the trio, despite his back turned to us. His tall, toned frame is clear even from this distance, dressed in black, tight, and tattered jeans, with the hood pulled up on his leather jacket.

I lean into whisper to Blush, my curiosity getting the better of me. "Who is the one in the middle?"

He turns to the side, retrieving a cigarette with calm movements and I take in the details of his side profile: the way his black, loosely curled hair shines in the moonlight, protruding from the front of his hood, almost covering his eyes and his jaw is sharp. Black face paint only highlights his cheekbones and darkens his eyes, streaking down his cheeks. He has a stitch design that stretches from the corners of his mouth to his cheek and a piercing on the bottom left side of his lip.

When he turns his head to take a brief glance in our direction, he double-takes as soon as he notices me, and I cannot stop my breath from hitching in my throat. His white and black, glowing spiral eyes seem to pierce through the darkness and me, locked with an almost hypnotic allure.

A shiver scurries through me, the hairs on my arms raising to attention as I find myself momentarily shook by his good looks, even if I can barely see them; I can only imagine how handsome he is beneath all the paints.

Blush hesitantly speaks into my ear, *"That's Hollow Hellion; The ringleader of The Hollow's. They are what you would call the daredevils in other places."*

Soul suddenly steps forward eagerly in my direction, catching my attention, "Fresh fucking pussy!" he chuckles, his approach predatory, and it causes tension to spike inside me.

Before I can fully process the situation and stand up for myself, he comes to a sudden stop as soon as a hand tightens on the scruff of his neck, yanking him back by force. My gaze follows the aggressive movement until Hellion comes into view, exuding dominance over him.

As Soul stumbles backward, hastily adjusting himself under Hellion's stern glare, I can still feel my pulse pounding, letting me know I must have some feelings inside me, after all.

Hellion suddenly turns his head swiftly, his glowing eyes flashing to mine in an unnerving manner. He comes toward me, every stride calculated, twigs snapping beneath his heavy boots, yet I hold his stare, refusing to let him see any of my vulnerabilities around his evil vibe. When he stops, he slowly crouches in front of me, and the silence hangs in the air, everyone falling quiet.

Despite the face paint obscuring some of his features and blackening his eyes, making them look hollow like a skull would, there is an undeniable magnetism about him, drawing me into his darkness involuntarily.

Now we're at eye level, we both analyse one another's features, a strange connection crackling in the small space between us. His spiralling contacts make it difficult for me to detect where he is looking, but mine boldly trace downward to the contours of his strong chest, noticing the ripple of muscles beneath his unzipped hoodie. The sight of his shirtless torso, decorated with swirling tattoos that wind their way across his tanned skin up to his sharp jaw, is both mesmerizing and menacing.

I become very aware of where his eyes are moving, when his head starts to tilt downward, tracing a heated path over my petite frame, tingling everywhere they move. His sight settles on my bare thighs, where the evidence of my pain is etched in slashes.

When I instinctively cover them with my hands so he cannot see me in any way as weak, his eyes flicker upward to meet mine. In a swift motion and without warning, he flips out a knife, positioning the sharp tip beneath my chin. I raise it slightly in response and even as adrenaline courses through my veins, pumping at an alarming rate, I narrow my eyes on his, ready to tell him to fuck off.

"Hell, please don't—" Blush's panicked voice cuts through the intensity, making me realize that there must be some kind of seriousness in this situation.

His eyes dart to Blush, and her words fade into the background as she looks away, obeying him without hesitation.

"Hell has found a toy." Soul's hyper tone comes from my left with an unbearable energy.

Fed up with their bullshit, I swipe Hellion's arm away with a forceful motion, causing the tip of his sharp blade to nip my skin, yet the pain does not faze me.

"I'm nobody's little toy." I scowl at him, gritting my teeth in frustration.

He meets my stern glare, his head tilting to the side expressionlessly. Then, he elevates his chin at my brave stance, clearly curious about me, before his eyes carefully follow the trickle of blood that trails down the front of my throat.

Amidst Soul's menacing laughter in the background, Hellion's hypnotic orbs swing to mine once again. "You'll be whatever the fuck I want you to be, Dolly." he states calmly, speaking for the first time.

His deep voice oozes threat, the words rolling off his pierced tongue like a powerful poison that is ready to kill me. My teeth grind together with irritation as he calmly rises, but I keep my gaze focused on the blistering flames of the campfire, refusing to look at him again.

From the corner of my eye, I see The Hollow's interacting among themselves, occasionally casting glances in my direction. Eventually, they settle down opposite us, on the other side of the campfire. Soul attempts to talk to Wrath, but my attention is drawn back to Hellion, whose intense eyes are already on mine, making me feel a variety of emotions. Fear, thrills, curiosity—yet they all seem to stir something inside me in the most deliciously fucked-up way and we hold each other's intense stare, the fire dancing between us.

"Hell is set on you, Noir." Blush says beside me, breaking the spell he has me under and finally drawing my focus away from him. I lift my chin, glancing at him again as he lights a cigarette. "Well, he can forget about it," I assert, my voice unwavering. "I'm not interested."

She shakes her head frantically beside me, "No, you don't understand. Hell doesn't do this and if he ever did, now is the time to be worried." I side-eye her, detecting fear in her voice, "He's fucking crazy."

I roll my eyes, knowing he is clearly insane; all of them are, I can feel it down to my bones, but I've dealt with much worse, I'm almost sure of it. He is nothing compared to the monsters I have faced.

"I am seeing someone, and he is here too," I murmur, using Eli as an excuse to escape the situation, even if he isn't technically my boyfriend.

She gasps loudly beside me, "Does he know how to fight? Kill?" she asks, her hand flying to her mouth in shock.

I notice the panic in her pink gaze, causing my brows to pinch with confusion before I chuckle, shaking my head, "Eli isn't like that."

"Well, he needs to be and quickly," she snaps back. My face falls from the seriousness of her words before my jaw sets tight, defensiveness seething through every fibre of my being and I look at Hellion, now knowing this is going to be a huge problem.

HOLLOW HELLION

After some time of getting to know Blush, I stand from the log and cast one final glance down at her as she remains seated. "I'll see you in a few days?" I ask, ready to head back to my trailer.

"See you then, Noir." she responds with a big, warm smile.

I give a small nod, then I turn away, making my way around the campfire, eyes following me until I am in the darkened woods, heading back toward the warmth of our trailer.

The sound of distant laughter and chatter fades behind me, my thoughts swirling with everything that has happened tonight. You can do this, Noir. Do not let them get under your fucking skin and intimidate you now.

As I stride forward, the chilly night air causes me to wrap my arms around myself and with each step, the path beneath me seems to stretch endlessly. As soon as I reach the midway point, a sense of unease settles over me, but I try to keep my focus on the distant silhouette of the circus in the distance.

Suddenly, a sharp crack behind me pierces the stillness, causing me to halt abruptly. I spin around in my converses, eyes scanning the shadows for any sign of movement. The forest is silent, except for the rustle of leaves above me stirring by the gentle breeze. A feeling twists my gut, feeling as if a presence is lurking among the trees, tracking my every move and I know it's him already. *He's fucking following me.*

"Stop following me creep!" I grit out.

When I get silence, I roll my eyes, tightening my grip on my upper arms and turn around to continue towards the trailer park. Each step quickens as I power ahead, a sense of urgency pushing me forward, eager to escape the unsettling sensation of being watched the entire time.

Once I am finally out of the woods, I quickly make my way through the trailers until I find mine. Pausing outside the door, I take a moment to scan the area behind me, searching for any signs of him. When I find none, I release a tense breath and open the door.

CHAPTER FOUR

As the trailer door softly clicks shut behind her, I step out of the darkness, a twisted sense of need coursing through me at her vulnerability toward me, despite her brave act. While thinking about my next move, I stand there, fixating on the door.

Should I break in now and fuck her senseless against her will, or should I play twisted games? This little dolly might not be an easy victory, but she is a challenge I'm eager to fucking conquer. The thought of having her as my prize fuels me like nothing I have ever encountered before.

The sickening desire to break her the fuck down has consumed me from the moment I first set eyes on her, like an unbearable force, driving me to reduce her to nothing more than my little fuck toy, to pleasure, to hurt, to dominate in every way my deranged mind can think of. Every fibre of my being wants to bend her to be mine only, to get off on the power I could have over her.

With a clenched jaw, I draw a cigarette from my pocket and bite it between my lips, attempting to stop myself from doing something psychotic and horrific. Once I have lit it with a match, I take a deep drag, the smoke swirling around me as I plot my plan of action.

My attention sharpens as soon as I notice a light switch on inside the trailer, causing me to take purposeful steps forward. While I draw closer to the window, I can hear water running from the shower. As I peer inside, I immediately spot her in the small space, her back turned to me while she lifts off her hoodie.

Her soft, wavy blonde hair cascades down her back, framing the curve of her spine and reaching to the top of her ass. My eyes linger as she pulls her black sports bra up her body, revealing a glimpse of the curve of her perky tits and the subtle bounce as they are freed. The sight of her threatens to unravel my lack of self-control, tempting me to give in to the urge to break in and break her. As she moves to remove her denim shorts, I find myself unable to tear my eyes away, like any normal man should, because it's wrong, but I'm not fucking normal, so I stay fixed on her like a predator stalking its prey.

She drags her shorts and panties over her rounded ass, swaying her hips from side to side and bending over slightly, offering me a perfect view of her peachy cheeks, until the fabric is dropping to her ankles. Once she steps forward, she holds her palm under the water, checking the temperature and the action offers me a side view of her exposed body.

An intensity surges through me that borders on addiction as she steps under the spray, turning to face me frontally. My growing cock suddenly expands in my tight jeans, straining against the fabric, my piercings catching as a low, involuntary growl escapes me and I have to adjust myself to be more comfortable.

Each movement she makes is captivating, compelling me to soak in every inch of her naked body, taking in the sight hungrily and my insane instincts scream at me to take what I fucking want.

Her good-sized pair of tits draw my attention first, and to my surprise, both of her little pink nipples have silver piercings. The look of her sends lust coursing through me like I have never felt before, making it difficult for me to stop myself any longer, fantasizing about the sound that my tongue piercing would make when it collides with them and how loud she would cry for me if I bit them.

As the water flows down her silky skin, she tilts her head back with her arms raised above her while she runs her fingers through her hair. My gaze continues to greedily roam down her flat stomach, tracing the path of the water until I land on her perfect pussy, glistening with moisture. The ache in my dick intensifies, and I clench my teeth, squeezing the tip in a useless attempt to squash the overwhelming craving I am feeling. *Fucking hell, I'm losing control.*

I analyse the slashed scars that decorate her forearms and inner thighs, like ladders drawn onto her tanned skin. Despite them being there, they only make her even more beautiful.

There is a twisted satisfaction in delivering pain, for me at least, but it's even more intoxicating when you find that your obsession seems to revel in the sensation of it. As soon as I looked into her icy blue eyes, a possessive hunger ignited inside of me, but the moment my gaze followed the contours of the pretty scars that mark her body, I knew she had to be mine.

Movement to the right suddenly catches my eye, and my gaze narrows as a guy enters the shower area, pulling his boxers down his legs. Rage surges through me at the sight, my insides burning with wrath as he joins her in the shower. With his back to me, he corners her, leaning in close to her throat to kiss it before he lifts her around him and presses her back against the tiles.

I know when he sinks his dick into her because her soft, plump lip's part. As he continues to screw her, she stares blankly, almost lost in a daydream, until she snaps out of it, her fingers taking his hand from beneath her thigh. With a gentle touch, she lifts it, whispering words I strain to hear.

She places his hand on her throat, and he raises his head, their eyes locking in a silent exchange. He gives a small headshake, then returns his hand to the back of her thigh, lifting her higher and disregarding her pleas for dominance.

He continues to fuck her with a gentleness that only stokes the flames of my fury. There's no violence, no pain—just a dull, pathetic fuck against the tiles, devoid of the pleasure my Little Dolly so desperately craves. I can see it in her eyes; she's not enjoying it—he's failing to deliver what she needs. There are no screams, moans, or even eyerolls, just a silent acceptance of his pitiful fucking performance.

When it's finally over after a matter of minutes, she lowers herself down, and I seethe with annoyance at the sight of her unsatisfied, betrayed by the motherfucker who couldn't even make her come. They both glance down toward his cock before they look at one another. She gives him a reassuring smile and then it dawns on me; he's not even hard for her. *Is this cunt fucking blind? What the fuck.*

He tilts his head down, capturing her lips with his, and when they part, she offers him another smile, but it's full of lies and emptiness.

As he starts to shower, her eyes suddenly catch mine with an almost magnetic pull. I notice her stomach muscles tighten, her eyes widening, but despite her reaction, I casually bring my cigarette to my lips, taking a deep drag, not fazed that she has caught me watching her getting miserably fucked in the shower.

Scream, little dolly and I will break in, kill him and then make sure you scream louder for me.

She doesn't indulge in my twisted games, unfortunately; instead, she stays unfazed, her gaze holding mine without a flicker of emotion, but the subtle rise and fall of her chest betrays the fear stirring inside her, a natural reaction to the danger lurking in my eyes.

After a moment of intensely staring at one another, her jaw tenses in annoyance as she slowly turns away, reaching for the soap, and with her back to me, she begins to wash herself, giving me a view of the perfect curve of her ass.

Brave, brave girl.

HOLLOW HELLION

Despite the murderous thoughts swirling in my mind, I stay and watch them for a few minutes longer, making her feel uncomfortable. When her curious gaze finds mine once again over her shoulder, my teeth clench and I reluctantly decide to walk away, leaving them to their empty charade.

After entering the woods, I continue deeper, my boots crunching over the brittle leaves beneath them. I take a deep drag of my cig before flicking it away, feeling the need to relieve some of this sudden anger and I have the perfect solution.

A woman getting under my skin from the moment I first laid eyes on her has never fucking happened before. I have an obsessive personality, but not for desperately wanting people. Hurting people, maybe, yet never like this.

Once I arrive at a clearing in the trees, I trail over the small field until I reach its centre, where I pause to peer down at the hidden door in the ground. A quick glance around confirms my solitude before I lean down, gripping the small handles and pull them wide open, revealing the entrance to my underground chamber.

I begin descending the stairs, the darkness engulfing me as I reach the bottom. The musty, earthy scent is all too familiar as I make my way towards one of the rooms below. Ripping my hood away from my head, I push down the handle and step inside.

As soon as I walk in, my eyes immediately land on him, exactly where I left him—secured tightly to the torture machine I constructed.

Chains hang from the ceiling like sinister ornaments as I walk through the dimness. Above him, a single bulb shines down on him in a sickly light, turning him into a centrepiece of execution. His frantic struggles and screams against the machine draw my attention, and I fix my gaze upon him.

A metal cage encases his head, screws aiming menacingly toward his eyes and temples, his bloodshot eyes held open by clamps. He is shackled by the wrists to the chair's arms, each finger connected to the vile apparatus.

Despite his desperate cries, his terror fails to move me. It's a horrific scene for someone of a normal mindset, but it's one I've orchestrated countless times, and I am now numb to it. As a member of the Shadow's Society, I am known for my cruelty, my methods sick. These victims are no more than pawns, feeding my hunger for suffering and nurturing the darkness within me.

Without wasting any time, I head over to the small camera sitting to my right, aimed directly at him. His screams stop abruptly as I press the button on top, the red light blinking to life.

Now, he is being live recorded, my client watching this horrific scene unfold, I take a calm seat by the back wall opposite him. His eyes fix on the camera, realizing that whoever placed the hit on him is now watching. As predicted, he starts shouting, desperate to get the last word in and the anger spills from him, but let's be honest, nothing he says will change the fact that he's about to be fucking murdered in the most brutal way possible. I release an unbothered sigh, hearing the same routine so many times before.

Finally, I press the button to my right, bringing the torture machine to life. I settle back in the chair, my arms draped over the armrests, legs spread wide. My gaze locks onto him as he thrashes in a measly attempt to escape, and the machine's metallic clinks and clangs echo around the room.

The sound is almost peaceful to me, a symphony of soon to be death. With each precise click, the machine activates, lifting his fingers upward, and stretching them to their limits. The screws spin at the same time, inching closer to his exposed eyes and temples. His bloodshot eyes, forced open by the clamps, dart frantically, searching for any sign of mercy.

I can't help but admire my creation. Every movement is calculated, designed to inflict maximum psychological and physical torment.

His veins bulge against the restraints as he struggles, muscles straining, but there's no escape. There never is. The screws inch closer and I savour the moment, the wait of his suffering rushing through me like a dark thrill. As his fingers are bent back brutally, I hear his bones snap, each crack is a sickening reminder of the machine's efficiency. His harrowing screams escalate, piercing the air with raw agony as the screws enter his eyeballs, spinning relentlessly. Blood spurts from his eyes, painting a gruesome scene as the other screws penetrate his temples.

The machine's finale begins now that he is securely clamped, and the cage slowly turns, forcing his head to an unnatural angle. I watch with detachment as his neck twists further and further. The tension in the room peaks, the air thick with his suffering and his screams, then abruptly, it's cut off with a final snap as his neck and the machine stops, its purpose fulfilled.

I close my heavy eyes, inhaling deeply, the dark satisfaction settling over me. The silence after his death is almost sacred and I throw my head back, allowing it to rest against the wall behind me.

Once I've fully revelled in the aftermath, I lift my hand and slap down on the camera button, shutting off the live stream. Rising from

HOLLOW HELLION

my seat, I grip the chair arms, pushing myself to my feet and I cast one last glance at his disfigured, lifeless body, before turning and leaving the room.

Walking down the short corridor, I push open another steel door and my eyes immediately land on the large pin board mounted on the wall, decorated with photographs of my victims—countless faces staring back at me, each representing a life I've taken. Retrieving a photograph from my jeans pocket, I approach the board, pinning the latest in its rightful place among the others.

Stepping back, my eyes wander over them all, each image telling a different story of how I murdered them, but smack bam in the middle of the sea of faces, one stands out, its presence like a thorn in my fucking side.

With a surge of bubbling anger, I tear the photograph from the board, holding it between my fingertips as I gaze down at it. With her head tilted down slightly, her long dark hair obscures most of her features in the photo. It's frustrating because it offers little to go on. This is the only image I have of her, but I've been told she has blue eyes. She's the only one that has ever escaped me—the killer of my cousin, Haze. And she will be the only woman I will ever murder. *Harley.*

CHAPTER FIVE

I'm chilling in the living room, and it's late. We've been here for a few days now, settling in before we both start tomorrow. Eli travelled to a local grocery store today and picked up some essentials for us. He seems to be less on edge since the first night we arrived, but I've had a problem finding my pills. They seemed to have disappeared out of E's truck. I know it's only a matter of time before I feel the full anxiety build within me without them, so I've been trying to relish the coziness of this trailer, enjoying that we finally have somewhere to stay.

I know I must find a doctor soon. Maybe I can speak to Madame about it. I am finding it almost impossible to fall asleep in bed, my routine is a mess. It seems my body had become way too comfortable with sleeping in chairs and the effects of craving my pills is keeping me up at night.

I rest my cheek on the comfy couch, my mind racing as I pull a thick blanket up to my chin. The air is cold around me tonight, but I continue to watch TV, the soft glow flickering in the dark trailer. Just as I'm about to drift off, something catches my eye in the window and my heart skips a beat, the hairs on the back of my neck standing to attention when I see his glowing, spiraling orbs staring back at me. He stands ominously, his silhouette still, yet I make no sudden movements.

I haven't faced Hellion since the night we met and he went on to invade my privacy by watching me in the fucking shower like a creep, but he came here again last night, watching me from outside until I fell asleep as well.

The man is fucking unhinged, his fixation on me becoming a disturbing game. He has only just met me, yet he's already crossed wild boundaries. I didn't entertain it the moment I saw him standing outside the bathroom window. It was too late to react; he had already seen me completely naked. There was a silent hope in his eyes for me to scream and panic, but soon enough, he will know that's not who I am. I've long shed any remnants of shame in being seen naked.

Did he really believe he could break me down by doing that? I'm pretty sure in that moment he learned that I am not like the other girls he has messed with, but I think that entire situation has made things so much worse. I worry how much did Hellion see. Did he watch E fuck me? Did he see how I asked him to grab my throat and he refused? Fuck. I think he did.

When I first met Eli, nothing about us was sexual. He didn't pressure me into doing anything, and when I first started riding in his car, I was nothing but a zombified shell that he didn't mind taking along on his journey. After some weeks or maybe months of constantly being with one another in the car or even in motels, one thing led to another, and we started sleeping together—but not often. It wasn't like we had a crazy connection or wild sex.

To be honest, it wasn't what I wanted. Sex is nothing to me; I don't really care for it, but I'm wise enough to know that's probably because I've never felt a connection with it. I can only imagine how great it must be to have feelings and love within a sexual relationship, but for me, I'm yet to experience that, and I worry that will never happen for me because I'm strange and cannot grasp it.

Eli hardly gets hard, and he isn't dominant, and I think sometimes I crave that to keep me grounded. My taste for pain and submission is far too great to ignore; my body screams at me that I need it to be able to feel or enjoy anything, but on my own terms. I will have to truly trust that person.

With Eli, the intimacy felt almost hurried, a simple routine we fell into rather than a passionate connection. He was gentle, which I appreciated back then, but it's continued even after months, and it has meant that when we have sex it's empty of what I need. I need someone who can match my darker desires, someone who understands the mix of pain and pleasure, someone that can make me feel truly alive. Because that's what I want. To feel alive.

Eli's softness and my own emotional detachment created a bridge between us that I can't seem to cross. I find myself aching for more—more intensity, more dominance, more of a raw, unfiltered hard fucking that would leave me feeling satisfied and maybe a little bit ashamed. It's not that Eli is bad at it; it's just that our sexual needs don't align at all, which is a shame because he is a good person.

My thoughts return to Hellion and how his eyes flickered with rage when I turned around to see him standing there. I could see it on his face, he was pissed; he is definitely a dominant male, and I was stupid enough to play his game and boy did I feel a strange sensation from his eyes all over me. A sensation that has me questioning my own sanity.

Am I just as crazy as he is because somewhere, deep down, I'm kind of into it? Like, why am I doing little to nothing to stop it? Why am I not marching to Madame's office to tell her that her golden boy is creeping me the fuck out? Why am I allowing him to watch me as I sleep? I'm starting to ask myself if I am more attracted to his danger than I want to admit.

I try not to entertain his strange behavior because the shivers and fright this man injects into my bones are unlike anything I have ever felt before, but at least he is making me feel something other than numbness. I've never had a man make me feel such an array of emotions before.

He just peers through the window, doing absolutely nothing else and I always wonder what the fuck is going through this maniac's mind. Is he tempted to come in and hurt me? Is he fantasizing about me? Fuck, of course he is.

God, I need to ask Madame to put some damn curtains in here. The thought of him lurking around out there at night, stalking me with those eerie eyes makes my skin crawl in the most fucked-up ways possible, yet I allow it.

As I try to concentrate on the TV, his overpowering dark presence is impossible to ignore. Every muscle in my body is coiled tightly, every instinct screaming at me to run, to hide, to do something other than lay here and pretend I am not terrified.

I take a deep breath and force myself to stay still, to keep my gaze steady. I will not give him the satisfaction of knowing how deeply he unsettles me.

Eventually, the weight of my exhaustion overpowers my fear, and my eyelids grow heavier. I know I need to get some rest, but the thought of closing my eyes while he watches me is almost unbearable. Yet, with a final, defiant glance at the window, I allow myself to sink deeper into the couch, the blanket pulled tightly around me, ready to sleep again under the watchful gaze of Hellion.

TWO YEARS AGO. . . .

Curled up in a ball on the hard, dusty floor, I shiver in nothing but a thin white nightie. The freezing cold bites my skin, and I gaze through a small crack in the boarded-up window, staring at the bright moon peeking through, the ray of light beaming down on me at a distance. In a daze, I slowly draw the tip of my finger on the wooden floor, quietly humming a song my mom used to sing to me when I was little. When she was alive. My body shudders, slowly shutting down from days without water and a week without food. A tear attempts to slip from my dry, sore eyes as I try to think about other things, but all my memories have been replaced with darkness.

Hearing heavy footsteps approaching from down the hall, I start to sit up, the shackle on my ankle rattling as I get onto my knees. I keep my head lowered, stars forming in my vision from the sudden elevation. The door creaks open, but I don't meet his gaze, his presence is so vile that it makes me want to puke. His heavy footsteps inch toward me, each step calculated, my heart pounding in my chest. He stops not far from me and suddenly pours water onto the floor, a lot of it. On instinct, I scurry forward on my hands and knees, desperate for moisture.

Just as I reach the puddle, he steps in it, his shoes caked in mud, mixing with the water. I halt, my body trembling, eyes wide. I shake my head frantically, tears struggling to fall, they want to, but they're unable too. I start hyperventilating, anger swirling inside me, and I stand quickly, my mind almost going blank. I scream, attacking him with my frail fists, hammering down on his suit-covered chest, each strike doing nothing against his solid frame.

He pulls his hand back and smacks me across the face with a hard blow. I spin and fall to the floor frontally, drifting in and out of consciousness. He flips me onto my back, kneeling between my legs. As I faintly hear his zipper drag down, his harsh words reach my ears, "Just like your cunt mother, a dirty filthy bitch that never learns."

I hear another pair of footsteps entering the room, stopping beside my head. "She wants water so bad?" Kai sneers above me.

Suddenly a dust bag is thrusted over my head, the string tightening around my throat. Panic seizes me, and I instinctively try to tear it off, but Kyro wraps the string around his hand, trapping me. Water starts to pour slowly on my face, seeping through the bag and suffocating me. I choke and cough, my body convulsing as I struggle for air. Kyro's presence looms between my thighs, a dark promise of what's to come, as he prepares to take full advantage of my helplessness.

My vision fades, the weight of their words pressing down as heavily as his body, and I slip into darkness, clinging to the memory of my mother's lullaby, the only light in this consuming abyss.

PRESENT TIME . . .

It's the next morning and it's our first day working here. As I hastily throw my hair into a messy bun, I steal glances at myself in the mirror on the wall of the bedroom and Eli moves behind me, pulling a white vest over his toned physique.

My mind drifts back to the past few nights, to Hellion's confusing ways and intrusion. I try not to dwell on it, but the unease lingers like a shadow. His unpredictability is a threat, one that could put Eli in danger, and I refuse to let him become collateral damage in Hellion's games. I can't keep letting him get away with it. I need to face him and shut whatever the fuck this is down.

Once I have finished with my hair, a knock on the door interrupts our morning routine. Eli and I exchange a brief glance as I turn to face him before he walks away to answer it and I follow behind him. When he has swung the door open, Blush stands there with two big bags in her hands, wearing a smile that stretches from ear to ear.

"Hey!" she says cheerfully.

I return Blush's smile, but when she moves to enter, Eli holds out his hand, blocking her path and her face falls.

"Do we know you?" He asks her sternly.

Her eyes flicker to mine, silently seeking guidance, and I gently shake my head for her not to tell him we've already met. She turns back to Eli, her brow arching inquisitively. "I'm Blush. I am here for Noir; to show her some costumes for Madame."

She raises the bags of clothing, but before Eli can respond, Billy appears, his gaze fixed on Eli and with the subtle gesture with his head, he speaks. "Come with me, kid."

Eli's eyes linger on mine for moment, and I offer him a reassuring smile before he moves past Blush. Once he's out of sight, I motion for her to come inside the trailer, but she shakes her head once. "Oh no, Noir. We're going to Madame's Chamber. She wants to see you."

I nod in response before stepping outside and locking the trailer behind me. As we make our way toward the circus, I take a glance around now that it's daytime. The air feels cold, and the sky is shrouded in cloudy, grey hues. I'm grateful for the warmth of my black tracksuit on a day like this.

"You didn't tell your boyfriend that you were out the other night, did you?"

I look at Blush beside me when she asks the question, reaching out to take one of the heavy bags from her hands. With a roll of my eyes, I turn my gaze forward, slinging it over my shoulder as I respond, "It's complicated and he isn't my boyfriend. We're just—"

As I trail off, I see her silently observing me from the corner of my eye, but I choose not to meet her stare and when I continue to stay silent, she changes the subject, "Hell followed you the other night. Did he say anything to you?"

Our eyes lock, my lips tightening into a thin line as I think about what he has been doing.

Her eyes widen, "Oh, fuck. What did he do?" she blurts out, a gasp escaping her lips.

I let out a tense breath before biting on my words with irritation. "That weirdo decided to casually watch me in the shower that night, then proceeded to watch me through my living room window two nights in a row."

A small giggle escapes her lips and I glance at her puzzled before her face falls again, an apologetic look in her eyes.

My brows pinch as I scan her. "You know that's not normal behaviour don't you, Blush?" I ask, confusion twisted on my face.

She responds with a raised eyebrow and a playful smirk, "Babe, you will learn that absolutely nothing or anybody is 'normal' here. This is Oddity Carnival and Cirque after all. Reputed as the most terrifying spectacle in the states."

The sight of a massive, glossy black double-story trailer catches my attention, not far from the circus. Bold red letters splatter across the surface, "The Hollow's," and beside it is a sinister white skull with spiralling eyes. The size could serve as a small mansion on wheels.

"Is that where they live?" I query, curiosity tingling in my voice.

She follows my gaze and nods before responding. "Yeah, all of them."

"Is there only three of them?"

"There were four, but Hollow Haze—" She pauses, glances at me, and searches my eyes for trust. When she seems satisfied, she leans in. "He was killed a while back. He was Hell's cousin," she states, her voice barely audible. My brows arch in surprise as she continues. "We don't talk about it. It's a sensitive subject for the guys."

I pause for a moment, curiosity piqued by the thought of delving further into knowing more about the psycho that's now stalking me. "Tell me about Hellion. What am I dealing with here?"

She takes a deep breath before beginning. "Well, Hell is cold, strangely calm, calculated, yet still not entirely sane, but it's Hellion you should be worried about. You've only met Hell."

A puzzled expression crosses over my face as I look at her.

"Did you just refer to him as two people?."

With a faint smirk playing at her lips, barely noticeable but enough to suggest a hint of devilish amusement, she answers, "That is exactly what I did. He has a character, and you need to know what you're being faced with. God help you when you finally meet Hellion. Lock your fucking doors and windows."

"Well, how the fuck am I supposed to know when he is Hellion?" I shoot back.

"Oh, you'll know. The entire atmosphere in this place is charged."

The unsettling revelations twist my gut, leaving me uncertain about what to make of it all, and I shift my gaze forward, allowing her to continue. "Luckily, Hellion, doesn't come out as much as you would think, it's mostly on Dark Night that he lets loose, but even then, Hell is going to terrorize the fuck out of you. You have been warned, Noir."

I draw a deep shaky breath, "And do you guys move around?" I ask, hoping that the answer is yes, but unfortunately she shakes her head. "Not often. We sometimes do small private shows in different states if requested at the right price, but most of the time we stay in this location because our Dark Night amusements are built here, and we own this land. It's protected."

I'm about to ask what Dark Night is, but we suddenly arrive at the circus with music blasting from the main tent, blurring out my lingering questions and Blush strides ahead, leading the way to Madame's chamber.

HOLLOW HELLION

When we enter, nobody is in here, but the candles and incense are lit. Making our way toward the back, we pass through a sheer, sparkling curtain, leading to another chamber.

My eyes take in the sight of a grand vanity that has a large mirror, bright lights bordering it. Neatly arranged racks display an array of colourful costumes and wigs. Along one side are plush lounge couches in rich red and gold.

While I am gawking, Blush's enthusiastic tone breaks my trance. "Okay, let's get started. Madame will be here soon, and she will expect to see you ready."

I eagerly follow her to the racks of costumes, and it feels like being a young kid again, playing dress-up for Halloween. As she selects pieces for me, I can't help but giggle and she starts to dress me in black fishnet tights, pairing them with a short, whimsical tutu and knee-high, laced, platformed boots.

Moving on, she wraps a black and white striped corset around me, tightening the back to pinch my waist and outline my curves. My breasts almost threaten to spill over the frilly trim since they are pushed up so high.

Finally, she settles me in front of the vanity, securing a sleek black bobbed wig atop my head after clipping back my hair. "I wonder if Madame will give you your own set of contacts and if she does, what color they would be." She asks curiously.

I gaze at myself in the mirror as she stands behind me, adjusting the black-fringed wig that enhances my features. It's not until I look at her peachy-colored lenses twinkling in the light that I answer. "Do you all wear contacts?"

She glances at me in the reflection, giving a small head shake. "Only us who work at Dark Night. I think you would suit black eyes since it would match your name perfectly."

"She's not wearing fucking contacts. Her pretty eyes are staying blue," a sudden deep male voice interrupts, startling both of us and prompting a swift glance over our shoulders.

My gaze locks onto Hellion, propped casually against the wall on the other side of the room. I gulp as take in his shirtless body, the sinister swirls of black tattoos writhing across every inch of his bronzed skin like living shadows. His black, tight jeans hang low on his hips, giving a view of the sculpted contours of his painted abs and the mesmerizing V that leads downward, drawing my eyes with an irresistible pull.

Despite the sheen of sweat glistening on his body from rigorous training, his face still has his usual haunting masterpiece. With his black and white coiled lenses still in place, he turns his head slightly, offering me a glimpse of his chiseled jawline. Now I am seeing him in the light, I find myself wondering what he really looks like beneath his scary act. What color are his real eyes? Light or perhaps dark like his hair.

"Get the fuck out." He demands icily towards Blush while facing aside.

She turns to leave without hesitation, and I swiftly stand from the stool, fighting the urge to grab her wrist to stop her, but I decide against it since I don't want him to see how unnerved I am by the thought of being alone with him. He cannot see me as weak because I'm fucking not. Also, this might be a good opportunity to shut this is down and quickly.

As she hurries out of the room, Hellion's gaze locks onto mine, and I shoot him a glare before turning to face the mirror. Each step he takes behind me sends a tightness of tension through my chest. When I sense his dark presence and heat looming against my back like a deathly shadow, I face aside, unwilling to look at him.

While trying to steady my racing heart, I steal a glance at him from the corner of my eye, only to find his head tilted downward, his lenses carefully tracing an unwelcome path down my collarbone until they settle on the curve of my breasts. I become annoyed and return my gaze forward, cocking my head to the side as his eyes meet mine in the mirror opposite us.

"Do you like looking at things you will never have?" I assert firmly.

He lifts his chin in response, and I counter with a raised eyebrow. "Whatever you're thinking, forget it. You clearly saw the other night when you decided to be a fucking pervert and watch me in the shower that I am seeing someone."

His jaw flexes again, showing his irritation, but he remains wordless. In the heavy silence that follows, he reaches behind me, seizing a handful of my wig and ripping it from my head before tossing it to the side. We hold eye contact as he frees my wavy blonde hair until it's tumbling down my back and framing my face.

"Keep yourself as you are. You're fucking perfect and you don't need all the extra bullshit," he commands, his voice carrying authority.

A strange sensation churns in my gut at his compliment, annoying me further because I don't want to feel it and I know it is all just mind games. Whirling around to confront him, I find my tits pressed against his solid abs. I tilt my head back, meeting his towering figure head-on and stare at him harshly.

"Flattery will get you nowhere with me, Hellion," I retort, my voice tinged with defiance.

"You're not fucking wearing that." He lowers his face towards mine, his words biting, giving me a taste of the monster that lives within him.

I inhale sharply as he takes a slow step forward until the bulge of his dick is pressing firmly against me, his lenses focused, and I place my palms on the vanity behind me, bowing backward to create some distance between us.

"Also, call me Hell, pretty girl, because you haven't met Hellion yet, but believe me, you will soon enough," he adds, his voice laced with a chilling promise. "And when that moment comes, the only time you'll be uttering his fucking name is when you're screaming it."

I lift my brows at his bold assumption, trying to remain calm until he suddenly moves my hair away from my eyes softly with his sharp knife. "Does that scare you, Little Dolly? Are you afraid of us?" he taunts, his tone filled with dark intent.

Adjusting my demeanor, I smirk slightly, allowing my gaze to trail from his strong chest until it meets his once again, ready to engage in his bullshit and I lift my mouth close to his, delving into his swirling depths. "No, Hell. You don't scare me, and neither will Hellion," I whisper seductively with a flutter of my lashes. "You're both big, fluffy bears compared to the men I have dealt with."

He tucks his bottom lip between his teeth, his eyes gliding over my features with a cold detachment as he ponders my brazenness.

"Brave words," he murmurs. "But let's see how brave you really are when my games begin, Noir."

Then, in a sudden move, he quickly thrusts his face unnervingly close to mine, the sharp edge of his blade grazing my throat. The action catches me off guard, and I am forced to tip my head back as he hisses, "Because you will be. I haven't even fucking started playing with you." My eyes frantically scan his, bracing myself for his next vicious words. "Limp dick too."

Anger flares within me, my brows pinching together, and I scowl before unleashing my venomous warning. "The only person who will be in danger here will be you if you hurt E."

I see the amusement dancing on his face as he responds. "Was that a threat?"

My jaw tenses as I stare at him squarely. "Yeah, it was. I'll stab you in the neck. You may scare everyone else here, but not me."

His gaze traces a heated path down my chest once more. "Fuck, I love it when you talk murder to me," he breathes out, a devilish grin tugging at the corners of his lips.

Without warning, he seizes the nape of my neck with a bruising grip, pressing his blade harder against my throat as he growls, "How about I just cut you from ear to ear and fuck your cold dead cunt instead?" My breathing grows erratic. I can no longer hide the fear he instils in me as he continues his terrorization. "My Dolly will be nothing but a stiff fucking corpse while I try to screw the life back into her."

My wide eyes stay fixed on him, panic coursing through my veins at the sight of this absolute maniac before me until he switches again and I start to wonder if I am experiencing Hell or Hellion or, both.

Coercing me to hold his knife, his grip around mine is vice-like as he places the blade on his throat, chin lifted. "Actually, slice my fucking throat since you want to speak of murder like it's nothing, brave girl. It's the only way you're going to stop what I do to you and him."

Still fighting against him, I manage to compose myself, clinging desperately to the shreds of my confidence. "You deranged psycho fuck. You're messing with the wrong girl."

"I know exactly what I'm messing with, Noir. I knew it from the night I first saw you. You're as fucked in the head as me. And every single night after, you allowed me to watch you has only confirmed it." Taking a deep breath, I narrow my eyes and remain silent, but he persists. "He can't even screw you right. He's a fucking embarrassment."

Defensiveness creeps up my throat. "He's a good person, unlike you. You sound jealous," I bite back, my words sharp.

"Yes, yes I am fucking jealous. I'm feeling murderous that he has the luxury of having his fucking hands on what's mine when he doesn't deserve it."

My face screws up with confusion, "Yours?" I scoff.

His hand tightens on the back of my neck as he peers deep into my eyes with seriousness. "Yes. Mine," he growls possessively, the way he said "mine" trembling down to my core.

I shake my head once, hardly believing this guy as he continues. "Good, don't make girls like you come or feel desired."

I quirk an eyebrow at his accusation. "Girls like me?"

With his knife still positioned on his neck, he brings his face closer to mine, his voice dropping to a menacing murmur.

"Yes, girls like you. The beautiful, yet broken kind that seem to blossom in the darkness of lust. They want to experience a scream ripping from their fucking throat rather than releasing a soft moan. They crave to feel the bite of pain rather than a gentle, loving touch. They possess an insatiable hunger to be violently screwed against the shower wall while being choked the fuck out until they can no longer stand it, rather than having to endure a slow, pathetic fuck."

His words hit me like a punch to the gut, raw and strangely accurate. They echo to the twisted part of myself that I've tried to deny, the part that craves darkness. As much as I want to fight him, to argue that I'm not what he says I am, a part of me knows he's right.

As I gather myself, I draw a deep breath. "So, this is a regular thing for you, is it? You do this to other girls?" I ask, my suspicions raised.

He shakes his head once in response, his spiraling orbs locked on mine. "No, Noir. I've been trying to find you my entire life."

Fuck, this needs to stop. He is saying all the right things. His way of words are stirring things inside me that I thought were long gone, things I didn't even know could surface.

Confusion.

Fear.

Arousal?

How can I feel this way about someone so fucked? He is everything I have tried to escape. Yet, unfortunately, there is definitely something about Hell that lures me in, and it's clear he feels it too. It's like a dangerous, fucked-up magnetic pull between us that I'm trying to resist with everything I have.

Maybe it's the pills; yeah, it has to be. I'm not feeling myself. I am not in control.

I decide to switch tactics, changing my demeanor and smiling widely. "Awe, Hell has found love at first sight. How sweet," I mock, trying not to show the effect he has on me.

He slides his hand up into the back of my hair, gripping a fistful and yanking it back forcefully, inflicting a teasing pain that entices a hiss from my lips. As his knife digs into my windpipe, asserting his dominance, a tremor of both agony and sick pleasure courses through me.

Seemingly reveling in my pain, he lowers his face, carefully running his nose up my jaw as he growls his response. "Love? No, Noir. What I possess for you is far more intense and deeply disturbing. Something that eclipses any form of love, leaving behind only a haunting stain of darkness in its wake." Lifting his head, his lips touch mine, sending a jolt of electricity through me, and he clenches his teeth viciously against them. *"Obsession."*

We pause, the tension thick in the air as I pant through my nose. His lips lightly brush over mine, igniting a twisted longing within me. Surrendering to the weight of it, my heavy eyelids close involuntarily, "But you don't even know me." I whisper in a haze.

His smoky breath mingles with mine as he responds, "I don't need to know who the fuck you were, Noir. Once I set eyes on you, I knew everything about your past would be lost. Your future, your fate—they're all mine now," he says, his voice is hushed. "They belong to me. That's the only Noir I will ever know—the one we shape. And in the process, she will become my obedient little slut."

Jesus fucking Christ.

His words are carving through me like his sharp knife, stripping away my defiance. I feel exposed, and vulnerable, as if he's peeling back layers of my identity with each syllable just because he knows he can. There's a dangerous edge to his tone, a vow of dominance and control that both frightens and intrigues me. Part of me wants to fight back at the thought of being reduced to nothing more than his obedient plaything, yet another part is disturbingly aroused by the thought of surrendering to his power.

He moves his blade slowly down the front of my throat, aiming toward the curve of my breasts and each passing moment becomes a threat, the possibility of its cut hanging in the air. The sexual tension solidifies, suffocating me in its toxicity. Feeling my heart smashing against my chest, we move our lips teasingly over one another's, almost as if they are toying with the possibility of giving in to our desires.

"I'm going to slice your beautiful body to pieces, Little Dolly, making every scar you own as mine. And you're going to come hard while I fucking do it," he vows.

Fuck.

Just as he leans in to kiss me, a woman's throat clears behind him, shattering the charged atmosphere. We both pause, lips still touching and my eyes snap open, locking onto his. His spiralling orbs search mine before he growls aggressively, showing his frustration. "Get the fuck out, Ma."

Just as he is about to lean in again, she suddenly raises her voice toward him. "Hell!"

Snapping back to reality and realizing what I have done, my teeth clench with annoyance, but he merely offers me the faintest evil sneer, knowing he almost had me before reluctantly stepping back and releasing my hair.

Withdrawing his knife from my breast, he grants me much-needed breathing space and I straighten myself, adjusting my outfit. He calmly turns away, giving me a view of his strong, tattooed back. My gaze then meets Madame's, finding her observing with a curious expression, her eyes darting between us both. While Hell rests against the wall, his gaze lingers on me, but Madame's approach captures my attention.

"Look at you. Amazing!" she gasps out.

She scans me from head to toe, a broad smile lighting up her face, causing me to peer down at myself. "It's not too much?" I ask, feeling self-conscious.

"Oh, darling. Nothing is ever too much here." She inclines her head toward the door, signalling for me to leave the chamber. "Now let's see if you can dance in it."

I offer an awkward nod before passing her, stealing a quick glance at Hell before exiting the chamber and making my way towards the main tent.

CHAPTER SIX

After watching Noir leave the chamber, my gaze flashes to Madame's, and I notice her suspicious glance. I keep my expression neutral although I am absolutely fucking reeling inside from her interruption.

When I sense her silent gesture for me to follow her, I push myself away from the wall with a growl, feeling the unbearable ache in my balls because of Dolly's teasing bullshit.

As we enter the tent, I take in the usual bustling scene: dancers training on the aerial silks and trapeze, fire dancers twirling flames, and the death wheel spinning with Soul practising on it. Beyond the pulsating music, there's a distant roar of Wrath's bike outside, training for our next performance.

My attention is momentarily caught by Noir as she approaches Blush, but Madame's hand wrapping around my wrist brings me back to reality. I shoot her a sharp look at the unwanted touch, but she simply pulls me to sit with her in the front row. As I settle in the seat, I sigh heavily, leaning back with my legs spread wide, bracing myself for the unwanted lecture.

"I want you to leave her alone, Hell." She orders as predicted.

I raise an eyebrow, fixing my eyes on Noir as she stretches in a way that almost gets me hard again, then reach into my jeans pocket to retrieve my cigarettes.

Once I have one lit and between my lips, I respond, my words muffled. "No can do. I'm fucking set on her."

Knowing I can't control my impulses when I say I am set on something, Madame shifts in her seat, facing me and I feel my jaw tense with agitation.

"I mean it, Hell. I like her, and she's good at what she does. She fits in perfectly here, and I don't need you playing your twisted games with her," she says, calmly trying to rein me in. My eyes flash to hers, a hint of confusion flickering in my expression at her words, and she continues. "Besides, she came with a guy. A weak guy, but a guy none the less. "

My teeth grind together at the thought of that pathetic cunt, every fiber of my being resisting the urge to unleash the murderous words building inside me.

"What makes you think I give a fuck?" I snap.

She shifts her eyes to Noir as she responds. "There's something off about him though, Hell. I don't think he has what it takes. I'm almost certain he will try to flee on Dark Night."

I take a long drag of my cig, gazing up at Noir while she climbs the silk, my obsession with her growing as she moves with such fluidity. She bends like something delicate that I could easily fucking snap beneath me. The range of sounds I could coax from her body—whether cries of pleasure or complete anguish—it's a symphony I'm desperate to fucking orchestrate.

With an exhale of smoke from my nostrils, I reply. "We'll lock him the fuck up for the night. Problem solved."

I notice her staring at Dolly with a curiosity, similar to my own. It's unusual to see Madame like this; usually, she only employs those who come from the Shadow's society. I have never known her to take in outsiders who are oblivious to what they're getting themselves into, only if it's the carnival, but never Dark Night.

Most of us came from the Shadow's Society, trapped in a world of horror and violence—a hidden underworld no one dares to mention. There, children are moulded within a sinister web of trauma and control. In my upbringing, I became obsessed with the thrill of killing while others took other routes of criminality. Each death surges through me like a shot of adrenaline, bringing an unsettling peace in my chaotic mind. I found my way to Madame when I was just thirteen, after my mother died. Though I can't be tamed or don't own a heart, I still share a bond with her as strong as the one I had with my own mother. It's similar to the one I have with Soul and Wrath—my brothers.

"You knew what the fuck you were getting them into as soon as you employed them both, Ma. Now they're in, there's no way out, unless it's by death, the same as it is for everyone here." I say firmly, reminding her of the rules.

She remains silent, still gazing up at Noir and I follow suit until she finally responds in a trance. "I know. But look at her—she's amazing."

"I want her to be our girl."

Madame now looks at me sharply, "But what about Pearl? She has been The Hollow's girl for years."

I sit forward, dropping my cig between legs and stamping it out with my black boot. "Things fucking change," I now turn my eyes toward her as I continue. "As you said, she's good."

"I know, but—"

"It's fucking happening, Ma."

"But she's not ready for Dark Night—She needs to be prepared."

As I get ready to stand with my hands on my thighs, I glance up at Dolly, twirling like an elegant beauty. "Don't worry about that. I have plans for her. She'll be more than prepared for Dark Night once I'm finished."

While standing and walking away, Madame attempts to whisper-shout to tell me what to do again, but I ignore her bullshit and head straight for the wheel of death. My eyes remain fixed on Noir as the wheel spins, with Soul flipping skilfully inside one of the rotating rings and my insane mind swirls with ideas of how to torment her.

When Soul reaches close to ground level, I leap up, catching the edge, and effortlessly pull myself onto the wheel as it turns before dropping down into his ring.

He breathes heavily as he steps forward while I walk backward, giving him a nod in Dolly's direction. "Light her the fuck up."

He glances her way before breaking into a mischievous smile, ready to wreak havoc like a cruel motherfucker. As soon as our rotating ring nears ground level again, he jumps down, landing with ease. While I continue walking backward, slowing the wheel down, I watch him head straight for her until he stops beneath her fabric. He flicks out a gas lighter, and I see her freeze, staring down at him with wide eyes as he ignites the flame. Seeing her panic is fucking breathtaking; she's no longer trying to hide it. She needs to understand exactly what the fuck we represent.

His green eyes flash with wicked intent before he finally places the flame to the fabric. As it catches fire, my gaze lingers on Dolly while she frantically shakes it in a pathetic attempt to try and extinguish the flames, but the fire only grows and climbs higher.

Soul steps back with a grin, and she scowls at him before glancing my way, her eyes narrowing. She spots another fabric within reach, sways, and grabs it, letting go of the burning one. But Soul isn't finished; he lights the end of the new one as well. Yet she continues to play the game, leaping from one to another, moving steadily in my direction, exactly where I want her.

When she runs out of material and clings to the last one, Soul moves to light it as well. She glances at a hoop hanging between us, then briefly locks eyes with me. I slow the rotating ring even more by stepping to the side, using my strong legs.

With the flames growing closer, she takes a final leap, catching the hoop and dangling beneath it. As she pulls herself up, I peek at her ass before she perches on it. Trying to catch her breath, she looks down at me with an eyebrow arched. A small smirk twitches on my lips; she thinks she's won, but I'm far from done playing.

I dig into my sweatpants pocket and retrieve my knife. Flicking out the black blade, I admire the white swirls engraved on it and the red letters spelling out 'HELL.' My evil orbs flash to hers above me before settling on the rope holding the hoop. I peer into her eyes once more, seeing her pupils dilate as she realizes exactly what I'm about to do.

Without warning, I swing my arm with force, releasing the knife in her direction. It slices through the rope with precision, and the hoop drops, a terrified scream escaping her lips as she plummets toward the ground. I reach up quickly, grasping the top of my ring before leaning out of it.

As she passes me, I stretch out my arm, catching her around the small of her back. She wraps her arms around my shoulders, her tiny body trembling as I pull her inside until she is standing on her feet in front of me.

"You bastard, you both could have killed me!" She shouts furiously.

Now looking up at me, she shoots me an angry glare while attempting to catch her breath which only amuses me, though I don't show it.

I press my face close to hers, searching her blue gaze as I respond coldly. "Not even death could take you from me, pretty girl." She squints her eyes even more, ready to deliver me another rejection, but I continue. "Besides, I saved your ass."

She now lifts her brow in defiance as she responds. "And what do you want? A fucking thank you when you're the one who did it?"

I lean down, sliding my hands around the back of her thighs, pressing my fingers through her fishnets and I feel her body stiffen against me as I snarl. "That would be nice, wouldn't it? But I have a feeling my stubborn Little Dolly isn't going to be so nice."

Tightening my hold on her thighs, I lift her in one swift movement, forcing her to wrap her legs around my waist. She places her hands on my chest, attempting to push back and break free, but she'll do as she's fucking told.

"What the hell are you doing?" she grits out through tight teeth.

"Whatever the fuck I want," I respond blankly, not giving a fuck.

She tries to wriggle out of my grasp, but when she fails against my strength, she releases a grunt of frustration as she faces aside, and I continue to piss her off. "Are you done?"

She ignores me, not entertaining my bizarre attempts at flirting. When I start to step forward, the wheel rotates slowly. I focus on her pretty side profile as she avoids my gaze, and then my eyes drop to the swell of her breasts. My wild mind starts thinking of all kinds of disgusting things as I admire them.

Those perfect fucking tits.

I have to see them bouncing as she rides every inch of my pierced dick.

I need to feel the warmth as I drop my balls into her mouth, jerking my cock off between them until I'm painting her body with my cum.

I crave to grab them aggressively, using them as leverage as I violently screw her tight asshole until it's gaping and pulsing for relief.

I want to suck and bite them, while twisting my entire fucking hand inside her cunt, bringing her to the brink of madness until she's coming for me.

Fuck, she drives me crazy.

With each step I take, I feel the heat of her pussy on my abs. A low growl escapes my throat, as I grasp her asscheeks roughly, my sense of control slipping, and I yank her closer until I can feel the damp fabric on my skin.

When her legs are forced further apart, she shoots me a severe look, her tone a clear warning, "I swear to god if you don't—"

"I can feel your wet little cunt, Noir." I cut her off, my eyes darkening from the feel of my cock swelling in my jeans. I notice her cheeks pinken before she looks away again, avoiding further interaction.

Smirking, I continue to terrorize her, enjoying every second of her discomfort, "Tell me, can Limp Dick make you wet without barely touching you? Actually, don't answer. I know for a fucking fact he can't."

Her eyes flash to mine, squinting them as she brings her face close to mine, attempting to assert her authority. "Why don't you stop talking about my sex life and get one of your own, freak," she bites back bitterly.

"I have one, she is rubbing her soaked pussy all over my abs right this second and it's getting me so fucking hard."

She rolls her eyes at my calm response, yet I catch the small smile playing on her lips before she faces away, trying to conceal it, but I know deep down she digs my psychotic shit.

"You're deluded, Hell. I'll never let you touch me, and I will never touch you," she says, but her voice is full of lies.

"Good thing I don't give a fuck about consent when it comes to you. You make me want to do terrible, terrible things." As soon as the icy words slip from my lips, her eyes snap to mine, but I maintain a stoic expression.

What does she want me to say? That I'll patiently wait like a good little boy until she lets me? Yeah. Fucking. Right. I see through her façade of loyalty to a man who can't even get hard for her. I know she craves the dangers that surround me, despite her little protests. It's only a matter of time before she surrenders willingly and drops to her knees but if she doesn't, I'll force her. My fucking patience is wearing thin already.

"Rapists make me feel sick and that says a lot about you," she declares with a frown on her face.

I lift a brow at her confession as I respond. "I don't need to rape you, Noir. You're going to push back on my cock, trying to take all of me. You can be in denial all you want."

She grins at my bluntness, shaking her head, but I am dead fucking serious. As I watch her, I zone in on her features with fascination.

"What the fuck. Honestly, your perception is warped," she finally answers, trying to fight her amusement.

"Everything about me is fucking warped, yet it clearly gets you off judging by your wet panties."

She stares into my eyes, now expressionless, lost in thought until she suddenly glances down to our right. I reluctantly tear my gaze away from her pretty face and turn my head to follow her line of sight, only to notice Limp Dick standing at the entrance, looking up at us.

As expected, she unwraps her legs, sliding down my body to land on her feet. As I stop the wheel, he stares at Dolly with a stern look on his face, fuelling my desire to kill the motherfucker. I slip my hand into my sweatpants to retrieve my knife so I can launch it into his fucking skull, only to realize it's not there.

He suddenly turns around and storms out causing Dolly to glance at me. "Just leave me alone, Hell. I don't want you." She declares coldly which makes my jaw tense with irritation, the need to control her seeping into my icy veins.

When our ring is low enough, she sits on it and jumps down. I watch her every move as she heads back to Blush and the girls, ready to train again.

CHAPTER SEVEN

After hours of rigorous training, I'm a sweating mess, my body is throbbing with exhaustion, and I am not feeling myself. I've pushed myself to the limit, perfecting a small routine for the performance hasn't been easy on my body or mind.

The tent is nearly empty now, darkness falling outside. Blush watches me intently as she backs away, her pink gaze reflecting admiration. "You did well today, Noir. You're a natural."

I follow her with a small smile, and as we make our way out of the tent, I look at Hell, who is now with Soul and Wrath. Our eyes meet briefly until I am out of sight.

As Blush and I head for the exit, the sounds of music and screams reach my ears, causing my brows to furrow.

"Wait, is the carnival open?" I ask as we approach the exit.

"Yeah, it's open to the public mostly every day of the week. The Cirque is open late Saturday nights, but Dark Night is once a month, and it's a private event, away from public eyes."

I cast a curious glance at her beside me as we draw closer to the bustling atmosphere outside. "What is Dark Night? I still haven't been told."

The carnival atmosphere is both exhilarating and chilling as Blush speaks beside me. "Well, think this but plus one hundred in fear."

As we come to a stop at the exit of the tent, I look around, taking in the sights of the horror carnival coming to life. The rides are all in motion now—the rollercoaster roaring along its tracks, the riders' shrieks filling the air and the massive Ferris wheel is full of twinkling lights as it slowly turns.

Workers jump out at visitors, their disfigured masks eliciting screams from the crowd. Tricksters perform daring acts with knives and fire, catching everyone's attention. Sinister laughter echoes from hidden corners, and shadowy figures lurk in the darkness, their eyes glowing with malevolent intent. Twisted amusements stands offer prizes, their gifts ranging from deranged toys, masks, and fake severed limbs, adding to the eerie atmosphere.

When a guy sluggishly strolls past us, my eyes widen and follow his every move. I observe the frightening scarecrow bag obscuring his head with a bloodied axe dragging behind him, the sharp noise of the blade against the concrete slicing through the air.

Nearby, a young woman with long red hair, dressed as a creepy clown, cackles, and skips merrily through the sea of people, swinging a baseball bat wrapped in barbed wire dangerously close to bystanders.

My eyes flash to Blush and she continues with a menacing grin. "This is tame compared to what Dark Night is about. The cirque, carnival, the glass maze, and the death rooms are open."

I shake my head, utterly confused. "What do you mean the death rooms? Where are they?"

She nods to the huge Ferris wheel. "It's hidden behind the wheel. It's closed right now, otherwise, I would show you, but you will see it next week, I'm sure."

"You didn't answer the first part—"

"Hey, isn't that the guy you're here with?"

My head turns swiftly as soon as she cuts me off and I scan the crowded area until I spot Eli standing by one of the rides, operating it.

I notice he is talking to a young girl and my brows pinch. "Who is she?" I ask before looking at Blush, and she cocks her head to the side as she answers. "Her name is Stephanie; she comes here often. She's obsessed with this place and visits every weekend."

I nod before looking over in their direction again but when I see him leaning in, tucking her hair carefully behind her ear, a strange feeling settles in my gut. The scene before me is more bothering that the monsters roaming around, and it's certainly not jealousy that I feel. It's something deeper, something that feels like a warning.

I tilt my head to the side, "How fucking old is she?"

"Hmm... Around seventeen I think."

My brow raises and my blood boils, but before I can react, I hear Madame's voice behind me. "I don't want you doing too much, Noir. After your small performance and introduction, you should enjoy the show."

I turn around to face her, desperate to escape the violent thoughts swirling in my mind. I offer a small nod and she continues. "Get some rest. You worked hard today."

I give her a half-smile before something springs to my mind. "I don't suppose you have any spare curtains for our trailer, do you?"

She gives Blush a brief glance before her eyes return to mine. "Sure. I'll have Billy come and fit some."

HOLLOW HELLION

It's late evening and I am standing in front of the bathroom mirror; I stare at myself with a dead look in my teary eyes. Tonight, I am feeling the full effects of having no medication. I am suffering. My mood is so low that I am finding it almost impossible to claw my way out of the depression. Eli isn't here, and it's driving me insane being here on my own, but also I know I need to be on my own.

As a tear drops down my cheek with a blink, I give a quick glance at the razor hanging up in the shower. My gaze lingers, and my mind screams for me to hurt myself just to relieve some of the pain that lives inside me. I squeeze my eyes shut, facing aside, trying to stop myself.

Images of my past life flash before my eyes as I drop to my knees. I kick my feet against the tiles, pushing myself into the nearest corner, covering my ears as I hear his voice repeatedly in my mind, whispering horrible things.

Kyro. My stepfather. The man who abused me from the moment my mom died until I escaped. The man who chained me up, never to see daylight or the outside world during my late teens. The man who destroyed everything about me just because he could, and he knew I had no one else. There was no one to come and save me from his cruelty because no one even knew I even existed. Except Arabella of course.

The memories flood back, each one a searing blade cutting deeper into my soul. His evil laughter, the feel of his rough hands on my body, and the suffocating darkness of the room where he kept me. The sense of hopelessness and despair that seemed to swallow me whole. Even now, months later, his voice still echoes in my head, a constant reminder of the trauma I faced.

I rock back and forth, trying to drown out the noise, but it's relentless. The weight of the past crushes me, making it hard to breathe. I want to scream, but I know no one can save me from these demons. They're a part of me now, embedded deep within, feeding on my pain. I can't give in. I won't let him win. I've come too far and fought too hard to be free of him, and I refuse to let his memory destroy me.

Slowly, I open my eyes, forcing myself to breathe deeply to calm my racing heart. I focus on the present and on the things I can control. I am stronger than he ever knew—stronger than even I knew.

When I suddenly hear the trailer door open and shut, I quickly wipe my eye's, knowing Eli is home. After I have fixed myself and slipped into my black tracksuit, I gently open the bathroom door and head toward the kitchen, where I hear him moving around.

As I enter, he has his back to me, busy preparing food. He side-eyes me, sensing my presence, and I go to the coffee pot.

Pouring myself a large mug, I decide to break the silence, feeling the tension already thick in the air. "How was your first evening at the carnival?"

He doesn't respond immediately, just keeps chopping vegetables and the sound of the knife hitting the cutting board fills the room, amplifying the uneasy silence between us.

After a moment, he finally speaks, his tone devoid of its usual warmth. "Yeah, good."

I take a sip of my coffee while observing him carefully, the heat spreading through me.

"Who was that young chick I saw pestering you?" I question, trying to probe him after the uneasy feeling I had when I first saw him with her. Wondering if that is what has triggered my downward spiral tonight.

He immediately stops cutting the vegetables, pausing to think about my question. "Who was that guy I saw you had your legs wrapped around?" he counters my question with a question, his voice sharp.

My teeth grind down hard before I slam the mug down on the counter beside me, "I work with him, E. That's Hellion, the ringleader of The Hollow's here. I'll be working with him a lot. He is not a customer." I bite back.

I know I am lying to him and probably myself. Hell is becoming so much more than just someone I work with. He is becoming my stalker and a pain in my fucking ass.

Eli suddenly faces me, clearly not convinced, "Really? It didn't look like just work to me. He had his hands all over your ass," he raises an eyebrow with his accusation.

As he turns back around, I draw a deep breath, trying to keep my temper in check, after the evening I've had.

"Neither did that girl. How old was she?" I tilt my head to the side my question laced with suspicion.

He suddenly snaps, his voice filled with bubbling anger. "Fuck off, Noir."

I narrow my eyes, scanning him more intently and I continue to press, the unease in my gut growing. "You're into younger chicks now?"

He suddenly turns, pointing the knife in my direction and my body tenses. His eyes are cold, his teeth clenched as he bites on his words. "I said fuck off!"

I stare at him blankly, masking the turmoil inside me. This reaction is so unlike Eli. He's usually so kind and sweet, but now he seems like I am looking at a stranger. We've only known each other for four months, confined to a truck, but is this who he truly is when we're living together? His entire demeanor has changed since we came here.

The silence stretches, heavy and uncomfortable, yet I know I need to make my feelings clear, "Don't worry, E, you're not bound to me. You can do what the fuck you want." I say coldly.

I take a step forward, my dark gaze unwavering. "But let me make one thing clear. If I find out she's underage, I will take your fucking balls off and replace your eyeballs with them."

My voice is steady, showing him a side of me he's never seen since he gave me the same courtesy. "I don't like child abusers," I declare through clenched teeth.

He stares at me, his eyes scanning mine as I lean over, unfazed by the knife in his hand and take a chopped raw carrot off the counter and pop it into my mouth. As I draw back, he turns away, showing me his back.

I chew on the carrot, closing my eyes, trying to reclaim my inner peace, to push away the shadows of the past that threaten to overwhelm me. The room is thick with tension, the silence oppressive.

When I open my eyes once more, I watch him for a little longer, then turn and head to the bedroom. As I close the door behind me, I lean against it, taking a moment to gather my thoughts before heading for bed.

CHAPTER EIGHT

It's way past midnight, and I am lying in bed, staring up at the dark ceiling. Eli snores beside me, loud and untamed, making it impossible to sleep. My mind races, churning over the past, the present, Eli, and the future.

After what feels like an eternity, I gently draw the duvet back and sit up, swinging my legs over the edge of the bed. Without waking Eli, I quietly sneak out of the bedroom and head to the living room. I grab my hoodie and Converse before slipping them on, then head for the door.

Stepping out of my trailer, the cold night wraps around me like an icy cloak. I gently close the door behind me, pulling my hoodie over my head and shoving my hands deep into my pockets for warmth. Once I feel prepared, I head toward the main carnival, eager to explore it.

The fog is thick and dense, obscuring my view of the ground beneath my feet and when I've made my way through the maze of trailers, I slow my pace, aware that I'm nearing The Hollow's trailer. Deep male voices drift from that direction, and I stop, pressing myself against a trailer. Carefully, I peek around the corner and see all three of them—Hell, Soul, and Wrath—talking, with Soul perched on his bike.

My mind races, trying to plan a way around them, when suddenly Hell spins around. I jerk my head back into the shadows, flattening myself against the trailer while my heart hammers in my chest. How the fuck did he spot me?

The murmurs of Soul's voice continues, but Hell's sharp instincts keep my nerves on edge. I risk another small peek, instantly seeing his glowing eyes sweep over the area, not quite looking at me but close enough to send a tremble through me.

The silence that follows becomes deafening until I hear Soul speak louder. "What can you sense, Hell?"

Hell's eyes continue to search, his posture is taut, coiled like a predator, ready to pounce at any moment.

After some time, he finally responds. "Nothing."

I notice Soul shifts, standing off the bike, his own senses now heightened by Hell's. His eyes dart around, analyzing every shadow and flicker of light. "You sure?"

Before Hell can answer, in the distance, a faint noise—a metallic clang—echoes through the night, drawing all their attention away from me. It's a small distraction, but it's enough and I take advantage of the moment, inching my way along the side of the trailer. After striding over the paths between the trailers, taking another route, I finally find myself at the edge of the carnival grounds. The mist thins and I pause, catching my breath. The silence is heavy except for the hum of the Ferris wheel and the occasional creak of the rollercoaster. The carnival, once a place of joy and screams, now feels like a haunted wasteland.

As I walk in deeper, I slowly pass a large, eerie carousel, creaking and groaning, but it isn't the cheerful ride of childhood memories; instead of the cute creatures that you would usually sit on, it has skeletal horses. Their empty eye sockets and gaping mouths give the impression that they are trapped in eternal torment, forever galloping on their circular path.

I continue, passing by the rollercoaster, its tracks rusted and twisted, and the Ferris wheel, its cabins swaying gently in the cold breeze, empty and abandoned. I notice a huge sign that reads: The Glass Maze, but I pass it, heading toward the death rooms behind the wheel and I feel my sudden fear teetering on the edge. My mind becomes hazy, screaming at me from the inside to turn back, to return to the safety of my trailer, but I don't. I push forward, wanting to find out about The Death Room's most of all. I have a feeling that I am being kept in the dark about this place on purpose. People are not telling me what Dark Night is, avoiding my questions, so, tonight I plan to get some answers.

HOLLOW HELLION

Once behind the wheel, I find myself confronted by a tall metal fence that is locked by a heavy chain. The bars are cold under my fingertips as I peer through them, scanning the area behind it. The fog is thicker here, the air almost suffocating, but in the distance, partially covered by the trees at the forest's edge, I notice a huge, black building. It stands with blacked out windows that have bars across them.

The building gives an aura of warning and the trees surrounding it seem to lean in, like they're trying to shield it or perhaps to scare off intruders. The forest itself is deadly silent, the usual night sounds of crickets are missing, as if even nature is too afraid to stir in this place.

Suddenly, a figure catches my eye from behind the fence, near the building, and my stomach drops, the hairs on the back of my neck standing to attention. I squint, pressing my face closer to the cold metal bars, straining to see more clearly in the dim light.

Then I see it's her. Her outline is faint, hidden by darkness, but unmistakable. *Arabella.* Her dark hair shines against the moonlight, and she moves slowly, almost cautiously, as if she knows she's being watched, but her eyes are fixed on something ahead of her. Not me.

She seems oblivious to my presence, and something awful settles in my gut. My breathing picks up, tightening my chest until she suddenly darts into the building. Not thinking clearly, I leap up, grasping the top of the fence, and climb it as quickly as I can, the metal clinking loudly with each movement. I drop down the other side before sprinting toward the building.

As I make it to the entrance, I pause, my breath ragged, my hand gripping the cold door handle. I glance back, half-expecting to see someone there, but the area is deserted. Taking a final deep breath, I pull the door open and step inside, the heavy door creaking behind me.

HOLLOW HELLION

Inside, the air is musty, the heavy scent of decay lingering, so potent that I have to cover my nose with my sleeve to stop myself from hurling. Shadows loom on the black walls, twisting and turning with each flicker of the dim overhead red lights. Thick, silver chains hang low, clinking as I walk through, attempting to push them out of my way. My footsteps echo softly as I move deeper into the building, my eyes scanning every corner for any sign of Arabella.

Once I am through the corridor of chains, I hear a gentle rustling ahead and I freeze, my pulse racing. Arabella's silhouette appears at the far end of the long hallway, her back to me. She stands still for a moment, then slowly turns her head, her empty eyes meeting mine. A chill runs down my spine, but I force myself to move forward, wanting to reach her.

"Arabella? What are you doing here? Are you okay?" I murmur through a shuddering breath.

As I get closer, her expression shifts—a flicker of something haunting—and she opens her mouth into a wide gape, like a huge black hole, before letting out a high-pitched scream that pierces through me.

The sound is unlike anything I've ever heard, a blood curdling wail that reverberates through the building, echoing off the walls. I instantly slap my hands over my ears, the pain in them unbearable, as I drop to my knees. The scream continues, a relentless assault on my senses, making my vision blur and my head throb. The red lights start to flicker, and Arabella's face is twisted in a distorted mask of agony and rage, her eyes wide, and locked onto mine.

I struggle to stay upright, the pressure in my head building. My heart hammers furiously in my chest, but through the daze of pain, I try to crawl toward her, to tame her, my movements sluggish.

Just as I think I can't endure another moment; the scream abruptly stops and silence crashes down around me, so sudden its disorienting. I remain on my knees, panting, my hands still pressed to my ears.

Slowly, I lower them, blinking rapidly, but I instantly notice through my blurred vision that Arabella is gone. The hallway stretches out in front of me, empty, the chains swaying behind me, and I push myself to my feet, trembling while I stagger ahead, still determined to find her. I can't lose her again.

My legs feel heavy with exhaustion, and I have to lean against the cool walls for support. Tears stream down my cheeks as I fight to maintain my balance, but when I turn a corner, I catch sight of her once more, standing beside a door on her right.

Her crystal blue eyes bore into mine, emotionless. I take a shaky step forward, but before I can get close enough, she darts through the door, slamming it shut with a loud thud. I sprint ahead and push open the door, my mind full of desperation, but as soon I cross the threshold, I suddenly feel myself tilting forward over an edge, hardly noticing the gaping chasm below.

Terror grips me as I feel myself falling, but a strong hand swiftly seizes the back of my hoodie, keeping me suspended over the abyss. My breath is caught in my throat as I hang over the hollow floor, my wide eyes scanning the deadly spikes below while my converses grip on the edge of the bottom of the door tightly.

The realization of how close I was to meeting my death by a trap hits me until I am yanked back to safety. I stumble backward as they release me, and I fall up against a wall.

Suddenly, the lights cut out, plunging me into darkness. My breathing quickens, becoming the only sound I can hear apart from the ringing in my ears. Panic sets in, and I start running, banging into walls as loud, heavy footsteps chase me from behind. My shrieks of horror echo through the building until I spot a set of red, swirling eyes far ahead.

Hyperventilating, I turn on my heel, only to see another pair of green, vortexed orbs closing in. I run again, my hands scraping down the walls in a frantic search for an exit. The eerie laughter of men surrounds me, growing louder, more menacing.

Suddenly, I bang into something hard, and I stumble backward from the impact, but before I can react, I'm hoisted over a strong shoulder. I scream and kick out as they carry me, still in panic mode, but they are seemingly unfazed by my fight, until we enter a dimly red-lit room.

HOLLOW HELLION

With a thud on my back, I'm lowered onto a hard surface, the impact knocking the breath from my lungs. When my vision clears, I'm met with the sight of Hell looming over me, his gaze stern. As I lie on a wooden table, he is positioned between my legs, his hands braced beside my head. After scrutinizing my frightened expression with curiosity, he lowers his face toward mine, and I draw in a quick breath. "What the fuck are you doing in here alone, Dolly?" He asks, biting on his words.

I shake my head once, not willing to tell him about seeing Arabella since it was clearly some fucked-up hallucination.

"Why were you guys scaring me like that?" I say, trying to catch my breath.

He tilts his head to the side, "What?"

I stay silent, wondering if my fear had made me imagine Soul and Wrath as well.

"You nearly got yourself fucking killed, Noir, and when the automatic lights cut out, you ran for your fucking life," he says, his voice harsh.

I quickly change the subject, shifting the focus away from my vulnerable moment, trying to unwind my coiled body. "I was just curious. What is this place?"

I look up and glance around me, taking in the surroundings. A small black room illuminated by a single red bulb, sharp spikes protruding from the walls and ceiling, with a table in the centre. Hell's presence above me feels oddly comforting even though he creeps me the fuck out as well.

"It's exactly what it's called. The death rooms." He responds.

I look at him, searching his eyes, "You guys kill people here?"

"In here, they kill them fucking selves. Hence the death traps."

My stare drops to his lips. "Again, your warped perception is shining through, Hell."

He suddenly grips the small of my waist in his large hands, pulling me further down the table until my crotch is pressed against his.

"And what would you do without my warped fucking perception, Noir? Your tiny body would have plummeted into those spikes if I didn't think or watch you like I do." His gaze hungrily wanders down my frame as he continues. "Nothing in this place is as dangerous as you being alone here with me though." My breathing quickens, my body tense, and the weight of his words sink in. "Me saving you is becoming a regular occurrence, don't you think, Dolly? I am now demanding shit in return."

"The first one was your fault, so it doesn't count." When I snap out the words, his black-painted mouth twitches with a small smirk, lowering his eyes again to my heaving chest before responding. "Maybe not, but this one definitely counts and I'm ready to collect the debt."

"So, you didn't just save me out of the goodness of your heart, Hell?" I ask, hoping for a lifeline.

He arches an eyebrow at my question. "Goodness? Heart? I have neither, pretty girl. I'm either completely empty or overflowing with darkness. Tonight, you get to decide which."

I swallow hard, "I did say I would never let you touch me." I attempt to protest.

His eyes flash to mine in an unsettling manner, and I can feel a swirl of conflicting emotions within me.

"Oh no, I won't be touching you if I can help it." He responds calmly.

I feel confusion before he murmurs close to my face. "You're going to make yourself fucking come in front of me. That's what the fuck I want. I want to see what you look like when you're actually coming apart."

As his dirty words hang in the air, I find myself stunned, my lips parting slightly in surprise. While staring back into the depths of his whirling lenses, I am reminded by the emptiness that exists within me when it comes to pleasure. It's a void that has been shaped by a history of trauma. One that E has never been able to fill. His struggle with medication doesn't help.

The truth is, I rarely find release by doing it myself either. Pleasure is non-existent in my life, a haunting memory that I have never truly experienced. It was stolen from me long ago, but now as Hell's heated gaze lingers on me with such ferocity, I am almost tempted to confront the reality of my own desires—or lack thereof. I could be rubbing or fucking my pussy with my dildo for hours and the orgasm might not strike, which is embarrassing. I would be humiliated if that happened in front of him.

"But this place, it's—" I try to say anything to get out of it, knowing I am not mentally sane after the shit I just went through tonight.

He brings his mouth dangerously close to mine, cutting me off, and clenches his teeth with aggression that shows his inner sexual frustration. "You either do it or I fucking will. I am not letting you leave this place until I know your pussy is dripping and satisfied."

I gulp down the lump forming in my throat, but he doesn't wait any longer. He grasps the waistband of my sweatpants and yanks them down my legs until they're at my ankles, trapped by my Converse.

"Hell, wait." He continues to pull my sweatpants off completely, but his eyes stay on mine. "This is the last time you ever come near me like this again. The watching and stalking shit stops. The fucking torment and weird ass behaviour stops. This obsession stops. I don't want you."

His jaw tenses, revealing his displeasure at my cold words, but I mean it. I didn't come here for this. My purpose was to fucking work and leave, not to entangle myself in a sexual relationship with a psychotic maniac.

His eyes trail down my body before returning to meet mine, a silent challenge in their depths before he finally speaks. "I better make the most of it then. Strip naked."

I shake my head once before responding. "What?"

"Strip. The. Fuck. Naked. Noir." His icy tone is full of dominance, a silent threat that if I don't do as I am told, he will still do it himself, which I think he wants; he seems to crave full control, but I know I need control too.

The command hangs between us, charged with tension as well as the strange connection we share. I inhale deeply before sitting up, then drag the zipper down on my hoodie. After shrugging it off, I move on to my white crop top, rising it over my head until my bare tits bounce free.

I can feel his feral stare all over me, analysing my movements and biting into my flesh, yet I refuse to look him in the eyes. I lift myself, dragging my black panties down my legs and as soon as I'm only in my Converse and my clothes drop to the floor, the room falls silent. A wave of self-consciousness washes over me, even though I know he's already seen me naked, but this time I am not in the safety of my trailer, so instinctively, I cover myself with my arms, feeling exposed and vulnerable.

Suddenly, Hell seizes my waist, roughly manhandling me and effortlessly forces me up onto my knees in the middle of the small table, positioning me exactly how he wants.

He leans down, delicately scooping my panties up with one finger and he raises them to his eye level, inspecting them closely before tossing them onto my lap.

"Stuff them inside your cunt. Let's see how wet you can get them." He demands.

I blink blankly at him, sensing that he's pushing my boundaries right away, but I am not sure how to react to his degradation.

"Now, Noir! I not going to hold myself much longer; I will force them inside your fucking pussy."

My body tightens as his powerful voice echoes through the dead silent building, and my eyes close briefly before I glance down at my panties.

I hesitantly take them from my lap, clutching them into my fist. With trembling fingers, I lower them between my thighs, gradually stuffing them inside myself until they're entirely engulfed.

"Now touch yourself. No shyness around me, pretty girl." He orders, "Your body is beyond beautiful."

I keep my head lowered, hearing his boots against the hard floor as he slowly walks around the table, taking in every inch of my naked body from all angles. The small room is thick with tension, my skin prickling under his greedy gaze. As soon I press my fingers through my folds and touch my clit, the sensation that is supposed to follow is non-existent, as usual. I push down, rubbing my bud, trying to coax some feeling from it. The circular motion is familiar, but it gives me no real pleasure. I keep my eyes screwed tight, focusing as much as I can, willing myself to gain something, anything so this can be over with.

His wicked presence looms over me, a dark and intense energy that heightens the pressure of the moment, making me wonder if he can sense that I am odd, not like the other girls he has probably fucked.

My thoughts swirl, anxiety peaking, not helping the fucking situation at all.

After some time, my hand starts to ache, and my clit throbs, but not in the right way. I hear him stop right in front of me, and the sound of his blade flicking out makes my heart jump. He places the chilly metal beneath my chin, forcing me to raise my head, and my eyes instinctively meet his.

"You struggle to find pleasure, Dolly."

His words hit me like a ton of bricks, the sting sharper than his knife could ever be. It hurts more than he could ever know. My movements freeze, and when he withdraws the knife, I lower my head again, avoiding eye contact, my body so stiff with humiliation that its ready to run out the fucking door.

He moves around me again and when he halts behind me, he suddenly cups his hand over mine between my legs causing them to tense. His other arm wraps beneath my breasts, dragging me closer to him and the table's edge. My heart races, my breathing picking, his grip is strong while he asserts control.

"Now rub your cunt," he orders with a snarl, his breath hot against my ear.

"But—" As I try to protest, he removes his hand from mine and roughly snatches my face, forcing me to look back at him.

His swirling eyes are filled with a darkness, and he tightens his teeth. "Do as you're fucking told, or I'll do it for you, and trust me, Noir, I won't stop. I'll keep forcing those fucking O's out of your tight pussy until you can no longer stand it."

His voice is full of honesty, his grasp on my face is so tight that it's almost painful, but it roots me to the spot, and I find myself obeying.

When I start to stroke my clit again, his eyes scan my features and he lowers his palm to my throat, almost stealing my breath with how hard he grabs it. His lips brush over mine, just as they did this morning, but this time, there is no one here to stop me from caving in. No one is coming to save me from his wicked embrace.

Tilting his head to the side, he flattens his pierced tongue at the edge of my parted lips, trailing it teasingly across them and instantly, the walls of my pussy clench around my panties, a surge of electricity surging through me. His grip tightens on my neck, the forbidden intimacy becoming consuming, pulling me deeper into a vortex of lust and danger.

As soon as he tries to lick me again, I do the inevitable and catch his tongue between my lips, sucking it hard, since I can't seem to stop myself, which instantly pulls a beastly growl from him.

Oh fuck.

As soon as I let go, our mouths merge and our tongues collide. The connection that storms through me sets my entire body on fire, and I start to stroke myself harder. He devours my mouth hungrily, his fingers digging into my jaw, anchoring me and with each flick of his piercing over my tongue, he delves deeper, attempting to taste every corner.

The flavour of him is intoxicating, a mix of tobacco and aggression, but when his hand glides down my chest, tracing the contours, I instinctively reach up, grasping his wrist, not allowing him to take any more than what he asked for.

"I swear to fucking god, Dolly if you don't start being a good little slut..." He snarls furiously against my lips, flicking my hand away.

Following his angry warning, his hand lands on my breast, giving it a tight, bruising squeeze, the sensation delivering a delicious pain, causing my brows to crease. He growls against my lips as his thumb flicks over my ridged, pierced nipple, then lowers his hand until he is grabbing mine. He takes it away from my bud, lifting my fingers to his mouth and he sucks the tips that were just on my clit, holding eye contact as he makes them wet for me. I watch through heavy eyes as he does it, the act driving me crazy. *Fucking hell.*

He returns my hand between my legs with his over it and presses his fingers down on mine, adding further pressure to my aching bud and he guides my movements.

As I feel his wetness on my clit, I start to become desperate for my release and for him. I fill my mind with dirty thoughts of him taking me as I keep my eyes closed and just when I think I couldn't want him any more than I do, I feel the cold steel of his blade dragging down my inner thigh, teasing and threatening me. How I was feeling tonight and what he said to me this morning returns to my mind, sending arousal through me at the possibility of him cutting me while he fucks me, and the fantasies start to consume my senses.

"Fuck, cut me, Hell." I demand, my murmur breathless.

Without hesitation, he slowly slices my skin, a sting followed by a warm trickle of my blood running down my thigh. The pain barely registers amidst the rush of adrenaline and desire it brings, eliciting a dragging moan from my lips.

"Again." I gasp out with my eyes rolling.

He moves on to make another cut beside it, this time firmer, and sharper, causing me to groan from the sensation. The friction against my clit starts to send shockwaves of pleasure through my veins and my body trembles, knowing that what he is doing is working in the most fucked-up way possible.

I surrender to my unhinged mindset, riding the waves of euphoria that is swelling inside of me as he continues to mark me. After dropping the knife onto the table, his hand moves over my hurting wounds with a possessive power, smearing the blood over my skin. When he grasps my breast again, painting my flesh with gore, he squeezes it viciously and my moans escalate into desperate cries against his lips.

The rougher he gets with me, the further I teeter on the edge of destruction. With a feral hunger, he sinks his teeth into my bottom lip so harshly that it pulls a scream from me, a raw sound of bliss. Once he releases, he licks away the blood he drew before plunging his tongue back into my mouth.

While he consumes me, his fingers and thumb press harshly over the slices he inflicted, the boundary between pain and satisfaction blurring into oblivion. I find myself riding both our hands, rocking my hips in the same rhythm as my pounding heart until I am utterly consumed by the most powerful climax of my entire life.

As a scream rips from my throat, my pussy and body convulsing with the force of my orgasm, I throw my head back, crashing against his chest as my spine bends inward as if an entity is trying to escape me. His hand strengthens around my throat, grounding me against him while with the other, he forces me to continue rubbing my throbbing clit, pushing me into overdrive.

"That's my good Little Dolly. I knew you had it in you," he growls, satisfaction evident in his tone.

Once I have ridden out my high, we slow down, my breathing steadying, and my sweaty, blood-dampened body gradually unwinds from the powerful release. I feel him reaching down behind me until he's gently pinching my panties that are still stuffed inside me, and slowly, he drags them out.

When he has them, he releases my throat before taking a step back and sliding them over my Converses. As the wet fabric meets my bare legs, I lift myself so he can continue putting them on me. He wedges them far up my ass crack before releasing them with a sharp snap against my hips.

Without warning, he seizes a handful of my hair, yanking it back, causing me to hiss and when I finally open my heavy eyes, I find myself locked in a silent stare with Hell, our gazes speaking volumes where words fail.

Slowly, he brings his mouth close to mine, his breath warm against my parted lips, "Now go back to him, wearing the sinful fucking mess you just made for me. Let every step remind you of how I degraded you tonight, and how you relished every filthy second of it."

My gut twists with guilt, but I don't show it as he searches my eyes before his sweep down the front of my body once more.

"You're fucking perfect, Noir. Every single part of you. Don't ever think otherwise," he says, his words genuine and raw.

A strange sensation overrides the guilt I just felt, but I continue to remain expressionless even if the insane connection between us has never been clearer. His sharp jaw visibly tenses, his demeanor showing his temptation to take more than what we agreed to before he suddenly releases me, his warmth dissipating from my body.

My eyes close, then I glance down at myself, noticing my thighs decorated with his slices. Turning my head to look for Hell, I find him gone, disappearing like a ghost in the night, leaving me alone in the aftermath of our depraved moment.

With furrowed brows, I call out for him, "Hell?" My voice echoes through the empty building, but there is no response.

I can still feel his burning touch lingering on my skin as I sit in the same position for a moment, wondering why he left so quickly until my thoughts turn to how he is the first man to ever accomplish that. I liked the way he guided the situation, but also allowed me to have full control of my pleasure.

Is Hell truly the monster he portrays? He breathes evil yet radiates a beautiful darkness that connects to my soul. Why do I have a feeling this is the beginning of the end and what's between us won't stop? I can already feel myself crumbling every time he wants to take from me. I need to avoid him at all costs or leave entirely. I can't get attached just because he's the only man who's ever made me feel things I never knew I could.

I also have to figure out what to do about E and make sense of what happened tonight. Maybe not taking my medication caused a psychotic hallucination when I saw Arabella, a gut-wrenching reminder of how much I miss her and that I'm here, in some kind of fucked up killing carnival and not searching for her anymore. Perhaps it's a sign that I shouldn't be here at all.

After some time alone, I gather my clothes and get dressed, starting to feel the unease settle over me at the thought of being here on my own again.

Finally exiting the death rooms, I make my way back to the trailer, each step weighed down by the confusion of the night's events, the wetness of my panties and the discomfort of the wounds etched into my flesh.

CHAPTER NINE

After making sure she gets home, I wait in the shadows, watching as she enters her trailer. Once the door closes behind her, my jaw tenses, and I linger for a moment longer, my eyes fixed on the spot where she disappeared.

I finally turn away, heading back to my own trailer, reaching into my leather jacket pocket. I pull out a cigarette and light it, drawing in the calming, toxic fumes into my lungs.

While admiring the bright red stain of her blood on my hand, the sight makes my aching cock twitch against my tight jeans, my thoughts crazy as I think about how close I came to losing control. I had to leave, but I'm far from finished. After tonight, I know for certain my Dolly has hidden demons and fantasies as predicted. I now know what draws me to her and I crave her fucking darkness.

Although she may think she was the one in control because I allowed her the power in that moment, the opposite is true. Her fight to push me away, only fuels my delusion to want her more. Imagine the depths of sensations I could evoke if I were to have her beneath me, her little body weakening and responding to my every whim. The thought of inflicting both pleasure and pain upon her, exploring the boundaries of her limits, makes my fucking balls throb. I want to show her the lengths of my sick desires, guiding her through a journey of dark euphoria.

With each sadistic game we play, I want her to know how beautiful I think she is, drawing her deeper into our shared world of depravity that knows no fucking bounds.

When she asked me to cut her, surrendering completely to my wicked fantasies without me even forcing them upon her, and the way she exposed herself to me deepens my obsession with her. She surprised me by agreeing to let me see her completely naked and vulnerable. I expected a fight, but instead, she seemed to relish the feeling. Her eyes shone with desire as she obeyed my commands with little hesitation.

The way her skin flushed under my gaze, the slight tremor in her breath—it was clear: Noir craves degradation and being controlled. The memory of her trembling body and the way I felt her greedy pussy pulsing against our hands while she bucked her hips run wildly in my mind. The way her breathing came out ragged after she screamed, her eyes rolling to the back of her head, how fucking soaked her panties were and the sight of the blood dripping from her thighs invade my perverted thoughts.

Fuck. I'll stop at nothing to take everything from her. I want to break her. I want to make her as insane as I am.

As I make my way back to my trailer, the realization that this is far from over settles in. Yeah, I reluctantly agreed that I would leave her alone, but I fucking lied. I lied so fucking hard just to get what I want. Things are about to get a whole lot worse for, Noir. This connection, this hunger I have for her, it's driving me even more crazy than I already am, and I can't stop myself.

Now that I've had a taste of the darkness that stirs inside her, there's no going back, I want it all; I want to see it all. She has ignited something insatiable within me, and I won't fucking rest until I have her completely, until she is mine in every sense of the word, even if I have to take it.

HOLLOW HELLION

While entering our trailer, I take in the familiar black walls and floor. Wrath's bedroom is downstairs, while Soul's and mine are upstairs. As I pass through the small kitchen area, I peel off my leather jacket, tossing it carelessly onto a chair. I continue towards Wrath's room at the back of the trailer, but I notice his door is slightly ajar. When I am within reach, I push it with my palm and I enter, only to stop as I take in the scene before me.

Wrath stands shirtless, only wearing black jeans, with a young woman suspended in front of him. Her wrists are shackled upward to chains fixed into the ceiling. Her pale, naked and unmoving body is hanging with her head lowered, her long dark hair obscuring her face. Small intricate words cover every inch of her skin, written in black script that I can't read from this distance. Wrath holds a pen in his hand, carefully adding to the markings on her figure.

Once he acknowledges my presence and turns to look at me over his shoulder, his red spiral contacts meet mine.

Jesus fucking Christ, what the actual fuck.

Feeling the usual mixture of disbelief and confusion when it comes to him, I've always known Wrath's madness knows no fucking bounds, and in this moment, he seems more unhinged than ever. He is probably the most psychotic person I have ever fucking met and that's saying something. Wrath has selective mutism, and he will only at times speak to me and Soul; anyone else gets complete silence from him. Well, from what I know.

As I watch him carefully from a distance, he blinks blankly at me, and I shake my head, "Is she fucking dead?" I ask, genuinely curious.

He doesn't speak, he just stares at me as if he is peering right through my existence and my teeth grind. "We spoke about this, Wrath. Why the fuck do you keep doing this shit?"

He lifts his shoulder, "They never do as they're told." He finally explains, completely unfazed by how horrifying he is.

I fight the urge to argue with him because I know I can't judge. After all, we're all messed up in our own disturbing ways, but sometimes, I think my brothers are even more unstable than I am or maybe that's just me being in denial of how far my own depravity goes. I try to keep them in check if I can, or they'd bring this whole place crashing down. Each of us has our own twisted story of how we ended up like this, how we ended up here, and none of them are pretty, but despite the darkness that binds us, we're still a fucking family. Our trauma bond runs deep, forging an unbreakable connection between us. I keep them closer than ever since Haze was killed and it sometimes keeps me awake at night thinking I could lose them too.

When I remain silent, not knowing what the fuck to say, he turns back around, continuing to write on her and I watch for a few seconds longer before finally backing away and leaving him to his insanity.

HOLLOW HELLION

Entering the kitchen, I spot Soul stepping into the trailer, his green whirling lenses catching mine, and he halts. I slump back into a chair at the table, my head thrown back, and close my eyes. I hear the scrape of the chair opposite me and lift my head to see him sitting down. He pulls down his black and neon green half-mask, revealing his painted nose and lips, his eyes never leaving mine. As he draws back his hood back, he ruffles his fingers through the top of his wavy blonde hair before resting his elbows on the table.

"What the fuck has he done this time?" he asks, knowing it's Wrath who has triggered me.

I let out a long breath, feeling the weight of the night bearing down on me. "The usual shit."

He falls back in his chair, eying me suspiciously. "Where the fuck did you go?"

I stay silent, staring at him and after a moment, a big grin spreads over his lips. "It was her you sensed, wasn't it?"

I sigh and face away, my jaw tense as I answer. "She was in the fucking death rooms, and almost got herself killed."

He raises an eyebrow, his grin fading. "Anything else?" he asks, seeking for information.

I mimic his eyebrow arch before responding bluntly. "What do you want, you sicko? All the fucking details?"

He throws his head back with a loud, evil chuckle, and I remain expressionless, observing him. Soul is what you would call the party in all of us. He's full of energy and a fucking menace, but no one should be fooled by his name. It doesn't mean he has a soul; he is in fact soulless. He may act like he has life in him, but he's just as dead on the inside as the rest of us. He just knows how to hide it with this crazy, fucking character.

When he finally stops laughing, he brings his head forward, a smirk still plastered on his face as he raises his chin. "So, she gave you her pussy?"

I shake my head once before responding, "I'm waiting for Dark Night."

His smile widens, a sinister glint in his green eyes. "I don't fucking blame you, Hell. That hot little thing deserves to be torn the fuck up for looking that good."

My teeth grind together as he leans in, his voice dropping lower. "Are you sure you don't want to share? I mean, we might fucking kill her in the process, but, bro, it'll be worth it, right?"

"Leave her the fuck alone, Soul. She's mine." I growl.

His lips twitch with a smile before he falls back in his seat again. "Fuck, what's this, Hell? Love? Are finally feeling something in that pitch-black fucking soul of yours?"

I glare at him with intensity in my eyes. "You know better than that. Shut the fuck up."

He throws his hands up in sarcastic surrender before standing from his seat. I watch his every move as he heads for the refrigerator, grabbing a couple of cold beers. He cracks them open with his teeth before placing one on the table in front of me, then takes a seat once again. I stare down at it for a beat, holding it in my hand and turning it slowly, but not drinking.

Noir's blood catches my attention again until Soul speaks. "She has some guy with her, doesn't she?" I raise my eyes to his, still turning the cold bottle in my hand, remaining silent so he continues. "Billy told me today that he's an ex-heroin addict. Well, he saw marks on his skin."

My mind begins to spin, realizing that I must not have noticed when they were in the shower together since I was too focused on her.

"Have you seen him yourself yet?" I ask, my curiosity piqued.

Soul gives a shrug of his shoulder. "Sort of. I noticed him working at the carnival tonight. He sticks out like a sore thumb. He doesn't fucking belong here."

He takes another swig of his beer, tilting his head back. "Is he gay? "I question.

His eyes immediately flash to mine as soon as the words escape me before he slams his bottle down on the table. I inhale deeply, sitting back, waiting for the anger I am about to feel.

"What the fuck, Hell?" He snaps.

I remain expressionless before responding casually. "Well, is he?"

His jaw tenses and his eyes flash with fury. "How the fuck am I supposed to know?"

I try not to roll my eyes as I look aside, knowing I should have kept my mouth shut. Soul is bisexual, yet he is completely in denial about the guy part. I don't give a fuck what he wants to does and neither does Wrath, so I don't get why he acts like this every time we mention it.

"What, you think I have some sort of magic sense of smell that tells me when a man is into fucking cock?" He bites in an agitated tone before releasing a scoff.

I try not to be amused by his choice of words as he flattens his hands on the table, getting ready to stand. "Why do you care anyway?" His tone has changed, interest replacing anger.

I glance up at him as I answer, "That motherfuck can't get hard for her."

He shrugs his broad shoulders before snatching his beer off the table. "Well, then he's definitely gay because she is some fine ass pussy, or it could be all those drugs in his system. That shit can do all kinds of things to a man's dick."

I give a small nod since it makes sense. He leans in, his voice quieting, "The real question is, why the fuck haven't you killed him yet if you're so hung up on this chick?"

I think about it for a second and silently question my motives, but I stay silent, and he scans my eyes before standing upright once more.

"Leave it to me. I'll find out what the little cunt is into." He winks with a big grin before walking away, leaving me alone with my thoughts. Soul will figure it out, he has his hands in all kinds of dodgy pots, he is smart as fuck and his hacking skills are top tier.

I know why I haven't killed Limp Dick; there's no fun in that. I want her to surrender to my every sick desire while she's still entertaining him. I like the thought of her going home to him knowing she's thinking about me, but facts are facts, Noir is mine regardless, and I won't let anyone mess with my plans for her. Sooner or later, he will only get in my fucking way and then after I've finished playing my games, I'll gladly kill him in front of her to show just how much she belongs to me.

After some time of staring at my beer but not drinking it, I stand up and head for my room.

HOLLOW HELLION

Once I get upstairs, I stroll down the hallway towards my bedroom at the far end. I push open the solid black door and step inside. Glancing around, I take in the sight of my round bed, centred in the middle of the room. Black sheets and pillows are strewn messily across it. Black fabric drapes down either side like a canopy, concealing the chains and shackles hidden beneath them. The room is entirely black—walls and floor—with a mirrored ceiling and a single red bulb centred above the bed. The only window in here is also blacked out as well. I fucking relish in darkness.

I kick the door closed behind me and stride to the bed, taking a seat on the end of the springy mattress. Leaning forward, I rest my forearms on my knees and gaze down at my hands, staring at the blood staining them, seeping into my pours. I can't get the images of her out of my fucking mind. She is living inside of me.

Lifting my head, I notice a piece of fabric on the floor not too far from me. I reach over and grab it before scrubbing her blood off my hand absentmindedly until an idea enters my mind. I look back at my bedside table and stand, heading towards it. When close enough, I open the drawer and retrieve my sewing kit. Taking a seat back on the bed, I begin to stitch the fabric, my hands moving with a knowing precision and each stitch brings me closer to her, becoming a ritual as I imagine her. The look of fright on her face when she first sees me, only to surrender to what we both want so quickly, makes me feel things. Things I haven't felt before. I'm addicted to the fucking feeling.

Since being at Oddity Carnival when my mom died, I've always taken what I want in life even if it means hurting people in the process. I am a hired torturous killer. People come to me for the most brutal ways I can murder. When we joined The Shadow's society, we made a vow. Sold our fucking souls to the devil if you will, with little in return but trauma and hollow hearts. I'm the monster I've been designed to be, yet I feel Dolly is someone who seems to yearn for something from me despite her seeing the evilness that dwells inside of me, and it does something to my crazed mind.

She lets me watch her, touch her, and take control of her. She could easily say no and make a big deal out of it. It probably wouldn't stop me, but just knowing she isn't willing to say it because she likes my twisted bullshit is even more thrilling than simply just taking it from her. Dolly is different. After some time stitching my masterpiece, I think about how she's mine in ways she doesn't fully understand yet, and I'm determined to show her the depths of my obsession.

Once I'm finished, I hold up the soft object, inspecting my work. It's a small gift, but it carries a weight of significance. A reminder of what she is to me—my perfect little toy. I place it carefully on my bedside table, a symbol of my deranged affection, ready to give to her when the time is right.

I lie back on my bed, one leg hanging off and my arm resting behind my head as I stare forward. My thoughts start to swirl with filth, and I flick the button undone on my pants, dragging the zipper down. I pull my growing, heavy cock free seeking relief before wrapping the chain from my jeans around my hand. The metal is cool and rough, adding a harsh edge to my grip.

I get a firm hold on my dick, jerking myself off slowly at first and the chain adds extra friction, scraping against my skin in a way that heightens my senses. My eyes drift close as I visualize her chained up, helpless and mine to destroy. I picture fucking her violently, her cries mixing with the sound of rattling chains. The image takes the edge off this built-up sexual frustration and the chain collides with my piercings as I become rougher, my hand moving faster. My breathing picks up, becoming ragged and shallow as my cock expands. When I finally explode, my hot cum leaks down my hand as I squeeze my pulsing dick harder, milking myself for every drop. I breathe heavily, my chest rising and falling as I slowly open my eyes again, staring blankly at the ceiling.

With a soft clink of the chain, I release my grip, my hand sticky with cum, but I make no attempt to clean it up, instead, I reach over, lifting the soft toy with my wet hand and place it on my stomach, leaving my scent on it. My eyes close, thinking about the next time I cum, it will only be because I am skull fucking her.

CHAPTER TEN

It's been a few days since I last saw Hell and it's my first night at the circus, and my emotions are a tangled mess. I crave him with a burning intensity. I want him to hurt and fuck me, to release this pain inside me, even though I know it's wrong. It defies everything I stand for, it's not fair on E and I feel so guilty for it, but I can't help it. I feel like he's turning all of my shattered pieces into a beautiful masterpiece, and it's a twisted sensation because it's dragging me back from my path to recovery, I think.

Surrendering to him last night and exposing my vulnerability, he saw I wasn't like other girls, but he wanted me anyway. In that moment, he helped me.

His blade relieved my pain, and strangely, it felt right because I wasn't inflicting it upon myself so I couldn't hate myself for it.

His pleasure gave me something I have never felt before, making me realize I have the ability to feel euphoria. His presence and words, they make me feel as if everything I believed was wrong with me, could never be wrong in his eyes.

Maybe he's right; perhaps I'm just as messed up in my head as he is and despite everything he makes me feel, I know I made the right decision by telling him to leave me alone. Hell is not good for me, even if sometimes it seems like he is. I am deluded. He cannot fix me—he is broken himself.

I've put up some curtains in the trailer to create some kind of privacy, yet I have a strange feeling that nothing will stop this man. He is, as he said, obsessed and I don't doubt he means it.

As I prepare for the circus, I lean into the mirror, painting my face with black makeup, transforming myself into a broken doll which is ironic considering what Hell calls me. Cracks spread from my heavily lined eyes, and I paint stitches from the corner of my lips, extending to my cheeks to create the illusion of a wide smile. I add two small red hearts beneath one eye and curl my blonde hair into loose waves.

While thinking about getting into my outfit since I am running out of time, I notice Eli enter behind me in the reflection. As his aftershave wafts through the air, I turn around to face him. Guilt creeps in as I think about our argument and then what I did with Hell hours later. I'm stuck in a limbo of telling him the truth or burying it in the past as fucked as that sounds.

I don't want to fight with E. He looked after me when I was at my lowest, and now I feel like I unfairly accused him of something so disgusting just because of my past. But in the aftermath of what happened between Hell and me, I can't shake the feeling that there's no future for me and E. He's been a great friend, but I need to be honest with myself that that's all we are. I can't keep letting him believe it can be more, because I wouldn't have surrendered to Hell so easily if it were. E didn't even enter my mind or stop me and that's the harsh truth. When things have calmed down between us, I know it's time to have that talk.

I look him up and down as he slips on some loafers. "Are you coming to the circus?" I ask with a hopeful tone.

Without looking at me, he tucks his blue shirt into his black pants. "Nah," he answers coldly.

I raise an eyebrow, pulling my hoodie tighter around me and crossing my arms. "So, where are you heading to?"

He turns his back to me, collecting the keys to his truck before he walks toward the door. "I'm going to a bar. I need a drink," he replies, his tone still distant.

My lips form a flat line, feeling slightly disappointed that he doesn't want to see me perform tonight and I decide to say something. "I would have thought you'd want to watch the show. I'm dancing for the first time tonight."

He stops at the threshold, his back to me, and keeps his eyes forward. "Why would I do that? We're not bound to each other, right?" he retorts, his words full of bitterness.

My jaw tightens, and I look away, but from the corner of my eye, I notice he glances over his shoulder at me. "Have a good night, Noir. Good luck."

With that, he walks away, and when I hear the trailer door open and shut, I close my eyes, taking a deep breath.

When I eventually turn around to face the mirror, I am startled, jumping backward as a petrified scream nearly escapes me. Arabella's reflection stares back at me with wide, haunting eyes, covered in blood, her mouth twisted into a silent scream. In the blink of an eye, she disappears, leaving me frozen in terror, my heart pounding like a drum against my ribs, questioning my sanity as I stare at my own reflection.

"*Weak,*" her loud taunting whisper in my left ear causes me to spin on my heels, my breathing frantic.

I stand there, worried with each inhale that she might return, but she doesn't. With a jittery breath, I quickly find my costume, and hurry to the living room to put it in a bag.

HOLLOW HELLION

Once I step out of the trailer into the cold night, I hike my backpack over my shoulder and make my way toward the circus. The breeze bites at my skin, freezing my bones, while a chill creeps up my spine. A single raindrop splashes onto my face, and I growl in frustration, yanking my hood over my head to protect my freshly done makeup and hair.

As I approach the circus, the distant murmur of an eager crowd grows louder and the glow of the lights pierces the darkness, and the smell of popcorn filling my nostrils. I focus on my goal: go in, get ready, perform, and fucking leave. As I pass by The Hollows' trailer, the roar of their bikes rumbles through the night. I keep my gaze fixed ahead, my pulse racing because I know it's them, but I refuse to acknowledge their presence.

As I draw closer to the circus, I watch Soul and Wrath whiz ahead on their bikes, their taillights flickering like fireflies in the night. The hum of Hell's bike comes up slowly beside me and I try not to pay him any attention, keeping my eyes fixed forward, but from the corner of my eye, I see him matching my quick strides, his engine revving aggressively in an attempt to startle me. The sound pierces the night, but I remain unfazed.

"Need a ride?" he shouts over his roaring engine.

I give him a brief glance, our eyes locking through his spiral lenses, and with a small, silent shake of my head, I look forward once again, my steps not stopping. He continues to follow me, and when I reach the back entrance of the tent, I can feel his eyes burning into my back as I slip inside, disappearing into the shadows, out of his sight.

HOLLOW HELLION

I march straight for Madame's chamber, hoping to speak to her before the show. I have questions about Dark Night, things I don't know, and I'm not sure why I'm being kept in the dark, but my frustration is mounting. Hell mentioned people kill themselves in the Death Room's, and my reaction to that wasn't what a normal person would be because of the situation I was facing.

Nothing usually surprises me, and death doesn't scare me, but what does fucking scare me is not knowing what I am facing before I face it, like the death traps. Ignorance is more terrifying than the thought of dying. Since Hell and I were too busy caught up in this twisted fucking connection we have, riding his hand until I was coming on my damn panties that were stuffed inside my pussy, I didn't have a chance to ask him what the fuck that place was and why it even existed. Sure, I could have asked him just now, but that would mean engaging with him again. Every time I am in his presence, my walls crumble like they're being shattered by a fucking earthquake, never to be seen again. That guy is dangerous, not just to my body, but to my mind too.

As soon as I enter, I spot her sitting behind her desk, a cigarette dangling from her lips, her head bowed over a spread of tarot cards. I stop in the middle of the room and clear my throat, but she doesn't look up.

"What do you want, Noir? You should be getting ready. You perform in less than twenty minutes," she states dismissively.

I inhale deeply, trying to rein in my irritation at her ignorance.

"Dark Night," I snap out.

She pauses, a tarot card held mid-air, her attention shifting slightly. "What the fuck is it, Madame? Am I part of it?" I demand, my eyes locked on her, refusing to be dismissed any longer.

She contemplates for a moment, the card still suspended between her fingers until her eyes finally meet mine, and she tilts her head to the side, a smile curling on her lips.

"Of course you are, dear. All my best performers are," she replies, her voice sweet with a sinister undertone. I stay silent, feeling my heart suddenly thumping against my chest, though I can't quite pinpoint why.

"Why do you ask, Noir?"

"The Death Rooms," I blurt out, "I almost got myself fucking killed last night because you failed to tell me such a place exists here." I point my finger at her accusingly. "It's your duty as my boss to tell me what I am facing," I seethe, my tone sharp with anger.

She keeps her dark eyes locked on mine as she drops the card onto the desk, her jaw set tight at my choice of words. I watch her every move as she places her hands on the wood and rises from her chair. She walks around her big desk calmly, her red dress trailing behind her until she stops in front of me.

At eye level, we stare into each other's eyes, and hers scan my features. "You know what you're facing though, don't you?" she asks calmly, and I stay silent, my eyes wide, my chest tightening, threatening to lose control. "You knew it the moment you met Hell."

She reaches out, softly taking a lock of my hair. "I wouldn't have let you work here if I didn't think you belonged here, Noir."

I back away from her touch, my face turning to the side as I try to calm myself down. "Why do you do it?" I ask before looking at her again. "Why do you kill people?" My voice is low, filled with fear and curiosity. "Are they innocent?"

Her eyes narrow, scanning mine, but suddenly she looks over my shoulder. I glance to the side to see Hell standing behind me, his dark presence sending a chill down my spine. I growl, shooting Madame one last look before turning around and storming past Hell, heading straight for the changing rooms.

HOLLOW HELLION

As I walk in, a row of mirrors catches my eye, surrounded by bright lights. A group of girls are scattered around, busy with their preparations. I quickly make my way over, trying to calm the storm raging inside me as I approach a mirror and Blush stands from her seat as she notices me.

"Noir?" she says with a concerned tone, but I just give her a small smile, dumping my bag on the desk beside her and starting to strip down.

"How are you feeling?" she asks curiously, but I avoid meeting her eyes. With a tiny nod, I continue to remove my top clothes and get into my costume. I feel the eyes of all the girls on me, as if I'm an intruder, but I ignore it; many of them I haven't even met yet.

As I wrap my corset around me, a girl suddenly steps forward, her eyes white, and her long black hair cascades over her bronzed skin. She's dressed in white: a tight corset, and a tutu, the complete opposite of my black attire.

"Oh, look who it is, it's the new Hollow's girl," she sneers as she folds her arms across her chest defiantly. Three more girls join behind her, mirroring her stance. I quickly look around, making sure no one is behind me before meeting her gaze.

"Were you talking to me?" I respond, my tone cool, but my grip on the corset ribbon tightens.

"Of course, I was talking to you! Have you dyed your head so much that you can't even tell when someone's talking to you? Fucking air head," she snaps, her words cutting through the air like shards of glass, while her minions cackle behind her.

My teeth grind down, not in the fucking mood for this bullshit, but I notice Blush taking a calm step beside me, which the girl picks up on.

"You want to become a traitor for an outsider, Blush?" she mocks, but I refuse to back down.

"What the hell are you talking about? Are you insane? Just back off and get on with your shit," I snap back.

Suddenly, she steps toward me, and instinct takes over, forcing me walk forward to meet her until we're nose to nose. I hold my ground, bubbling with anger after everything that has happened recently.

"I suggest you get the fuck out of my face before I give you a new one," I growl, "I'm not the one you want to fuck with."

Suddenly, the ribbon on my corset is yanked back, and I collide with a hard chest. I keep my head low, knowing it's him, feeling the unbearable anger radiating from his aura.

When the girl speaks, I glance up at her scowling at Hell behind me. "You want me to just be okay with this, Hell? Her stealing my job? I have been the Hollow's girl for years!"

Before I can even open my mouth to ask what the fuck she's talking about, his deep voice vibrates on my back. "She didn't steal your job, Pearl. I fucking did." Her face falls at the revelation. "I was the one who requested she be the Hollow's girl."

My brows pinch in confusion, "You did what?" I breathe out, my eyes flicking up to him behind me, but he keeps his harsh gaze fixed on Pearl.

"Are you going to argue with me?" he aims toward her, and I look to see her give him a small head shake in response, dropping her arms beside her in surrender.

"Good, now get the fuck out there and work." He glances around, his dark eyes meeting every single girl in here but me, "Now!" he shouts aggressively causing all of our bodies to tighten.

They scurry out of the changing room like ants, including Blush and when it's just me and Hell alone, I pull my ribbon out of his grasp and face a mirror. "I don't need your help," I mutter, refusing to meet his eyes, though I can feel his crawling all over me.

I reach around to tighten my corset, but struggle without assistance. From the corner of my eye, I see him edging closer until he's standing directly behind me. He suddenly presses his hand against my back with a hard shove, forcing me to brace myself with my palms on the vanity.

"I said I don't need your help!" I bark, but he simply ignores me, wrapping the ribbons around his tattooed fists and presses his crotch against my ass. With a swift, powerful yank, he pulls them so tight that I groan, the air leaving my lungs.

"Shut the fuck up and let me help you, stubborn Little Dolly," he demands. With my head down tilted down, he continues to tighten the corset, clearly unaware of his own strength.

"I didn't mean with this, I meant in general. I could handle her..." I manage through shallow breaths. "Besides, what's with all the secrecy around here? Why does no one tell me anything?"

"I have no doubt you could handle her, pretty girl. I was just telling her the facts."

My teeth grind as I respond, "That I am somehow the new Hollow's girl?"

"That's right."

"Why?"

"Because you're better than her and because I fucking said so," he answers bluntly.

I roll my eyes, "That's unfair, Hell."

"Life ain't fair, Noir." I don't argue with that statement because he is absolutely right.

"And what exactly do you want to know?" he questions, his tone sharp as he gives another tight yank on the ribbon. "I think deep down you know exactly what the fuck we are and what this place is," he takes a brief pause before continuing. "It's no secret what Oddity is once you're in it, but tonight's show is just a mirage of normality. It disguises what really lurks beneath the surface."

I wince, the corset digging into my ribs. "What does that even mean, Hell? I want to know why the fuck you think this is normal. Why you all act like it's just another day at the circus when it's clearly one big farce."

His grip on the ribbons relaxes slightly, but his intensity doesn't waver. "Normal? There's nothing fucking normal about this place, Dolly. We live in the shadows, thrive in the mayhem. Every performer here has a story, a reason for being part of this twisted show and for most of us, it's all that we know."

"And what's your story, Hell?" I challenge, turning my head slightly to catch his eyes in the mirror. "Why are you here?"

His vortex eyes darken, and for a moment he ponders before he continues with tying the knot. "My reasons are my own," he says, his voice low, "But I won't let anything, or anyone hurt you, Noir."

I scoff, trying to hide the unsettling warmth his words bring.

"I don't need your protection, Hell. I need answers."

"You'll get them," he replies, tightening the corset one last time. "But you have to earn them. Trust isn't given here, it's fucking earned."

I meet his gaze in the mirror once more. "And how do I earn it?"

He pauses, his spiral eyes flicking up to meet mine in the reflection, "By surviving. By showing that you belong here, that you can handle whatever the fuck this place throws at you."

I take a deep inhale, my tone hardening, "And if I just want to leave?"

He suddenly whirls me around to face him as soon as I say the words, snatching my throat to keep me steady. Tilting my head back, the pad of his thumb presses down on my bottom lip, his face so close that I can feel his smoky breath on my skin. Panic rises as I struggle to breathe, both from his proximity and the corset's tight grip on my lungs.

His gaze bores into mine, his jaw set tight. "You can't," he orders, his voice chillingly calm compared to his unpredictable demeanour. "Once you were declared part of Dark Night, there was no way out." I look at him confusingly as he continues. "Oddity owns you now, Noir. The only way you'll ever leave this place is in a fucking body bag just like the rest of us."

My gaze widens in shock, but fury quickly replaces it, "No one fucking owns me."

A dangerous twitch of a sneer spreads across his lips, "Oh, my Little Dolly, that's far from the truth."

As I roll my eyes, I push myself up onto the desk and he releases my throat but stays standing between my thighs, his presence overwhelming.

"In your dreams, Hell, maybe." I murmur.

Ignoring his gaze as he watches me carefully, poised to pounce again at any moment, I grab my bag off the vanity and pull out my black tutu and fishnets. I slip the tutu down my body until it's fixed on my hips, then draw my jeans down my legs. As soon as they reach my ankles, he yanks them off with an aggression that sends a jolt through me.

He steps forward, grabbing the back of my thighs, pulling me closer to him and forcing my legs his waist in an animalistic act of frustration. I have to lean back on one hand while the other pushes against his chest. His warm palms move up the back of my thighs, my skin igniting under his touch and his spiral contacts lock onto my lips.

"You think I didn't notice your choice of face paints tonight, Noir?" He acknowledges. "Are you trying to tease the fuck out of my cock until I end up destroying you? I think you want me more than you'd like to admit."

I scoff and look away, "Yeah right. Your head couldn't get any bigger."

As he lowers his face to the side of my neck, his hands reach my bare hips and when he gives them a tight, painful squeeze, I feel the throb in my pussy again.

"Your little cunt came hard the other night, and you're still as frustrated as ever? Does my Dolly seek more pleasure and pain from me?" he asks with a growl in his throat.

Yes! I internally scream. Yet, I stay silent, knowing better than to tempt him. My chest heaves with every breath I take from pure arousal and fear, but eventually, he draws back, our dark eyes instantly meeting.

He stands upright, snatching my fishnet tights from the desk, then crouches between my legs. I watch curiously as he slips them over my feet, but he pauses when he notices the scars on my ankle, and panic strikes me.

"What are you doing?" I manage to breathe out, my voice barely audible, but it makes him withdraw from his lingering thoughts.

"Like I said, I do whatever the fuck I want, and I get whatever the fuck I want," he responds calmly, his wicked gaze fixed on the movement of the nets ascending up my smooth legs.

"I wonder how it feels when the big bad monster isn't getting the pussy that he desperately wants," I taunt.

He stops, his eyes flickering up toward mine, a sinister aura in them and I instantly regret my words.

Without warning, he aggressively spreads my knees wide apart with his hands. Before I can stop him, he dips his head, and his pierced tongue moves harshly over the ladder of fresh slices on my inner thighs, punishing me for my backchat.

My eyes roll and I groan loudly from the pain, my hand instantly latching onto his black, soft hair, in a pathetic attempt to stop him, but he persists in his untamed movements, sucking on the wounds and biting them to inflict immense discomfort. He edges toward my core, and I begin to pulse with need.

With a sudden motion, he plunges his face into my panties, aggressively devouring me through the fabric. My head snaps back, a loud gasp tearing from my throat and my legs shudder involuntarily from the intense violation. The heat of his tongue and piercing working in unison as he savagely gnaws on my pussy lips like a wild beast tearing into flesh which sets me on fire. My grip on his hair tightens, as his hands move to my inner thighs, spreading me wider while he digs his fingers into my cuts causing a delicious blend of pain and pleasure that electrifies my senses.

His mouth detects my swollen, aching bud, and he starts to suck on it through the delicate lace, igniting a fiery sensation that consumes my entire being.

Oh god, please don't come. Don't come when he's eating you out through your fucking panties. Please goddamit! I internally plea with myself, holding onto everything I have.

I start hyperventilating, the overwhelming feeling of bliss building inside of me. I can't control it—his mouth is too skilled.

Too wild.

He's too good.

Fuck, I'm going to come!

When he abruptly stops, I tilt my head forward, staring down at the back of his head with expanded eyes, my breathing frantic, my clit one flick away with his tongue from an earthshattering climax.

"It seems the pussy I desperately want is betraying her owner," he murmurs over my throbbing core, his tone detached.

In my dazed state he rises suddenly, his fingers digging into my wounds, adding to the intoxicating agony that causes me to hiss, while his other hand sneaks into the back of my hair, yanking it back forcefully.

Then, he presses his lips against mine. "Don't. Ever," he growls, his sexual frustration palpable, "Think you're the one in control, pretty girl." I pant through my nose as his lips tease mine and his fingertips scrape down my slices causing my brows to knit. "The only person in control here is me. If I weren't, I would have violently fucked every single tight hole you have from the moment I laid my fucking eyes on you."

I swallow hard, my body shaking for release as he continues. "You have no say in the matter. You're my little toy, my fucking game, and I'll keep playing with you, keep teasing you until I decide when it's time to take what the fuck I want."

He tilts his head to the side in an unnerving manner, breathing heavily, "I don't give a damn," he bites out fiercely, "how many times you say no. You're going to be mine and you fucking know it."

He suddenly releases me roughly, and as I lift my head, he takes steps backward, adjusting his hard cock in his tight jeans, and I watch the movement before our eyes lock in a silent battle. His gaze is wide, almost crazed, a threatening promise of the things to come between us.

When he finally turns his back to me, heading for the door, a surge of defensiveness and sexual refusal floods through me. "You said you would leave me alone, Hell!" I shout after him, my angry voice echoing in the empty changing room.

He ignores me completely, his stride unbroken as he exits and the door swings shut behind him, leaving me on the edge of an orgasm on purpose. I let out a frustrated growl, hopping off the desk and my hands tremble as I pull my fishnets up my shaky legs before stepping into my knee-high, platformed black boots.

My mind floods to Hell, the way my body betrays me, desperate for him, despite my mind and soul screaming for distance. He knows I'm weak for him, just as he is for me, and he's now taking full advantage of the situation. The pull I have towards him is irresistible, making my body ache with desire and fear, a deadly concoction.

"Just one more time, Noir," it whispers every fucking time, but my mind warns me that Hell will drag me to a place of no return, a literal hell from which I may never escape, yet the strangest part is, I worry that I might not want to escape. I might get cozy from the warmth of his hellfire, finding my place in his insane world and willingly obey his every command.

Deep down, there's a nagging feeling I can't ignore: despite Hell's deranged behavior, I'm beginning to trust him against all odds. Trust him with my pain, with my pleasure, and with my safety, and it's a scary place to be.

He has a way of blurring all my internal suffering away, giving me respite just for a while as he taunts, pleasures, or hurts me. His twisted games and darkness somehow provide a distraction from the havoc of my thoughts just like my meds did. It's like he knows exactly how to pull me out of my spiraling mind and ground me in the present, even if the present is filled with his insanity.

Maybe it's because he's never pretended to be anything other than what he is, unlike the other men I've unfortunately faced. From the first moment we met, he has shown his true self, and even during the mayhem of his actions, there's a strange consistency, even if it feels like he switches a lot, it makes me feel, against everything, that I can rely on him.

The way I feel safe when he watches me sleep from the window, the way my body responds to his touch, his obsession with me—all of it stirs something deep inside and for the first time in my life, I feel *desired.*

I know he is making it clear that this might be purely sexual; the way he talks and manhandles me tells me he wants to fuck the life out of me, but there's more to his obsession. It's not just about having me and using me like everyone else has; he wants all of me. I just can't afford to get attached to him or anyone else; it's far too dangerous for everyone.

Fuck this is toxic. Yet here I am, stuck in this place with him every day, feeling my will weaken with each passing second and I know it's only a matter of time before I break and give in to Hell's wicked ways. I just dread how much I'll enjoy every second of his sweet depravity. I worry that once I get a taste of Hell, there's no going back to any kind of innocence. I will be officially corrupt.

When I have tied the laces, I finally head for the main tent to preform and watch tonight's show.

HOLLOW HELLION

The night is thick with anticipation as I perch high above the crowd on the trapeze platform. The big top of the Circus loom's around me, the smell of smoke mingles with the faint tang of sweat and fear. Madame's voice booms through the tent from the speakers, introducing my act. "Ladies and gentlemen, prepare yourselves for a brand-new chilling performance that will haunt your dreams! Presenting Noir, our broken dolly!"

The music starts and I take a deep breath before I leap from the platform, my body arcing gracefully through the air. The audience gasps as I catch the trapeze bar. Swinging back and forth, I gain momentum, each one higher and faster than the last, eyes glued to my every move.

Releasing the bar, I soar and reach out to grasp a pair of red aerial silks hanging from the rafters. The silks twist around my wrists, and I began to climb, feeling my muscles straining. The silks seem to come alive as they wrap around my limbs and the spotlight follows my every move as I reach the pinnacle of the tent. I hang upside down for a moment, my hair cascading like a light waterfall. With a sudden burst of energy, I begin my descent, spinning and twirling down the silks in a blur of motion.

They create a visual of black and red, but as I near the ground, I stop abruptly, hanging mere inches from the floor. The tent is plunged into darkness, and for a heartbeat, all is still. Then, a circle of fire ignites around me, the flames dancing wildly.

With a flick of my fingers, the flames grow higher, the fire following my every command, then I begin to spin once more. The flames lick at my skin, but I remain unaffected, acting like a master of the inferno as I perform daring flips and spins in the centre.

As my performance reaches its climax, I release the silks and land in the center of the burning ring. The flames roar higher when I raise my arms. My chest heaves until the fire dies down, leaving only a faint glow on the ground. I take a deep bow, my eyes meeting those in the front row and as I stand upright, Madame's voice booms through the speaker once more.

"Ladies and gentlemen, a round of applause for Noir, our broken dolly!"

The crowd roars, their applause echoing through the tent and just as it reaches its peak, suddenly red paint is released from above me, splashing down over me and almost catching me off guard. The crimson liquid flows over my body, mixing with my sweat and smudging my makeup, creating the illusion of blood. I stand there, drenched in it, the paint dripping from my hair and tutu, pooling at my feet like a crimson river.

My eyes met the audience's once more, a chilling smile playing on my lips, and I give one last, slow bow before finally, heading back to the changing rooms again to fix myself.

HOLLOW HELLION

After washing myself down as much as I could and getting changed, I find a seat in the crowd beside Madame at the front row.

She nods at me approvingly, "You did well, Noir. The crowd loved you, as predicted."

"Thank you," I reply, my voice hoarse as I settle into my seat, ready to watch the rest of the show unfold.

Blush and a few other girls take the stage next, their costumes glittering under the spotlight. They move with grace, performing fire-breathing and eating acts that stun me. The flames dance around them, and the audience watch in awe until Blush exhales a plume of fire so close to the crowd that they are forced to bow backward, almost burning them alive.

Next up is a man I have never seen before, dressed as a creepy looking clown, who confidently walks to the center of the arena, a long, gleaming sword held in his hand. He opens his mouth and slowly slides the blade down his throat. The tent is silent, all eyes fixated on him and the whole thing makes my stomach turn into knots, but with ease, he withdraws the sword and takes a bow.

Next, a pair of clumsy clowns stumble into the ring, meeting the other one, their makeup smeared and their eyes hollow. They juggle sharp knives, their movements crazy, keeping me on the edge of my seat until one slips, the knife slicing through the air and embedding itself into the other's arm. Blood spurts pulling horrified screams from the crowd, yet the injured clown just lets out a high-pitched giggle, yanking the blade free and continuing the act as if nothing had happened. *What the fuck.*

The tension in the tent grows when one of the girls are brought out and strapped forcefully to a spinning wheel by another two clowns. The spotlight focuses on her, illuminating her anxious face which is probably fake. The man who swallowed the sword now holds a set of axes; his expression emotionless and as the wheel starts to spin rapidly, he launches the axes at her causing my toes to curl. Each one lands dangerously close, but luckily never touching her. The crowd hold their breath with every throw just as I fucking do, only exhaling when the act is finally finished.

I lean closer to Madame, whispering, "I wonder how they manage to stay so calm when they're doing all of this."

Madame smiles faintly, her eyes never leaving the ring. "Years of practice, trust, and a lot of insanity. It takes a certain kind of person to thrive here, darling."

When the ring is cleared, a dark, huge figure enters from the shadows, each step he takes makes the ground thump beneath him. His body is a patchwork of horrific scars and stitches and chains rattle around his ankles as he is led into the ring, his black eyes simmering with rage. On the other end of the chain is Hell and he has them tightly wrapped around his strong, tattooed arms in an attempt to control him.

As my gaze lingers on his shackled ankles, a sense of sadness washes over me, sparking my own harrowing memories of how I was once chained in the same fucked-up way.

Madame leans in beside me, catching my attention, "He is Hell's pet. The Monster."

My brows pinch as I turn my head, "Pet?" I respond with a shudder. She gives a small nod before looking forward, "He is the only person in this place who is able to control him."

The ringmaster's voice booms through the speakers, "Feast your eyes upon The Monster! Who here is brave enough to tame him?"

A volunteer in the front row is chosen, a trembling old man reluctantly stepping forward and The Monster roars, the sound vibrating through the tent, making my body tense. The man is handed a whip, his face pale with fear and he cracks it once in a stupid attempt to assert control.

The Monster lunges forward, chains snapping and dragging Hell forward, his eyes burning with murder. The lights suddenly flicker, then plunge the tent into total pitch black. The screams that follow are piercing, a sound of bloodcurdling pain, but when the lights came back on, the ring is completely empty, and my mouth drops open in surprise.

As I observe all the performances, I can't help but reflect on my own place here in Oddity. The danger, the thrill, the constant dance with death—it is all amazing, but there is a dark feeling of the thought of being trapped in this place, also, Blush's words that this performance tonight is not even remotely as horrifying as Dark Night will be gnaws at me. How the fuck can it get any more terrifying than this?

After some other acts, I can sense the final act is approaching, and the anticipation in the air is electric; The Hollow's are about to take the stage with their motorcross bikes. The lights dim, and a hush falls over the crowd.

The roar of engines fill the tent, echoing like a thunderstorm and the spotlights swing around to show the Hollow's, helmet-less and lacking safety, but I expect nothing less. Their painted faces and spiralled contacts glow with menace and every single one of them are shirtless, exposing their ripped, tattooed skin; all alike, yet so different from one another. They rev their bikes, the engines growling like caged beasts ready to be unleashed.

When they're ready, the Hollow's speed around the ring, weaving in and out with incredible speed. They perform deathly ramp tricks, soaring high into the air, twisting, and flipping through rings of fire. The heat is intense even from where I sit and with each leap they land with a perfect execution.

Next comes the death wheel, the massive rotating structure that the Hollow's use to defy death itself. They ride along the vertical walls of the wheel with speed, and it causes it to spin faster and faster. I hold my breath, the tension almost unbearable. One wrong move, one fucking slip, and it would all be over, but the Hollow's prove me wrong.

Then, the death dome is descended from the ceiling—a giant metal sphere with a skull logo. The Hollow's ride into the dome, their engines roaring even louder within the confined space. They circle inside, crisscrossing paths in a dizzying display while it flickers wildly with red lights and the dome pulses as they barely miss each other.

Suddenly, ascending from below the center of the death dome, bound and vulnerable, is Pearl. Her eyes wide with a mix of fear and defiance, her body rigid as the bikes speed around her. The roar of their engines is deafening, and the sight of Pearl in the middle of the chaos only adds an extra layer of tension.

The Hollow's continue their cruel stunts, weaving around her with terrifying perfection. As the act reaches its end, the Hollow's begin their finale, and the dome is engulfed in a ring of fire, the heat and light almost blinding. Then, as quickly as it had begun, it is over and the lights cut out, the fire dims and the engines cut off, leaving a silence in their wake.

When the lights are switched back on, The Hollow's and Pearl are no longer there, all that's left is a gust of dust and smoke.

The audience erupts and I find myself clapping along as well with a big smile on my face. As I think about my performance and everyone I watched tonight, I feel a small sense of pride inside of me that I am a part of this mad world.

CHAPTER ELEVEN

Standing in Dolly's closet, since she decided to put fucking curtains up to stop me from watching her, I wait impatiently for her to return home. The rain pelts down hard on the trailer and drum against the windows. I know Limp Dick is not here tonight, so I broke in after the show.

As I listen intently, my senses are on high alert, until I finally hear the door open. I peer through the thin shutters and watch as she enters. Her long blonde hair is soaked and now has a tinge of red in it from her performance. Her broken dolly face paint streaks down her cheeks, darkening her piercing blue eyes, but even in this dishevelled state, she is still a stunning sight.

She pauses, her focus fixed on the black rose I left on the bed, confusing her. Her brows knit together, walking quickly toward it. She halts at the end of the bed, continuing to stare at the flower for a moment more before finally leaning over to lift it, but as soon as she does, she drops it with a hiss, her lips curling in pain.

I smirk slightly as she gazes down at her pricked finger, a bubble of blood now forming and she growls softly before placing it in her mouth, sucking on the small wound.

The sight of her reaction, the mix of pain and confusion, stirs something dark within me. I continue to observe her every move, savouring the moment, knowing that she is now fully aware of my presence and the games I intend to play. She quickly turns around, dashing through the trailer, probably trying to see if I am still here, hidden, but when she returns to the bedroom, it's clear she thinks I'm gone.

Still not taking her eyes off the rose, she drags her cropped leather jacket down her arms, tossing it to one side before moving on to her tight black jeans. After unbuttoning them, she pulls them down her legs, the wet fabric peeling away from her skin, and she winces as my inflicted wounds on her thighs sting.

Once she has stepped out of them, I keep my full focus on her body. She is now in black panties, the strings sitting high on her curvaceous hips, and a black cropped t-shirt sits just below her nipples, offering a mesmerizing view of the curve of her tits. I have to stop myself from pouncing on her, from taking her in this vulnerable state.

She heads for the small bedside table, muttering things I cannot understand, but I can sense her anger. My frantic eyes move all over her figure, the roundness of her peachy ass and how it wobbles with every step she takes until she opens a drawer, pulling out a pack of makeup wipes before tossing them onto the bed. Then she gazes inside again, pondering, before finally reaching down to withdraw something else. When she lifts out a black, medium-sized dildo, I shake my head once, the sight of it stirring something within me, a blend of jealousy and possessiveness.

Looking at it curiously, her small hand wraps tighter around it, until finally, she decides she is going to fuck herself with it and tosses it onto the bed. My cock throbs painfully in my wet jeans; there's no fucking way I'm just going to be able to watch her screw herself right in front of me.

My palms sweat, balling tightly into fists and my leg starts shaking, my control dissipating as she strides to the end of the bed. She bends over, crawling up it before stopping and positioning herself on all fours, reaching for her dildo. She gives me the perfect view, which is unfortunate for her and for fucking me.

My patience wears thin as she turns on the plastic dick, the sound of vibrations rippling through the air, merging with my heavy breathing. She reaches around, sliding her finger beneath the string of her panties that is wedged between her ass cheeks, pulling them to one side. I have to stifle the growl crawling up my throat, my hand immediately grasping my cock as the throb intensifies.

Hold on a little longer, Hell. I tell myself.

Placing her cheek on the bed, only her ass in the air, she starts by teasing clit with the vibrations before slipping it inside her pussy. She thrusts a few times but seems unsatisfied, then she does something that almost breaks my will to live. She moves the toy to her asshole, and my eyes involuntarily close, my forehead gently resting against the closet door, my jaw tense. I'm seconds away from punishing her for driving me so fucking insane.

When I finally open my eyes, I see her easing it into her little pink ring, her brows pinched together, and her mouth dropping open as she stretches her tight hole out, inch by inch.

Fucking hell. I can't stop myself. I start stroking my hard cock over my jeans, trying to relieve the unbearable ache building inside me.

Once the dildo is all the way inside, she keeps her fingers pinched around the base, waiting a moment to adjust to the sensation, then, when she's ready, she begins fucking herself, her thrusts becoming erratic, driving the toy deep inside her and the sweet melody of her moans fill the air.

She reaches between her legs with her other hand, frantically rubbing her clit at the same time, her eyes closed tight and with a gasp, she finally becomes lost in her pleasure.

"Oh, fuck," she cries out.

My strokes over my dick grow rapid, my hand moving roughly over the curve of my hardness in the same rhythm as her thrusts, almost tempted to flop my fucking cock out so I can get a better grip and come up the closet door if I have to.

As her breathing picks up, so does mine in perfect sync, almost ready to bust, until she suddenly screams something that stops me entirely. "Oh yes, Hell, just like that!"

My blood ignites, my eyes widening, and finally, I snap.

Without a second thought, I smash through the door, interrupting her near orgasm. I stand there, struggling to breath, my gloved hands opening and closing like an utter maniac.

She's instantly startled, jumping off the bed with a wobble in her legs, and her dildo falls out of her ass, dropping to the floor with a thud. Her breathing is erratic, her chest heaving with every breath she takes, matching my own, and her pretty blue eyes are expanded with terror. I take a small step forward, causing her to push herself closer to the window.

"Run, run, run, little dolly. Run as fast as you can. Because if I catch you, I'll make you obey my every command," I bite out, the poisonous rhyme rolling off my tongue.

With a flick of my blade, she bolts to the door without hesitation. I pause, taking in the aftermath of how she moaned my fucking name. As the sound of the trailer door being swung open reaches my ears, I turn my focus to her dildo lying on the floor. I bend down, my fingers closing tightly around it as I lift it, then I calmly step toward the door, ready to pursue her.

Exiting the trailer, half-naked and exposed to the downpour, I feel the weight of the rain on my flushed skin as I dart around the trailer, my bare feet skimming over the sodden ground. With each step, the squelching mud, and sharp twigs tear at my feet, but I continue, driven by sheer desperation. The darkness of the woods engulfs me as I plunge deeper, my heart pounding in my chest with every cold breath and panic claws at my throat, knowing I have to escape him at all costs. Why did he have to hear that? What the fuck was he doing in my closet? This is the worst possible scenario, and his crazed demeanor showed me that there's no turning back now. He has officially cracked, and I am the prey he is hunting.

When I throw a glance over my shoulder, I spot his shadowy figure calmly trailing behind me, his blade glinting menacingly in the dim light, hood drawn over his head.

Suddenly, I lose my footing, crashing frontally to the ground with a thud. I ignore the mud soaking through my little clothing and scramble to my feet, pushing forward in a frenzied attempt to get away from him, even if deep down I know I won't outrun him, it's worth a fucking try.

In a bold move born of desperation, I stop and turn to face him, his glowing eyes piercing the darkness, almost like they're floating towards me as he closes in.

My heart races as I frantically search my surroundings until I spot a sturdy tree nearby and I dart behind its massive trunk. I begin to climb, my fingers and toes struggling to find grip on the slick bark, but despite the difficulty, I refuse to give up, inching closer to the branch above.

Just as I reach for it, I hear the sounds of him getting closer, his heavy boots crunching over the undergrowth, but with a final burst of adrenaline, I hoist myself onto the limb while feeling the wind of his grab strike my leg. I scramble to safety just in time with a terrified squeak escaping me.

I balance upright on the branch and gaze down at him, my heart pounding in my chest as fear courses through my veins. His face, streaked with rain and paint, exudes a haunting aura that sends a shiver through me.

For a moment, we lock eyes in a tense standoff, the weight of unspoken threats hanging between us. Then, breaking the silence, he makes a gesture with his fingers. "Come on down, Noir. I'm going to show you what Hell looks like," he taunts.

I give a defiant shake of my head, lowering myself into a crouched position on the branch, fixing him with a glare that dares him to come closer.

"Just leave me alone, Hell. We agreed you would!" I yell, my voice quivering from the cold.

His eyes glint with wickedness as he tilts his head down slightly, shadowing his face beneath his hood as he responds.

"You either come the fuck down, or I'll climb up and—" his voice trails off, leaving the threat in the air like a dark cloud and he positions the knife's tip against the rough trunk, dragging the blade along the surface as he carefully circles the tree, chanting a twisted melody of his own creation.

"Noir and Hell, fucking in a tree. F-U-C-K-I-N-G," he jeers, his lips curling into a malevolent smirk.

My eyes roll with frustration, my jaw set tight, the urgency to escape him pulsing through my veins. Without thinking clearly, I wait and as soon as he comes into view, rounding the corner, I swiftly drop down, my hands instinctively latching onto the branch. With a forceful swing of my legs, my feet collide with his strong chest, the impact momentarily stunning him, causing him to take a step backwards. Yet, he is still unaffected, and he quickly snatches my ankle, his grip brutal and strong. I frantically shake my leg, desperately clinging on, my fingers slipping against the soaked wood.

A sinister grin spreads across his face before he suddenly yanks me down, sending me crashing to the ground with a resounding thud and pain shoots through my back, knocking the wind out of my lungs.

I groan from the impact as I struggle to gather my senses, but before I can even understand what the fuck is going on, I can feel myself being dragged across the muddy earth. My eyes expand in terror, my hands clawing at the dirt, grasping for anything.

"Hell!" I yell, my voice a desperate plea, the syllable trembling with urgency.

Debris from the forest floor clings to my body as I am mercilessly pulled, my attempts to stop him are only met with his calm strides. As I hyperventilate with fear, I start thrashing and kicking out in a frenzied attempt to break free, but he stays unbothered, his gaze fixed forward as he continues his hallowing pursuit.

"Silly, silly little Dolly," he mocks, his voice drenched with darkness. "Did you really think you could outrun your fate?"

Suddenly, we emerge from a clearing in the forest, the ground beneath me transforming from mud to grass. Above me the trees thin out, allowing the full force of the rain to drench me and wash away some of the muck on my cold skin.

Hell, finally stops, turning to face me while maintaining his firm grip on my leg. He pulls back his hood, his vortex eyes scanning the length of my body, his head tilted to one side.

"But you don't want me?" he breathes out against the crisp air.

I sigh and face aside, now knowing he definitely heard me moan his name, but from the corner of my eye, I notice him reaching into his pocket. When he pulls out my black dildo, my attention snaps back to him.

He examines it curiously, his eyes tracing the length of the similar shape as he speaks, his tone dripping with twisted amusement, "I heard you, Dolly. You were imagining me drilling into your asshole." My lips press into a thin line as he continues. "But this little thing is nothing like my fucking dick. Maybe double its size and add thirteen piercings."

My jaw drops, my eyes widening at his confession before I screw my face up, not believing a word of it, "Yeah right." I scoff.

His eyes snap to mine, expressionless and cold, making me wonder if he's telling the truth. Without warning, he drops my leg, leans over, and swiftly grasps my wrist, yanking me to my feet. My front crashes into his, but I twist, trying to run, yet I barely get a step away before he grabs my hair, jerking me back.

Pain shoots through my scalp as he forces me to face him, my body pressed against his, treating me like his little toy. He keeps a firm grip, and I clutch the lapels of his leather jacket, trying to steady myself and regain control.

"Dirty slut. You can't even take plastic dick in your fucking ass, let alone my monster cock screwing you." He pulls my hair back further, his mouth inches from mine. "Don't make me show you how soulless I can really be, Noir," he snarls, his breath hot and quivering over my lips, teetering on the edge of losing control.

I swallow hard before I respond, my entire body trembling from sheer coldness and panic, "I didn't say your name, Hell." I protest.

He now hisses viciously against my lips, his teeth exposed with frustration, "No, you fucking screamed it, pretty girl. You screamed it and almost fucking came."

He licks his tongue from my chin to my lips, tasting me before whispering, "Do you want your ass fucked Noir? How bad are you still throbbing?"

I struggle to get air into my lungs, lost for words, rain falling on my face, the entire situation rendering me stiff. With an untamed growl, he suddenly yanks my hair downward, forcing me onto my knees in front of him.

"Get on your fucking knees and suck me," he commands, his tone leaving no room for refusal.

As they sink into the sludgy grass, he drops my dildo and my face paint starts to sting my eyes, the colours smudging from the tears welling up. I gaze up at him, trying to keep my composure under his intense stare. They bore into mine as he swiftly unbuckles his belt with his free hand, the metallic clink of the buckle and chain echoing in the damp night air.

"Let's see just how much of my cock you can take down that slutty throat," his words are laced with dark desire.

While having me bound, he releases one end of his chain from his jeans before securing it tightly around my throat and with a harsh tug that pinches my skin, he wraps it around his fist, making sure I cannot escape him. He then, drags his zipper down, and I don't find myself saying no. The word crawls up my throat, begging to be released, but it doesn't come. Instead, I wait with anticipation and dread swirling inside me, a confusing state of mind, but kind of curious to see if he is telling the truth about his size and piercings.

He buries his hand into his black boxers before finally flopping his dick out and my eyes immediately lock onto it.

Holy fucking shit. He was not lying.

His cock is impressive and thick. The veins that ripple down his length pop out from how hard he is, a clear sight of his arousal for me, but it's the piercings that truly catch my attention. A ladder of gleaming metal studs runs up the underside and top of his shaft, each one catching the light in a way that makes my breath hitch.

He begins to stroke himself slowly, the skin pulling back to reveal two silver balls that go straight through the tip. They glisten with a mix of pre-cum, and I can't help but feel my mouth water involuntarily. This man is not only gifted in length and girth, clearly blessed by Satan, but he decided to weaponize this snake as well? The sheer fucking audacity is shocking.

When he smacks it against my lips, the weight and force almost split them open and I flinch, snapping out of my trance. He runs the tip over my lips and his slickness coats them, a demand dangling in the air, urging me to take him in.

"Part those plump lips for me, Dolly," he orders, his tone carrying hunger, "Let me skull fuck you before I force them open and do it anyway."

A furrow forms between my brows as I contemplate how the hell he plans to force my lips apart. I shake my head frantically, but before I can challenge him with words, he shoves himself inside, his piercings clinking against my teeth and catching me off guard.

He drives in, plunging to the back of my throat instantly with one swift stroke, stretching my mouth to its absolute limit. I instinctively clutch at his wet jeans, attempting to regain my composure as he seizes my hair with both gloved hands, anchoring me as he keeps his dick lodged in the back of my throat.

My stomach heaves, threatening to rebel as I choke repeatedly. Tears blur my vision, rushing down my cheeks with each blink and he closes his eyes with a twisted sense of satisfaction as he growls above me, "So beautiful when you shed tears for me." He peers down at me once more through darkened eyes, continuing his torment, his voice breathless yet intense, "Cry, cry, cry, pretty girl. Show me how much you despise being degraded by me. Let me see how much you fucking hate me for stuffing my cock down your throat." He does not stop, his sadistic delight clear as my tonsils contract with each gag.

Finally, he withdraws slowly, granting a brief respite as his piercings trail along my tongue and the roof of my mouth, offering a fleeting chance to draw some oxygen into my lungs.

But the reprieve is short-lived.

As soon as he reaches the tip, he dives back into my throat with force. His aggressive thrusts show no mercy as if he aims to fit his entire cock down it. It's an almost useless task, his size making it physically impossible, yet he persists undeterred.

"You will learn to swallow every fucking inch of me, Noir," he dictates, his tone seething with dominance. "Every snug little hole you have will be reshaped to take all of me and only me."

His gloved hands flatten on the back of my head, holding me in place as he begins to brutally fuck my face. Each ram is harsh, smashing into my windpipe with unrelenting power. I've never experienced such ferocity, feeling like I might pass out from the intensity.

My vision starts to black out, my jaw aching, as if it might shatter. Saliva fills my stretched mouth, dribbling down my chin as tears pour from my eyes and I try to draw back, my fists curling tight against his thighs, but he keeps me firmly in place, showing no compassion toward me and offering no leniency.

After some time, his breathing grows heavier above me, his cock swelling with each passing second until, finally, he pulls out with a swift motion, yanking my hair back with one hand.

Gasping for air, he jerks his cock off and releases his cum over my face, the thick liquid warming and coating my cold skin. I watch through blurred vision as his eyes close momentarily, a slight sway in his posture as satisfaction passes over him before he refocuses, staring down at me once again.

As he looks at me expressionlessly, he rubs the tip of his dick over my tingling, swollen lips, a cruel reminder of his dominance and my submission. We both breathe heavily, the tension crackling in the air between us and with one hand, he releases my hair, while the other moves to my face. "Look at you, covered in my cum like my pretty little fucking whore," he smirks wickedly and with his gloved fingers, he smears his juices over my skin.

"Stick your tongue out, Dolly," he commands, and I hesitantly obey, feeling exposed and vulnerable, knowing he knows how to force mouths open. "Wider." I push my tongue out further, opening my mouth wide.

He growls in satisfaction at my obedience before gathering spit, allowing it to fall from his lips in a gleaming string until it hits my tongue. Again and again, he repeats the disgusting act until my tongue feels coated with his saliva, each drop feeling like a mark of his control over me.

Then, leaning down, he orders, "Swallow my fucking spit." I lock onto his glowing gaze as I reluctantly draw my spit-filled tongue into my mouth and swallow it down, feeling a wave of degradation wash over me.

"Such a good slut," his teeth tighten on my lips. "Good sluts get what they want. Your turn."

As his lips crush against mine, he releases his chain and tugs on my hair, pulling me to my feet. With his arm wrapped tightly around the bottom of my back, he holds me close, his heat a stark contrast to my numb body, and I am almost tempted to cuddle into him. Tremors course through me as the cold seeps into my bones when suddenly, the metallic rasp of his knife slicing through the air cuts through the silence, causing me to freeze.

With a quick action, he swings his arm, hurling the blade, and I turn my head, stunned as it embeds itself deeply into a nearby tree trunk. Confused, I lift my wide eyes to meet his and they roam over my tear-stained face. With strange gentleness, he moves the damp strands of hair clinging to my skin.

Then, he seizes my face, his grip firm on my jaw, his expression taut with frustration, "Ride it." His voice cuts through the air like a lash, his eyes burning with intensity.

My eyes expand further, but before I can protest further, he presses his lips against mine, his kiss aggressive, his tongue intertwining with mine. As he guides me backward, each step feels like a surrender to his will, his touch igniting a fire within me despite wanting to stop him.

"Bounce all over it with your tight asshole," he murmurs with a hostile tone over my lips. "Stretch it the fuck out and take it as deep as you can."

He pushes my face with sudden force, and I stumble backward over the slick ground beneath my bare feet. Once I find my balance, I continue to walk backward, but with predatory strides, he follows me. Taking the opportunity, I whirl around trying to flee, but his grip on my panties yanks me back before I am slammed frontally against the tree. His hand clamps down on the back of my neck, my cheek pressed hard against the sharp bark.

My breath comes in heavy gasps, my heart pounding fiercely against my ribcage, threatening to break free and from the corner of my eye, I see him biting the tip of his finger, pulling off the leather glove before it drops to the ground with a soft thump.

"You keep being a fucking brat, Noir. You keep fighting what we have, and trust me, I like it. But if you don't start doing as you're fucking told, I'm gonna do extremely unforgiving things to you. I am being tame right now," he growls.

With a bold move, his hand lowers between my thighs from behind, roughly, and possessively, his fingers move over the fabric covering my pussy, aiming to feel every part of me.

My body tenses at the intrusiveness, a strange mixture of terror and arousal coursing through me, but despite my initial resistance, I find myself yielding to his touch, my legs gradually relaxing as I push my ass back, granting him better access.

He forcefully snaps the string of my panties wedged between my ass cheeks, tearing them apart and without hesitation, he shoves his two long, cold fingers deep into my pussy, his silver rings scraping along my walls, stretching me with one brutal thrust. I scream, rising onto my tiptoes from the sudden invasion, but he yanks my hair back, his snarl a clear warning to take it, before he aggressively bangs his fingers into me repeatedly.

Twisting and curling them, he coils them deeper, trying to loosen my pussy, causing my legs to shake. The intense feeling ignites a raw desire within me, and my cries escalate, a mix of pain and overwhelming pleasure.

"Such a tight little cunt. I would love to force my entire fucking hand inside you," he growls through clenched teeth against my ear with raw desire, "Stretch you out so you can take every inch of my cock with ease."

His dirty mouth sets my veins ablaze, and I can feel my climax building inside me at an alarming rate, a rapid sensation I have never experienced before.

As soon as he starts ripping his fingers out of me, scraping the tips down my walls before plunging them back inside again, I cry out, my orgasm slamming into me like a tsunami and my come rushes down my legs and his hand, warm and slick.

While my body convulses, he slides his fingers back inside me one last time, desiring to feel my pussy contract around them until I come down from euphoria.

With my eyes closed, trying to catch my breath, his thumb presses down on my puckered hole and the rumble in his chest indicates that he is still going to force me to fuck his knife.

He suddenly pulls his fingers out of me, smearing my come over my asshole before tightening his grip on my neck, demanding me to manoeuvre. On trembling legs, I reluctantly follow his lead around the tree until he turns me, and I feel the cold handle of his knife, aiming at a slight upward angle against my ass.

Bringing his face is close to mine, his eyes are feral as they search my heavy-lidded gaze. Leaning down, he grabs my ass cheeks, splitting them wide apart and I cling to his soaked leather jacket, my fingers digging into the wet material as he pushes his body against mine, making me take his knife.

I shift slightly, ensuring the handle is centred to avoid it slipping into my pussy or cutting me. With every movement, it slowly enters me, it's cold, firm surface an unnatural intrusion and my brows pinch together, my mouth dropping open at the same time as a gasp escapes. The shape is odd, completely out of place inside me, but he continues steadily, stretching me as each engraved ridge of the handle immerses and glides down my forbidden walls.

As soon as I feel the edge of the cold steel blade, I push against his chest, stopping him and I take a moment, trying to adjust to the strange sensation, but his hands tighten on my ass, his fingers digging into the flesh, taking power, giving me little time to get used to it.

Suddenly, he slides me all the way up to the tip and forcefully pushes me back down again, almost reaching the blade.

"I said, fucking all of it," he growls.

The feeling elicits a shamefully, loud moan against his lips, beyond my control and his grip moves to my hips, becoming firmer, guiding my thrusts to become more erratic and aggressive. His eyes scan my face, absorbing my heavy gaze and parted lips. The further I lose myself in his swirling eyes, the more I find myself surrendering to him and with shaky hands, I lower them, slipping my fingertips beneath his wet, black tank that clings to his skin. Hesitantly, I lay my palms on his hard abs, unable to stop myself. I need to feel him. I need to touch his incredible body, despite knowing this is so wrong. The strong muscles beneath my fingertips ripple with each movement, solid and tight.

"You're touching me, Dolly."

Lost in my insanity of lust, my eyes are so dazed they close. "Fuck, I know," I gasp out with a breathless whisper. "I don't want to, but I can't help it."

I move my hands up further, skimming over his pecs, feeling the hard lines of his muscles and his nipple piercing slides over my palm, the cool metal contrasting against the heat radiating from his skin, causing me to shiver.

His grip on my hips tighten as he pulls me closer. "I know you fucking can't. You're mine, pretty girl, and there's no turning back for you. For us." I shudder at his words, the weight of them sinking into my veins.

My hands continue to explore his tattooed body, tracing every contour and despite the handle still inside me, the discomfort mingles with an undeniable pleasure, making me crave so much more. I arch against him, surrendering to the storm of emotions that are taking over me, knowing there's no escape from this dark, irresistible connection.

As one of his hands snakes up the front of my body, he captures my lips, and I accept, our tongues merge in a feral and devouring kiss. When he has a firm hold on my breast, squeezing brutally, I hiss against his lips.

Once he realizes he no longer needs to control me since I am fucking his knife of my own free will, his other hand slips into the waistband of my ripped panties. The tips of his fingers instantly press through my pussy lips, finding my sensitive clit.

He rubs me out forcefully, heightening my pleasure, and I once again feel my peak approaching. The intensity of his touch is overwhelming, and my moans grow louder, blending with the primal sounds escaping him as our kiss deepens.

"Oh yes, just like that. I am so fucking close, Hell. Don't stop." I groan, letting him hear the words he undoubtedly wants to hear, but with a vicious snarl against my lips, he suddenly plunges three fingers into my soaked hole without warning.

I let out a loud cry, not caring who hears and his other hand clings to the back of my thigh, lifting it to his hip, allowing him to delve even deeper into my dripping pussy. Now with both of my holes filled, I know it will be everything I need to be pushed over the edge.

As we kiss wildly, I fuck his fingers and the knife with desperate, animalistic bounces and the intensity builds rapidly, my body trembling with the effort. Feeling my climax peaking inside me like a ticking time bomb about to detonate, my breaths become ragged and frantic against his lips. My eyes roll back, the pleasure so intense it borders on pain.

"Fuck, I'm going to come!" I scream out.

With a sudden, vice-like grip on my throat, he wrenches me forward, the knife tearing out of my ass with a brutal tug. I stumble, his strength propelling me until I crash onto my hands and knees on the mud below.

His hand presses on my back, forcing me face down into the sodden ground as he kneels behind me. The sharp sting of the knife's handle pierces my violated ass once more, eliciting a cry from my lips as he thrusts it deep inside me. Simultaneously, he drives all three of fingers back into my wet pussy, the attack unstoppable and wild, like a crazed beast unleashed.

As he begins fucking both my holes once again with unbearable force, my thighs shake, but despite the ferocity of his sickening assault, his control works. Within moments, pleasure explodes within me like a violent tempest, my fingers claw at the mud, a cry ripping from my throat, reverberating into the darkness of the silent forest.

In the midst of my orgasm, he swiftly withdraws his fingers and the knife, only to spread me wide apart with his fingers and thumbs, his face diving into my dripping pussy. His tongue lashes out with a predatory hunger, ravaging my pulsating core with fierce strength.

With each untamed moan that leaves me, he heightens the ecstasy, his piercing teasing, and tormenting with expert precision. His movements are ruthless as he feasts on me with a growl before his tongue flattens against my swollen flesh before sliding upward to my asshole, collecting my come, where he continues to eat.

He forces his thick tongue so deep into each of my openings, stretching and desperate to taste my inner walls, that I can feel his piercing inside of me. My eyes drift shut, starting to see spots forming behind my eyelids, seeking refuge as I try to steady my erratic breaths, allowing him to do whatever he wants to me since I am absolutely immobile.

After what seems like hours of his unrelenting gnawing on my holes, unable to get enough of the taste of me, he withdraws, the absence of his touch leaving me feeling oddly deprived and needing for more already.

A sharp smack against the side of my ass with his big hand jolts me out of my hazy state, eliciting a wince of pain from my lips. He leans over, his fingers tangling in my wet hair as he pulls me upright, my exhausted body collapsing against his solid chest.

With my head resting on his shoulder, I feel his warm breath ghosting over my skin as he trails his nose slowly along the curve of my neck, sending shivers cascading down my spine. His hands roam upward at the same time, skimming over the contours of the front of my body until he pushes them firmly over the swells of my breasts. He toys with my pierced nipples, latching them between his fingers before pulling until he cannot tug anymore.

A low, primal growl vibrates from his torso as his teeth graze my jaw, igniting a whirlwind of feelings within me, feelings I struggle to understand but cannot deny.

When he speaks into my ear, I am still in a stupor, but my eyes gently open. "I want to take you home with me and use you as my little fucking toy all night, but Hellion will be unleashed on you on Dark Night, Dolly."

His warning sends a chill through me and as I ponder the unsettling truth, the difference between Hell and Hellion becomes clear. Hell, for all his brutality, yet he still possesses a twisted form of passion, a dark allure that draws me in despite the danger, such as in this moment, but Hellion... There is something sinister lurking beneath the surface. In the wake of Hell's intoxicating dominance, the thought of facing his character leaves me worried and confused.

After touching me as much as he can while I am in my tired, freezing-cold state, I feel him shrug off his leather jacket before placing it over me, in an attempt to keep me warm. When he shifts, he scoops me up in his arms, effortlessly and before I know it, he is carrying me back to my trailer.

CHAPTER TWELVE

When I carry Noir back inside her trailer, she suddenly wriggles out of my arms, landing on her feet. I watch curiously as she speeds toward the bedroom, and I follow slowly behind. When I enter, she has her back to me, tossing my jacket onto the bed before heading to rummage through her wardrobe for something to wear, but she hasn't told me to leave.

I reach for my jacket, sliding it on while standing there, observing intently before drawing a cigarette out of my pocket, and biting one out of the packet. She strips completely naked, now not shy at all around me, and I raise an eyebrow while lighting the end. She spins around at the sound of the gas lighter's click, facing me completely nude, and I growl.

"Not in here!" she yells, panicked.

My cold eyes flash to hers as I take another long drag, the smoke curling from my nostrils and I ignore her stupid rules, probably set by Limp Dick, because they mean nothing to me.

She rolls her eyes, knowing I am not going to do as she asked and I continue to watch her as she dresses in a baggy black hoodie and jeans to match, finishing with leather platform boots. As she throws her hair into a messy bun, I start to wonder what the fuck she is doing.

"Going somewhere?" I finally ask, my tone cold. She doesn't answer until she's done looking in the mirror and then turns to face me. As she takes steps forward, my eyes rake down her beautiful figure.

"Will you take me to meet The Monster?" she asks, her voice steady.

I'm caught off guard by her question, but when I have thought about it, I give a small head shake, "He doesn't like people." I respond truthfully.

Her plump lips twitch into a smile. "And neither do you."

I sigh and look away, knowing it's not safe to take her there. If he breaks through those bars, she's fucking dead and then I'll have to kill him for taking my Dolly from me.

"Please," she pleads gently, placing her small hands on my chest in an attempt to sway me. I search her eyes, trying to think of a way to get around it without triggering him.

I inhale deeply, readying myself for what's to come. "If I take you, you need to listen to me," I say firmly. "If he starts kicking the fuck off, you need to leave right away. Don't try to act like a hero and think you can take him, because trust me, you can't."

Her eyes widen slightly, but she nods. "I understand," she whispers.

"No, you don't," I growl, taking her hand away from chest and holding it. "This isn't a fucking game, Noir. One wrong move, and it's over."

She swallows hard, determination still on her face. "I won't make any wrong moves," she promises.

I let out a frustrated sigh, knowing there's no changing her mind and give a head gesture for her to follow me.

HOLLOW HELLION

As we walk to where he is kept, the rain continues to pour down on us and Noir strides beside me, her curiosity evident in her voice. "What's his story? Has he always been here?"

I side-eye her, noting how much shorter she is compared to me even with her platformed boots. Gazing forward, I give a small head shake. "Nah, he was owned by another circus in another state around six years ago," I explain. "But when I visited for business to plan a possible joint horror performance, I saw how badly he was abused there during their show. It pissed me off." She listens carefully, her blue eyes wide with interest and I continue, "Instead of working with them, I burned the entire place down and fucking took him."

Her mouth opens slightly in surprise, the questions swirling in her mind, "So, you saved him?"

I snicker, the memory of that night still vivid. "I'm no fucking hero, pretty girl if that's what you want to hear. I'm the villain through and through. He is just better off here, but he's still a danger to everyone around him and to himself."

She nods in understanding. "And now you keep him locked up?"

"It's the only way to keep everyone safe," I reply, my voice hard. "He's a ticking fucking time bomb, and if he ever gets loose..." I don't finish the sentence, letting the threat hang between us.

We continue walking in silence, and as we approach the place where he is kept, I can see the nervousness in Noir's eyes, but she's made up her mind, and there's no turning back now.

HOLLOW HELLION

When we get to the steel door on the outskirts of the trailer park grounds, I pull out the key and unlock the padlock before removing it and placing it in my pocket. I pull the heavy chain away, letting it fall to the floor with a loud thump before yanking open the door. I enter first, the candle lit area making it hard to see. Leaning over Noir, I bring my face close to hers as I reach for the handle, slamming it shut behind us. She gives me a small, shy smile from the close proximity between us and my gaze shifts to her lips briefly before I turn around.

Our footsteps crunch over the hay-covered ground, and we move forward until he comes into view behind the bars to our left. He sits in his makeshift "bedroom," hunched on the floor in the corner, reading a book, his favorite thing to do. As he notices me, he lifts his head, unfazed by my presence, but as soon as Noir steps into view behind me, he bolts upright, charging straight for the bars with frightening speed.

"Fuck's sake," I mutter, knowing what's coming.

He collides with the bars, denting them, the entire building shaking from the impact. Dust rains down from the cracks above as he lets out a deafening roar, his blackened teeth exposed in a terrifying grimace. The force of his breath sends Noir's hair flying back, her face whitening at the raw power and fury emanating from him.

I step between her and the bars in a protective stance, my gaze locked on his wild eyes as he slams against them again.

"Easy, M," I say, my voice steady despite the chaos. "She's good."

Suddenly Noir walks around me, coming into his sight again and his face falls. "Good?" he asks, his deep, gruff voice now strangely curious by her. She holds out her shaking hand, slowly heading towards him, her eyes fixed and focused.

I'm ready to stop her until she speaks gently, "You're beautiful."

My eyes flash to M to see his reaction, and it's not what I was expecting at all. He shows no sign of wanting to hurt Noir anymore, which is shocking. Their eyes lock, mesmerized by each other as she continues her approach. When she is close enough, her hand sneaks through the bars, and before I know it, her palm is laid gently on his deeply scarred cheek. M's eyes widen in surprise, his rage seemingly dissipating under her touch, and he leans into her hand, a low, rumbling purr vibrating from his chest.

Noir's fear is replaced with a look of wonder as she strokes his face softly. "You're not a monster," she whispers, her voice trembling. "You're just... Misunderstood."

I watch, stunned, as M closes his eyes, savoring the gentle contact. It's as if, for a moment, the beast within him is tamed by her touch. I can't believe what I'm seeing. I've not even seen him like this with Madame. Her bravery, her kindness, it's doing something to him. It's fucking doing something to me.

HOLLOW HELLION

When we're finished, we leave the chamber, and I padlock it shut behind me. As I turn around, Noir's eyes are already on mine and I set a cigarette between my lips, pulling my hoodie over my head to shield it from the rain, still bewildered by how the fuck she managed to do that.

"Maybe we can train him enough so that he can live closer to the circus and have freedom," she speaks up beside me quietly as we head back to her trailer.

"We?" I question coldly, not looking at her, the scepticism evident in my tone.

"Yes, we. I think he trusts me, and he definitely trusts you."

I take a long drag from my cigarette. "You think it's that fucking simple?" I say while exhaling. "He's dangerous, Noir."

"Aren't we all?" she murmurs.

As we stop by her trailer, we turn to face one another, and she continues. "We all have our demons, Hell. Some are just more visible than others. Maybe he's dangerous, but so are you. So am I. We all have a darkness inside us."

My brow raises at her words. "You're not dangerous, pretty girl," I growl, closing the gap until she's wedged between me and the trailer. As my big frame presses against hers, she sucks in a sharp breath and I bring my face down to hers, her head tilting back to meet my gaze. "You're my gentle Little Dolly."

I flick my cig away before slipping my cold hands under her wet hoodie, grabbing her bare waist roughly, and she exhales a breath against my lips, her skin breaking out in shivers under my touch.

"Aren't you?"

"No," she whispers, her heavy eyes shutting.

I hiss, baring my teeth against her lips at her stubbornness.

"Little. Fucking. Liar."

I plunge my tongue straight down her throat and she welcomes it this time. She wraps her arm around my shoulders and draws me in closer as she devours my mouth with a moan. It's clear after tasting the fires of Hell, she now craves the full fury of my inferno. My dick hardens as I push myself firmly against her, showing her exactly what she does to me.

My hands sneak upward, gripping her braless titties with a harsh grasp and she arches toward me, a seductive gasp escaping her lips, until suddenly, a male throat clears from behind us.

She pauses, her eyes snapping wide open before she pushes on my chest. I growl, wiping my thumb over my wet lips with my head down while I take a step back.

"So, I leave for one fucking night and you're already jumping on the next cock?" Limp Dick shouts at Noir drunkenly behind me.

I seethe as she walks around me, her hands out in surrender. "No... I..." she stutters out in protest.

He suddenly throws his bottle of beer, narrowly missing her head by an inch, shattering against the trailer, and I snap, whirling around. My angry eyes flash to him, and he seems startled that it's me. Murder floods through my veins at an alarming rate and before Noir can stop me, I pull my fist back, smashing him in the face with one sledgehammer punch. As soon as I connect with his nose, he's out cold, stiff, and falls back on the wet grass with a loud thud.

"Hell!" Noir screams out, but as she passes me to get to him, I quickly reach out, catching her throat, and I pin her against the trailer. I breathe heavily, fuming with rage, and press my face close to hers, squeezing her neck tight.

"What the fuck are you doing?" I grit out viciously. "I will fucking kill him!" She looks at me with broad eyes, and I continue. "He's fucking hurting you like that?"

She shakes her head frantically, "No, he has never... He's not usually like that. He's drunk. He just saw us kissing... He..."

I growl loudly, cutting her off. "So fucking what," I raise my voice. "He needed to know he is not allowed to hurt you!"

I see the defensiveness swirling in her icy blue eyes. "But you're allowed to, right?" she asks, her brows creasing with anger.

I squeeze her neck a little more, my voice dropping to a lethal whisper. "Yes. Yes, I fucking am. That's the whole point, Dolly."

She snickers in defiance. "So, you're allowed to force me to my knees in the woods, almost suffocate me with your dick in my throat, or maybe shove a knife in my ass? Hm? What did you think that shit doesn't hurt, Hell?" She tries to excuse his actions by turning them around on me.

I lean in closer, my breath against her ear. "The difference is, you want me to hurt you. You fucking crave it. He doesn't understand that, but I do."

When I draw back to meet her gaze, I notice her face has fallen at my words, and I seize the moment. "And I would never hurt you out of malice or fucking anger. I would never harm you intentionally. The only time you're ever allowed to shed tears is when the delivery of my pain and pleasure gets too intense. No one, and I mean fucking no one on this earth, is allowed to hurt your beautiful body or soul but me. Not even you."

She shakes her head once, disbelief etched on her features. "You're out of your fucking mind."

My jaw tightens, and I lean in closer. "Are you only just noticing, Noir? Because I don't think it's been much of a fucking secret that I am insane since the day we met."

Limp Dick stirs behind me, regaining consciousness, and Dolly tries to peek over my shoulder, but I grab her face, squeezing her cheeks, forcing her to look into my swirling eyes as I press my lips against hers.

"Either leave him, or I'll fucking kill him," I growl.

Her eyes widen in shock. "What?"

"You fucking heard me."

She shakes her head once. "I can't. He was there for me when no one else was," she admits.

I stare deep into her eyes, my grip tightening. "And now you have me. Get. Rid. Of. Him."

Her eyes glaze over with moisture. "I hate you," she chokes out.

I try not to roll my eyes as I respond, "Tell me something I don't know."

"You can't just control everyone and everything, Hell."

I lower my mouth to her ear, "Fucking watch me."

As Noir and I maintain intense eye contact for some time, it seems she is starting to calm down, as if a reluctant acceptance is stirring inside her. When Limp Dick stumbles past us, heading for the trailer, her eyes drift to follow him, but I quickly move her face back to mine, retaining her focus. "Come back to my place. I don't want you here."

She scans my gaze before giving a small head shake, pulling my wrist to release her. "I'll be fine," she murmurs. "Please just leave this to me, Hell."

I growl and look aside, dropping my hand, but she tiptoes, placing a gentle kiss on my cheek. "Don't ever underestimate me. I now say who is allowed to hurt me," she whispers close to my ear. I turn my head quickly confused by her words, our eyes connecting, and she continues expressionlessly, "I'll see you soon, I'm sure."

She slips past me, and I stand rooted to the spot, an internal battle raging within me—whether to let her handle this herself or to kidnap her and take her home with me.

 When I enter the trailer, I close the door gently behind me, taking a deep breath with my eyes closed. I hear Eli in the kitchen, his movements unsteady. Composing myself, I head towards him and as I step into the kitchen, I spot him immediately. He is leaning against the counter, a tissue pressed to his bloodied nose and guilt creeps up my spine, knowing he's not alright after what Hell did to him.

"E? Are you okay?" I ask gently, my voice soft and concerned despite knowing the obvious answer.

He remains silent, the blood dripping steadily from his nose. I step forward, "Here, let me help..."

Without looking at me, he stands straight and brushes past.

"Just leave me the fuck alone, Noir," he snaps.

I instinctively sidestep, "But..." Before I can finish, he storms into the bedroom, the door slamming shut and the bang reverberates through the trailer, leaving me standing there, guilt and worry churning in my gut.

I let out a heavy sigh, feeling defeated and tangled in confusion knowing where both guys are coming from. Eli is angry because of what he saw which is justified, but throwing a fucking bottle at me wasn't. Hell just went into protective mode which is also justified. Fuck, I need to get myself out of this mess. What am I doing?

I stroll toward the couch, taking a seat, and slowly pull off my boots and jeans, leaving only my oversized hoodie and socks on. My mind races with thoughts of how to talk to Eli tomorrow, and my eyes flicker to the window hidden behind the curtains.

I stand and move toward it before gently pulling a curtain aside. The night outside is pitch black, and his swirling orbs, absent, leaving a hollow ache in my chest.

Turning away, I head back to the couch, dragging a thick blanket with me. I curl up into a ball, my head resting on the armrest and minutes stretch into what feels like hours, my thoughts refusing to settle. Then, something by the window catches my eye and I carefully lift my head, seeing him standing there, smoking a cigarette.

A strange wave of calmness washes over me, and I lay my head back down, maintaining eye contact with him through the glass. His presence, even at a distance, brings an unexpected comfort, a huge difference to how I once felt when he used to watch me. As the tension eases from my body, I finally drift off to sleep, knowing Hell is watching over me, my deadly guardian in the night.

CHAPTER THIRTEEN

It's been a few days since everything went down and Eli is still giving me the silent treatment. His anger is understandable, but we're fucking adults. I believe we should be able to talk about it. Today, I plan to visit Blush. She is going to dye my hair, and I hope to get some answers about what to expect at Dark Night, which is fast approaching in a few days.

Deep down, I know it won't be pretty and I truly believe it's something sinister, but the thought of innocents dying unsettles me, and I hope that's not the case. In a twisted way, I hope they deserve it because that might make it easier to stomach. The way these acts and murders might be committed, along with facing Hellion, makes me anxious, and I have no idea why I haven't run for the fucking hills yet. What is keeping me here? Why am I so attached to these people and the atmosphere?

In some strange way, this place is starting to feel like a home. A messed-up home, but a home, nonetheless. It's more of a home than what I had to endure for years after my mother died.

Sitting on the end of the bed, I slide on my boots when Eli suddenly walks into the room and I lift my head, noticing the bruising around his eyes, but he still avoids me, heading for the wardrobe. I keep my gaze on him as I tie my boots and he slips on a jacket.

"You're working tonight?" I ask, hoping to break the ice after the hundredth attempt, but he continues to ignore me.

"You can keep avoiding me, but it's not going to change anything," I say, frustration creeping into my voice. "We need to talk, Eli."

He stops for a moment, his hand pausing on the wardrobe handle, and I can see the tension in his shoulders, but then he continues as if I haven't spoken at all, rummaging through his clothes.

I stand up, crossing the room to stand behind him. "E, please. This isn't helping either of us. I get that you're angry but shutting me out is childish."

He finally turns and looks at me, his eyes hard and filled with a mixture of hurt and anger. "What do you want me to say, Noir? That I'm okay with everything? Because I'm not. You put me in danger, and this ruins everything."

I swallow hard, knowing he's right. "I know and I'm sorry, but we can't move forward if we don't talk about it."

He exhales sharply, shaking his head. "You're into fucking clowns now? Does this mean we're done?"

I tilt my head to the side. "Nothing I say will explain or justify what you saw, but I will be honest with you because you deserve the truth."

Eli stands there, arms crossing over his chest, finally ready to listen to what I have to say, and I sigh before facing aside. "I can't resist him," I admit, almost bluntly.

He lets out a loud scoff, "What the fuck, Noir!"

My eyes return to his, and I give a small shoulder shrug. "Again, I am just being honest. You've been a great friend, but..."

"Friend?" he barks. "A fucking friend? We've been together and fucking for months. Is this because I'm having problems?" He glances down at his crotch before returning his eyes to mine.

I shake my head, my brows pinching together. "No, of course not. I just have never felt romantically connected to you, E."

My honesty makes his face fall. "You used me," he breathes out.

I shake my head again. "No, I..."

"What was I? Just to pass the time? What the fuck, Noir. I was there for you when you had fucking no one. You would have died without me!"

I narrow my eyes, hating the fact that he said that. Although he might think that's true, I would have still found a way of survival regardless because that's me, but I brush it aside, not wanting to argue.

"I appreciate everything you have done for me, and I want to stay friends, but I think it's best if we're not like that anymore. I am not going to feed you any more false hope. Whatever we were, ends now."

His fists clench, and he storms toward me, but I stand my ground and when he is entirely in my space, I stare up at him blankly while he simmers on the edge of wrath. The intensity in his eyes burns, and I can feel the heat of his anger radiating off him.

After a tense silence, I shake my head once. "He will kill you," I say softly, my voice barely above a whisper. "You need to be very, very careful with threatening me. If you can't control yourself, then I suggest you leave this place altogether because if he finds out you're even getting in my face like this, I won't stop him."

His eyes flash with disbelief and he takes a step back, his fists still trembling. "You'd let him kill me?" he gasps out.

I hold his gaze steadily. "If you keep doing this bullshit, yes. I won't protect you from him. I won't even protect you from myself."

His face contorts with frustration. "You're choosing him over me?"

"I'm choosing myself, E," I reply firmly. "And you should choose you. This isn't a fucking game. You need to decide what's more important: your pride or your life."

He stares at me, his expression torn, and then he lets out a defeated sigh. "Fine," he mutters. "But don't expect me to stick around and be there when you self-destruct, because you fucking will, and he won't help you. He's only using you for your pussy."

My jaw tenses, but I'm smart enough to know he's being nasty because he's hurt and I can't blame him, I am being pretty emotionless right now, but he needs to know the truth.

"I think you should ask Madame to give you another trailer," I suggest.

He pulls his head back, his face scrunched up. "Fuck no. I'm staying. You don't get to dictate where I go when you're the one who put us in this mess."

I sigh, looking aside, and without another word, he passes me and storms out, slamming the door behind him. I stand there, the echoes of his departure ringing through the room. Taking a deep breath, I try to steady myself. The atmosphere in the trailer now feels heavy, and as I glance around, the familiar surroundings suddenly feel uncomfortable. I turn around and head out the door, making my way towards Blush's trailer.

HOLLOW HELLION

The cool night breeze hits me, a stark contrast to the heated tension I just left behind and the ground beneath my feet feels uneven, each step anchoring me more in the reality of my decisions. Is this me choosing Hell? Or is this just me being truthful with myself finally and Hell has been the wake-up call?

Once I arrive at her door, I raise my arm and knock my knuckles against the glass. A moment later, the door swings open, revealing Blush standing there in a black crop top and high-waisted leather pants, a big smile plastered on her pretty face.

"Hey, girl!" she greets enthusiastically.

I smile back and take the two short steps to enter as she stands aside, allowing me in. The interior of her trailer immediately captures my attention. "Wow, it's fucking amazing in here," I gasp, taking in the chic black and pink decor.

Blush giggles behind me. "Thanks. It's taken me a while to get it how I want."

I nod while she passes me, gesturing for me to follow her to her bedroom and as we enter, I notice how much bigger it is compared to mine. She suggests I sit at her vanity, and I slip my leather jacket down my arms before taking a seat. Blush places a towel over my shoulders and begins preparing the dye.

"I always thought you weren't naturally blonde. Your dark eyebrows give it away," she remarks, her eyes meeting mine in the mirror. "What made you dye it? I mean, it suits you, but I bet you look amazing with dark hair."

I think about how I dyed it to be less detectable to Kyro and so far, it has worked, I guess.

I shrug my shoulders. "I just wanted a change," I tell the lie, trying to sound casual.

She nods, not pressing further. "Well, you're going to look beautiful when we're done."

As she starts applying the dye, I relax into the comforting atmosphere as she continues our conversation. "So, what's been going on with you?" she asks.

I let out a heavy sigh, "Well, Eli caught me and Hell..."

I trail off, my eyes meeting hers in the mirror and they widen with surprise. "Fucking?" she says out, attempting to finish my sentence.

I shake my head. "Not that far, but enough to hurt E."

"But he isn't your boyfriend, right?"

I give a small nod. "He isn't, but he was there for me when no one else was and I was in a very bad place."

Blush nods a few times before rolling her eyes with a deep exhale. "Ah, trauma bond," she declares knowingly.

"Yeah," I agree, the weight of her words settling in. "I guess it is."

She applies more dye, her hands working through my hair. "It's tough, you know. Those bonds can feel so real and deep, but they're built on shaky fucking ground."

I nod in agreement. "I know. It's just hard to get around all of this."

Blush gives me a sympathetic smile. "It always is, Noir, but you're strong, and you'll get through it. Just make sure you take care of yourself first. Fuck guys."

Her words make my brows pinch, sparking curiosity about her personal life. "Do you have a boyfriend?"

She scrunches her small nose in disgust. "Hell no. I eat pussy," she says bluntly, causing my eyebrows to shoot up in surprise. She throws her head back with a laugh, which makes me laugh along with her.

"Don't worry, you're safe, but only because Hell caught you before I did," she teases, winking at me in the mirror and I shake my head with another laugh as she continues. "Saying that, there is only one man on this planet I would gladly fall to my knees for."

"Who?" I ask, tilting my head to the side, intrigued.

She leans in closer, a mischievous sparkle in her pink eyes.

"Wrath," she whispers.

I blink, taken aback as I respond. "Wrath?"

Blush nods, a dreamy look on her face. "He's... something else. You know when you just know they're beyond dangerous, but you're drawn to it anyway? I've heard some things. Terrible things, but a girl can dream. Apparently, he's into girl on girl too." She shudders out, "Fuck, I would love to eat pussy in front of him while he screws my ass from behind."

I roll my lips inward with a smile, "Jesus, Blush." I giggle out.

She gives me a big grin and a shoulder shrug. "Although I know it will never happen, a girl can fantasize, right?"

I lift a brow, "Why won't it ever happen?"

She lets out a long breath before explaining, "When I say he is dangerous, Noir, I am not fucking lying. He is worse than Hell. I would be putting my life in danger, and I like my life better."

"But does he know you're interested?"

She lifts her shoulders again. "I don't know, he is mute and doesn't speak, so I have never approached and flirted with him if that's what you mean."

After covering my hair, she slips off her black latex gloves. "I'm going to make us a drink. I think we could both do with one or two."

As she heads to the small kitchen area, I take a moment to process what she said. Wrath—more dangerous than Hell. It's hard to imagine anyone more dangerous, yet here we are, talking about it so casually and as if all this insanity is fucking normal.

Blush returns with two glasses filled to the brim with a vibrant, neon pink cocktail. "Here," she says with a big smile, handing me one. "To surviving murderous men or women and living to tell the tale."

I chuckle and clink my glass against hers. "Cheers to that."

We take a sip, the sweet alcohol burning beautifully down my throat, and I continue the conversation. "So, you've never even tried to get close to him?"

Blush shakes her head. "Nope. Like I said, I value my life. Plus, he's got this crazy aura that just screams 'stay the fuck away.' But it doesn't stop a girl dreaming."

I nod, understanding more than I let on. There's something intoxicating about the red flags, about the forbidden. Hell has that same allure, and despite my better judgment, I'm drawn to it like a moth to a flame, especially now he has had his hands all over me, showing me exactly how dominant he can be and what he can do to my body.

"So, what's the plan for Dark Night?" I ask, changing the subject.

She narrows her eyes, and I instantly know she isn't going to tell me in full detail what Dark Night is about, just like everyone else here. It's like they're telling me, but only in code, keeping me on the edge of my seat so I don't know what to truly expect.

"The usual stuff," she answers cryptically.

I sigh, the familiar feeling of frustration stirring inside of me. "Yeah, I figured," I murmur.

Blush suddenly brightens up. "Hey, after this, we should head over to the carnival for a few hours!"

My eyes meet hers in the mirror, and I think about it. Why not go and have fun for the night? Maybe it's needed. A distraction and a break from all the bullshit, so I give a small nod in response with a smile. "Sure, let's do it."

 Leaning against my bike, I take in the sight of the bustling carnival as I smoke a cigarette. While being hidden out of sight, I watch Soul in the far distance trying to engage with Limp Dick, who's busy working a stall. The urge to murder him in the most inhumane way imaginable gnaws at me, but I'll give Dolly the small opportunity to get rid of his ass before I step in. Still, a little push isn't going to hurt.

As Soul strides toward me, I drop my cigarette onto the ground, stamping it out with my heavy boot. He leans up against my bike, lifting his chin in Limp Dick's direction. "Nah, I don't think he's into it," Soul says.

My teeth grind as I stare at Limp Dick from a distance, watching him serve a customer. "There's something up with him though. I can sense it. I don't fucking like him," Soul continues. "I will find out for you, bro, don't worry."

I inhale deeply, knowing I feel the same way about this cunt. "Well, he should be gone soon. If not, I'll just fucking kill him."

A regular strolls by on his own and I whistle, "Hey!" I yell quietly. He stops, raising his chin in acknowledgment and I make a head gesture for him to come over. When he steps forward and stops in front of me, I glance behind him to make sure Limp Dick isn't watching. Seeing he's still busy working, I look at the guy. "Wanna make a quick fifty bucks?"

His eyes light up before narrowing in suspicion. "What do I have to do?" I reach inside my leather jacket, pulling out a small bag of heroin and a couple of needles.

I nod towards the visitor. "Hold out your hand."

He hesitates but does, his hand shaking slightly as I slap the drugs into his palm. "Pretend you're going to sell this shit over by that stall,"

I say, gesturing toward where Limp Dick is stationed. "Soul will come over and hit you for dealing on our grounds."

The guy's eyes widen as he looks from me to Soul, who stands beside me with a dark chuckle. "Don't worry, I won't hit you too hard," Soul reassures, slapping his hand down on the guy's shoulder a couple of times.

The visitor ponders for a few seconds, glancing nervously between us and I reach into my jeans, flicking out fifty bucks, holding it out to him. "Here."

He takes a deep breath before reluctantly taking the money and turning around. As he walks toward Limp Dick, I keep a close watch on him and Soul nudges me in the arm, and I side-eye him.

"What are you up to?" he asks, a devilish grin spreading across his lips.

"When you hit that guy, pick him up and escort him out," I respond. "But before you do, give Limp Dick the smack and tell him to take it to Madame."

He snickers, pushing himself away from the bike. "Got it."

Soul moves in, his pace steady and the moment he reaches them, he swings a hard punch that lands squarely on the guy's jaw. The guy stumbles before Soul grabs him by the collar, stopping him from hitting the ground.

"What the fuck are you doing selling this shit here?" Soul growls, his voice loud enough to draw attention. He reaches into the visitor's hand, yanking the heroin and needles out, then shoves them toward Limp Dick.

"Take this shit to Madame," he orders.

Limp Dick looks confused but takes the drugs, his eyes flicking between Soul and the visitor.

"Erm, okay," he stammers.

I turn around, facing the other way, and peer behind my hood as he gazes down at his newfound treasure. He glances around, eyes darting to see if anyone is watching and when he's satisfied that no one is paying attention, he sneakily shoves it into his pocket. *Stupid fucking cunt.*

I can feel the tension in his shoulders from here. He's nervous, but the pull of his habit is far too strong for him to resist. He doesn't realize he's walking into a fucking trap, and that ignorance is going to cost him tonight. I have horrifying plans for my Little Dolly.

I watch as he hops over the counter and blends into the crowd until he is no longer in sight and I inhale strongly, turning around to face the carnival again. Tonight, the vibrant colors and screams of terror are merely a facade for the darkness that will soon unfold on Dark Night, and I think about how I will finally have my dick deep inside Noir. Claiming every inch of her and destroying her for any other man but me.

Suddenly, her familiar scent wafts close, and I sniff the air before looking to my left. I spot her right away, walking beside Blush, a slight wobble in her posture.

She's fucking drunk.

I observe closely, and when she is passing me, she makes brief eye contact, a small smile playing on her rosy lips before continuing ahead, entering the carnival.

A low growl escapes my throat as I stare at her perfect, round ass in those tight black jeans, imagining how her soft cheeks will bounce against my hips while I fuck her from behind. Her blonde hair swings just above it, springing in the same rhythm as her footsteps. She looks back a couple of times, knowing I am watching her intensely, and she loves the fucking thrill of it.

I flick the cigarette butt away, my eyes locked on her every move and as she laughs at something Blush says, she throws her head back, the sound carefree. It's the total opposite to the dark, brooding thoughts in my sick mind, but that's what makes it all so much more arousing. She doesn't know what the fuck is coming. She doesn't know how tightly I'm weaving her into my world and how badly I am going to fuck her up on Dark Night while enjoying every fucking second of it.

Suddenly, my phone buzzes in my pocket and I dig for it before glancing down, noticing his name flashing across the screen. I snarl, knowing I haven't heard from him in weeks, but I answer and press the phone to my ear, waiting silently to hear his deep, gruff voice.

"We think we have a sighting of her," he says casually.

I stand straight, my attention buzzing, and I turn around, my eyes scanning the crowd. "Where? I can go there now," I say, agitated to get my hands on her.

"I think we should wait until it's confirmed," he retorts, and I growl in frustration. "Don't worry, you'll get your fair share of her, but you know to bring her to me, right?"

I draw another cig out of my pocket and place it between my lips. "I'm not sure I'll be able to stop myself once I get my hands on her," I answer truthfully, my words muffled by the cigarette.

"That wasn't the deal, Hell. I find her, and you go get her, so stick to the fucking plan." With that, he hangs up, leaving me reeling.

I take a long drag from my cigarette, the smoke curling around my face as memories of Haze flood my mind. His brutal murder still haunts me. I remember the call that changed everything and the horrifying sight that followed. Even for me, it was fucking gruesome. His throat was sliced with a machete in the kitchen, his cock and balls stuffed down his throat. It was a savage act of hatred—typical of a woman's way of killing, but I still don't have answers. Maybe he crossed the wrong woman. Who knows? All I know is he was fucking family.

Haze didn't live here; he moved between this place and his home state, usually working here during the summer for about six weeks. We were close—practically brothers and he was a lot like me; we had a lot of fun together. His death left a void, and apart from my uncle, I was alone again, family wise.

Before my mom died of cancer, she finally told me my father's name, but I was placed in foster care for six months while they searched for my other family. They found an uncle, my father's brother, but he refused to take me in at first. Eventually, he agreed but with a catch—I had to join the Shadow's Society. At the time I was desperate to escape the foster system as a kid, so I agreed, not realizing the darkness I was walking into. I thought I'd be a soldier or a fucking drug dealer, not a hired killer.

The training was brutal. Abuse, torture, and sexual assaults were routine, meant to break us and rebuild us as insane, ruthless killers. Once you were in, there was no way of getting out and we were conditioned to accept this twisted life as normal. I have two more years until a retrial, where the Shadow's will decide if I've contributed enough to their corrupt system to earn a normal life. But what the fuck is normal now? I've been so deeply warped that the idea of a decent, normal life feels impossible. My brain is fried, my soul twisted. This is my normal now. The dust of my old life with my mom is just that—dust, shadows of a past that no longer exists.

CHAPTER FOURTEEN

 After a night with Blush, filled with laughter and drinks, I return to my trailer, feeling lighter and more at ease. Unlocking the door, I smile to myself, grateful for the fun I had.

The darkness inside welcomes me as I lock the door behind me, and I shrug off my jacket as I head straight for the bedroom. The moonlight filters through the shutters, casting a glow on Eli's figure in bed and he has his back is to me, snoring heavily as usual. I don't care about his presence tonight—I just need the comfort of the bed. Stripping down to my long, baggy t-shirt and panties, I drunkenly attempt to be quiet, gently pulling back the duvet and slipping under it. I lie on my back, staring up at the ceiling as the room spins slightly from the alcohol.

While the night deepens, my thoughts wander back to Hell and the memory of his heated gaze on me tonight. The way he watched me, was as if he could see right through me, stripping away all of my clothes with his enigmatic eyes. God, I can't wait for him to fuck me. The thought of how he will feel deep inside my pussy. How much pleasure and pain we could ignite. Oh, how things have changed just by him taking me in those goddamn woods like he did. It set something unstoppable inside of me.

In the quiet of the night, with Eli's snores filling the room, I find myself giving in to the pull of my fantasies and I imagine Hell's touch, his hands on my body, his lips on mine. The thought of our bodies entwined sends a wave of heat through me.

Suddenly, I feel a gust of cold air strike my exposed leg and my dazed eyes slowly open. Swirling, glowing eyes meet mine, hovering ominously above me, and my heart skips a beat, but before I can react, something is stuck over my mouth. As his hand wraps around my throat, my head tilts back involuntarily, and I realize it's duct tape sealing my lips.

"Shut. The. Fuck. Up," he whispers close to my face with a harsh, threatening rasp. My heart pounds in my chest, each beat a frantic reminder of the unsettling situation and with Eli sleeping just beside me, makes it all the more intense. Hell's grip on my throat loosens, and I raise my head, watching his tall, shadowy figure move to the end of the bed.

He reaches over, grabbing my legs, his touch firm as he starts to slowly drag me down the bed and panic surges through me, my body stiffening. My mind races, trying to comprehend how I can stop him. As he pulls me further, the bedsheets rustle, but the tape on my mouth muffles any sound I might make. When I am close to him, I glance up at Eli, but luckily he is still sound asleep, his snores uninterrupted, yet the thought of what Hell might do fills me with dread. The idea of this happening right beside Eli is so fucking wrong. Hell's presence is overwhelming, his eyes burning with an intensity that makes it clear he intends to have his way with me, regardless of the circumstances.

The room feels charged with an electric tension as my wide eyes watch him calmly take off his leather jacket, then lift his hoodie over his head, discarding both items onto the floor.

The moonlight filters through the shutters, shining rays on his ripped body. His spiralling tattoos seem to writhe with each movement, and he ruffles his curly, black hair with his fingers, letting it fall just enough to shadow his glowing gaze.

My chest heaves from a strange mixture of worry and undeniable arousal as he takes a step forward. He places his hands on my knees, spreading them wide apart before kneeling softly between them, his eyes never leaving mine.

I hold my hand out with a head shake in protest, but Hell merely catches it and pins it to the bed with a firm grip. He moves closer, his body pressing on top of mine and my breathing quickens, the heat radiating from him, his weight and size in comparison to mine, sets my pussy on fire. I can't fucking help it.

With his breath hot against my ear, his growing cock presses firmly against my core as he flexes his hips and instinctively, my legs lock around him, pulling him even closer.

"If even so much as a peep escapes your pretty fucking lips, waking him up while I am violating and brutalizing your tight cunt, I'll kill him and still unleash havoc on your beautiful body, but instead, in a pool of his spilled blood," he says in a dangerous whisper.

I turn my head quickly, my eyes expanded as he lifts his head to meet mine. I feel his calm gaze scanning my panicked face before he rises slowly.

After delivering my warning, I sit back on my knees, gathering her shirt before lifting it up her body and over her head. I watch as her perfect tits bounce from the movement, her nipple piercings glistening in the light. I then move on to the strings of her panties, drawing them down her smooth legs.

She complies, knowing I am fucking serious, the panic is clear on her face which only arouses me. Her breathing is shallow, and her eyes are wide, darting between me and the door behind me as if looking for an escape that doesn't fucking exist.

When she is entirely naked, I take a moment to admire her beautiful body, each curve, and every detail. Then, leaning over, I take her nipple into my mouth. She breathes deeply through her nose at the sensation—the small clink of her piercing meeting mine. Her body responds with a tremble, arching her back to be closer as I suck and roughly tug, tightening my teeth on the metal and dragging it back before consuming it entirely again. While I savage both of her tits, I slip my hand between her thighs.

My aim tonight is a disturbing game, something I can't get off my deranged mind, and I will achieve it. A sadistic preparation for her to take me on Dark Night and while I do it, somehow, she is going to have to stay silent if she wants Limp Dick to live.

My fingers slip through her slick pussy lips, finding her clit instantly and I begin to rub hard in circular motions, my touch unrelenting. Her legs instinctively tighten around me, but I flick them away with a firm shove, demanding she keep them wide open for me.

I raise my head, my lips tingling from ravaging her tits, and bring my mouth close to the tape.

"The more you resist me, the more you'll tempt me to wake him up and make him watch what I do to you," I murmur, my voice a quiet, stern threat. "Now, be a good Little Dolly and keep those fucking legs spread wide for me, no matter how intense this gets."

Her eyes expand with fear, but she nods, the air thick with the scent of her arousal betraying how deep down she is into this warped shit.

I lower myself down her body, sinking my teeth into her stomach, testing her pain threshold. Her sharp breaths and whimpers fuel my wicked desire as I continue until I position myself between her legs. My hands trail down her inner thighs, pressing into her soft flesh, my fingers digging into her skin before I attack, diving my face into her.

I devour her cunt violently, savoring her taste with a primal hunger. I could suffocate in this pretty pussy and kill over a happy fucking man. Her body writhes, her back arching, the curve of her tits casting shadows in the dim light, her rigid nipples pointing upward. I am brutal, doing everything I can to make her squeak, but my Dolly doesn't give in. I bite down on her swollen clit, gnawing on it, drawing mute cries of pain and pleasure from her, but I don't eat her come yet; I'm saving that. I need her to be fucking soaked for what I am about to do.

When she starts pushing on my head, trying to reduce my savagery, I grab her wrists and pin them to her thighs, forcing her to remain exposed and vulnerable to me. I go harder, my tongue and teeth working in sync until finally, she reaches her peak. My eyes flicker upward as I watch her body clenching, her attempts to stifle the powerful orgasm almost impossible.

Limp Dick continues to sleep, oblivious to the scene unfolding beside him, out of his head on smack. Meanwhile, I feast on Noir's perfect cunt, consuming her with an intensity that leaves no doubt who the fuck owns her.

I release one of her wrists, snatching them both with one hand. My cock strains so hard against my jeans that I have to drag my zipper down for relief, shoving my hand in my boxers to draw it out, thumping, dripping, and fucking heavy with need. I begin to jerk myself off, unable to hold the arousal she stirs in me.

I make her come again while I continue the persistent strokes on my dick. As she descends from her second high, I lift my head, kneeling once again between her legs. Keeping my grip on her wrists, I shuffle on my knees until they are pressed against her inner thighs, keeping them spread for what's next.

She tenses up as I lean over once again, attacking her tits while jerking my cock fast against her sensitive clit. Until, finally, I shoot my warm jizz, aiming for her pussy. I press my forehead against her chest, breathing heavily as my entire body tingles.

Once I am finished, I tuck myself back inside my boxers and lift myself up. I raise her arms, pinning her wrists above her head, my knees brutally pressing against her inner thighs as I hover over her, my lips close against the duct tape. I stare into her glazed eyes, her spirit and dignity broken but not yet shattered.

This is just the fucking beginning. She will learn that her fight only fuels my need to control her, to break her completely and when she finally gives in, fully and utterly, only then will I be satisfied. Until then, my sickening games continue.

I move my hand between her legs once more, feeling her soaked pussy hole dripping. I slide two fingers inside her quickly and a whimper escapes her against the duct tape as I shove them as deep as I can,

then I add *another* finger,

and *another,*

then my *thumb.*

Her eyes widen, her breathing becomes frantic, realizing I am about to press my entire hand inside her, just as I said I would. She shakes her head, but I release her wrists, grabbing her throat, squeezing tight, silently ordering her to take it.

She struggles to fit me inside of her as expected, her pussy is so fucking tight, but I don't relent. Knowing I need lube to do this, I release her throat and draw out my knife from my jeans pocket. As she lifts her head I press the blade against my palm, slicing deeply and swiftly across it until a steady flow of my blood is dripping onto her pussy and the pool of my cum. I clench my fingers, attempting to squeeze more out and then I roll my hand in a mix of my own blood and cum.

She stares at me with wide eyes like I am utterly insane and I fucking am, I know.

Now my hand is ready, I press my fingers and thumb inside once again, feeling her pussy stretching until all five of my top knuckles are inside her. She has her head tilted back, her eyes squeezed shut as I slowly rotate and push.

Inch by inch I extend her to the absolutely limit, but she doesn't stop me, she just scrunches the bed sheets into her hands, holding her breath until finally, her little cunt hole is tight and clenched around my wrist, her pussy swallowing my hand whole. She lets out the shuddering breath she was holding in through her nose, her chest heaving with each inhale and exhale.

I allow her to accommodate to the size of my hand because although this is probably the hottest thing I've ever felt and seen, and I would love to aggressively ram inside her, I don't want to tear her completely apart. I still want this pussy for Dark Night without fucking stitches and internal damage.

The muscles inside her clench around me, resisting my intrusion and I lean over her, bringing my mouth close to hers. "You need to fucking relax, or you'll be ripped the fuck apart," I growl quietly.

I press my forehead against hers, maintaining eye contact as I slowly twist and push my hand further inside her. She reaches down, grabbing my wrist tightly, the tension in her body is obvious, every muscle taut with a mix of pain and pleasure.

"Keep your eyes on mine," I command against her lips. "Focus on me. Feel every inch of my hand inside you and how well you're taking it."

She takes a quivering breath, her eyes never leaving mine as I attempt to guide her through it. The power of the moment is fucking electrifying, and her body begins to yield, her tightness gradually giving way as she follows my orders.

I can feel her surrendering, her walls relaxing ever so slightly as she accepts me deeper. "That's it," I praise breathlessly. "That's my good Little Dolly."

Eventually, I find my hand moving faster as I start to lose control, rotating with a rhythm that she seems to enjoy. The sight and feel of her body responding to me, the way her soaked pussy takes my hand and some of my wrist repeatedly, has me rock fucking solid again, and I am tempted to fuck her asshole at the same time.

Each time I thrust my hand deeper, she loosen a bit more, yielding to my untamed invasion. The deep wound on my palm stings, the wetness of our shared cum and my blood making every movement smooth and fluid. My breathing becomes ragged, matching hers, our shared dark sadistic delight filling the room.

Her hips begin to buck with more confidence, meeting my thrusts, her hand squeezing my arm and I growl with approval. "Fuck," I mutter, my voice thick with lust. "Fucking take it all, you little slut. Show me how much you want to ride my fucking fist."

She moans against the duct tape, her eyes rolling back as she loses herself. Lying beside her, I lean over, my free hand reaching and gripping her thigh to hold her open as I drive my fist in and out of her with increasing power, attempting to make her scream for me but all I hear are the wet sounds of her pussy echoing in the room.

Feeling her titties bouncing against my bare chest, I glance down before teasing one of her nipples with my tongue. Her body arches off the bed, her back bowing as she chases her release, her breathing growing more frantic. I can feel the pressure building inside her cunt, the way her muscles clench and flutter around my hand. The sight of her surrendering to the pleasure, her body writhing beneath me, is almost too much for me to witness.

With one final, forceful drive, I push her over the edge.

Her body convulses, the bliss crashing over her like a wave. I keep fucking her with my hand, drawing out her orgasm as much as I can, feeling every spasm and contraction as she comes apart around me.

I release her nipple, lifting my head to gaze down at her, seeing her restrain the scream she desperately wants to let out, and it only makes me admire her more. She has willpower. As always, a stubborn Little fucking Dolly.

As she gradually comes down from her climax, my hand slows down inside until finally, I ease it out of her. I possessively rub her twitching wet cunt with my hand, staring down at her as if I've won a prize I've desperately always wanted.

"You're so fucking perfect," I rasp. "You're made for this, made for me."

In an orgasmic daze, she runs her fingers through the back of my longish hair, searching my eyes as we share a moment, then I rise, standing off the bed.

As I gather my hoodie and jacket, she hurriedly pulls on her shirt and when I turn to face her, she's already seated at the bed's edge, stealing a glance back at Limp Dick, who's still out of his head and she looks confused by it.

I kneel in front of her, drawing her attention back to me and my eyes linger on the duct tape she hasn't pulled away, silently waiting for me to allow her to remove it. I lift my hand, pinching the edge of the tape, and peel it away, eliciting a sharp hiss at the sudden sting.

A smirk tugs at my lips as I look down briefly, retrieving something from my inner pocket. I hold it in my hand for a moment, scanning its bizarre features: a deranged plush dolly with black stitched cross eyes, a tiny button nose to match, cream-colored yarn pigtails, and a small pink dress. When I raise my gaze to hers, she is staring at the soft toy intently, her expression a mix of curiosity and awe. I offer it to her, and she accepts it cautiously, cradling it in her palms. Her thumbs press into its rough fabric as she holds it in her lap, her eyes glassy when they meet mine.

"It's for you, my Little Dolly," I murmur.

She nods faintly, a silent acknowledgment of the gift, her emotions playing across her face as she absorbs the weight of its meaning.

"You made it?" she whispers back with a tremble in her bottom lip.

I give a small nod in return, and she pounces, her lips slamming against mine which catches me off guard. She wraps her arms around the back of my neck while slipping her tongue into my mouth, instantly merging with mine and I growl, sliding my hands up the sides of her thighs beneath her shirt.

I'm not the mushy type, and Dolly knows exactly how twisted I am, but I need her to understand that I want her. If baring these little parts of myself means I get to see that look on her pretty face again— the one that just sent a tremor down my fucking spine—then I'll do it. It's now the same intoxicating rush I get when I pleasure, hurt, and degrade her. I am utterly addicted to every emotion she has, every reaction she gives.

CHAPTER FIFTEEN

Waking up in the morning, the brightness of the day filters through the shutters. I gradually open my heavy eyes, my head thumping, a hangover creeping in. I lift my head, glancing around at my surroundings until I spot E still beside me in the same position as last night, facing away from me. Rolling onto my back, my head sinks into the pillow as I replay how Hell took me last night in ways I didn't know my body could handle.

After everything I endured in my childhood and early twenties, Hell is the only man I've ever met who I'd willingly allow to do these unholy things to my body under his control. No man has ever wanted both my body and my soul. Except for E, but it's not the same. Hell is far more superior in that respect.

When I feel something beside me, I peek under the duvet to see the mini dolly he made for me. My eyes ease, and I gently lift her out, analyzing every inch of her strange looks, noticing how much she resembles me. It's things like this, knowing he made this for me, it brings intense comfort to my shaded heart. Little does Hell know, I was on the edge of bursting into tears when he gave it to me. He will never understand how much it meant. I can't even remember the last time I was given anything, let alone something made with such meaning. Growing up, I often didn't know what day or time of year it was. Birthdays and Christmases were all non-existent; gifts disappeared after my mom died. So, this tiny dolly means the entire world to me.

I lie there, placing her on my stomach, moving the arms like a little girl with her favorite toy, a tear slipping down my cheek. While lost in thought for some time, I find myself thinking about tomorrow, Dark Night, and how I will finally face everything. I have a twisted sense that I want some kind of control over the situation. I want to play games. So, tonight, I will be plotting a way to take Hellion before he takes me, because I can play too, right?

I visualize scenarios where I outmanoeuvre him, where I can hold the upper hand, if only for a moment. I imagine the look on his face when he realizes he had underestimated me. I want to show every single one of them that I belong here. This isn't just about the physical act—it's also about proving to myself that I am not weak and that I can stand up to any darkness within any man and meet it head-on. It's not about power; it's about survival, about reclaiming some part of myself that's been lost in the chaos of my past.

If I am ever going to fully trust Hell or even Hellion, then this is how it needs to be. I need to face everything on my terms. I will not be a fucking victim; I will be a force to be reckoned with.

Eli suddenly stirs beside me, and I quickly hide mini dolly beneath the duvet. Wiping the tear off my cheek, I start to sit up. He groans, rolling onto his back, and as I rest against the headboard, I side-eye him, feeling awkward. He turns his head, giving me a brief glance before facing away again.

"You came to bed?" he asks, his voice gruff.

I throw the duvet off me. "Yes," I answer before standing up. I walk around the bed, his eyes following my every move as I head toward the wardrobe, wanting to find some clean clothes to wear after a shower. As I search through it, I give him a sidelong glance and he sits up with another groan, looking hungover.

"I didn't see you at the carnival last night. Didn't you go to work?" I probe, trying to keep my tone casual.

Eli rubs his temples and sighs, "Yeah, I did, but I just finished earlier than usual." His eyes narrow slightly as he studies me. "What about you? Looks like you had a rough night."

I pull out a shirt and jeans, avoiding his gaze. "Blush and I decided to have some fun and headed to the carnival. I needed a break from everything," I say, hoping he doesn't press further.

He tosses the duvet off himself, and I avoid eye contact, my mind consumed by the events of last night with Hell and how uneasy I feel. As he walks around the bed, I hear him suddenly gasp and I whirl around.

"What the fuck is all this blood?" he exclaims, his eyes locked onto the stain—a mixture of Hell's blood and our dried cum.

Panic floods me. Why didn't I think about this last night? He bends over, lifting the sheet to inspect it more closely, and I cringe before bolting forward, slapping it away from his hand. "You know what it is, Eli," I say flatly, my cheeks burning with shame.

His eyes meet mine briefly before they fall to my bare thighs, hidden beneath the long shirt I am wearing. I cleaned myself up last night, but I can feel his scrutiny. His gaze hardens before he stands tall, but something catches my eye on his arm. *A red dot.*

I reach out, but he quickly pulls away and my wide eyes flash to his, then narrow in a scowl.

"But I am the one who will self-destruct, right?" I hiss, knowing exactly what it is.

He scoffs, waving me off before walking away. "Your time is coming, Noir," he shouts back, the warning lingering in the air as he exits the room. I stare blankly at the door, confusion and frustration churning inside me, but my instincts scream that I should be there for him, especially if it's my fault he's like this, maybe it's a cry for help. I just can't keep holding someone else up when I'm barely carrying myself most days, especially without my meds now. I need to start putting myself first.

HOLLOW HELLION

With Eli out again tonight, I decide to do my own kind of investigating and as I weave in and out of trailers, I am quiet as I head towards the Hollow's trailer. The trailer looms ahead, its silhouette barely noticeable in the dark except for the haunting painted skull.

Once I have stopped, I peer from behind an empty trailer, waiting for his appearance and after some time, I finally see the front door opening. Hell steps out, closing the door behind him and lights a cigarette, the brief flare illuminating his painted face before he pulls his hood over his head.

When he is ready, he starts to walk, and I gradually back further into the shadows until he is passing me. While following him, I don't make a sound, like a ninja in the night, my breath held as I maintain a careful distance. He moves with a sense of purpose, his tall, toned figure cutting through the dim light like a phantom.

What does he do when he's not watching me? I want to know. I need to know what I am truly up against.

When we enter the woods, I slow down, but the glow of his cigarette serves as my beacon, guiding me. Once he walks through a clearing, I stop behind a tree trunk, ducking and peeking around it. My heart skips a beat as I realize this is where we were the night I rode his knife. The bright full moon casts a glow upon him as he strides across the small field. My brows knit together in confusion as he stops dead in the center.

Leaning down, he grasps something with both hands with his cig tucked between his lips. When he pulls open two doors hidden in the ground, I am shocked. *What the fuck. A hidden entrance that leads underground?* He stands still for a moment taking one last drag of his cigarette, the ember glowing bright before he flicks it away, watching it soar through the air until it lands with a soft hiss on the damp grass.

Without hesitation, he descends into the darkness, disappearing from view and I remain frozen, my mind racing, but I am not stupid enough to follow him. I'll hold out and when he leaves, I'll go down there.

I wait for what feels like forever, sitting on the cold, dirty floor, hidden behind the trunk, but when I hear his heavy footsteps crunching over the grass, my body tenses and I remain utterly still until he has completely passed me. It's strange because he usually senses my presence no matter where I am. Maybe he has things on his mind. Probably Dark Night.

When the coast is clear, I gently stand, my muscles stiff from holding the same position for so long. I move cautiously around the tree, my eyes darting in every direction to ensure Hell is truly gone and as soon as I am satisfied that I am alone, I make my way toward the hidden door.

My heart pounds in my chest as I approach and once, I reach them, I gaze down for a moment, then bend over, fingers curling around the cold handles. I pull them apart, the hinges groaning softly in the night, revealing a set of steep steps leading down into total darkness. A musty, damp smell wafts up, and the air feels colder as it meets my skin. I hesitate, listening for any sign of movement below, but all I hear is the faint rustling of leaves in the breeze.

I grasp the edges of the doors and begin to descend into the abyss. The walls are rough as I steady myself, and the stairs narrow, forcing me to move carefully and cautiously. My eyes gradually adjust to the dim light, and I see a passageway that has some doors. I glance around as I walk forward, my senses heightened, pushing down on every handle of every door I pass, but they're all locked until I reach one and it softly clicks open.

As I step inside, the dim light automatically comes to life, and I feel a chill run down my spine. Thick, long chains hang low, rusted, and heavy, clinking softly with the draft. Metal units line the walls, each one covered in dark stains and strange, sinister-looking tools lie on top of them.

In the center of the room stands a metal surgeon's table and it's fitted with restraints. The air is thick with the scent of iron and something else, something far more sinister. I take a step closer, my eyes darting to every corner of the room, trying to understand what the fuck Hell uses this place for. My gaze lingers on the table, imagining Hell bringing someone here, strapping them down, and possibly hurting them. The thought makes my stomach churn, but I can't tear my eyes away. I need to understand, to know what Hell is hiding down here although it is becoming pretty clear cut. Taking a deep breath, I reach out and touch one of the chains, feeling its cold, rough texture beneath my fingers.

Knowing I can't be here long because he might return, I dash toward the units lined along the back of the room and with careful yet swift motions, I pull each one by one, every drawer revealing an array of weapons and devices until finally I come across a med drawer, and I halt. My eyes scan over the neatly labelled vials, my mind sparking with ideas until they settle on a name I recognize all too well: *Etorphine.*

I quickly grab a clean, unused needle from beside the drugs and draw the tiniest dose of the liquid into the syringe. Carefully, I cap the needle and hide it away in my pocket, making sure everything else remains undisturbed and is still in its place. Then, I turn around and quietly leave the room, pulling the door shut behind me with a soft click.

CHAPTER SIXTEEN

Tonight is the night, and I'm getting ready with a mix of nerves and anticipation. A constant spike of anxiety pulses within me, but it's matched by a thrill. It feels like I've been waiting for this moment for such a long time, for the answers I desperately need. As I slip into my outfit, I gaze at my reflection in the mirror, taking in the sight of myself transformed.

Tonight, I'm dressed entirely differently from my usual costume. I snuck into the circus's changing rooms this morning, scouting for something that would make me undetectable to Hellion. Something to throw him off when he tries to hunt me down.

Black knee-high boots fit snug around my legs, paired with white fishnet stockings, the lace trim sitting just below my small white tutu with a black and red frill. A matching corset snaps my waist, contouring my curves and I've styled my hair into a bun, with loose red curls framing my features. My makeup is my usual broken dolly look, but tonight, I have a white porcelain doll mask with black cracks around the hollow eyes and red lips to complete my disguise. Long, finger-tipless, silk, white gloves conceal the scars on my arms.

Once I'm finished with my clothing, I lift the eye contacts I stole—black and white swirls, just like Hell's. A smirk curls at my lips before I struggle to place them in each eye, but with persistence, they finally fit onto my blue pupils, transforming my gaze into something horrifying.

Ready and unrecognizable, I take a deep breath, preparing myself for what's to come. This is it—the night I've been waiting for, the night everything changes.

After one more glance in the mirror, I turn around and head for the bedside cabinet. Pulling open the drawer, I push everything aside until I find the needle and I lift it out, then stuff it deep inside my boot. Grabbing my mask off the bed on the way, I head for the front door.

Just as I reach it, I hear the shower running, knowing Eli is in there and a thought crosses my mind: what will he be doing tonight? Will he be working? Will he be watching this entire thing unfold as well? I hope he doesn't. I'm not sure if he would handle it well. I press the handle down and exit the trailer, closing the door behind me.

The night air flushes against my hot skin, instantly reviving me. I glance down at my mask before raising and fixing it to my face. Then, I walk toward the bright lights of the huge circus and carnival in the distance.

HOLLOW HELLION

After creeping past The Hollow's trailer, the park is eerily quiet, as if everyone is already inside, and I start to wonder if I am late, even though it's almost eleven o'clock. No, I can't be. Madame said that time.

As I slip silently into the back of the tent, the music is loud in my ears, the lights pulsing through the cracks in the fabric, a huge crowd already inside the arena. Then I hear Madame's voice on the mic just as I enter, causing me to stop at the threshold.

"Ladies and gentlemen, welcome to Dark Night, where fear isn't just a sensation—it's a dread that seeps into your bones and lingers in your final breath. Here, death isn't merely a threat; it's an experience, a macabre spectacle that will haunt your very soul and claim you as its own."

I peek around the entrance, the audience on the edge of their seats, but I quickly notice that these aren't the usual visitors. They are men and women in luxurious outfits, a sea of suits and elegant dresses and my brows pinch with confusion as my eyes skim over the strange crowd.

Center stage, Madame stands draped in a blood-red gown, spotlights shining down on her, demanding the attention of everyone in the tent.

"Tonight," she continues, "you will witness the unthinkable—the beauty of horror. We present to you a performance like no other, where the line between life and death is a nothing but a tightrope, ready to be cut at any moment."

Madame raises her arms almost elegantly. "Remember, our dear guests," she says with a chilling smile, "there is no turning back. Once you enter the realm of Dark Night, you become part of our sinister symphony, where every scream, every drop of sweat and blood, belongs to us. From this moment forward, you're tangled in our web, fighting for your life." The crowd laughs, but something dreadful settles in my stomach from her words.

Cautiously, I slip into a seat in the back, not near anyone, ready to watch the show unfold since I have been told I am not to perform tonight and just be a watcher. The lights dim further, then the tent plunges into darkness. When a spotlight pierces the blackness, it illuminates a cage that is being descended from above. I glance up to see a figure trapped inside, his face full of fear and when the cage reaches the ground, his desperate pleas for mercy echo.

Performers dressed in bizarre costumes enter from the shadows, each one more terrifying than the last. A man with a painted skull face juggles flaming knives, while a woman in a tattered, ghostly dress twists her body in impossible ways across the dusty floor, and a horrifying clown on tall stilts, holding a long, black whip all creep toward him. Each one moves in a strange, haunting way—like nothing I have ever seen before.

The woman slithers up to the bars of the cage, her arms and legs wrapping around them like a snake as she leans in close to the man, her hot breath visible against the cold night air. His eyes are wide with terror before she suddenly lets out a high-pitched chilling laugh and tosses something onto his face, a liquid. He instantly lets out a blood-curdling scream, trying to wipe his face desperately, but as he moves his hands away, I see it is melting. I hold my breath, my eyes wide as he continues to try to escape, knocking into the cage because he is now blind.

The crowd erupts in laughter with sadistic amusement and the other two performers step forward. They whip him harshly, each lash drawing blood, while flaming knives are thrown into his flesh, embedding themselves with sickening thuds. His screams are horrifying, but they only seem to fuel the audience's enjoyment.

My stomach churns as I watch, the reality of the situation sinking in. This isn't just a performance; it's a ritual of torture, a display of human suffering dressed up as entertainment. The audience, dressed in their finest clothes, it all makes sense now. This isn't for just anyone; this is for those who crave the macabre, who find delight in the pain and death of others.

As his cries fade out, his body barely clinging to life, the crowd rises to their feet, clapping and cheering. The sound is full of glee, the total opposite to the horror that has just unfolded, and I just remain seated, my pulse pounding in my ears, unable to tear my eyes away from the gruesome scene.

As the night progresses, I can't shake the feeling that I'm in way over my head. The darkness of this place is more dangerous than I could have ever imagined.

I watch many performances, each one more shocking than the last, where people are tied up and murdered in front of everyone. Unlike the acts from the other night, each one ends in death. A woman on a spinning wheel is axed to death, her screams drowned out by laughter. People are burnt alive by fire breathers, then let loose to run around in agony until they're just fried meat lying on the ground.

Guys on bikes ride in the death dome, not The Hollow's, and the woman standing in the middle isn't Pearl and as their bikes spin around her, they slice her to pieces with machetes or chainsaws until she's nothing, but a pile of human remains in the middle. This place is fucking ruthless.

One man is forced onto the tightrope high above, and I silently pray for his safety, hoping against everything that I have witnessed tonight that he will still somehow make it to the other side, but the clown on the platform deliberately shakes the rope with an evil cackle, sending the man plunging to the ground with a splat, his body torn apart, guts flying everywhere.

I turn my face away with my eyes closed, taking a deep breath through my nose. Despite the rising urge to run for my fucking life, I remain stuck to my seat, trying to not let this place get to me and I can't help but wonder when Hellion will arrive. What role he will play?

After what feels like forever, it seems to be ending, and confusion sweeps over me. Just as I begin to wonder about Hellion once again, the Hollow's finally emerge from the curtains.

Their faces partially hidden by black, lower half masks with swirls in the colors of their eye contacts and they have tools in their hands. Behind them, enter a line of girls, including Blush and Pearl, holding blow torches and flame throwers, their identities concealed by full creepy masks, but they are detectable to me because of their hair.

Madame takes center stage once more, the Hollow's and girls circling her as they face the audience. Her grin stretches wide, eyes darkening. "I trust you found the show enjoyable?" she asks, her voice carrying a chilling undertone. "But now, we come to the grand finale of Dark Night," she gestures with her hands toward the crowd.

"This final act is one we've all wanted you to witness. It marks the end of your laughter, your speech, your breath." Her words hang like a dark cloud, murmurs circling the tent as more performers enter the ring, carrying an array of weapons, their expressions grave.

"You see, Oddity has always served a purpose, but you know that," Madame continues, her tone growing more sinister with every word. "Each of you have come here for a reason. To revel in the death of someone you despise, but have you ever considered your own sins and why you were given that black ticket in the first place?" A deafening silence falls over the crowd as Madame's words sink into my bones. "This final act is a retaliation for your deceit, my darlings. This final act will cost every single one of you your lives. On Dark Night, no one escapes. Not even YOU!"

My eyes widen in realization, but when Madame chuckles loud and menacingly into the mic, throwing her head back, the crowd stupidly erupts in laughter with her. I gently stand, my pulse racing, watching the performers closing in on the crowd.

As soon as Madame's laughter stops, weapons are unleashed. The atmosphere shifts from cheerful to deadly in an instant as they understand the truth: this is not a performance; it's a fucking massacre.

As people are burnt alive and knives are thrown into skulls, nail guns are fired, and chaos erupts. Everyone tries to flee, coming my way, scrambling over the seats, desperate to reach the exit near me. My eyes dart to Hellion, and I find his already on mine. My breath hitches in my throat, my body stiffening, wondering how the fuck he spotted me in the middle of absolute madness. His eyes are wide and crazed, his broad chest expanding with each breath as if he is about to pounce while he stands completely still. I can see it in him. He is Hellion tonight; there is no shadow of a doubt that he is going to fuck me up and enjoy every sickening second of it.

As the crowd gets closer to me, I bolt, heading for the exit beside me. I run down the passageway, aiming for the carnival, trying to stick to my plan. Frantic screams and heavy footsteps echo behind me, but as soon as I am outside, the crowd surrounds me, pushing me toward the main exit.

I try to break free and get out of the pull, but I am trapped between hundreds of panicked people. Looking ahead, I see the tall, spiked gates are locked, with a huge sign that says in bold red painted words,

"No way out."

Once I'm finally able to stop, the crowd continues forward, desperately trying to get through the gate and my heart races as I watch them all, struggling to breathe.

I glance down, noticing black circus tickets scattered across the cracked ground. When I lift my head notice more I spot carnival performers on the other side and I tiptoe to see what they're doing, and my heart stops completely when I see it—they're handing out weapons to fight back.

What the actual fuck.

As the crowd arms themselves, I worry that I have nothing to defend myself with, but still dressed as part of this wicked show, a fucking target. Thunder and lightning suddenly crackles through the air, heavy rain plummeting down on me. Panic rises inside my chest, feeling surrounded by madness and violence, wondering how I'm going to fucking survive this night.

As soon as I hear motorbikes closing in behind me, I turn on my heel, seeing performers finally exiting the circus, armed and ready to unleash even more bloodshed. When the Hollow's round the corner, I run fast, hoping Hellion doesn't see me yet. The crowd scatters and people begin to fight. I weave in and out of the mayhem, as if I am on a battle field, trying to get around the circus and back to the trailer park, but every way I go, it's blocked.

A guy with a chainsaw suddenly jumps out in front of me causing me to stop abruptly, my heels skidding across the wet ground. He's middle-aged with grey hair, dressed in a suit and he licks his lips. "Well hey there, gorgeous, are you lost?" he growls, his eyes glimmering with murder.

I take a step back as he takes one forward, and then he lunges, attempting to slice me apart. I bow backward and sidestep, narrowly avoiding the blade, but without warning, a knife whizzes past my head and plunges brutally into his eye. My expanded gaze stays locked on him as he falls to the ground, dropping the chainsaw, but it continues to run, hacking at his leg.

I throw a glance over my shoulder, and my eyes instantly collide with Hellion's. He sits on his bike at a distance, watching me intently. The chaos around me seems to blur as if the world is narrowing to just the two of us. The violent, blood-soaked carnival fades into the background as I see the darkness in his swirling orbs.

I remove my mask, tossing it to the ground to reveal mine, but before I can see his reaction, a woman charges towards me with a scream, an axe raised high in the air. Without thinking, I lean down, grabbing the heavy chainsaw lying nearby and while spinning around, I thrust the jagged blade forward, catching her in the stomach. Her cry mingles with the revving of the saw as her guts spill out onto the ground. I feel the warm spray of her blood hit my face, arms, and chest as I hold my breath.

She drops to the floor, and my wide eyes meet Hellion's once again across the carnival. He's holding a knife, positioned to throw it at her. His gaze flickers to mine, and an evil smirk tugs at his lips.

I understand his silent message: only he is allowed to hurt me as he said the other night, but he will still protect me in his own twisted way even if he is within his character. His presence is both terrifying and oddly reassuring, a reminder of the strange bond we share. When his face suddenly falls and he flicks his blade closed, my heart skips a beat and I drop the chainsaw.

He starts to rev his engine and I spin around, running as fast as I can. The sound of his bike gets closer with each step until he whizzes past me, skidding sideways to block my path. I look around frantically, trying to find a way to escape him until my eyes land on the sign for The Glass Maze. As Hellion stands away from his bike, I bolt again, pulling on the door and heading inside the unknown building.

CHAPTER SEVENTEEN

The entrance door closes behind me, and I'm plunged into a brightly lit labyrinth of glass that stretches far and wide. Ahead of me, I faintly see other people, desperately trying to find a way out. When I glance down, I notice a thick sea of blood at my feet, confusion momentarily paralyzing me, but I know I can't stand around for long; Hellion is right behind me.

I start to run through the maze, blood spraying up my legs as my heavy boots land with each step. I bang into the thick glass panels, the impact hurting my entire body. The mirrored walls and ceilings, make it hard to tell where I am or where I need to go next. As I weave through the narrow passageways, the blood on the floor seems to become thicker, the stench of iron, death filling the air and I start to wonder where the fuck it's all coming from.

As soon as I hear the entrance door closing behind me, my head snaps around and not too far away, I see Hellion has entered. Suddenly, a screeching siren screams through the building, making me slam my hands against my ears. The lights turn red when it stops.

What the fuck was that?

Hellion catches my attention once again, calmly strolling through the maze, knowing the route perfectly, his corkscrew orbs fixated on mine, his jaw tense.

Fuck.

Without warning, the glass walls start moving, some much quicker than others, and panic surges through me. As soon as I hear a woman screaming, I look in that direction and watch her running for her life, a glass panel sweeping across the passageway she is in at an alarming speed. With nowhere to go, it crushes and flattens her against the wall with a loud crack.

Holy shit. It's a whole mindfuck death puzzle.

The sight of her lifeless body, mangled and squashed against the glass, sends a shiver down my spine, but I don't have time to process it. I need to move, and fast.

Hellion's deep voice reaches me, low and mocking. "Running won't save you from me or this place, my pretty Little Dolly. I designed it and I will fucking catch you."

He designed this place? What the hell?

As a tremble runs through me at his words, I notice other traps, like fire shooting out of the walls as you pass by, and I start to slow down, wondering if it's better to just face Hellion than go through this deathly obstacle course.

A sudden noise behind me snaps me out of my thoughts. A pane of glass is moving toward me at a frightening speed, and I run, but my feet slip on the blood-soaked floor, sending me skidding across the passageway frontally until I crash against the wall. Just in time, I throw myself into another passage on my right, narrowly dodging the glass as it smacks against the wall. I breathe heavily, my heart pounding, stuck in fear until I see Hellion is only one passage away from me, calmly navigating the maze.

I scramble to my feet, but he starts running, seizing the opportunity and I stumble over the blood, my clothes now drenched in it. As I hear his heavy footsteps right behind me, I let out a loud, petrified scream, but before he can get me, he slips too, crashing to the floor but not before grabbing my leg, making me fall as well with a hard thud, blood splashing up my face and the glass. I turn as he yanks me down towards him, kicking and thrashing, but he simply lets out a wicked chuckle.

His jaw suddenly tenses in irritation as he positions himself between my legs, grabbing my waist and forcefully dragging me closer, his movements swift and effortless. I swing at him with my fists, determined to give him a fucking fight, but he grabs my throat with his bloodied hand, squeezing tightly, restricting my airway. He reaches up under my tutu, yanking my red panties and ripping them aggressively down my legs. The realization hits me—he's going to violate me right here in a pool of other people's blood and guts. Fuck, he is wasting no time at all.

"Hell!" I try to yell through strangulation.

Ignoring me, he forces my legs wide apart before dipping his head and sliding his pierced tongue all the way up my exposed pussy. A loud gasp escapes me, my head tilting back as my soaked, bloodied hands find the glass on either side of me, gripping for dear life.

He eats me out so fucking violently and with such force that I begin to slip upward on the blood with each flick of his tongue. His face smothers my pussy like a crazed animal, his mouth working miracles on my clit in just the way I like it. Every time I slide away from him, he grabs my thighs and yanks me back down aggressively with a snarl, my pussy slamming against his face.

My untamed moans flood through the glass maze, mingling with terrified screams, moving glass, and the sound of footsteps running over the blood-slick floor. The entire scenario is fucking wild, being eaten out so deliciously in such a place and around people dying, but

I can't contain the undeniable thrill running through me. The wet sounds of his tongue lapping up every drop of my come that I release, and the roughness of his movements drive me to the edge quickly.

My body tenses, my hips bucking uncontrollably against his mouth, and I feel the bliss swelling inside me, my cries growing more desperate. His grip tightens on my thighs, his growls vibrating through my core as he pushes me to the brink of ecstasy. With one final, powerful thrust of his tongue, I shatter into a million pieces. My orgasm rips through me, intense and overwhelming, and my screams echo throughout the maze.

Suddenly, the siren screams throughout the maze again, startling me mid-orgasm and without warning, Hellion grips my hips, pushing me away with force, causing me to slide across the bloody passageway until I crash into a wall behind me. I groan from the impact before sitting up to see him still on his knees some distance away. A sound from above grabs my attention, and I look up to see a glass pane descending rapidly. It lands vertically, barely touching the floor, effectively separating me from Hellion and I think about how it could have just cut me in half if he didn't know.

My wide eyes meet his and he is breathing heavily, his jaw set tight. This night is far from over, but I realize I now have the upper hand but for a moment, we just stare at one another through the glass, the sexual tension thick between us. Hellion's eyes burn with frustration and desire, and I know he's already plotting his next move, just like I am.

Taking advantage, I get to my feet, scanning my surroundings, but his calm demeanor from the corner of my eye as he stands captures my attention. I turn to face him fully, and he takes a step forward. His big, solid dick is now out, his blooded hand tightly wrapped around it as he slowly strokes himself.

"Do you see what you do to me, Little Dolly? I'm so fucking hard for you." he groans, his eyes rolling back as he cracks his neck from side to side, his movements on his cock not stopping for a second.

Fucking hell.

He places his hand on the glass, smearing blood from his bare chest and face, his eyes lock onto mine with a distant gaze. Slowly, he sets his pierced tongue onto the glass, licking it seductively upward in a way that makes my thighs clench. A wide smile spreads across his face, a smile I haven't seen before—handsomely terrifying.

"You have around five fucking seconds to run from me again, pretty girl," he growls, his face suddenly falling into a serious expression. "The next time I get my hands on you, I am going to fuck you so hard and in such a ruthless way that you might not make it out of my embrace alive."

My muscles tense as soon as he drives his fist into the thick glass with a menacing laugh, and the glass cracks ever so slightly. My eyes widen, and I turn, running through the maze, stepping over body parts along the way.

Behind me, I hear the sound of glass breaking, Hellion forcing his way through the barrier and panic surges through me, fighting to keep my focus, but I have to keep moving, I have to find a way out.

I dodge flames emerging from the walls, narrowly avoiding moving glass, but then, I finally spot a faint light ahead—a possible exit. I push myself harder, my legs burning with the effort and with one last burst of energy, I dive through the door, tumbling onto the ground outside of the maze.

I stumble to my feet, my breaths coming out in heavy gasps. The rain pours down on me, lightning flashing and crackling across the sky, washing away the blood from my soaked body but I only feel a brief respite from escaping that horrifying maze. Hellion won't stop until he has his dick inside me, breaking me, but I need to stay one step ahead. I need to get him where I have plans for him.

I glance around as I run forward, hearing screams coming from the death rooms as I pass the fence and I continue, making my way toward the bright lights of the carnival. As I run through it, bodies are scattered everywhere on the ground, some amusements caught on fire. It feels like I am on a strange warzone, but hardly anyone is fighting here anymore. I try to ignore my surroundings, running around the circus to get to the trailer park.

Once I enter, I hear a motorbike in the distance, and I instantly know it's him. As he gets closer, I stumble across the soaked grass and gravel, desperately wanting to get to the woods, my body lacking energy. When I become enveloped by woodland, Hellion's bike gains on me in speed, he whizzes through the trees, as do I, until finally, I am at the clearing of his hidden basement. *Just a few steps further.*

I cross the field until I stop, hovering above the doors as I catch my breath. The cold rain pelts down on my hot skin as I wait for Hellion to emerge from the woods and when he does, his bike flies through the air. He lands, his eyes locking with mine as he skids across the soaked grass from a distance, then he dismounts, both of us panting heavily, and we stare at one another for a beat.

Knowing he is waiting for my next move; I give him a huge smile before leaning down and pulling open the doors. I hear his heavy footsteps jogging across the sludge as I descend into darkness, rushing toward the room I entered last night. The dim light flickers to life as I close the door, then hop up on a small unit out of view behind it, waiting for him to follow me in here. I swiftly dig into my boot, grab the needle, and uncap it.

He smashes through the door causing me to flinch, but as he steps inside, I scream, soaring through the air. He spins around, catching my throat in mid-jump and cocks his head to the side, seemingly confused by my antics. Holding me off the ground, my feet don't even touch the floor, and his grip on my throat tightens, almost squeezing the life out of me.

I smile menacingly before raising my arm and without warning, I stab him in the side of the neck. I press down on the syringe just in time as he releases me, and I drop to the floor, gasping for air. Lifting my head as the needle hits to the ground in front of me, I watch Hellion stumble backward and collapse onto the surgeon's table.

Rising to my feet carefully, I keep my eyes locked on him, his spiral eyes meeting mine with a blend of confusion and fury. His hand reaches up to his throat, struggling against the potent drug coursing through his veins.

Despite his resistance, his eyelids grow heavy, and I take a cautious step forward, pressing a finger to my lips, "Shhhh." I whisper softly, leaning in closer. "When you wake up, I'm going to make us both feel so fucking good."

CHAPTER EIGHTEEN

"Hell, or is it Hellion?" The soft voice echoes in my mind.

Suddenly, I feel small, warm hands sliding up my chest, a thumb toying with my nipple piercing and my eyes snap open to see Dolly is straddling me. I lunge forward instinctively, but my movement is violently restricted. She stares at me with calm eyes, and I glance down to see my arms wrapped in chains, leather straps binding me to the propped-up surgeon's table in my underground chamber.

"I'm sorry, Hellion," she whispers, and my eyes flash to hers, full of burning rage. "You understand, don't you?"

My jaw sets tight, seething with fury. I can't fuck her, can't have my hands on her, can't hurt her. This little minx has the upper hand, and the contradiction rips through me—part of me wants to hate her for it, yet another part can't help but admire her fucking audacity.

"No one," I growl through tight teeth, "has ever fucking dared to do this to me, Noir."

She smiles, but it's full of uncertainty. "I know," she responds. "That's why I had to do it."

I raise an eyebrow. "Are you sure you're ready to face the repercussions?" I ask with narrowed eyes, sniffing out any vulnerability. Her spiraling contacts search mine, mirroring my own as she tucks her bottom lip between her teeth, pondering.

"I knew what I was facing the moment I stuck that needle into your neck, Hellion," she says with confidence. I inhale deeply, hating every second of this scenario, but she continues unbothered. "I am willing to feel your full control after I get what I want first."

I tilt my head to the side, "And that is?"

She lifts her chin, her fingers finding the hooks on the front of her corset. "I want control the first time we do this," she answers, her eyes never leaving mine. "Even if it's just for this moment that you're entirely mine."

I pull against the chains, the leather straps biting into my skin.

Her fingers continue undoing the hooks, one by one, exposing more of her soft skin and the curve of her breasts. My muscles bulge, every instinct screaming to break the fuck free and reclaim my dominance, every fiber craving control, yet here I am, fucking chained in the same way I would have done to her. I am forced to wait, forced to feel, forced to acknowledge her taking control. I have to witness a reflection of myself in her eyes, the same dark urges I possess, which confuses the fuck out of me, because I've never seen this side of her.

"I want to feel what it's like," she murmurs, unfolding her corset, revealing both of her perfect tits. "To have you at my mercy. To take, just as much as you do."

She is playing with fire, and we both know it because once I am out of these binds, she's fucking done for. I will be uncontrollable. Un-fucking-stoppable. Fuck, I might even kill her by accident.

Her hands move over my abs, her touch igniting a primal hunger in me. The room is charged with a dangerous energy that crackles between us.

"I'm going to ride your big fucking cock, Hellion," she purrs seductively enough to make me rock hard in an instant beneath her hot pussy. "Every single inch until you cum inside me," she continues as she bucks her hips against me, and my teeth grind together, my dark gaze traveling down her beautiful figure.

She reaches for the button on my jeans, flicking it open, her eyes fixed on the movement. Once she has the zipper down, she starts to strip entirely, pulling her tutu up her body and tossing it to the floor leaving only her blood-soaked stockings and boots on. As she frees her hair from its bun, letting it flow down and frame her face, I become mesmerized by her.

Keeping her eyes locked on mine, she slides her hand into my boxers, her fingers wrapping around my throbbing cock, sending a jolt through me. She pulls me free, breaking eye contact to gaze down at my dick, standing to attention, showing her exactly how much I want to feel her warm cunt on me. Betraying my fucking anger.

As she starts to pump me up and down, my legs tense from the sensation, my fists clenching in their restraints and her eye contact doesn't relent, a silent challenge in her gaze. Without taking her hand off my cock, she licks her other before lowering it to her pussy, making herself wet and ready at the same time.

She jerks me off harder, her grip firm and demanding, and I groan, my eyes gradually closing. The pleasure is fucking torture, and I can't help but give in to it.

"Fuck," I mutter, my dark eyes locking onto hers. "I'm going to destroy you, you little fucking slut, I hope you know that."

With a sway of her hips, she positions herself above me, her wet pussy teasing the pierced tip of my cock. She descends slowly, lowering herself onto me inch by inch. I can feel her tight cunt stretch around me, the sensation driving me to the edge of madness. The look on her face tells me she's struggling to take me, her body fighting to accept my size which only turns me on even more. Although I had my fist in her pussy the other night, she's still having difficulty taking me now. She's going to have a rough fucking night.

"God, you're so big," she groans, her eyes fluttering shut.

When she opens her dazed eyes, not even halfway down my shaft yet, I can see the strain on her face as she pushes herself to take more of me.

"Fuck," she breathes, her voice quivering. "You're stretching me so much."

Not being able to manage the slowness of her movements because they're driving me utterly insane, I flick my hips upward, my cock penetrating her cunt as deep as I can get inside her. She lets out a loud scream, her palms slamming against my chest as she steadies herself. My eyes gradually close, the satisfaction of being buried inside her and having some kind of control buzzing through my dark veins.

When I open them once again, I observe her with her head tilted down, her long blond hair obscuring her face, cascading over my chest as she breathes deeply through the pain.

"Now ride me, greedy Little Dolly, before I fuck you senseless seeing as you were stupid enough not to strap my lower half down," I growl.

She slowly lifts her head, her eyes wide when they meet mine. "There's no way you're going to fit inside my ass, Hellion."

A small sinister smirk tugs on my lips. "Good. I don't want it to, but we'll make it fucking fit, pretty girl."

With her expanded eyes fixed on mine, she sits back, and my gaze flicks downward to see my dick completely immersed inside of her. The sight of my cock disappeared makes my pulse race with raw, animalistic desire. I keep my eyes locked on her stretched pussy as she slowly rises my length, leaving a trail of wetness in her wake and as her soft, warm walls brush against my piercings, my toes curl.

Fucking hell, I'm going to fuck this tight cunt so fucking hard.

Her eyes grow heavy, her tits bouncing with every thrust downward, and her moans turn untameable as she becomes lost in the lust of having me inside her. My breathing picks up, and I find myself pulling my chains, desperate to get free while she rides me hard and fast. Tingles sweep through my body, every nerve electrified by the friction, the heat, the tightness. Our connection.

I watch how her body moves, her facial expressions twisted with pleasure and with each rise and fall of her hips, her pussy slams down onto me, our skin smacking together, echoing in the confined space. I can feel myself striking her cervix, pushing her to her limits, but she takes all of me like she promised. Her screams grow louder, more urgent, and I can sense her climax peaking, her pussy becoming wetter, looser.

When she reaches up, wrapping chains around her wrists and hands for more leverage, she rises all the way up my length to the tip before slamming down onto me, and a guttural groan escapes my lips. The feel and sight of her is too fucking much; I can sense myself building already.

When she finally explodes, a cry rips from her throat, her head thrown back in ecstasy. The sensation of her pussy convulsing around me in a powerful grip is enough to make me release too, and with a deep, primal growl, I eject my hot cum deep inside her.

She moans again from the swell and pulse of my cock, but her thrusts continue, determined to milk me for every fucking drop, pushing us both into overdrive and my eyes roll while my legs twitch.

When she has finished, she releases the chains, her tiny body flopping down onto mine as we both fall limp. Our chests heave as we struggle to catch our breath, her warmth seeping into me, anchoring me in the aftermath of our raw moment, but despite the temporary unwanted surrender, my mind starts to race with thoughts of the degrading, disgusting shit I'm going to do to her once I'm freed.

Every dark fantasy, every twisted desire—she will experience most of them.

"Now release me," I bite out through clenched teeth.

She starts to sit up, her sweaty skin unsticking from mine. Her sparkling eyes widen with a petrified gaze as realization sets in— she's crossed a line, chaining me up like this and taking what she wants like a greedy fucking whore. And so she should be afraid. She better keep me locked up for eternity because if I'm freed, my Little Dolly will never be the same once I'm finished with her.

"Don't worry, Noir," I murmur menacingly, watching her eyes relax. "I'll let you live, at least, but barely."

Her gaze expands again, and I lift my head and body quickly, straining against the chains with all my power. I roar loudly until finally one of the binds snaps and my arm is free, the chain loosening. She shrieks, jumping off me in panic, but as soon as I pull my arm free, I reach out, grabbing the back of her hair just in time. I yank her until her back falls against my chest and I wrap my arm around her throat, holding her close to me. I dip my head, looking at her panicked side-profile.

"Be a good girl and undo the other one," I growl viciously against her ear. Her chest heaves with every breath until we hear movement inside the small room, and I inhale deeply, recognizing the sound.

"What the fuck was that?" she whispers, her voice trembling with fear.

I lift my head, peeking behind me to see one of my victims stirring under a sheet, awakening from his drug-infused coma. His wrists and ankles are bound, but it's not enough to stop him from fighting against Noir if he needs to. Even though I could easily free myself from the second strap and chain, I decide to scare her even more.

I peer down at her, my voice unnervingly calm. "My victim is waking up." Her breathing ceases altogether, amplifying his groans and movements. "You have less than ten seconds to release me, or he kills us both, Little Dolly."

She hesitantly and shakily lifts her hands.

"One," I whisper.

Her hands find the strap on my arm, her fingers trembling.

"Two."

She works quicker, the guy's movements behind me getting louder.

"Three."

As soon as the strap is loose, I rip my arm free but keep her held around the neck while I sit up and swivel my body. When I step down off the surgeon's table, I walk her backward until she is at the end of it. I forcefully bend her over, slamming her down against it with my hand on the back of her neck.

"Hellion..." she pants out, her tone laced with fear and panic.

Unable to hold back any longer, the entire situation getting me hard again, I reach down, grabbing my heavy shaft before slipping back inside her cum-filled pussy with one forceful stroke. She shrieks, rising to her tiptoes. I grab the top of her hair, lifting her head, forcing her up on her elbows. As I start to give her slow, hard thrusts, my eyes grow heavy, watching my cock being swallowed whole by her wet cunt repeatedly.

Her moans grow louder, becoming lost in the pleasure, but as soon as movement from across the room catches my attention, my eyes flicker in that direction, seeing him attempting to stand.

When she sees him getting to his feet as well, her breathing grows frantic. I let him watch me fuck her for a few seconds, his eyes wide with confusion, before I dig into my jeans pocket, retrieving my knife.

He assesses his surroundings, looking for something to free himself with, and I make Dolly stand by her hair, her back slamming against my front with a slap, a hiss pulling from her lips. As I wrap my palm around the front of her throat, holding her close to me, I tilt my head down, running my nose up the side of her cheek with a growl. A shudder runs through her, her pussy gripping around my dick.

I flick out my blade and force her to hold it in her hand before whispering in her ear, "Kill him."

"What?"

"Fucking kill him," I repeat, more strongly this time.

Noir's shaky fingers compress around my knife as I raise my head, and we both observe the guy backing himself against one of the units, trying to reach for a tool.

"But what if I miss?" she whispers, her voice breaking with uncertainty.

"Then you miss, and we're fucked," I lie. There's no way this motherfucker is killing either of us while I'm in the room, but I know my Dolly loves the fear I instill in her. She loves living life on the periphery of horror just as much as I do. We're made for one another. She is my twin fucking flame.

With each passing second, her pussy gets wetter around me, our cum dripping down my balls, and her breaths grow heavier. As he starts to free himself, I gaze down at her terrified side profile.

"What are you waiting for? Fucking do it. You're part of us now."

As soon as his hands are free, he smiles widely, and I raise an eyebrow just as Noir's arm lifts. His face falls, and she pulls her hand back, releasing and launching the knife. With a nauseating thump, it inserts in his chest, piercing his heart.

I grin as he slumps against the wall, slowly descending until he's on the floor. I know I've now pissed-off a client, but that was fucking worth it. I look down at Dolly, then snatch her cheeks, forcing her to gaze into my feral eyes. Hers are wide with shock, and I glance at her lips before dipping my head, slipping my tongue into her mouth. She welcomes it, her body melting against mine instantly.

We devour each other's mouths for a while until my dick grows rock-hard inside her again. Grabbing her hair, I force her back down onto the table. My breath becomes ragged, my inner beast raging within me.

"Stay," I growl the demand.

I reach for a small tool trolley to my right, dragging it over toward me. Opening one of the compartments, I retrieve barbed wire, the metal glinting against the dim light. Taking her arm, I wrap the wire tightly around it before binding it to the other, securing both behind her back. As the wire bites into her skin, she winces, blood oozing from the fresh wounds instantly, but she doesn't stop me, of course. Noir is a fucking masochist, relishing the pain her sadist brings.

"I'm going to make sure you feel the full force of suffering and bliss, Dolly," I promise. "After tonight, you'll never be the same girl you once were. You'll crave my sadism, begging for me to hurt you in unimaginable ways, whenever your body or mind needs it and I'll gladly deliver every single fucking time."

As soon as I finish, I withdraw my drenched cock from her pussy and flip her onto her back. A scream rips from her throat, but I continue to manhandle her, enjoying her pain, her agonizing screams, wanting to hurt her more with each passing second. I drag her closer by the tops of her thighs until her ass is hanging off the edge. Reaching up, I grab the chains and pull them down, wrapping them behind each of her knees before linking them back up, forcing her legs to sit high and wide for me.

My greedy eyes wander over her, blood now spilling onto the cold metal of the surgeon's table. Her body is placed perfectly for me to do as I please, with no hesitation and little room for resistance. She is in an extremely dangerous position, giving me full power over her. My sick mind swirls with possibilities and scenarios, driving me insane.

I move my hands down her spread inner thighs, and she peers down at me through heavy-lidded eyes. Lowering myself into a crouch, my gaze fixes on her glistening cunt. I press my tongue against her asshole, licking up to her pussy hole before taking a bite at her clit. She cries out, her legs tensing, but I don't relent. I suck and nibble roughly, drawing all kinds of sounds from her little body.

At the same time I press my fingers into her pussy, getting them doused before easing them into her ass. She clenches, but I continue until they're knuckle-deep. Thrusting them in and out, I eat her out, then slide two fingers into her cunt. I fuck both her holes simultaneously until she gives me an orgasm, but I don't stop. Each time she comes for me, I add another two fingers into her pussy. Her fluids drip down my hand and wrist as I give her swollen clit no fucking respite.

Her body responds to my touch, yearning for exactly what I'm giving her. With four fingers buried in her pussy, I rip the other two out of her ass and lower my tongue. It flicks over her pulsing, puckered hole before I give a sharp spit. Slowly, I stand, my eyes crawling over her sweat-dampened body. Her tits heave, her face a perfect picture of satisfaction, eyes closed in blissfulness.

I reach over and grab her cheeks, forcing her eyes open.

"Keep your fucking eyes on mine, Little Dolly. Watch what I do to you and how much you turn me the fuck on." I demand.

When she looks at me, darkness stirring in her gaze, my palm moves down her throat, between her breasts, and over her stomach. My eyes drink in every inch of her as I reach for my throbbing cock. Centring the tip on her asshole, I press forward and immediately, her body strains to take me. A cry gradually escapes her throat, but it only fuels my sadistic mind. I don't stop for a second, stretching her little asshole out to the fullest until her tight pink ring is gripping the base of my cock.

The warmth and feel of her around me is so fucking good that I waste no time. I don't let her adjust; I just drag back and plunge straight into her with full force. The more she screams in pain, the rougher I become, inching my way deeper and deeper. My fingers plunge into her sloppy pussy simultaneously. The symphony of her cries, my cock slamming into her ass, and the shameful sounds of her wetness echo through the room like a tune that will burn into my mind forever.

"Fuck, I can feel my cock in your ass with my fingers," I growl, staring down at the movement.

A wild impulse takes over me, and I slowdown in her ass, pushing my thumb into her soaked pussy before slowly easing my hand into her again. My eyes flicker upward to see her back arching, trembling, and struggling as expected. But with time and persistence, my hand fully slides inside her once more.

"Good fucking Dolly," I shudder out with satisfaction because she is being so fucking obedient.

The sight and sensation of her tightness drive me to the brink of madness, and I fist her cunt roughly right away while fucking her ass with my dick at the same time. My fingers deep inside her move over my piercings, and I attempt to jerk my cock off at the same time.

"Do you feel that Noir? How I'm jerking my fucking cock off in your ass with my hand inside your eager pussy?"

Being so full of me pushes her into a climax within minutes. Her holes convulse around me, a scream tearing from her throat, and I lean over, continuing my harsh penetrations while I attack her jiggling tits with my mouth and teeth, drawing out all the sensations from her overwhelmed body.

"Oh, my fucking god! Yes!" she screams out in ecstasy, letting me know that she is enjoying every degrading fucking second of this.

My movements never cease. Again and again, my hand sinks into her loosened pussy, twisting and thrusting while my entire length violently destroys her ass. Her juices coat my hand and shaft, and the room is filled with the raw, primal sounds of our disturbing ways of fucking.

After some time of absolutely ruining her, I decide to change positions. I slide my hand out of her pussy, my dick slowly withdrawing from her ass at the same time. Reaching up, I release her legs from the chains before wrapping my arm around the bottom of her back. The barbed wire stabs my skin as I pull her limp body upward and her forehead crashes against my chest as she breathes heavily. I cup her face, tilting her head back, and her dazed eyes meet mine. Seizing her neck roughly, I tilt down, shoving my tongue straight down her throat. She arches against me, moaning, her legs wrapping around my waist, desperate for more.

Raking my fingers through her sweaty hair, I grab handfuls before pulling her away from the surgeon's table. When she lands on her feet, her legs buckle, and I quickly catch her before turning her around and forcing her to bend over again. I grab some duct tape, ripping two piece's free with my teeth before sticking them to her ass cheeks, pulling them apart to keep her slit wide open for me. I kneel, my hands on her cheeks, pushing upward to expose all of her, before starting to eat her ass and pussy out again, plunging my pierced tongue deep inside each of her openings, exploring and tasting her inner walls. She moans, her body quivering as I ruthlessly soothe her with my tongue.

I growl, my cock, leaking and thumping, ready to cum as I stand straight. My eyes take in her bloodied form, the way the barbed wire has pierced her arms and back. Then I glance up, noticing the heavy chain above her. I lift and push her further up the surgeon's table until her entire front is on it, her legs spread and dangling down each side, with only her ass and pussy hanging off the edge. I reach up, grabbing the chain, and take a handful of her hair, lifting her head.

As soon as I start wrapping it around her throat, she whimpers in panic, but she can still breathe, for now. Once the chain is securely around her neck, I tighten it round my fist and tug, arching her back.

Now she is in the position I want her in, both of her openings exposed and vulnerable to me, I grab the base of my dick and flick the tip over her dripping pussy before aiming for her asshole. Breathing heavily, I hear my violent, evil thoughts coming into play, my sanity completely slipping.

With one forceful push, I glide into her ass and when she shrieks in agony, my eyes close in disturbing delight before I yank on the chain, cutting off her cry. As I start to aggressively wreck her asshole, her screams are limited by the chain. The more satisfaction I get out of her struggle, the more I pull on the chain and cruelly pound into her, showing absolutely no mercy to my Little Dolly.

I growl and throw my head back, reveling in the sensation of her entire body stiffening under my control. Her legs are rigid, her fingers straining, and her breathing is completely cut off as I straighten the chain to its maximum restriction. I continue destroying her, her body spasming from lack of oxygen, her face turning a deep purple, her skin paling. Yet I don't sympathise—this is what I crave, this is me.

I wait for her to give me exactly what I need to push me over the edge, "Come for me, my pretty girl. Surrender to pleasure and pain as you dance on the edge of death. Come for the man who holds your fucking life in his hands while he fucks you into oblivion." I growl.

Her body starts to grow limp, almost losing consciousness, but then I feel it: her asshole throbbing around me, her cum dripping onto the floor beneath us and finally, I let go of the chain.

She drops down onto the metal table with a loud thump, taking a huge gasp of air, her body in a state of shock and euphoria, teetering on the boundary of life and death as she comes hard. I roughly squeeze her waist with both hands, fingertips driving into her flesh and give one last brutal thrust, my cum blasting deep inside her. I toss my head back, the overwhelming sensation driving me to utter lunacy as I continue to pound into her lifeless body until I am completely thru.

I lift my heavy head, gazing down at her wrapped around my dick, a slight beat still ticking through her walls. My eyes flash to her, noticing that she has hers closed, her hair partly veiling her face as she tries to regain her breath.

Slowly, I slide my cock out of her, my hands gliding over the curves of her peachy ass as I kneel behind her again. I push her cheeks higher, admiring my cum oozing out of her asshole before I lean forward. My tongue meets her swollen cunt, and I lash at it, sucking her pussy and drinking every bit of sweet arousal she just released for me even though I almost killed her in the process. She gasps, her legs shuddering, and I slide my thumb into her cum-filled asshole, reminding her that the night is far from over for her. For us.

CHAPTER NINETEEN

Waking up in the morning, my body feels like it has been through ten rounds in the gym. I groan, rubbing my eyes before I slowly open them. As my vision clears, I see Hell staring down at me and my gaze widens as I realize I am in his dark bedroom, lying in his bed, not knowing how I ended up here, my mind still hazy. I dodge him as I sit up swiftly, feeling my naked body beneath the sheets, and as I attempt to get out, his hand tangles in my hair before yanking me back down.

"Get the fuck back here," he growls, his voice a menacing rumble. I hiss from the sudden pain in my scalp, my heart pounding and he props himself up on his elbow, gazing down at me, his orbs scanning my face with a curiosity.

I breathe heavily through my nose, memories of last night flooding through my mind as I look into his hypnotic eyes. The way he chased me, the way he fucked me, the way he spoke to me—all of it rushes back in vivid detail.

Hellion absolutely annihilated me in every way he could last night. At one point, I thought I was going to fucking die at his hands. But he didn't disappoint— even if most of the time I was fearing for my life, he gave my body exactly what it needed.

Climax after climax.

In some strange way, I relished every second of it. The fear, the pain, the lust, the passion—everything made my mind explode in ways I never knew were possible. He brought me back to life in that moment, even if I felt half dead at one point.

I glance down at myself, seeing and feeling the full effect of where the barbed wire was cutting my skin, keeping me bound while he did as he pleased to me. The bruising around my throat becomes apparent when I swallow, where my breathing was constricted by the chain. Little slices scatter over my arms, but I realize they're clean. I am almost entirely cleansed.

My eyes meet Hell's above me once again. "How am I clean? I don't remember getting in the shower," I ask, my voice quiet.

He lifts an eyebrow, staying silent, but I feel him moving his warm hand across my stomach causing butterflies to flutter inside me and he stops when he reaches my hip. Clutching it firmly, he forces me onto my side, dragging me closer to him.

At first, I am stiff under his touch, but with his naked form against mine, the heat, and the strong muscles, I find my body melting against him. My cheek gradually rests on his chest under his chin while he lies back, his arm resting lazily around my shoulders.

"I cleaned you up. I didn't want any of your wounds getting infected," he says casually. My eyes ease, then I lift my head, resting my chin on his pec and his lenses immediately collide with mine.

He lifts his hand, gently flicking my hair over my shoulder before he wraps it around the side of my neck. "I need some fucking answers."

"Oh yeah? What do you need answers about?" I ask.

He tilts his head to the side, his eyes scanning my face with curiosity. "Why is all of this nothing to you?" His warm thumb moves down my jaw as he continues, "All that you saw last night. You were not as fazed as I thought you would be, you played the fucking game and played it well. Does this shit not scare the fuck out of you?"

I think about his questions carefully before I respond. "It does. Of course, it does, but I relish feeling anything other than emptiness, I guess." My truthful answer makes his thumb pause on my jaw as he thinks carefully about my words, but I continue. "I've got questions too, Hell, and I need answers now that I have made it through Dark Night."

His teeth tighten as he rests his head back on the headboard, sliding his hand down to my shoulder. "Ask, Madame," he instructs bluntly before facing aside.

I move my body further up his, my tits sliding across his skin and when my lips are close to his, we stare into one another's eyes. "I'm not asking, Madame. I'm asking you." I push quietly while searching his gaze. "Why is this all normal to you? And who were those people? Were they innocent?"

He inhales, starting to sit up and as he rests his back against the headboard, I sit up as well, swivelling my body to face him and wrap the sheet tightly around my front. He briefly considers how to respond before his eyes meet mine.

"We don't ask fucking questions; we just do," he answers coldly and my brows pinch in confusion. "We're a secret society. There are thousands of us across the network. It's not just us here. We're merely one of the cleaners of the society," he explains, his tone flat and unfeeling.

I shake my head, shocked by the revelations, a shiver scurrying up my spine. "What?" I shudder out, realization settling over me like a cold blanket.

He shrugs his shoulders carelessly, "You could say they're innocent to someone, but not to the fucking society they aren't. They're traitors, witnesses, or rivals lured here to lose their lives for their betrayal against their vows."

My mouth drops open to speak, but he continues. "They believe coming here means they're getting their own revenge on those who have deceived them, and they do, but by the end of the night, they also meet their own fate in the worst ways imaginable. They feel the sting of their own wrongdoings in the society," he finishes, his eyes locking onto mine. I lower my head, fiddling with the sheet, taking his words in carefully, but I feel his dark stare all over me, observing my reaction.

"You shouldn't even be here, Noir. You owe nothing to the society," he says, and I lift my head.

"Yet here I am," I respond quietly. "Do you even want to be here, Hell?"

He raises his eyebrow at my question, "It's all I know. I've been here since I was a fucking kid."

I offer a nod. "And that place you have underground?"

He takes a deep inhale before looking aside and grins, "You fucking had me, Little Dolly, I'll give you that."

I smile slightly, but then his face falls. "How did you know what drugs to stab into my neck without killing me?"

When he asks, my face falls as well, and I avoiding eye contact. "I studied meds once or twice," I breathe out the lie.

"And where the fuck are your family, Noir? What was your life like before all of this mayhem?" His voice cuts through the silence, pressing for answers, seemingly trying to get to know me and my mind races frantically.

When my eyes meet his, I finally speak. "They're dead. Well, I have a sister somewhere, but…" I shrug my shoulder, not wanting to delve into much. He raises his chin, studying me before giving a small nod in understanding.

"And you?"

"Dead," he answers without hesitation, devoid of any emotion.

"All of them?"

He squints his eyes before glancing away, "The ones that mattered."

Talking to him like this makes me realize that we're not much different from one another after all. Maybe that's why we click. We've clearly both had fucked-up childhoods, and even now, we're stuck in darkness in ways the outside world might never understand. But I know, deep down, I can't stay here. After him saying that this circus is linked to a criminal society, it's only a matter of time before Kyro finds and takes me. I dread to think what he might do when he finally gets his hands on me. I doubt I'll make it out alive twice.

The thoughts of leaving here and Hell fill me with a sorrow I have never experienced before because I feel like I have found my place, but I don't want him tangled up in this horrifying web.

If Hell has no say over this society, he certainly won't have any say over Kyro. Kyro is powerful; he is an acknowledged man in the criminal underworld of the United States. No one, not even Hell, can save me from his cruel clutches, and that's the harsh truth.

Hell's loyalty will always lie with this place, his society, because that is just the way it is, and I am nothing but an intruder who will make things harder for everyone here. How the fuck, out of all the places I could have gone and stayed, have I ended up here? A killing carnival that cleanses a hidden society in the underworld.

"I should get going," I say, turning around to get off the bed, but his firm grip on the nape of my neck stops me. He pulls me back down and flips me onto my front. I breathe heavily as his chest presses against my bare back, and he brings his mouth close to my ear.

"Now that I've had a taste of my pretty Dolly, I'm not letting her go. You're staying here with me from now on," he murmurs, and panic surges through me. He grabs the back of my hair, lifting my head before wrapping his palm over the front of my bruised throat, peering down at me.

"You can't keep me here, Hell. I will run from you as soon as I get the chance," I whisper breathlessly.

He sets his lips against mine, exposing his teeth against them. "And I will fucking catch you every single time," he hisses.

I challenge him, "But what if I just knock you out again?"

I feel his lips curl into a wicked smile against mine. "Then I'll fucking find you and after I awaken, I'll do unholy things to your body again, just as I did last night, but so badly next time. To the point that you're never able to escape me again. I'll cut your fucking legs off if I have to. As long as I still have your perfect cunt, hot tits, and pretty face, I'm fucking satisfied. You'll be my little nugget."

"You're sick," I say, grinning slightly.

"I know," he growls, shifting between my legs from behind. "You don't have to tell me, pretty girl. You should be asking yourself why it gets your pussy so fucking wet."

With his palm still wrapped firmly around my throat, he keeps my head tilted back, our breaths mingling, lips brushing against each other. His other hand moves between my thighs, and as soon as he touches my pussy, I wince, the pain from last night's brutality sharp and evident. Ignoring my discomfort, he slides his lengthy fingers into me quickly, and just as I am about to scream, his lips crash against mine, drowning it out.

His tongue slips into my mouth, exploring and dominating, as he gives me a few hard thrusts with his fingers. The sensation sends shockwaves through my body, and his dick, hard and heavy, bobs against my asscheek with every movement he makes.

I moan into his mouth, my body responding despite the lingering pain. His fingers curl inside me, hitting that perfect spot, and I lift my ass, giving him better access to delve deeper.

As soon as come starts to ooze out of my soaked entrance and all over his fingers, he pulls them out, breaking the kiss. Then, he sits back, yanking my hair, forcing me to follow. With my back against his front, both of us up on our knees, he wraps his arm around my neck, holding me close to him and guiding his cock to my pussy from behind. I feel his piercing slip down my slick folds before he suddenly slips into me with one forceful shove. My eyes widen, a scream escaping me as my pussy clenches around him from the pain.

He groans in delight at my agonizing shriek, squeezing my breast viciously with one hand before giving it a hard slap.

"Fuck, I love it when you scream for me. Do it a-fucking-gain," he demands, his voice a guttural growl as he presses his forehead against the side of my head.

He starts to pound into me, each thrust deep and forceful, his piercings creating a delicious friction against my inner walls. His movements are wild and untameable, each one driving me closer to the edge, my ass bouncing and slapping against his hips. As his arm tightening around my neck, my nails dig into the skin of his forearm, leaving angry red scratches.

My cries grow louder the harder he gets, smashing his cock into me with relentless force, but as soon as we're both teetering on the edge of a climax, he releases me, and I collapse forward, my hands meeting the bed. He harshly presses me down, forcing my ass to stay in the air, the position making me feel utterly exposed and vulnerable. His hand pushes against the top of my ass, spreading my thighs wide, while his other hand stays on the back of my head, holding me in place, asserting his dominance.

With his cock still buried deep inside me, he removes his hand from my head, gliding it down the curve of my sweaty back until it's positioned on my ass. He splits my cheeks and lets a trail of spit slip from his tongue, the warm liquid landing on my puckered hole. The sensation is both humiliating and arousing as he prepares to invade me further.

When he starts to ease two fingers into my ass, I reach back with one hand, the whimper escaping me muffled by the sheets as the pain from last night becomes apparent.

I turn my head to the side, breathing heavily, and from the corner of my eye I can see he is watching me intently, his gaze gleaming with sadistic pleasure as he takes in every pained expression and sound I make. Still easing his fingers into me, ignoring my pleas, he catches my wrist with his free hand and with a firm grip, he stretches my arm before pinning it against my ass, restricting me.

"Shut the fuck up, Dolly. You're going to take everything I do to you, or I'll chain you up again," he threatens, his voice a chilling calm yet breathless.

He spits again, the warm liquid dripping onto his fingers before shoving them all the way inside me, causing me to scream.

"Such tight little fucking holes, no matter how many times you're stretched the fuck out and wrecked by me." He grits out with frustration.

I feel the heaviness of his dick still inside me and with every thrust of his fingers, it twitches, but he doesn't attempt to fuck me in my pussy yet. He focuses on my asshole, his fingers coiling and twisting relentlessly as deep as he can get them, bringing a mix of immense pleasure and sharp pain.

My fingers strain and clench, my knuckles turning white as he shows me no leniency, and my screams seem to mix with moans continuously. Despite the blend of sensations, he is, once again, building me up to something beautiful.

"I can feel it, pretty girl. Go on, fucking explode on me. Let me feel you pulse around me again."

When my orgasm shatters me, I bury my face into the sheets, my entire body trembling. As my legs shudder, he stays still, savoring the sensation of my convulsing muscles gripping him tightly. He growls from the intensity, a primal sound of satisfaction, before slipping his fingers out.

After releasing my wrist, he slides his two pointer fingers inside me, stretching me out. I wince, clutching the sheets tightly as my climax slowly ebbs away. He spits straight into my open asshole, before sliding his fingers back in with a rumble of pleasure in his chest.

"Such an obedient little slut for me, ain't you, Dolly?"

When I don't answer because I am in too much of a euphoria-infused state, he aggressively pushes my ass down further with his free hand, making me lower until my legs are spread as far as they can go beside me, my pussy touching the sheets.

With only the tip of his cock now inside me, he twists his fingers upward as he leans over causing me to shudder. He brings his mouth close to my ear, and I side eye him. As he breathes heavily, his warm breath skating over my skin, he slides his dick back inside me and I moan, my eyes closing.

"Tell me what you are, pretty girl." He growls into my ear.

Thrust.

"Fucking say it."

Another thrust, but so much harder.

They are slow, yet deeper with each strike and it makes it hard for me to answer, because they are not only painful, but they feel so fucking good.

"This is the last time I ask you, Noir and if I don't hear it, I'm ramming my dick in your fucking ass, and it won't come out all day."

Fucking hell. He knows I'm stubborn and that is exactly why he's doing this. He wants to break me down to be his and his only with confessions voiced, but there is no way that monster cock is staying in my ass all day.

"I'm an obedient little slut for you, Hell." I grit out with shame.

He slides his tongue slowly up the side of my face with a possessive snarl, his piercing moving across my skin.

"Such a good fucking girl." He murmurs, his tone carrying his satisfaction at my surrender.

Then, he starts to fuck both my holes again. His grunts and heavy breathing, mix with my cries as he pounds into me in the steepest position.

When we both cave into the pleasure, he slams his cock into me one last time, pushing inside me and holding himself there as he releases. While my body quakes beneath him, he slides his fingers out of my ass and brings his hand to the back of my hair, taking a handful, as his other takes my jaw. With his body heavy on mine, he rests his forehead against my cheek, both of us trying to control our erratic breathing.

"I mean it, my Dolly, he pants out. "Get your shit from that trailer, you're staying with me."

I stay silent as he continues, "You owe nothing to him. If you really wanted him over me, you wouldn't fucking be here getting fucked this hard by me." His words are punctuated by a purposeful forceful thrust, and I gasp, my objections dissolving in the heat of the moment.

"He chooses needles over you," he growls, his voice a harsh whisper against my ear. "While my only high is you, and I've never felt anything as blissful as your dark fucking ecstasy."

I freeze, thinking about his words carefully. "What did you just say?" I breathe out completely ignoring how beautiful the second half of his speech was.

He pauses, and awareness hits me. "Get off me, Hell."

When he doesn't move, I bite my teeth in frustration. "I swear to god, if you don't get the fuck off me, I will never grace your presence again."

He growls, but finally listens, pushing himself away from me. As soon as he is sitting back on his knees, I turn and sit up, gathering the sheet and wrapping it around myself.

"You gave him that shit, didn't you?" I say, my gaze narrowing. He just raises an eyebrow, expressionless, not denying my accusation. Fury bubbles up inside me, and I begin to get off the bed.

"Asshole," I spit out.

I stand up, passing him, and search the room for my clothes, but I don't even remember how I got here last night. When I spot one of his black hoodies on a chair, I drop the sheet and quickly slip it over my body, getting ready to leave. Pulling the hood over my head, I turn, but I am startled to see him standing right in front of me, his eyes full of intensity. As he takes a step forward, I stand my ground, not weakening to his intimidation.

"What did you expect me to do, Dolly? Just allow him to keep being around you?"

I glare at him, "I told you to leave it to me, Hell. That was so fucking wrong of you," I reply, my voice raised.

When I try to pass him to get to the door, he steps in front of me, and I sigh, my patience wearing thin.

"Yet he still took that shit. What does that say? I'm just trying to protect you, Noir. There's something fucking weird about that guy."

I fold my arms over my chest in a defensive stance, my chin raised. "And you're Mr. Perfect, are you?"

He brings his face down to mine until it's close enough to feel his breath. "I'll be whatever the fuck you want me to be, pretty girl. I'll be your weak little bitch. Put your heels on, stamp all over my fucking dick, drag me through the mud with it still attached and I'll still worship the ground you walk on."

His hand slides around the side of my neck and I turn my face to the side, closing my eyes against the whirl of conflicting emotions inside me because he can be oddly sweet all the fucking time.

"These are the lengths I'll go to make you mine, Noir. I couldn't give a single fuck if that motherfucker dies with a needle embedded in his arm. He is fortunate he is still breathing. He is lucky that deep down I know you don't want him. You want me."

My eyes flash open, meeting his swiftly. "You'll be whatever the fuck I want you to be, remember? So, stay the fuck out of this." I assert firmly.

His jaw tenses in irritation. "And let me make one thing clear," I continue, my voice steady and unyielding, "whether you think I am yours or not, whether I surrender to you while your cock is inside me is the total opposite of what you can expect from me outside our sexual fantasies, Hell. No one will ever own me again, and if you have an ounce of respect for me, you would..."

"Again?" he asks, cutting me off.

I realize my slip instantly, my gaze widening in panic. My heart thumps in my chest as we stare into one another's eyes. He stands tall, his hand sliding to the back of my neck where he takes a firm grip.

"What the fuck do you mean, again?"

I keep my eyes low, trying to avoid his intense gaze and think of some way to lie to him.

"Noir!" My body jolts from his powerful voice, and my eyes close.

"Nothing," I breathe out, tears almost welling up in my eyes.

When they lift to his, he searches mine, looking for something hidden.

"Can you just let me go, and I'll see you later?" I plead softly.

He slowly and reluctantly slides his hand away from my neck until it drops down beside him. I gently place my palms on his strong, bare chest and tiptoe, bringing my lips as close to his as possible.

"Thank you," I whisper, my gaze locked on his vortex stare, but he remains silent, his jaw set tight.

I lean in, placing a gentle kiss on his mouth before lowering myself down and walking around him toward the door. I turn the handle and step out, the door closing quietly behind me, leaving a silence that echoes the unspoken words between us.

HOLLOW HELLION

As I exit The Hollow's trailer, I head directly for mine, my head stirring with clashing emotions. Hell is determined to make me his, but how he is doing it in this situation is below the belt, even for him. I just wish he had trusted me to handle this. Now, I must deal with Eli, who could potentially go on a downward spiral once again. The chilly winds envelop me as I shamefully stroll across the trailer park, barefoot and dressed only in a hoodie. As I pass Blush's trailer, I suddenly hear her call out to me, and I halt. I take a few steps backwards until she comes into view, and she walks toward me with a big smile on her face, but when she stops, her expression changes.

"Wow, you look like shit," she says bluntly.

I roll my eyes and glance aside. "Thanks for the compliment, Blush."

"I take it you finally faced Hellion?" she asks, her tone tinged with amusement.

I look at her instantly, and she chuckles. Not in the mood to stand around and chat about how Hellion obliterated me last night, I start to walk away. "I'm sorry, I need to go."

"Wait!" she shouts.

I stop with a heavy sigh, hearing her jogging toward me and I turn to face her, noticing the concerned now in her eyes.

"Are you okay?" she asks, her tone softening.

I give a small nod in response. "I'm fine, I just need to get back."

"I'm not sure if..." She trails off, her lips creating a thin line.

"Not sure if?" I mimic her words, lifting an eyebrow.

She fiddles with her sleeves and looks in the direction of mine and Eli's trailer. "I walked past last night, and I'm sure I heard..." I shake my head in confusion, prompting her to continue. "I don't think you were the only one doing the dirty last night."

My lips purse together as I inhale deeply and lower my head, nodding a couple of times. "I just wanted to warn you, Noir. I think it's that chick from the carnival the other week. He must have snuck her in."

Her words make my eyes dart to hers, "What?" I bite out, fury building inside me.

I give her no chance to respond, whirling around and heading straight for the trailer with Blush in tow. When I reach it, I try to open the door, but it's locked. I bang my fist against the glass.

"Eli! Open the fuck up!" I shout, anger seething in my voice.

I start hearing male and female voices from inside and continue to bang until finally, the door opens. They both stand there before me, and as she takes a few steps down, my eyes follow her while she slips on a hoodie. When she tries to pass me, I grab her upper arm.

"How old are you?" I question almost aggressively.

Her brown eyes flash to E's behind me and I stand in her line of sight, releasing her arm. Her gaze meets mine, and she straightens her back. "I've just turned eighteen," she says with confidence, almost proudly.

"You know he is in his thirties, right? Do your parents know you're here?" I ask her calmly.

"Noir, what the fuck..." E shouts behind me.

I whirl around to face him. "Shut the fuck up, you," I yell.

He scowls at me, and I keep intense eye contact with him while hearing her sneak away, but I am so angry, I let her.

I point my finger at Eli. "You're leaving here. Today," I assert strongly.

He crosses his arms over his chest. "I still have a week left here according to Madame, but after that, I'll be glad to leave this dump."

I seethe with rage, his attitude almost making me want to kill him. His green eyes drag up and down my frame with judgement. "You're pissed because I'm getting pussy when you've clearly been with that fucking clown all night."

Blush scoffs behind me. "Oh boy, I would be very careful who you're talking about, because my loyalty is all for The Hollow's. You won't last a fucking hour if I tell that 'Clown' you're talking about what you just said, let alone a week."

"I don't give a fuck where your pathetic dick has been, E," I say bitterly through tight teeth, drawing his attention back to me and his eyes narrow.

"There is not one ounce of jealousy inside of me, trust me, it's not even about that," I declare, stepping forward slowly. "But I warned you about her age."

He snickers, looking aside. "She's a woman."

"BARELY!"I shout, and his eyes flash to mine. "You're what? Thirty-four?" I shake my head in disgust.

"Fuck off, Noir, you're not far off her age," he tries to justify.

"I am sure as hell, not eighteen!"

Feeling fed up with his bullshit, I step ahead and push past him, entering the trailer and proceeding to the bedroom to gather some things.

"Noir…" Eli's warning tone follows me as I enter the room, with Blush slowly trailing behind.

I go straight to the wardrobe, grabbing a bag. As soon as I have it, he yanks it from my grasp. I turn around quickly to see Blush standing in front of him, glaring fiercely. "Keep your hands off her, motherfucker, or I swear to god."

She tries to take the bag, but he pulls it back, shoving her aside before stepping toward me, anger blazing in his eyes. On instinct, I lift my hand and deliver a hard blow across his face, fuelled by rage.

With his face turned to the side, I close the gap between us, breathing heavily. "One week, and I don't want to see you ever again, E."

His eyes meet mine, softening. "Noir, please."

I shake my head firmly. "No. I can accept a lot of things—drugs, habits, weird-ass behavior—but what I will not accept is underage fucking. It makes me sick."

"She's not underage," he insists, straightening his back defiantly, the red mark on his cheek becoming apparent.

My eyes flash to Blush, who steps into my view behind him, her pink gaze loaded with fury. Suddenly, she raises an empty glass bottle.

"Blush! No!" I yell, but it's too late. She whacks it over his head, the glass shattering everywhere, and he drops to the floor, knocked out.

My mouth gapes open, eyes meeting Blush's and she simply shrugs her shoulders, "He had it coming."

I let out a shuddering breath, watching as she leans down to take the bag from his hand. She tosses it to me, and I catch it. "Get what you need. You deserve better than that piece of shit."

My eyes water as I gaze down at Eli, feeling confused. Four months of my life, and it has come to this. Am I the problem for allowing my past to influence me like this? Or has he truly gone too far? All I know is, I am wise enough not to put him or me in this shit situation. Without my meds, I cannot be around someone who is triggering my past this way. It's a painful awakening that we're not compatible for a relationship and even a friendship, but it's the sad truth. A tear rolls down my cheek, and Blush steps forward, her hand finding my shoulder with a reassuring squeeze.

"Noir," she says softly, and my watery eyes dart to hers. "Don't be upset. Your stance on this is valid. I don't know you well, but this subject clearly bothers you. Your feelings matter."

I sniffle and give a small nod before turning to the wardrobe to pack some things, including my mini dolly. When I'm ready, I step over Eli, noticing he is still breathing, but a sob builds in my throat, guilt creeping in as I pass him. Blush slides her arm around my shoulders and guides me out of the trailer.

CHAPTER TWENTY

After getting out of the shower, I stand in front of the mirror, carefully applying my face paint as I do every day, my swirling contacts still in place. My thoughts drift back to Noir and what she let slip.

"Own again?" I murmur to myself. "What the fuck does that mean?"

My Little Dolly clearly has hidden secrets. Maybe she has been with other guys. Well, of course she fucking has, and I hate the thought, but it is what it is. It wasn't the idea of others that bothered me so much; it was the pain in her voice when she said it. I saw it in her pretty blue eyes as they glazed over, and it gave me a fucked-up feeling in my gut.

Now, more than ever, I crave to unravel everything about her. I want to know who she was before all of this. I want her to trust me. She needs to know that with me, she will have someone she can confide in. I'm no longer just chasing to fuck her; I'm chasing to understand her.

Once I'm finished, I run my fingers through my damp, curly hair, letting it fall over my eyes before turning around and exiting the bathroom. I pause as I enter, pulling my black towel around my waist tighter, when I notice the door opening. Noir steps in, and my eyes lock onto the bag in her hand before meeting hers. She closes the door behind her and leans against it, her intense gaze never leaving mine.

She pulls her hood down and pushes away from the door, tossing her bag onto a chair as she passes. She stops in front of me, and I look down at her, my mind already screaming to take her pussy for walking into my bedroom like she fucking owns it. But she does. She can own every damn part of me, and I'd willingly allow it. This girl has my balls in a fucking vice.

"I'm sorry," she says, and my eyes scan hers. "You were right all along."

My brows pinch, ready to ask what she is talking about, but she speaks first. "Can I use your shower?"

I give a slight nod and gesture to the en-suite bathroom, but as she passes me, I catch her upper arm, stopping her and she slowly turns around.

"He didn't put his fucking hands on you, did he?" I ask, my eyes boring into hers.

She arches a brow, her expression unflinching. "Quite the opposite, Hell."

My brows knit together, my head tilting slightly in confusion. She walks closer and reaches for my towel and with a swift tug, she exposes my cock, then grabs my balls, making me jolt.

"Are you going to show me how a real man fucks in the shower or what?" she taunts, her voice dripping with challenge.

A wicked glint flashes in her eyes while she bites her bottom lip and without warning, I clamp my hands around her throat, squeezing tightly. She tilts her head back, a defiant grin playing on her lips.

I lean in as I murmur, "I hope to fuck I don't end up killing you while you're here. I like you too damn much."

Her smile widens, her eyes gleaming with a mix of fear and excitement. "Show me, then," she whispers, her voice a breathy dare. With a growl, I push her backward into the bathroom, capturing her lips with mine, the heat between us igniting into an inferno.

It's been a couple of days since I have been here and I'm alone in Hell's room. He said he had some things to take care of, which I understood, but my mind is stressing me out tonight. I stupidly start thinking about E and whether he's okay. I have been hiding inside this trailer, so I don't face him. I don't know why, but I feel like he needed that wake-up call.

He can't keep up the threatening behavior just because he's not getting what he wants. He can't keep fucking these young girl. It's disgusting. I guess him putting his hands on Blush was the final line crossed. She holds no prisoners, and honestly, when I think about it, he's lucky. She kills for a living, and a bottle to the head was the least of his worries—and mine.

I just feel so disappointed, in him and in myself. It's really dragging me down tonight, making me wonder if I'm the problem. Did I drive him to this mad state of mind because of what I was doing with Hell? I feel a war inside me because I didn't feel like I was exactly his girlfriend, yet maybe I should have spoken to him more openly about things before I did what I did. As a friend at least.

"Or maybe he wasn't the problem after all." A voice whispers in my ear and my head snaps to the right.

"What?" I murmur.

"Maybe it's Hell. Maybe you chose the wrong man." The whisper responds.

"No, I…"

"I mean, Hell isn't much different to Kyro, right?"

Tears well up in my eyes and I shake my head.

"The way he abuses your body is just as bad as what they did to you."

"No, you're wrong." I mutter, my bottom lip trembling.

"No, you're wrong. You were conditioned to take abuse and now you accept it by disguising it as a form of pleasure because it's all you know.. "

A sob rises up my throat as I continue to cry.

"He is everything that you don't want or need. He weakens you. Kill him."

I slap my hands over my ears and squeeze me eyes shut, "No."

"Kill him before he kills you."

"No, he isn't like them."

"No, he's worse. Fucking kill him and get out of this place."

"Kill him!"

I shake my head frantically, "No!" I yell.

"Kill him!"

The whisper continues over and over again, repeating the same two words, growing louder in my ears and it drives me insane until I let out a high-pitched scream, jumping to my feet. In my crazed state, I grab my hoodie and head for the door. I swing it open until it hits the wall and I storm out of the trailer.

HOLLOW HELLION

As I pace quickly over the gravel, I throw my hoodie on, my wide gaze fixed on the circus ahead, glowing from on the inside. When I enter the back entrance, I wipe the tears off of my face and head for Madame's chamber, hoping she will be there.

When I enter, luckily I spot her sitting behind her desk, a glass of wine in her hand as she smokes a cigarette with her head titled back. I stop in the middle of the room, and she slowly lifts her head, her eyes meeting mine.

"Noir," she says with a soft smile before gesturing to the seat opposite her. "Take a seat."

As always, somehow, I feel strangely calm in Madame's presence and I shuffle forward, tugging my sleeves further down my arms. She sits upright, placing her glass on the desk, and I sit in the chair.

"What can I help you with, darling?" she says in a motherly tone that almost makes me burst into tears.

I lower my head, trying to push the thoughts away, and I fiddle with my fingers.

"Have you been crying, Noir? It's not Hell, is it?"

I shake my head, "No," I say and when I lift my watery eyes to hers, she scans them with genuine concern. "I'm just having a rough night. It's a lot to take in, you know? After Dark Night."

She gives a small nod of understanding. "I get it, but you'll get used to it."

She gradually stands, walking around the desk with purposeful steps before stopping in front of me and leaning against it.

"Eli gave me the keys to your trailer today," she says, and my brows pinch in confusion. "He didn't tell you he was leaving?" she asks.

I shake my head once before wiping my nose with my sleeve. "No, he didn't."

My heart aches in my chest, and I don't know why. My emotions are all over the place right now, reminding me why I came here in the first place.

"Do you guys have access to a doctor?"

She tilts her head to the side with perplexity before nodding. "What do you need?"

"Anti-depressants," I answer, my voice unwavering.

Her eyes scan the length of me, not in a judgmental way, but she gives another nod when her gaze returns to mine. "Of course, I'll have him drop some off."

I feel my shoulders relax for the first time today as I lower my eyes.

"Most people here don't try to tame their mental state of minds, Noir. We simply embrace the madness," she admits almost proudly, and my eyes flick up to hers.

"The difference between me and everyone else here, Madame, is that you're better off having me in my sane madness than in my insane madness, trust me. It's not very fun hallucinating and seeing your sister running around the carnival when she isn't actually here," I confess firmly.

She analyzes me briefly before drawing a deep breath and pushing away from the desk. I can't exactly tell her that the voices in my head are also telling me to kill Hell. I don't trust anyone here enough to let them see my vulnerabilities in that light.

"Where are you from, Noir?" She enquires as she takes a slow seat in her chair.

I feel anxiety tighten my chest, and I lie, "Erm, Vegas."

She raises her chin, as if she knows I am lying then moves her eyes to the bottle of red wine, lifting it and pouring some into a glass.

When she is finished, she lifts it and offers it to me, "Here is some of my anti-depressant."

A small smile plays on her lips, and it makes me grin slightly as I lean over, taking it from her hand. I bring it to my lips as I sit back in the chair, taking a big gulp. Once the alcohol hits the pit of my stomach, I sigh, relishing the warmth it brings.

"Are you staying with Hell now?" She asks curiously and I look at her before giving a small nod in response. "For now."

I see another smirk on her lips as she takes a long sip of wine. "It's nice to see him happy," she says, lowering the glass.

"Happy?" I ask, my curiosity piqued.

Her eyes swing to mine before she smiles widely. "That's probably the wrong word," she admits with a soft chuckle. "You know what I mean."

I give her a slow nod before I stand from the chair, leaning over to place my half-empty glass of wine on the desk. "Well, I better get going," I say, turning to leave.

"Noir…" I stop in my stride when she says my name and glance over my shoulder at her.

She stands and walks toward me, speaking with genuine concern. "I hired you because you're not only an amazing dancer, but you radiate a darkness that fits in perfectly here. I know that may feel like a curse rather than a blessing, but here, it's not. We accept you for all that you are. Inside and out."

Her words make me turn around, facing her fully and she continues, "We may not know each other well yet, but we are one big crazy family. All of us. And if you ever need me, I am here. I care about every single one of you, even with what we do here."

I lower my eyes, pondering because what she said strikes a chord deep within my soul. When I have finished processing her words, I lift my head, my eyes finding hers.

"Thank you," I say gently, showing my gratitude.

She gives a small nod in return, then I turn to leave, feeling a strange sense of belonging that I haven't felt in a long time. As I walk away, her words echo in my mind, making me realise that even in the darkest places, there can be light and acceptance.

HOLLOW HELLION

Not feeling ready to go back to the trailer, I head to the silent carnival. The dim surroundings of this terrifying place bring a strange sense of calm to my chaotic mind. The eerie stillness blurs out all the intrusive thoughts as I focus on the possibility of something jumping out at me. After some time of aimless strolling through the vast, deserted area, I find myself stopping a short distance away from the carousel with a sign saying, "Ride closed." I tilt my head to the side, gazing at it before taking gentle paces forward.

I step up to the platform, my hand grasping one of the cold poles attached to a skeleton horse. I lightly graze my fingers over the bones, lost in thought. Vague memories of my mom bringing me to places like this surface, though they were, of course, not horror-themed.

When she was alive, it was her ultimate goal to give me everything. She wanted to fill my head with beautiful memories and ensure I had a childhood I could reflect on and smile about. She wanted me to have the best. She pushed me to bring my talents to life, entering me into contests, and when I won, she would shower me with love and tell me how proud she was. She was the perfect mother.

Her laughter, her encouragement, the way she made me feel like I could conquer the world, the way her love seeped into my bones—those memories are bittersweet now and they are the total opposite of the darkness that envelops me, both in this carnival and in my life.

When my mom and I were in that car crash, I lost her, and my life spiralled into a living nightmare. I ended up being nothing but a slave to my stepfather. When she was alive, he wasn't the cruel man he became, that I knew of anyway. We didn't exactly have a father-and-daughter relationship, but he also didn't treat me like he did the moment she wasn't here. Every word, every touch was so full of hatred, and I couldn't understand why.

What had I done that was so wrong? I didn't cause that crash, and he never blamed me for it either. I used to scream at him, begging for answers, but he would just respond with meaningless phrases that confused me. They didn't explain shit to my innocent mind. The only thing I knew from his words was that he despised me and my mom suddenly. He said I was going to be trained to be the perfect little whore and be sold to a man or men as brutal as he was so I could suffer for the rest of my life.

Over the years, I realized everyone who knew me, and my mom thought I had died in that crash as well. He did something to convince the world that we were both dead, but in the shadows, he was killing me himself—physically and mentally. Before I left, I was months away from being "perfect" for my next abuser. Around one year before I escaped, I discovered someone was in the room beside me, another girl, and I would speak to her through the thin walls. She told me she was my half-sister on my dad's side that I never knew about. I was initially shocked because I never really knew my father, but deep down, it didn't surprise me. From the moment my mom passed, I learned there were so many secrets being held; I was presumed dead, I had a secret sister, and I am sure there is a lot more.

That crash had devastated my entire world, but it was the aftermath that truly broke me. My stepfather's change into an evil bastard was swift and brutal. He became a man I didn't recognize. His cruelty was endless, the physical abuse horrific, but it was the mental suffering that left the deepest wounds. He would whisper vile things in my ear, breaking down my soul piece by piece. I was isolated, cut off from the world, and forced to accept his twisted form of "training."

The discovery of my half-sister was a spark of light in the darkness. She was a mirror of my own suffering, and our conversations through the walls became a lifeline.

I wish I could find her. The day she got me out of there is all a blur. I can only remember the bedroom door swinging open, the sudden rush of freedom as the fresh air touched my skin for the first time in years. I remember running through the dark woods, the branches clawing at my clothes and skin, his dogs barking in the background. She screamed at me to go the other way from a distance, and I regret listening to her because I escaped that night, but I don't know if she ever did.

I never got the chance to hug her, to touch her, to thank her for saving my life. Everything happened so fucking fast. One moment we were prisoners, and the next, we were running for our lives. I can still hear her voice, urgent and desperate in my ears, urging me to keep going, to not look back. But I did look back, and the image of her fading into the night still haunts me.

I wish there were some way to know if he still has her, if she's still suffering under his control. I owe her my freedom, and the guilt of leaving her behind is a heavy burden to bear.

If I were strong enough, and if it weren't just me, I would fight him. I would do anything in my power to take him down, but I just don't hold that power. He will always be above me, someone I can't escape. He was always stronger than me, both physically and mentally. There is no fucking comparison. The thought of confronting him fills me with a mix of rage and helplessness. I can only imagine how furious he was when he discovered I had escaped.

As I walk around the carousel, I take in the vintage-looking painted decor, the way they peel and crack, revealing the aged wood beneath with every slow step I take. Suddenly, I feel the ride dip on the other side as if someone has stepped on it as well, and I freeze. My heart pounds in my chest as everything goes still. Tiptoeing, I begin to creep around it, peeking around the corners, but when I don't find anything, I stop, letting out a tense breath.

The moment I turn, a figure stands in front of me, and I scream. His hand slaps over my mouth, pinning me against the carousel, and my eyes swing upward to see Hell's spiraling orbs. My body relaxes instantly, and he removes his hand only to grab my throat with a firm grip.

He tilts my head back, dipping down to bring his lips close to mine. "Hello, my pretty girl. What are you doing here all alone?" he asks with a deep murmur.

My eyes ease, my stomach fluttering and I whisper in response, "I just needed to clear my head."

His eyes scan mine for a moment before he gives a small nod, slowly releasing me. As I stay leaning against the carousel, I observe him turn his back to me, wandering around between two horses.

"You know this shit is haunted, don't you?" he states calmly.

I roll my eyes, "There's no such thing as ghosts, Hell."

He stops and side-eyes me, "I wouldn't be so sure about that, Dolly." As I stay silent, he walks around a little more. "This carousel has been around for over a century. It's been through wars, it's been through fires, people have died on this fucking thing in brutal ways. Many years ago, they used to tie people to it as it rotated and leave them there to rot until their last breath," he explains, and my eyes widen.

He turns to look at me and offers me his hand. I push myself away from the wood and take cautious steps forward, sliding my hand into his. He yanks me toward him, my front crashing into his, and he grabs my waist, lifting me onto one of the horses.

He mounts the back behind me, and I side-eye him as I wrap my hands around the pole. When he is comfortable, he moves his warm hands up my thighs, sending shivers through me, then cloaks my midsection with his strong arms. I melt against him, feeling safe, my head resting back against his chest, and he turns his head to look down at me.

"They closed it around ten years ago because strange shit started to happen," he continues.

I smirk, "Strange shit? Like what?" I query, not believing a word of it.

"People reported seeing figures moving around, hearing whispers that weren't there. Some even said they felt cold fingers touching them when no one else was around. Kids were fucking pushed off the horses, bones broken. And then there were the vanishes. A few workers went missing, never to be seen again. The last straw was when a child disappeared while riding this carousel. After that, they shut it down for good."

I inhale deeply wrapping my arms around his, "That sounds like just typical ghost stories to me, Hell."

He gently runs his nose up my ear before responding into it, "There's always some fucking truth behind all stories, Little Dolly."

"That's true, but nothing is as terrifying as actual reality," I confess, my voice barely a whisper. He stills, the weight of my words hanging in the air between us.

After a moment of silence, he finally speaks again. "What's on your mind, pretty girl?"

The ache to reveal everything to him hurts me, and I ponder opening up to him just a little bit. "My sister," I whisper, my eyes threatening to water. "I'm finding it hard being here. I can't settle because I know I need to find her."

"Well, where is she?" he asks, and I shrug my shoulders with a sniffle. "I don't know."

I can sense his confusion. "Do you want me to find her?"

My brows knit, and I turn my head until our eyes meet. As my gaze wanders over his painted face, I worry that any information I give him might lead him to Kyro.

"How could you do that when I don't even know where she is?" I lie. I could be sending him on a hunt for someone who is still in that vile man's hands, but I am almost tempted to let him because I am so fucking desperate.

"All I need is a name, Dolly." His warm breath kisses my lips as the words escape him.

"Arabella," I say without thinking straight, but he gives a simple nod. "Anything else?"

Unfortunately, there isn't anything else. I don't even know if she has the same last name as me. I don't know where she is from. Changing my mind and shutting down, I give a small headshake. "There isn't. Just don't worry about it, Hell. I'm sure I will find her one day," I declare while looking away. "Or maybe I have to accept I have lost her forever."

"I'll do what I can for you, Noir," he promises, and I smile softly.

"You lost someone close to you recently, right?"

When I feel his body tighten behind me, I warily turn my head until I am looking up at him again, and his eyes flash to mine.

"What happened?" I ask.

He inhales before responding, "He was killed."

As he faces aside, I can tell it's something that still bothers him, a wound that hasn't healed.

"Did you find who did it?" I question, and he shakes his head, his eyes not meeting mine. "No."

I can only imagine how it eats away at him, not getting revenge on someone who took something from him. Hell likes control. He likes answers. He is so straightforward and doesn't pretend to be something he isn't that he probably expects the same in return. Mixing his cousin's murder with him knowing I am holding secrets; I can only imagine it's driving him insane, and I feel so guilty for it.

If I don't leave this place, and I choose to stay with him, I can only hope that one day, I will find the confidence to open up to him. I lift my hand, bringing it to his cheek, turning him to face me. As I glance at his lips, he dips down, crashing them against mine. His hand finds my throat as he devours my mouth, making my feelings for him grow stronger with each stroke of his tongue. He tastes like sin, a toxic pleasure that I can't resist. He is a drug, potent and addictive. I can't get e-fucking-nough.

When his other hand trails down the front of my body, I moan into his mouth, the sound swallowed by his feral kiss. As soon as he reaches my jeans, he flicks open the button, dragging down the zipper. Without hesitation, he slides his big, warm hand down into my panties. My stomach somersaults from the sensation as his fingers press firmly between my pussy lips, rubbing from my entrance up to my clit repeatedly and roughly. His fingers are so fucking skilled, knowing exactly how to drive me wild.

When he suddenly stops, he tears his lips away from mine, leaving me breathless and tingling. "I don't know about you, but I need a violent fucking. I'm taking you home to absolutely shatter that perfect cunt in a way it deserves," he growls against my lips.

With a swift motion, he pulls his hand out of my panties, the sudden absence of his touch leaving me aching for more, but I don't argue. I allow him to pull me away from the horse, my legs still trembling and his grip on my hand is firm, and possessive, as he drags me back home.

CHAPTER TWENTY-ONE

TWO YEARS AGO....

I sit huddled against the wall; my naked body smeared with blood. Closing my watery eyes, I lean my head back, wrapping my arms around my legs and holding them close to my bare chest. As I sniffle, the metallic tang of blood fills my mouth, a taste I've grown accustomed to after enduring ten years of violent abuse. I wipe my possibly broken nose with the back of my hand, my mind growing hazy, likely from yet another concussion.

Suddenly, a distant whisper reaches my ears, and I slowly open my eyes. "Are you okay? I heard what they were doing to you." I rest my chin on my knees in silence as she continues. "We need to get out of here. It will only get worse when he gets what he wants."

I glance down at the shackle that is attached to my ankle, as it is most of the time. "It's no use, Ara. We've been trying for months now, and we need to accept that there is no escaping him." I murmur back.

"Pull on the chain. I have been doing it for the past week now and the bracket on the wall is coming loose." She says with determination and my eyes follow the thick, silver chain until they land on the heavy metal bracket that is screwed tightly in the solid wall. I brim with tears, feeling like giving up already and I throw my head back, my eyes closed. "I am just ready to die, Ara. I'm sorry."

Suddenly she shouts at me in a demonic voice that pierces close to my ears, thumping my brain. "Fuck that! We're getting out of here!"

PRESENT TIME . . .

Tomorrow night marks another Circus performance, and Hell has had me in vigorous training so I can perform for the first time as the Hollow's girl. I'll be dancing and performing with him on the wheel of death, along with other terrifying stunts. To say I am not nervous would be an understatement, but in a way, being around him this much and with the training, it has taken my mind off things. When I am with Hell, he seems to calm my crazed thoughts. Despite them shouting at me to do horrendous things when he isn't around, they go silent when he is.

The more I get to know him, the more I find myself entangled by feelings I never knew existed within me. It's an intensity that steals my breath, but only in the most powerful way. He makes me feel like the most beautiful woman in the world. His touch is an enigma, both rough and tender, igniting my veins like an addictive drug. But I've noticed his growing curiosity, the way he asks more and more questions, as if he senses I am hiding things, and he wants to decipher the darkness I don't show. It's clear I am confusing him.

As always, reluctance takes over, and I shut down. What's the point in telling him everything that has happened? What could he do? I'd rather he remain in the dark, so I don't have to relive it all over again.

I worry his view of me could change, that he'll treat me like a fragile doll instead of the woman I am. I want him to stay true to himself, to continue being the brutal man I've grown obsessed with.

Yeah, it would be nice to talk in him, to share my burdens, but it would change so much between us. The dynamic we have would be altered, and I don't want that. I need him to see me as strong, as resilient. Telling him everything could strip that away, and I just can't bear the thought of it.

As I flip and dance on the death wheel, I feel his heated stare on me from below, seated in the front row, beer in hand, barking out orders now and then. This circus isn't for the faint-hearted, and I know it will take time to get used to it, but right now, I am also torn between staying, hoping to blend into the shadows, or leaving altogether and that decision cripples me.

"Straighten your back!" he yells from a distance.

I halt, slowing the wheel, breathing heavily, my lungs starving for oxygen. Hell is a tough fucking trainer; he is a perfectionist. After swiping my sweaty brow with the back of my arm, I place my hands on my hips and stare down at him. Tilting his head back, he takes a big swig of his beer, his eyes locked on mine, then lowers the bottle. Leaning forward, he hooks his finger at me to come down. I take a deep breath, somewhat relieved he's giving me a break.

As the wheel descends, I jump, my muscles aching, and then stroll toward him through the empty tent. It's just us. It's late, it's silent and the lights are dim. I take my hair tie from my wrists and gather my sweaty hair before creating a messy bun atop my head.

I stop in front of him, behind the barrier as he sits back, legs spread wide and shirtless. His devious eyes rake down my body with a wicked intensity, taking in the silky, black bodysuit that sits high on my hips, wedging up my ass, and the black fishnets covering my legs down to my knee-high, platformed boots. When his gaze meets mine, his lips lift into a devilish sneer.

"Dance for me, pretty girl."

I tilt my head to the side, and he waits patiently, never breaking eye contact. "There's no music," I say.

He lifts a brow, "Use your imagination and let your beautiful body flow."

With his forearms resting on his thighs, he points to the floor between his legs. "Here," he demands through tight teeth.

He wants a private show, and I have a feeling it won't end there. His entire demeanor tells me he is seeking some form of dominance. I don't know Hell well, yet, but I know him well enough to sense when he is eager to rearrange my organs, which is often. I let out a tense breath before walking around the barrier and passing all the front-row seats. I halt between his legs, freeing my hair as he rests back lazily.

When I think of a tune in my head, I allow my body to move to the music. I dance slowly, sensually, letting my hips sway and my arms trace patterns in the air. His eyes follow every movement, a predatory gleam in them and the sexual tension between us thickens.

I arch my back, letting my hair cascade down, my body bending and twisting to the rhythm. He drinks in every curve and motion as he drinks his beer, every part of me, he devours.

The imaginary music takes complete possession of me, and I swiftly turn, lowering myself onto his lap. I roll my neck before laying my back against his powerful chest. I rotate my hips, pressing my ass against his cock, my hands tight on his thighs. I feel and hear him inhale deeply, gradually losing control. I place my palm on the side of his tattooed neck, continuing to grind against him. He gazes down at my moving body, sweeping his palms up the front of me, but when I turn my face to the side, he follows, forcing our lips so close they lightly brush, sending electricity through me.

Maintaining eye contact, I bring my lips closer to his, taking his bottom lip between my teeth, sinking them in before sucking and dragging back. A deep growl escapes him and when I release, I push myself off him, whirling around.

I bend forward, resting my hands on his broad shoulders, and lift one leg, then the other, descending my pussy onto his clothed cock. I feel it strengthening beneath me as I flex my body back and forth like I am riding a wave. His eyes darken as I continue to buck my hips, wrapping my arms loosely around the back of his neck and flinging my head back.

He reaches up, flicking my hair over my shoulders casually before pulling the zipper down the front of my bodysuit. He stretches it, freeing my tits as expected. He glides his palm up and between my breasts before taking my throat, keeping my head tilted back, while his other hand squeezes my ass.

I continue to grind down on his hard length, the friction and heat between us building and his grip tightens, a primal need evident in his touch. The room feels charged; every sensation amplified.

As soon as he has had enough of the teasing, although it's his own fault for asking, he suddenly grabs the back of my hair, tugging it back. Then, leans forward and I instinctively wrap my legs around his waist as he stands.

HOLLOW HELLION

Soon, we enter a room somewhere within the circus, and my ass is dropped onto a table. He releases my hair, grabbing my jaw firmly, and his lips collide with mine. We kiss savagely, my hands moving up his firm torso, and he squeezes my ass, dragging me forcefully closer to him. He stretches my bodysuit over my shoulders, roughly ripping it down my body until it's on my hips. His big hands find my tits, groping them bruisingly, setting my body on fire. I gasp against his lips, my arm wrapped around his toned shoulders, arching closer to him.

Our movements are frantic, unable to stop ourselves as our bodies crave each other's touch. His breath is uneven against my lips as I claw at his back, feeling the powerful muscles flex beneath my fingertips.

"Fuck, I can't get enough of you. Just when I thought I had reached the depths of my fucking madness, you appeared, plunging me further into insanity." he snarls before completely pulling me away from the table again.

He walks a few steps before lowering me to my feet, our lips never leaving one another's. He suddenly snatches my throat, pushing me back until I crash against something at a slight angle. His hard body presses against mine, and my thighs part wider to let him grind against me. He grabs my wrist, lifting it until I feel something metal lock over it. I break away from the feral kiss abruptly, looking up to see my arm stretched and shackled. Before I can confront him, he takes the other, doing the same thing and my eyes flash to him, confused.

Realizing he has bound me to the swirling wheel, I stare at him in bewilderment. A small smirk twitches on his lips. "Do you trust me, Little Dolly?" he murmurs, a brow arched.

Still trying to catch my breath from sheer arousal, I give a small nod. "Yes," I manage to say.

Without hesitation, he steps back, tearing the rest of my bodysuit off me and tossing it aside, leaving me in just my fishnets, panties, and boots. He lifts the bottom of the wheel, tilting me further back. Then, he takes each of my legs, splitting them and buckling leather straps over them, locking me in place.

Hell steps back, his eyes roaming over my body with a mixture of lust and possession. His smirk deepens, letting his fingers trace lightly over my exposed skin, sending shivers through me. "You always look so pretty like this," he mutters, his voice dripping with dark satisfaction. "Bound, helpless, and all fucking mine to violate."

As his face grows more serious, he flicks out his knife, extending his hand to place it firmly against my throat. I raise my chin, our eyes locked in an unbroken stare. Slowly, he glides the blade down my neck, chest, over the curve of my breast, and stomach, sending tingles across my skin and stiffening my nipples.

When he presses the knife against my pussy, my breath hitches, and he glances down, hooking it between the strands of my fishnets. One by one, he cuts through the gaps, creating a larger hole.

As soon as he has access, he slips the blade beneath my panties at an angle, the cold metal threatening to slice my tender lips. With a swift movement, he cuts through the fabric like butter, but when he becomes dissatisfied, he reaches out, ripping the remnants from my body. His eyes lock onto mine, and with gentleness, he glides the knife between my slick folds. My breath gets caught in my throat, eyes widening.

When he withdraws, the blade glistens with wetness and he lifts it to his lips, dragging his tongue along the metal, his eyes closed and a soft moan escapes him, savouring my taste as if I am the most delicious thing that has ever graced his taste buds. My body responds to his danger, my core tightening with hunger, the ache for him to fuck me into oblivion unbearable.

"Hell, please..." I beg, my voice trembling with desperation.

His eyes, dark and swirling, snap open in an eerie manner, instantly colliding with mine.

He studies me, then shakes his head slowly, a wicked smile playing on his lips. "Only if you're a good girl for me."

He turns away, his muscles rippling beneath his tattooed skin as he strides past the circus props, fingers lightly grazing over them as he contemplates. He stops and gathers three small, gleaming axes. I start to hyperventilate, each heartbeat louder than the last.

Suddenly, he storms back toward me, gripping the wheel and spinning it with force. I scream, the world blurring into a whirl of colours and through my disoriented vision, I see him step back, raising an axe.

"Hell!" I yell, my voice cracking with panic.

He ignores my plea, swinging his arm with power. The axe embeds itself with a solid thump into the wood between my legs, the rush of air kissing my exposed pussy. My thighs clench involuntarily, terror coursing through me.

A sinister chuckle escapes his lips as he launches another axe, the blade whistling past my head. I scream again, my hysteria echoing through the small room. The final axe lands with deadly accuracy beside my right breast, and I sag in relief, my breath coming in gasps for air. He approaches and stops the wheel abruptly. As I hang upright, my vision clears, and I fix him with a harsh glare, my mind still reeling.

"You fucking asshole!" I shout, trembling with outrage.

He bites his bottom lip, his eyes glittering with dark amusement, "I thought you trusted me?" he says while tilting his head to the side.

"It's hard to trust you when you don't tell me what you're going to do next. I need to be prepared," I reply, still panting.

He reaches up, softly brushing a strand of hair from my lashes. "Oh, my Little Dolly. When have I ever told you what the fuck I'm going to do next? Where's the fun in that?" His mouth hovers close to mine. "The more I fucking scare you, the wetter your precious cunt gets for me."

He drops to his knees suddenly and leans in with a predatory hunger. I watch as his tongue snakes out, tracing a slow, firm path up the slit of my pussy. Then, as if a switch flips, he becomes feral, devouring me with a greedy hunger. His mouth works so desperately that the sensation makes my muscles tense, and my moans fill the air as I close my eyes, lost in the overwhelming pleasure.

Suddenly, I feel the sharp edge of his blade on my pubic area and my eyes snap open, looking down at him. While sucking on my clit with a strength that borders on madness, the knife pierces deeply into my skin. I hiss, my eyes squeezing shut as I throw my head back. The blend of pain and pleasure is beautiful, and I pant heavily as he slowly carves into my skin.

When he seems to be finished, I look down at him once more through a daze, seeing my blood streaking down onto his painted face while he mauls my pussy violently. The word "HELL" is engraved into my skin, a claim of ownership. I want to say something, to yell at him for fucking branding me, but I can't. The way he eats my come and blood has screams ripping from my fucking throat continuously. His disgusting, depraved actions always turn me on in ways that should not be possible. In this very moment, I am in fact, entirely his and I'd proudly admit that.

Without warning, he withdraws, grabbing the bottom of the wheel and rotating me until I am hanging upside down. The world tilts, my pulse-pounding, as he unbuckles his belt, the metallic clink echoing in the room. He drags his zipper down and his hand disappears into his boxers before he frees his heavy, throbbing cock. He rubs the pierced tip over my lips, and I part them eagerly, my breath hitching as he growls, shoving himself deep into my throat.

As he begins to fuck my mouth with a slow, relentless rhythm, he lowers his head between my thighs, his tongue lashing out to eat my pussy with the same ferocity. Pressure rushes to my head as his thrusts grow stronger, ramming himself inside, and making me gag repeatedly. I feel my warm blood slowly streaking down my stomach from the wound as he gnaws on my clit, until he pulls back, leaving me swollen and pulsing for relief.

I notice him reach for a juggling pin beside him and then lift it. As he presses it against my wet entrance, my legs tense, and I try to speak around his cock, but he doesn't stop, of course. His thrusts in my mouth become rough, each one a punishing stroke, shutting me up as he eases the juggling pin inside my slippery pussy. The stretch is intense, a delicious agony, and he snarls, pushing slow and deep, each time pressing the pin further inside me. He fucks my face and screws my pussy with the pin, "Such greedy fucking holes," he bites out with frustration, showing how much he is enjoying his depravity.

Saliva, blood and come drip from me, mingling in a slick mess, and his movements grow savage. When I climax around the pin, my body convulses, and he slows down in my mouth, my loud cry vibrating around his cock, sending shivers through him.

He pulls the pin out, the sensation leaving me aching and empty, then drags his dick from my mouth, each of his piercings running across my tingling tongue. With a sudden spin, he turns me upright. As I gather my senses, I feel him unbuckling my legs, leaving me suspended by my arms. He stands, his menacing gaze trailing a heated path over my body, soaking in every inch until he is looming over me. He dips down, capturing my mouth with his in a savage kiss, our tongues battling with a fierce hunger.

Suddenly, he grabs me by the back of my thighs, lifting me with ease and wrapping my legs around his waist. Without breaking the kiss, he sinks his cock into my dripping pussy, the sensation causing me to moan loudly against his lips. He starts to fuck me with a harsh pace, his strong, ripped arms rising above us to grip the wheel for more leverage.

Each thrust is powerful and deep, spreading my legs wider beside him. My tits bounce against his chest, his breath warm against my lips, cut off by occasional kisses. When he starts to pound me into the wood, each stroke drives me closer to the edge, making me scream in ecstasy.

With one final, strong drive, he cum's inside me, the sensation making me come at the same time. My body shudders violently as we ride out the waves of our shared climax, his cock pulsing deep within me.

I rest my forehead against his shoulder, my body spent as his slows to a halt. He reaches over and releases each of my wrists, the restraints falling away with a small clink.

"Never trust me when it concerns me fucking you, but anything else, pretty girl, I've got you." He murmurs through heavy breaths before placing a hard kiss on the side of my head.

He lifts me further up his body effortlessly, my legs still wrapped around his waist, and I cling to him as he takes me toward the exit. As we leave the room, he throws a thick blanket over my almost naked body, and I snuggle against him.

CHAPTER TWENTY-TWO

It's the night of the circus performance, and I am getting ready in the changing rooms beside Blush, both of us applying our makeup.

"So, the little weasel just left without saying a thing?" she questions about Eli, her voice a tone of shock. I side-eye her, my lips curling into a wry smile as I lean forward, carefully drawing the cracks around my eyes.

"That's right."

"You're staying with Hell now, huh?" she probes.

I sit back, dipping the brush into the paint as I ponder her question. "Yeah, I am," I admit, the words feeling heavier than they should.

"And he's being nice?"

I pause, meeting her gaze, and we both burst out laughing, the sound echoing off the walls. "Yeah, real fucking nice. My pussy hasn't been the same since," I say through a chuckle.

As the laughter dies down, I find myself thinking about Hell. Despite his insanity, there's a strange kindness in the way he treats me, and I can't fault him for how he is with me. He may be rough and completely unhinged, but it almost seems like he cares.

"You know, he actually treats me alright," I say, my eyes lowering as I speak. Blush smiles, nudging my upper arm with hers.

"Is Noir in love?" she teases, her eyes sparkling with mischief.

I turn my head to look at her, my face expressionless. "I wouldn't even know what love felt like," I respond, the words tasting unfamiliar on my tongue.

She nods in understanding, her gaze shifting to her reflection. "Well, I've heard it's when you feel things you've never felt before, an intense pull, as if you've known that person your entire life and everything flows between you effortlessly."

I think about her words, a sigh escaping my lips as I look ahead. Why does that description match everything I feel?

"Also, the thought of losing them shatters your heart into a million pieces. That's a big one," she continues, her voice softening.

I inhale deeply, leaning closer to the mirror, my breath fogging the glass. "I haven't known him long," I mutter.

"So fucking what. When you know, you know. There's no fighting it, it just happens. Time doesn't mean shit," she responds firmly.

Suddenly, there's a tap on my shoulder, and I pause, my heart skipping a beat. I turn to see Madame and Soul standing there, their presence commanding the room. I glance between them, my confusion clear, until Madame speaks.

"There's a slight change in the performance tonight, Noir," she says, her tone calm but firm. I furrow my brow, confused, and she continues, "Hell has been called away to something important, so he won't be here for the show."

I inhale deeply, the weight of her words sinking in, and I drop the paintbrush, thinking that my performance might be cancelled.

"So, instead, you will perform with Soul," she announces, her eyes shifting to him. I meet his gaze, his green swirling eyes locking onto mine as he gives me a big, wicked smile. I've been with Hell for a while now, but it seems I barely see Soul or Wrath. I'm still not sure who or what either of them are, but I'm certain I'll find out in time.

"Everything will still be the same. Soul knows the routine," she explains. "So the dance on the death wheel and the finale kiss will go ahead as planned."

When she turns to leave, I stand abruptly, my voice tinged with panic. "Will Hell be okay with that?" I ask, knowing how possessive he can be.

She turns back to face me, a smile playing on her lips. "Noir, you work for me," she asserts, her authority unmistakable.

I glance at Soul when he chuckles, his laughter deep and intimidating. "It's okay, Noir, I don't bite," he says, suddenly sticking out his tongue. It's split, with two piercings on either side, and my head jerks back, my eyes wide with shock. "I fucking lick." He winks with a big grin, and I shake my head once, my gaze meeting Madame's.

"What the fuck is that?" I exclaim, my tone mixed with disbelief and curiosity.

"Baby, that's my fucking weapon," he responds.

Madame rolls her lips inward, suppressing a smile, before turning around and leaving me stunned, with Soul trailing behind her.

Once they're gone, I slump back into my seat with a heavy sigh. "Hell is NOT going to like this," I say to Blush beside me, my voice filled with dread.

CHAPTER TWENTY-THREE

As I enter the nightclub on the outskirts of town, I raise my chin in a silent gesture, and the bouncers let me through without a second glance. A cigarette dangles from my lips, the hood of my leather jacket pulled up, casting shadows over my face as I travel through the bustling crowd. Eagerness courses through my veins; this is the first lead I've had since my cousin's death, the first phone call telling me where she might be.

Apparently, she's here with some fucking guy. My plan is simple: kill him if I need too and kidnap her. I have to take her to my uncle, but my instincts scream to slice her throat and be done with it. This past year has been consumed with trying to find her. Whoever the fuck she is, she knows how to hide, which raises my suspicion that I might be dealing with a hit-woman who will put up a fight. I don't usually fight or kill women, but this one is different. Family is fucking family, and she will die for what she has done.

As I head for the bar, the bass from the music pounds in my ears, a relentless thump that matches the anger in my chest. Although I work and live at a circus and carnival, which is pretty busy most days of the week, there is nothing I hate more than stepping out of those grounds I call home to come to shithole places like this.

While ordering my drink, my phone vibrates in my pocket. I retrieve it and glance down at the lit-up screen. Seeing it's my uncle, I answer and hold the phone close to my ear. "Yeah?"

"She's in the VIP section," he states calmly.

I turn around, my eyes scanning over the sea of people until they land on a dimly lit corner on the other side of the enormous space. A small area is cornered off, and I squint to see a few people seated there. One of them is a young woman with long, straight dark hair cascading down to her hips. She's wearing a short white dress that hugs her petite frame, and she's sitting on a guy's lap, sipping a drink. From here, I can't confirm if she's the girl in the picture or not.

"Are you sure it's her?" I ask, not wanting to kidnap the wrong girl.

"Yeah, it's her. It's Harley," he answers unwaveringly.

"Are you fucking sure?"

"Yes, Hell. Now bring her to me." He hangs up like the rude motherfucker he is.

I keep my angry eyes locked on her as I snatch the beer off the bar, taking a long, bitter swig. I despise my uncle. If he weren't family, I would have hacked his head off his fucking shoulders already, but luckily for him, he is. He's an obnoxious cunt who thinks the world owes him a favour, living his luxury life in his mansion while he dictates to criminals who hate him as much as I do. He is the reason I am the monster I am today and no; I'm not fucking thankful for it.

My gaze remains fixed on her until I see her getting up. I straighten, lowering my beer onto the bar, tracking her every move as she heads in the direction of the restrooms. This is my opportunity.

I creep through the crowd and once I reach the door, I push it open with a force that sends it swinging. I spot her not too far ahead, talking to another girl. I slow my pace, lowering my head, concealing myself behind people in the busy corridor. When she finishes her conversation, she continues forward. As I draw nearer, she suddenly glances over her shoulder and as soon as her blue eyes meet mine, I'm certain it's her. Her gaze widens in recognition before she starts walking quicker. I fasten my pace, shoving people out of the way to get to her. I flick my blade out, the metallic click causing some women to scream, but I remain unfazed. She looks back again, noticing the knife in my hand, and attempts to run in her tall heels. I close the distance until she dashes into the women's restrooms.

As soon as I'm close enough, I smash open the door without hesitation. The girls inside scream at my unsettling presence, their shrieks echoing off the tiled walls. My gaze sweeps across the room as they run past me to escape. When I don't see her, I know she's hiding in one of the cubicles. As the room empties, I use my foot to boot the doors open, one by one, each crash reverberating through the restroom.

As soon as I hear a noise a few doors down, I walk toward it with deliberate steps before smashing my foot against the door. It swings open with a resounding crash, and I see her perched on the toilet seat, shivering in fear. Her blue eyes are wide and brimming with tears.

"Please don't hurt me, mister," she pleads, her voice trembling.

A growl of anger rumbles from deep within me as I storm forward, my patience worn thin. I don't waste a second hesitating, and I grab her roughly, throwing her over my shoulder in one swift motion. Her small frame feels fragile against my solid build, but I ignore the pang of guilt that tries bubble inside me.

As I stride down the hallway with her, she screams for help, her struggles against me frantic and desperate. But her cries blur into the background noise of the nightclub. My focus remains unyielding, my grip on her tightening. Her fists pound against my back, her nails clawing at my jacket, but I remain unfazed as each step brings me closer to the exit.

ᚼᛟᛚᛚᛟᚹ ᚼᛖᛚᛚᛁᛟᚾ

After hurling her into the trunk of my car, I finally arrive at the destination and turn off the engine. As she screams, I draw a deep breath. What the fuck is wrong with me, just do it. Pushing past my doubts, I open the door and step out, heading for the back of the car. I flick out my blade before popping open the trunk and she now lies still, her gaze wide and petrified.

I take a step back and calmly lift my fingers, "Get the fuck out." I order, calmly.

"Are you going to rape me? Please don't rape me." She whispers through sobs.

My jaw tightens, but I don't give her an answer, I give another gesture. "Get the fuck out or I'll get you out."

Gathering herself, she slowly sits up with hesitation before she finally jumps out of the trunk. When she attempts to run, I snatch her upper arm and drag her back toward me with force, making my knife be known.

"Stop fucking with me, Harley." I grit out with anger, and she looks up at me, "Harley? I'm not Harley, I'm Star."

I lift a brow with a growl and push her forward, "Yeah fucking right."

"I mean it, mister. You have the wrong girl!"

"Shut. The. Fuck. Up." I bite out viciously before turning around quickly and point the knife in her face. "I will fucking kill you!"

She swallows hard at my sinister threat, her lips clamping shut as her mascara runs down her cheeks. Once I'm satisfied that she's taking this seriously, I continue to pull her toward my uncle's mansion, her resistance now stopped.

When entering, I drag her inside with me, immediately spotting my uncle with his back to us, engaged in conversation with a man I don't recognize. He turns at the sound of our entrance, his eyes instantly locking onto the whimpering girl beside me. I take a moment to size him up—wearing his usual gray tight pants, polished shoes, and a half-buttoned white shirt with the sleeves rolled up. My uncle looks nothing like me; he's far shorter but a bit broader. The only similarity is our black hair.

He takes calculated steps forward as we stop in the middle of the huge, gleaming white foyer. When he halts, his eyes never leave her. With her head bowed, she avoids his intense gaze, but I can feel her body shaking beneath my grip on her upper arm. He reaches out and snatches her face, forcing her to look up at him. Their eyes meet, and he just stares at her, a silent tension crackling in the air. I glance between them, impatience gnawing at me.

"Well, is it fucking her?" I ask, annoyance buzzing through me.

He pushes her face away roughly with a growl, and she sobs, lowering her head in defeat.

"No, it's not," he finally answers, seething with frustration.

I inhale deeply, pissed off at the realization that I now have to take this random chick back to where I found her after thoroughly petrifying her. As I turn to leave, his hand clamps down on my shoulder, stopping me in my tracks. My eyes drop to it before meeting his gaze. His eyes drag up and down her body as he takes a step back, a wicked hunger lingering in his expression.

"Leave her with me," he says, his tone dripping with malice.

I narrow my eyes at him, my voice a low growl. "Get fucked." His eyebrow arches in response, a silent challenge.

"You had me kidnap this chick because you don't know the fucking difference between her and the cunt that killed your son?" I spit out, my anger barely contained. His jaw tightens, the muscle in his cheek flexing as he folds his arms across his chest.

"I am taking her back," I say firmly, my voice brooking no argument. "I'm not leaving her with you, motherfucker, for you to traumatize her even more."

He raises his chin, his eyes scanning mine with a cold, calculating gaze. "I would be very careful who the fuck you're talking to, Hell," he says, his threat delivered with a chilling calmness that should mean something, but it doesn't fucking faze me.

I take a step forward, overshadowing him, bringing my face close to his. "Stop fucking with me, you old fuck. I don't give a flying shit who you are, and you fucking know it." My teeth clench with each word.

We stand there, locked in a silent battle of dominance, murder gleaming in both our eyes. "You have no authority over me, remember that. I may have given a shit about Haze, and that's why I'm doing this, but you…" My eyes rake down his form in disgust. "I wouldn't fucking piss on you if you were on fire, Unc's," I snarl.

With that, I tear my gaze away, turning around and forcing the girl to follow my lead. I can feel his eyes burning into my back, but I don't look. My focus is now on getting her out of here, and away from his twisted grasp.

CHAPTER TWENTY-FOUR

Once I return home, still reeling from tonight's events, I can't shake the anger boiling inside me. That cunt must be stupid, why send me somewhere when you don't know for a fucking fact it's her? The sheer recklessness of it all gnaws at me. It's not how I operate. That could have gone so wrong. If I had been out of control, I could have killed her.

As soon as we find the right girl, I'll be glad not to see his face ever again. My fists clench and unclench as I enter the back passageway of the circus, the urge to punch something almost overwhelming. The memory of her terrified eyes, the way she trembled, it all plays on a loop in my mind. I could have ended an innocent life tonight because of his foolishness.

I stride into the main tent as the acts are in full swing. The lights flash intensely around the ringside, but when my gaze lands on the death wheel, I halt at the threshold. I observe Soul and Noir performing together in one of the rotating rings, much like Pearl and I used to do. I tilt my head to the side, watching as their bodies move in perfect sync. Knowing it's the finale, I keep my eyes locked on them. When the wheel stops, Noir jumps, wrapping her legs around

Soul's waist and as he catches her, his fingers dig into the back of her thighs.

My brow lifts until, suddenly, they kiss, and my jaw tenses instantly. A wave of possessiveness surges through me, ready to unleash chaos. The crowd roars and my fists tighten, while Soul grips the back of her neck, devouring her mouth with ferocity. I hold onto my anger, waiting until they're finished.

When they finally break away, I see her eyes wide with shock—not expecting how his tongue felt, I suppose. This only brings me great pleasure that she didn't like it, because now, I'm going to do something that will fuck with both of them.

I turn around and head outside, waiting in the shadows by the back exit of the tent. When I finally hear the usual group walk out and past me, I fixate on Noir with an intense gaze before pouncing. Creeping up behind her, she somehow senses me and spins around, but it's too late. I lift her by her waist effortlessly and hurl her over my shoulder. A scream escapes her before her breathing quickens.

As I start to head toward our trailer, I shoot an angry glare at Soul and make a head gesture for him to follow me. He rolls his eyes, knowing I'm about to give them both hell, but he does as he's told regardless.

HOLLOW HELLION

Entering, Noir starts to struggle against me, clearly picking up on my pissed-off demeanor. I smack her ass hard, causing her to shriek.

"Shut the fuck up, you little slut," I seethe through clenched teeth.

I release her onto the table, her back slamming against it with a hard thud. I grab the small part of her waist, roughly yanking her down to the edge, her legs splitting wide to accommodate me between them. "You want to kiss my fucking brother like that, huh?" I grit out angrily.

She shakes her head frantically, her eyes expanding. "No, Madame said it's part of the act, I—." She protests breathlessly, "It didn't mean anything, Hell."

Of course, it fucking didn't, but I am a nasty, sick motherfuck who likes to see fear in her eyes, but there is nothing more I like to see than her being degraded.

When I hear Soul pull out a chair behind me, I side-eye over my shoulder as he takes a lazy seat, his back resting against the wall while he watches us from across the small kitchen.

My eyes then dart in an eerie manner to Noir beneath me, watching her chest heave with rapid, panicked breaths and my fingers find the hooks on the front of her corset.

When she reaches out to stop me, I grip her throat hard without warning, squeezing until her breath becomes restricted.

"Want to act like a fucking slut? You'll be treated like one," I growl, my tone drenched with dominance.

Her black pointed nails dig into my hand, desperately clawing for release, but I remain unbothered. Carefully, I unhook her corset one clasp at a time, my movements unhurried. Her face deepens to a purplish hue, but I wait until the final hook is undone before releasing my grip.

She gasps for air, her body shuddering as colour floods back into her cheeks. Seizing the moment in her vulnerability, I gently peel open her corset, exposing each of her perfect tits. Leaning in close, I let my breath ghost over her lips. "Stop fucking with me, Noir. You know what the fuck I am. I will kill you both," I hiss.

She stays silent, her jaw set tight, still fighting for air as I draw back and reach between her legs. Sliding my fingers into the gaps, with a harsh pull, I rip her fishnets into a single, gaping hole. My fingers sneak beneath her lace panties, and with one swift tug, I snap them, exposing her pretty cunt to me. I keep my eyes locked on hers, watching a myriad of emotions flicker across her face.

She shakes her head once, glancing down at Soul behind me. "But—"

I give her no chance to continue, dipping my head between her thighs. I place a soft kiss on my name carved into her skin, reminding who owns her before flattening my pierced tongue against her and tracing a slow path up the slit of her pussy. She gasps loudly, her head tilting back as her legs cradle my head. My palms glide over her inner thighs before I violently force them wide apart until they are pressed against the table and start eating her out aggressively, my mouth devouring her with a ferocious intensity.

Her legs shudder as I dip in and out of her pussy hole, then glide up to gnaw and bite at her clit. She can never hold her moans when I touch her, each sound she makes igniting a fire within me, my cock already swelling and dripping in my pants.

Digging my fingers deeper into her thighs with a possessive growl, she reaches down, taking handfuls of my curly hair, completely surrendering to the situation as always, encouraging me to continue.

I feast on her pussy like she is my favourite fucking meal because she is, and when she is throbbing for release, I draw back, my gaze lingering on her soaked, swollen cunt before I spit directly into her little leaking hole.

Gradually standing, my darkened eyes trail up the center of her body, relishing every inch of her. As she struggles to compose herself, I snatch her wrist and yank her upright. Gripping the back of her hair, I forcefully turn her around and bend her over the table, her face slamming against the wood with a thud.

"Hell!" she shouts followed by a groan.

I wrap her hair tightly around my fist, ensuring she keeps her head down as I swiftly release my belt buckle.

"You're not seriously going to fuck me in front of him, are you?" she gasps, her voice trembling with a mixture of fear and arousal as she squirms beneath me.

Ignoring her protest, I plunge my hand into my boxers, feeling the pulsating heat of my hard dick. With a rough motion, I pull it out, revealing myself. As I slide the tip up her pussy, I sense the involuntary shudder that courses through her body.

"Hell, I—" she pleads before I press her head down further, cutting her off with an aggressive snarl. "I swear, Dolly, shut the fuck up."

Positioning myself on her soaked hole, I slide into her in one swift, brutal movement, hitting her cervix instantly, eliciting a scream from her lips as her pussy clenches around me. I groan at the sensation, my eyes growing heavy before tugging her hair back, forcing her to lift her head. My other hand slips beneath her thigh before I lift it and place it high on the table, holding it in place.

I waste no time banging into her cunt, driving myself as deep as I can with each rough penetration, determined to teach her a fucking lesson. Despite her cries, she succumbs to bliss within a matter of seconds, her pussy gripping me in a vice-like tightness.

But I don't stop; I ram my cock deeper, aggressively hammering into her until she cannot take any more, her peachy ass rippling and bouncing against my pelvis, her come smothering my balls with each powerful thrust.

After a relentless session of brutal fucking, I finally release inside her, my climax shaking me to the core. I pour my hot cum into her pussy with uncontrolled force, each pulse of ecstasy reverberating through my body. My legs almost give way, and as I loosen my grip on her hair, her head falls down, her cheek hitting the table from exhaustion.

Breathing heavily, I press my forehead against her sweaty back, my heart pounding like a drum. I kiss and bite her skin with fervor, lost in the primal intensity of the moment. I revel in the sensation of emptying myself inside her every damn time, consumed by the obsession of our connection.

As I come down from my high, my awareness sharpens, and I run my tongue up her spine, savouring the taste of her sweet and salty skin. I kiss her shoulder, my desire unabated.

Once I reach her ear, I speak low and breathlessly, "Such a good girl for me."

I lift myself but keep her leg in place as I gaze down noticing her eyes closed, trying to relegate her breathing.

Glancing back over my shoulder, I spot Soul still sitting there, his eyes fixed on Noir with a darkness that matches my own. When our gazes finally meet, he lifts a brow inquisitively.

"Was that my punishment, to watch you drill her?" he questions with a hint of amusement in his voice. "I wouldn't say that was much of a bad thing, Hell."

My teeth grind together in annoyance at his nonchalance before I take a step back and to the side, allowing my dick to slide out of her now cum-filled cunt, then tuck myself back into my boxers.

"No, Soul," I reply calmly. "You're going to be degraded tonight at my command as well."

I draw my wicked eyes away from his, peering down at her pussy, glistening with our shared moisture. I slowly, but firmly move my palm down the split of her ass until it is covering her, and I pull it back before giving her pussy a swift slap. She squeaks from the pain, her body jolting as she is brought back to reality, but still not fully recovered.

I slip my two fingers between her lips before fanning them out, revealing her exposed cunt hole to both me and Soul.

When I hear him take a deep breath as my juices ooze out of her, my gaze lifts to his and they instantly dart to mine.

"You're going to eat my cum out of her pussy." I grit out with bitterness.

Soul's expression changes, falling completely, realizing exactly what I meant by both of them being humiliated.

"You wanna touch my girl when I told you to stay the fuck away from her?" I stand tall, covering her wet pussy with my palm again. "The only time you will ever get the luxury of tasting this sweet cunt is when it's pumped full of my jizz."

His jaw flexes with irritation, knowing I am doing this because of his sexuality. In all honesty, this is not what I'm into, I'm a straight man and I don't share what's mine, but what I do enjoy is the fact they are both feeling uncomfortable by what I am doing here, just as I felt uncomfortable when he had his tongue down her fucking throat.

I'm on my deranged bullshit right now and they are both going to face the consequences of their actions. But I would only ever do something like this with Soul, one time only. No one else gets to touch my Dolly like this. He is lucky my bond with him runs deep or he would be dead already, my knife launched into his fucking skull.

He just sits there staring at me, unmoving until I make a head gesture. "Be a good boy and eat my cum out of my girl's pussy, Soul."

His eyes narrow. "Fuck you, Hell," he snaps back.

I raise my chin in response, unwilling to argue. Reluctantly, he stands with a heavy sigh, well aware he owes me for doing something so fucking stupid.

I watch his every move as he stalks toward us. When he is close enough, he lowers onto his knees behind her, and I remove my hand, revealing her to him. I shift my eyes to Noir, who still has her eyes closed, completely shattered from me screwing her so violently. Reaching over, I carefully move her blonde hair away from her sweaty face, a strange tenderness in the midst of this twisted act.

When Soul shoves his split tongue into her pussy, her eyes fly open, a loud gasp escaping her lips, "Holy, fuck!"

I snarl, pressing my hand down on her neck with a bruising grip. "Was that a fucking moan I heard from my brother licking your cunt?" I bite out the words, my tone edged with fury.

Her eyes roll back, her lids fluttering shut as she stutters a lie, "No. Never. I—"

I lean in, my voice a chilling, venomous whisper in her ear. "You better not come, you slut, or I swear, I will tear you apart."

She stays silent, but it doesn't matter. I'm going to do everything in my power to make her come. I want to make her feel dirty, to hate the fact she had her mouth on someone else that wasn't me. She won't do it ever again once I'm finished.

Keeping my hand on her neck, I stand upright again, my eyes locked down on Soul as he works his pierced, lizard tongue on Noir's pussy. I try to hold onto my jealousy and not murder him, because let's be real, this is my own fucking doing, but the point I'm trying to prove will be satisfying.

He twists and dips inside her, eating and sucking out her and my cum before he wedges her clit between the slit of his tongue, kneading it.

I have heard about what his tongue can do, and Noir's shaking legs betray her pleasure. Despite her best efforts, she is clearly suppressing the sounds she would usually make with everything she has.

The sight fuels my rage and determination. "You think you can resist, pretty girl?" I press down harder on her neck. "We'll see how long that fucking lasts."

I whip out my knife, suck, and spit on the handle before lowering it, slowly easing it into her asshole. She whimpers instantly, her body tensing as it slides down the inside of her tight walls, inch by inch until it is buried completely, hitting the base.

As I start to fuck her asshole in the same rhythm of Soul lapping at her pussy, her breathing picks up, but I can tell she's still holding on for dear life to not come.

"You bastard, you fucking bastard," she pants out between gasps.

My lips twitch into a sinister grin as I tangle my hand in her hair once again, pulling hard. As I twist and shove the handle in and out of her, her fists clench, but still, she resists. My frustration mounts, and with a rumble in my chest, I rip my knife out of her ass, splitting her cheeks before spitting on her puckered hole and forcing her leg down.

With my dick now rock hard again, I hop up on the table, lowering myself with my knees on either side of her ass.

I glance down behind me, locking eyes with Soul, and lift my chin in a signal. He nods in understanding, turning his body to work on her clit from underneath.

I flop out my cock, aligning with her little hole and as I start to press into her, she quickly reaches back to me, knowing I am pushing her to her limit. I snatch both her wrists, locking them tightly behind her back with one hand, and lean over, resting on my elbow beside her head.

As I continue to sink my dick inside, each piercing gradually entering one by one, she chokes back a scream. I breathe heavily into her ear with a taunting whisper. "You're not going to come, Little Dolly, are you?"

Her lips roll inward, eyes squeezed shut, but I catch the subtle shake of her head. "That's my good girl," I praise. "You know better than to come on my brother's face."

When I start to screw her precious opening, I feel her body stiffen beneath me. My eyes stay locked on her side profile, scanning every expression as she tries not to betray me. But as soon as I begin fucking her much harder, almost hitting her spine, her moans grow loud and untamed.

"Hell, I don't know if—" she screams out, her voice breaking.

I lift myself on one hand, still keeping her bound as I continue to pound into her tight hole. "Fucking hold it," I growl with a warning edge.

Her entire body shudders, her screams turning into desperate, frantic cries. I can feel her getting closer, her resistance weakening with every thrust.

"Don't you dare," I hiss, increasing my pace, smashing into her with full force, each movement calculated to push her right to the brink but not beyond.

"Please," she whimpers, barely able to breathe.

"Hold it," I command again, my grip on her wrists tightening, my strikes inhumane. I know she's fighting with everything she has left, and the tension is charged, her desperation feeding my sick, sadistic mind.

I lean down, my lips brushing against her ear, "You're mine, Noir. Don't ever forget that." I whisper harshly, feeling her body strain under my dominance, teetering on the edge of submission and release.

She continues to beg me, and while sensing my own climax building, my balls tightening, I aggressively grit out the word that she needs to hear. "Come."

Her orgasm crashes over her like a tidal wave instantly, her raw scream tearing through the trailer as she gushes all over Soul's face, the squirt of her come hitting the tiled floor.

Her asshole pulses around me, prompting me to slow down so I can feel it. I observe her little body rocked by the intense climax, spasming under me, and I sit back, keeping my eyes locked on her.

"Soul, get out," I bark the order, side-eyeing him as he rises to his feet, wiping her wetness off his face. Without meeting his gaze, he walks out, leaving Dolly and me alone.

I get off the table, sliding out of her before flipping her onto her back, grabbing her waist, and dragging her closer to the edge.

When I slip my dick back deep into her ass with one quick stroke, she shrieks in pain, but I simply lift her legs, placing them over my shoulders as I incline, bringing my mouth close to hers.

Her glazed-over eyes lock onto mine as she scans them as. As soon as I start fucking her ass again, she now doesn't hold onto her sounds, but I just continuously kiss her parted lips, allowing her cries to mingle with my breath. "Fucking say it, Noir," I whisper between kisses, "Tell me I own every part of you."

My hips slap against her ass with a persistent rhythm that echoes through the room. "Yes! I'm yours, Hell," she screams out, her voice a symphony of surrender.

I snarl before plunging my tongue into her mouth, and she responds by sucking hard on it, becoming lost in the moment between us.

I hammer into her vigorously until, with a final, hard thrust, I bust inside her, my entire body tingling. My cock swelling and twitching elicits one last satisfied moan from her throat.

As she lets go of my tongue, I rest my sweaty brow against hers, eyes closed, trying to catch my breath and gradually slow my movements.

When I pry open my eyelids, her blue orbs are already looking into mine. I study her face as I lower her legs from my shoulders and rest my forearms beside her head. Hovering over her, I give her a soft kiss on her lips, but she doesn't reciprocate.

I arch a brow, "Say whatever the fuck you need to say, Noir," I murmur, readying myself for her bullshit.

She tilts her head to the side, her eyes narrowing. "I always thought you were the possessive type, yet here you are, sharing me with your fucking friends," she states, confusion lacing her words. "Tell me, Hell, what did you actually get out of that?"

"You." I growl without hesitation, sliding one arm around the small of her back and the other hand beneath her thigh. She clings to me as I lift her with minimal effort, carrying her upstairs to my bedroom.

HOLLOW HELLION

When I enter, I kick the door shut behind me, taking her over to my bed. As I lay her down, I follow beside her, leaning over on one elbow while reaching for the black silk sheet. I pull it over us, then slip my palm up the back of her thigh, making her wrap her leg around me.

Slowly, I trace the tips of my fingers up and down her skin, feeling goosebumps scatter beneath my touch. Gazing down at her, she looks at me expectantly to follow on the conversation.

"I think we've established that I'm not exactly sane," I explain before continuing. "I don't think like a normal person would. Degradation is my thing. I thrive off it. I fucking love it. Anything immoral and sick pleases me."

Her eyes widen as she inhales deeply. "So, you're into threesomes now?" she asks.

I pull my head back, shaking it once. "No. I just liked seeing you both uncomfortable, just like I was when I saw you two making out. It's how my odd mind works. I'm a calculated motherfucker, and everything I do has its reasons, whether it's deranged or not, it makes perfect fucking sense to me."

Her heavy-lidded eyes trace a searing path up my chest as she glides her palm over it. "Hmm, how?"

When her gaze swings to mine, I draw my face closer to hers.

"Will you do it again, my Little Dolly?" I question, my breath skating over her plump lips.

She studies my swirling orbs before giving a small smile and a head shake. My jaw clenches, and I grab her ass cheek, yanking her harder against me, "Exactly."

"Just don't make a habit out of it," she exhales, her blue eyes flicking to my mouth, "I only want you, Hell."

My lips twitch, fighting a smirk, "Point proven."

Her gaze softens as she presses her fingers into the back of my hair, "Sometimes I don't think you're the monster you think you are, Hell." I just stare at her, my expression unreadable. "Yeah, you're a bit abnormal by society's standards, but who's to say the "normal" ones aren't the real crazies?" she protests, her tone carrying sincerity.

I grin slightly before looking down, "I wish I could tell you I'm not a monster, Noir, but I am. You know that and you don't need to try to find excuses for me."

When my eyes meet hers, she analyses every feature of my face with a tender intensity. "But you can be so gentle with me," she murmurs.

I lift a brow in question, "Can I?" I run my hand over her ass again, giving it a squeeze.

She continues with curiosity, "You can be. I have never met a monster who can switch like you can. You confuse me. I thought all monsters were pure evil toward everyone and everything."

I think about her words, delving into the depths of her gaze. "We are, but it seems monsters are not always monsters to the things they deeply want, Noir," I reply truthfully "Why would I push away the one thing I truly want to keep? I have never known the feeling of want before." Her hand pauses on the back of my hair, a silent acknowledgement of our shared understanding and I glide my palm up the curve of her body.

"I know sometimes what I am terrifies you, but even in the darkest depths, there's always a flicker of light that solely belongs to you. That's why I'm so fucking obsessed with you, pretty girl. You're the only person who has ever stirred something inside me other than darkness. And I am addicted to it." I confess, the words slipping out like a forbidden secret.

Smiling gently, she draws me down to her lips, "Point proven."

CHAPTER TWENTY-FIVE

Leaning against the headboard of my bed, I stare down at Dolly as she sleeps on my chest, her breathing soft and steady. As I become lost in my thoughts, I stroke her hair, the silky strands slipping through my tattooed fingers. The quiet is shattered when the door suddenly swings open and my eyes dart to Wrath as he stands at the threshold, not even fucking knocking. His gaze momentarily lingers on Noir before he looks at me, giving a silent head gesture for me to follow him.

As he leaves, I inhale deeply and when I sit forward, Dolly stirs, her eyes fluttering open. I lean down, giving her a kiss on her lips. "I'll be back," I murmur. Her eyes are barely open, but she nods before snuggling deeper into my pillow.

I close my bedroom door behind me, heading down the stairs until I spot Soul and Wrath in the kitchen. I look between them both suspiciously as I stride forward, pulling a chair out to sit opposite Wrath.

"I found out what's wrong with that fucking guy she was here with. I got this emailed to me last night," Soul says, his tone full of irritation. He sighs deeply, grabbing a file from the counter and tossing it onto the table in front of me.

"Eli Simmons, thirty-four from Florida," Soul continues. Opening the file, it reveals his mugshot, his eyes staring up at me from the page. As I read through the details, Soul's voice cuts through the silence once more.

"Nonce," he spits out the word with disgust, and my jaw tightens in response, sharply looking up at him.

"What?"

"He's a fucking paedophile, Hell. Got bailed out on a bond, but he absconded. Now he's on the run," Soul explains, his words fuelling the rage building inside me. I stand abruptly, the file slipping from my fingers and hitting the table with a thud.

"I'll fucking kill him," I growl through gritted teeth, my hands balling into fists at my sides.

"Kill who?" Dolly's gentle, sleepy voice interrupts the tension and my eyes close briefly as I lower my head. She approaches from behind and walks around my tense frame before stopping in front of me, her eyes drawn to the paperwork spread across the table.

My gaze can't help but linger on the black sheet that is wrapped around her, held tightly with one hand concealing her naked body beneath, before tracing all the scars on her body. When my eyes flicker to her side profile, she reaches out for the file, but I quickly snatch her wrist, stopping her and her blue gaze meets mine with a questioning look.

"Nobody," I tell the lie, my eyes boring into hers, worried about how she might take this. She pulls her wrist from my hand, confusion etched on her face.

"If it's nobody, then why can't I know?" she asks, raising an eyebrow, suspicion creeping into her voice. "It's not like we're not all murderers now, right?"

My teeth grind together, and I face aside. "Wrath, Soul, can you..." I trail off, but without needing to finish my sentence, they leave me and Dolly alone.

She stares down at the files, her fingers trembling slightly as she gently lifts a piece of paper. I examine her facial expressions as she reads, searching for any sign of recognition or shock.

When there is no shift, I speak. "It's Eli. Soul looked into him." Her eyes dart to mine, a flicker of confusion and concern in their depths. "I had a hunch he was strange from the get-go. I mean, who the fuck wouldn't get hard for a woman as beautiful as you?"

She tilts her head to the side before I continue, "He is currently on the run for a crime, Noir. A very bad crime."

"What?" she gasps, her eyes flashing back to the paperwork in front of her.

"He's a fucking paedophile."

As soon as I say the word, her face drains of all color, her eyes widening in horror. Her hand flies to her mouth, and she suddenly turns, bolting to the sink. She starts heaving violently into it, the sound echoing in the quiet room.

My brows knit together, concern washing over me, and I take slow steps forward. I gather her blonde hair as she throws up, sweat beading across her skin, her body quivering with each retch. I wait for her to finish, and when she does, she breathes heavily, wiping her mouth with the back of her shaking hand.

"That disgusting piece of..." she sobs quietly, her head lowered.

I reach for the back of her neck, my touch gentle but firm. "Come here."

When she stands, she crashes her face into my chest, her cries uncontrollable and I cradle my arms around her, placing my lips on her head, allowing her to let it all out. Her reaction confuses me. Yeah, it's sick, but anger was my first emotion, not throwing up and crying, but then again, she was fucking him, so maybe that's it. My mind is a mess as I try to figure her out. Noir is like a puzzle piece, and some of those pieces are hard to fit together. The end picture is never clear as you cut corners to try to slot them in.

"It's okay," I murmur.

She pulls back slightly, her eyes red and swollen, her face a mask of distress.

"How could I not see it?" she whispers, her voice breaking. "How could I be so blind?"

"This is not your fucking fault," I say firmly, lowering myself to her height, eyes locking.

She nods, but the guilt and shame in her gaze remains. I can see the weight of it bearing down on her, crushing her spirit. "I just... I feel so dirty," she admits.

"There is absolutely nothing dirty about you, Noir. You are fucking perfect," I assert sternly. "Don't ever turn this around on yourself. He is the fucking dirty one. How the fuck was you supposed to know?"

"I had a hunch when he was flirting with a young girl at the carnival, Hell. I should have listened to my fucking gut. I should of..." Tears streak down her cheeks as a sob builds in her throat again before she presses her face against my chest.

I sigh, drawing her closer to me, now knowing more than ever that I need to find and kill that dirty cunt while enjoying every second of it. It seems my own personal hit list is growing day by day.

CHAPTER TWENTY-SIX

It's late at night, and I am sitting on the floor in Hell's shower, the cold tiles pressing against my back as I cry. The water cascades over me, but it does nothing to wash away the filth I feel inside. I feel sick, so fucking sick. It's gnawing away at my insides that I allowed a child abuser to be near me again in such a way. Hell has done his utmost to convince me otherwise, but he doesn't know why I feel this way, why I feel so fucking dirty all over again and I can feel myself spiralling out of control.

The truth has resurfaced my trauma to its highest level, my dark thoughts becoming deafening. I press my hands to my ears, fighting and whispering to them, trying to convince myself it's not my fault or Hell's. None of this is, but the voices won't stop; they are relentless. They claw at my sanity, dragging me deeper into the abyss.

I feel like screaming, the urge to release the pent-up agony almost overwhelming. The thought of slicing my body to pieces, letting the pain drain out of me, anything to relieve it, crosses my mind.

As the voices get louder, I quickly reach up, desperately trying to find the razor. My fingers fumble, shaking as I tear through the plastic. Without hesitation, I press the blade to my arm and swiftly slice across, again and again. My blood mingles with the water, a crimson river pouring onto my thighs and swirling down the drain. My sobs grow more erratic, the whispers in my mind telling me I am useless, weak, and that I will never be anything more than a victim because of how these men have treated me.

I continue frantically, slicing the other arm, but the pain doesn't help; it seems to grow worse, amplifying the torment inside me. Feeling numb, I drop the blade, the clatter of metal against the tile echoing in the small space. I rest my head back, my eyes closed, and inhale deeply. My arms sting, warm blood trickling from them as they rest beside me, and when I finally start to feel myself calm down, a tingling sensation sweeps over me.

After a brief blackout, my eyes snap open, and I stand. My mind goes numb, so quiet that I cannot even hear my own thoughts. I move toward the door in a trance, my body acting on autopilot. The world around me blurs, the edges of my vision darkening as I walk forward as if I am in some kind of dream.

HOLLOW HELLION

When I stroll into the bedroom, I stop at the end of the bed and blankly stare at him, asleep. I tilt my head to the side and then my eyes gradually drift to the right of him where I see his knife, lying on the bedside cabinet. I absentmindedly go toward it and once within reach, I gently lift it. Squeezing the handle tightly with both hands, I face Hell, gazing down at him through a blur.

"*Kill him.*" Finally a voice enters my head.

I raise the knife, tears wetting my cheeks before I thrust downward. Almost entering his throat, he swiftly grabs my wrist just in time, his eyes flying open. His looks at me angrily as I continue to use all my strength to push down, but he suddenly disarms me, grabbing my throat, lifting me effortlessly, and slamming me down onto the bed.

"What the fuck, Noir!" he shouts aggressively, "what the fuck are you doing?"

"Killing you," I say without emotion.

He cocks his head to the side, confused before he lowers his face close to mine, searching my eyes.

"Why." He growls, his fury arising within him.

"Because you're just like them."

He looks at me like he doesn't recognize me before his eyes trace down my cut arms.

"What the fuck have you done?" his gaze meets mine and I just stare at him. He shakes me by my throat to make me respond, and I suddenly scream at him.

"You made her like this! You treat her like nothing but a fucking animal when you fuck her and then call it pleasure!"

He pulls his head back slowly, his hand loosening on my throat and I continue, "You chain her up and use her just like they did for your own enjoyment, not caring about the damage you leave in fucking your wake!"

He shakes his head from side to side, "Noir…"

"You're just like them." I whisper.

"You're just like them."

"You're just…"

Suddenly my eyelids drop, darkness enveloping me, and I feel him gently tap on my cheek with his fingers, "Noir?"

 As she lies between my legs, her back against my front, I peer down at her now and then while she sleeps, gently wrapping her sliced arms with bandages. It's clear that my Dolly was out of her fucking mind. I didn't recognize her. The way she looked into my eyes with no emotion, the way she spoke didn't carry her usual voice. It was like a fucking entity was living inside of her.

Everything she said was hollow, yet somehow true. It twisted my fucking gut. I've been around madness for many years to know the signs of someone losing their sanity, and in that moment, she lost hers. Everything is triggering her to its highest peak; she's dangerous and broken. And the more I spend time with her, the more she reveals it. Day by day she is showing me the darkness she tries to mask. Just like them? Who the fuck does she mean? All I know is when she said it, it fucked me up. I wanted to move away, not touch, or hurt her anymore.

She suddenly stirs, and when she slowly opens her eyes, they fix on me bandaging her arms.

"What the fuck happened?" she murmurs sleepily, trying to move.

I pull her back down. "Almost done."

She avoids eye contact with me as we fall into silence, her emotions clearly conflicted. "You don't remember what happened?" I ask, curious.

She shakes her head. "No, I remember being in the shower, and then everything went blank."

I let out a big breath, the weight of her words settling heavily on my shoulders. As soon as I am finished, I lift her, lying her beside me.

She faces away, and I roll onto my side, gazing down at her until gradually, she falls back to sleep. The room is filled with a deafening silence, suffocating. I watch her intently and my mind races with thoughts that I can't seem to untangle.

CHAPTER TWENTY-SEVEN

As I sit at the kitchen table in the Hollow's trailer, I stare down at the lukewarm mug of coffee that my hands are wrapped around. Blush stands, leaning against the corner to my right, trying to convince me to go out with her tonight.

"Come on, Noir. It'll be fun. It's just a quiet bar not too far from here," she reassures me, her tone persuasive.

I take a deep breath, bringing the mug to my lips. "I'm not sure, Blush. Why don't we just hang out here?"

"Because it's shit," she responds bluntly, and I can't help but smile while lowering the mug after taking a sip, but the smile feels foreign, almost forced.

I feel the cuts on my arms rubbing against the fabric of my hoodie, a constant reminder of everything I went through just a couple of nights ago, the blackout I had. Ever since that night, I have felt a shift in Hell's behaviour. He is quieter than usual and not as hands-on; we haven't even fucked. I've asked him if he is okay, but he just responds with a simple nod, as if he doesn't want to talk to me. The atmosphere is making me feel uneasy, a tension that I can't shake and want to escape from. Maybe going out with Blush will be what I need.

"It'll only be for a few hours," she adds, her eyes pleading.

I look at her, sighing as I sit back. "You're not going to drop this, are you?"

She shakes her head with a big, wide smile. "Fuck no."

Suddenly, Wrath walks in shirtless from the direction of his bedroom and we both fall into silence. His eyes meet mine briefly, but he doesn't say anything as usual. He continues forward, and my gaze shifts to see Blush staring at him, lust evident in her pretty pink eyes, her cheeks literally blushing.

As he stops in front of her, his tall, broad frame overshadows her and presses against hers very boldly as he reaches for the refrigerator beside her. She sucks in a sharp breath, her head tilted right back as his red orbs stay fixed on hers. Without them breaking eye contact, he reaches inside for a bottle of water, his jaw flexing with every chew of his gum. His expression is blank, but the intensity pours from him as if darkness is seeping from his pores and suffocating the room. He is clearly unbothered that he is intimidating the fuck out of her, and I can't help but grin at the sight.

When he has the bottle, his eyes gradually move down to the swell of her breasts before he steps back, turning around and returning to his bedroom. The air is thick with unspoken tension, and Blush's breath comes out in a shaky exhale before she looks at me with expanded eyes.

"I think I need to change my panties." She says in the most serious tone, and I can't help but laugh.

"Please, Noir." She begs once again, and I think about it before giving a small nod. "Fine. But I'm not staying for long."

She squeals, "Be ready for eight pm."

With that she walks out with a spring in her step, and I sink back into my chair, lost in stillness. When the door opens, I don't look until Soul comes into view.

He tosses a small box onto the table in front of me, "Madame said to give these to you."

I lean forward, reaching for it, noticing it's the anti-depressants I asked for, and a wave of relief sweeps over me.

"Thanks," I say when my eyes reach his. He gives a small nod before walking away, leaving me staring at the box blankly.

 It's early evening, and I walk into my bedroom after a long day of plotting another hit for a client. The music blares, and Dolly's perfume assaults my senses, a heady mix of sweetness and danger. I hear her singing along to the tune playing from the bathroom, the door left open. I peel off my leather jacket, tossing it onto the bed before pulling my hoodie over my head. When I am finished, I stride toward the bathroom door, peeking around the frame with one eye.

My gaze travels down the length of her back as she leans over the sink, scrutinizing her reflection in the mirror while doing her makeup. She's wearing a tiny black, skintight mini dress with thin straps on her shoulders, paired with her usual black platform boots. Her blonde hair, thick and loosely curled tonight, cascades down her back to her ass.

When she stands straight, I notice she has long black, silk gloves that reach up to her upper arms, covering her pain from the other night. I start wondering what she is up to until she turns around, and I dip back, leaning against the wall, thinking how to confront her.

Beside me, I spot a small white box on the chest of drawers, and I gently reach over. I lift it before bringing it in front of me, my eyes scanning over the text and realizing they're anti-depressants. I open the box, seeing she has already taken two, and then place it back down.

A heavy sigh escapes my lips as I feel the weight of the past few days pressing down on me. Since the other night, I have had to withdraw from things to assess them for what they are. The words she said to me, even if she was clearly out of her fucking mind and not remembering she said them, they rocked me. They have made me think I might not be right for her, even if I feel like she is the other part of me. It makes me believe those words that were spoken were still from somewhere deep within her and they had truth in them. I am a violent asshole, I know this, and if something has happened to my Little Dolly before her meeting me, am I just adding to her fucking trauma? Am I just like "them" as she said? I guess some form of guilt is creeping in. Something I've never felt before, but it just shows what this girl does to me. There's a war within myself because it seems like she likes who and what I am whenever we're together which has me fucking conflicted. I know, soon, I am going to have to speak to her about it, but only when she is feeling herself. I don't want her having another psychotic episode.

The way I was so rough with her when internally she has been so broken makes me shudder. I've done terrible things and hurt people without a second fucking thought, but with her, it's different. I care about her in a way that fucking scares me. Yeah, me, the man who has never been afraid of shit in his life. The man who kills people for a fucking living in the most horrific ways without feeling a single ounce of remorse.

I run a hand through my black, curly hair, frustration bubbling to the surface. When she suddenly walks in, she doesn't see me, and I watch her every move while she leans over the bed, reaching for her small black bag with a shoulder chain. My eyes move down her again, knowing I have been unfair by being so closed off.

"Going somewhere?" I say, my voice low and deep.

Her body jolts before she spins around to face me. She lifts a brow in defiance, clearly annoyed with how I have been.

"I'm going out for a few hours with Blush," she responds, sliding the chain of her bag up her arm.

I push myself away from the wall and take slow, intimidating steps toward her, noticing how her breathing has picked up, but her chin is raised with confidence. When I stop in front of her, I take in her pretty face, the black makeup decorating her blue eyes, making her iris's pop. Her full lips, glossed, draw my attention and I find myself wanting to slide my dick between them for looking so goddamn beautiful. She tries to pass me, but I grab her upper arm, pulling her back in front of me.

"Now you want to bother with me, Hell?" she asks, hurt flashing across her features although she tries not to show it.

I move my hand up the curve of her back until it's on the nape of her neck, and she tilts her head, "Tell me, Dolly, do you like the way I fuck you?" I ask.

She searches my eyes, "Yes," she whispers without hesitation.

"Why?"

She thinks about it for a moment, her eyes scanning mine. "Because you're the first man I've met in my entire life that I fully trust," she breathes out honestly. "You're the first man who has ever given me not only the pain I crave but the beautiful bliss that comes with it. In your presence, the ache in my heart is replaced with your agonizing pleasure. I am safe, even if safety hurts like hell."

My eyes close as I rest my forehead against hers, allowing her to continue. "At first, I was skeptical. I felt like it wasn't right, like I was wrong for wanting it as much as I did." I open my eyes and stare into hers, the intensity of her words striking me. "But then I realized, it was okay to give in to your dark desire for the man you trust and..." She pauses for a moment, taking a deep inhale, "You show me there is a twisted form of good in you, when you don't show it to anyone else. It makes me feel.."

I lift my head, my gaze scanning her face, wondering if this is the truth and she slides her hands up my chest. "You make me feel things my cold insides have never felt, Hell. *Fire.* When I feel dead, you have always made me feel alive again. You breathe life back into my soul every fucking time we're together and when you touch me."

I take in her words carefully before asking something else that weighs heavily on me. "Why do you like receiving pain, Noir?" My eyes bore into hers, and she inhales sharply before facing aside.

"What makes you think there is a reason?" she responds, her voice barely above a whisper. I don't answer immediately, my gaze fixed on her pretty side profile as she tries to avoid eye contact.

"There's always a fucking reason," I finally say. "I have hundreds of reasons why I am who I am, yet not one of them really justifies my lack of self-control to want to inflict pain on other people."

She looks into my eyes finally, her expression a full of vulnerability and defiance. "I guess you and me aren't so different."

My eyes harden as I take another step forward, my voice dropping to an intense growl. "You're nothing like me. You could never be." I slip my arm around the middle of her back, pulling her close to me, my face inches from hers. "For the last fifteen years, I have been built to deliver immense pain and suffering, Dolly. And I fucking love how it feels."

She remains silent and blank, her eyes searching mine. "Why do you like to receive pain? Why the fuck did you mark your pure skin before you even met me and why are you doing it again now?" I probe for her to voice the answers, even though deep down I think I know why, yet my frustration still mounts that she claims to trust me but won't tell me the truth.

I notice her eyes brim with tears before she turns her face aside, her voice trembling. "It doesn't matter," she murmurs in a low tone.

I suddenly grab her face, squeezing her cheeks, and force her to stare into my intense eyes once more. "It does fucking matter to me," I declare through clenched teeth. "When I said you're mine, Noir, I meant it. That doesn't mean just your pretty face and beautiful body— that means your soul, too. I want it all. Your hurt, your tears, your fucking laughter. I don't want to just give you pain; I want to give you more. You need to feel more."

Her tears spill over, tracing paths down her cheeks. "I don't know if I can," she whispers, her voice breaking. "The pain helps."

That's when it hits me—it's this fucking trauma thing. Noir has never experienced anything other than what she is used to, just like me. She's never experienced that fluffy shit, and although it doesn't bother me as much, it clearly bothers her.

Without warning, I grab the back of her thighs, lifting her quickly and dropping her back onto the bed. A squeak escapes her from my sudden dominance, but before she can say anything, I shove my tongue into her mouth while lying on top of her.

Her body tenses for a moment, then melts against mine, her hands gripping my back. I drag her thin dress straps down her shoulders, the fabric slipping easily under my fingers. With a swift yank, I pull the bust down until her breasts are freed, the cold air causing her nipples to harden instantly. I push her dress up her thighs, my hands rough and urgent.

Her moans vibrate against my tongue, as my hands roam over her exposed flesh, feeling the softness of her curves, the way she arches into me, craving more.

I grab the strings of her panties, dragging them only halfway down her thighs, not wanting to peel my skin away from hers to rip them off fully. As I free my belt and drag my zipper down, I slip my hand into the back of her hair, taking a handful and tugging it back to expose her neck to me. Flopping my hard cock out, I press the tip against her wet entrance, breathing heavily over her parted lips, then sink into her.

She lets out a dragging gasp as I stretch her, her eyes rolling back, but I don't ram into her like I usually would. I make her feel every fucking inch of my dick and piercings as I gradually slide down her walls. The sensation is intense, her warm cunt enveloping me, and I savor every moment of it. As soon as I am balls deep, I dip my head and do something I've never done—I smother her delicate neck with my tongue and lips.

I feel her shudder from the sensation, and I slowly start to fuck her in a way that is absolutely foreign to me, but not to her. Except this time, it's not with Limp Dick, it's with me and I will make her fucking come for me.

While dipping into her over and over again, I deliver no pain, and surprisingly, it's not as shit as I thought it would be, but it's undoubtedly because it's with her. Nothing could ever be shit with her. She digs her nails into my back, her nipple piercings sliding up and down my chest with each stroke, one clashing with mine. Her moans as well as her come leaking down my fucking balls tell me she is enjoying what I am doing to her.

"We're so much more than depravity and pain, my pretty girl. Our connection is what forges us, not our twisted fucking mindsets," I murmur in her ear through heavy breathing.

I lift my head, taking her plump lips to mine again, and she eagerly kisses me back while I continue to grind my cock into her soaked pussy with a steady, deep rhythm, bucking my hips against her and spreading her legs further apart. I move one of my arms beneath her knee, lifting it so I can drive further, and after some time, we both cave into the pleasure.

Her body and pussy tighten around me, her orgasm shaking her to her core. I press deep, my cum shooting into the furthest depths, and I let out a growling groan against her lips from the sensation. I continue to fuck her slowly until we're both finished and then I rest my face against the crook of her neck, giving it a couple of breathless kisses.

But then I suddenly hear her sob, and I raise my head swiftly. As I look into her watery eyes, she just stares at me with a wobble in her lip. I tilt my head to the side as she slides her arm around my shoulders, drawing me down to her lips.

"Thank you so much," she whispers, her voice trembling.

My eyes ease, and I lean my forehead against hers, sweeping my thumb down her jaw.

She closes her eyes, a tear slipping from her eye into her hair. "I never thought I could feel that way."

If I do actually have a heart, I felt the ache in it when she said that. What the fuck has my Dolly been through? Who the fuck has done this to her? I'll fucking kill them. I'll make them suffer so horrifically. I'll burn the entire fucking world down for her. I need to know, but I also know I must wait to confront her about it. She's so fucking fragile right now.

"I don't want you ever doing that to yourself again, pretty girl." I murmur over her lips, "If you feel like everything is falling apart, you need to fucking come to me. I might not be the best of men, but I'll try to be the best for you."

She breathes in deeply before giving a small nod in agreement. After a moment of silence, I push myself off her, slipping my arm around the middle of her back and drag her with me. While standing, I buckle my belt and she pulls her panties up her thighs before adjusts her dress.

I watch as she passes me, striding into the bathroom to fix her makeup that I ruined, seemingly now a lot happier. When she returns, she heads straight toward me. She throws her arms around my shoulders, drawing me down to her lips, and devours my mouth so fucking hard with a moan that I feel like I might tie her to my fucking bed and ruin her pretty asshole all night long.

I lift her dress, giving her soft, peachy cheek a rough squeeze, enough to make her squeal and smile against my lips. The sound of her now giddiness is music to my ears.

I glance all around her face, taking in every detail, every expression, before I speak. "Later, I can't promise I'll be so nice, Noir."

She gives a sinister smirk, her eyes glittering with mischief. "Promise?" she raises an eyebrow, biting her bottom lip.

I growl, my hunger for her flaring up again. I give her ass a sharp slap, the sound echoing in the room. "Get the fuck out of here with my fresh cum smeared all over your cunt before I chain you to my damn bed," I grit out, my voice filled with frustration.

She giggles, sending a shiver down my spine, and dashes past me. I watch her every move, my dark eyes following the sway of her hips and ass until she smiles back at me before walking out the door.

CHAPTER TWENTY-EIGHT

I'm chilling outside the trailer with Soul and Wrath beside our bikes, smoking a cigarette when my phone vibrates in my pocket. I slide it out and glance down at the screen to see it's my uncle again. My teeth grind together in annoyance, and I press the button, placing it to my ear.

"What the fuck do you want." I snap.

"I'm going to text you an address, call me when you're outside." He says before hanging up.

"You good?" Soul speaks behind me, and I give a small nod.

When I receive the text almost instantly, I look at it before shoving my phone back into my pocket, then mounting my bike.

I kick the stand, rev the engine and ride forward, heading to where he said.

HOLLOW HELLION

When I arrive at the destination, I cut the engine across the street from a bar not too far from Oddity. I stare at it, noting that the area is more or less empty, but I can hear music thumping from inside and see people moving around within. I pull my phone out of my pocket, swiping to his number, and I call. After a few rings, he answers.

"You there?" he asks, his voice deep and gruff.

"Yeah, I'm fucking here, but why am I? This better not be some kind of fuck around again."

"Oh, it's not. She's in there," he responds in a menacing tone. "Look through the window if you don't believe me."

I sigh, stepping off my bike and walking toward the bar. I stop at a window, gazing through one of the squares, my eyes scanning over everyone.

"Far right, at the back."

I look in that direction, but it's not Harley.

"What the fuck is this, Kyro?" I say through tight teeth, my eyes focused on Noir beside Blush.

"The blonde girl is Harley," he replies calmly.

"No, it's fucking not. It's Noir."

I hear him let out a soft chuckle, and my brows pinch in anger.

"She's been right under your nose, and instead of killing her, you ended up fucking your own cousin's killer?" he says with seriousness.

My blood runs cold, my stomach dropping as I stare at her. "You're fucking lying."

"I'm not, Hell. That is Harley. Ask her if you don't believe me."

"You told me she had dark hair," I protest.

"She did until she dyed it to hide from me, just as she changed her name," he says steadily. "Now bring her to me."

My pulse pounds in my ears, my palms growing sweaty, everything blurring around me.

"Put those soft feelings aside, Hell. She is not who or what she says she is, trust me on that. She killed Kai."

"Fucking trust you?" I yell down the phone with bitterness. "How long have you known she's been at Oddity?"

When he falls silent, irritation takes over me and I whirl around, "How fucking long?" I shout.

"I've known where she's been the entire time," he admits.

My body tightens, and I gaze ahead as he continues, "You and me aren't so different, Hell. See, you like playing games with your prey, and so do I. It must run in our bloodline."

Reality starts to hit me. "You pushed her into my arms on purpose. That little nonce that she was with was your doing?"

"Ahhh, Eli, yes. He did well."

Rage almost explodes inside of me, and I clench my teeth. "I will fucking kill you, you cunt."

"You were only supposed to kill her, Hell. I pushed her right into your hands. When you chose your dick over your commitments, I let it ride out a little bit. Can you blame me? You shouldn't have been so blind."

I close my eyes, trying to breathe through the shit swirling through my insane mind.

"Now bring her to me."

"Get fucked," I bark.

"You cannot protect her, Hell; she killed a member of the Shadow's, and you are to carry out the hit. Rules are rules."

I roar and launch my phone against the pavement, shattering it to pieces. I turn quickly, peering through the window again until I see Noir laughing at Blush dancing, so carefree and pretty.

My Little Dolly.

My jaw clenches, my thoughts a mess as I question my morals, my feelings for her, who I am, who I will be, and where I go from here. The one woman I actually give a fuck about, the one who has made me utterly obsessed, is the same woman I am supposed to kill.

The lines between right and wrong blur, and I am left standing in the middle, torn between my loyalty to the Shadow's and my addiction for Noir. Not knowing what to do, I turn around, heading for my bike. I wait for a while in the shadow's and when I see her get into a cab with Blush, I head back to Oddity.

CHAPTER TWENTY-NINE

I wake up in the morning, stretching my arms above my head with a yawn. I glance around the dark room to see Hell isn't here still. When I came back last night, he was missing. I tried to stay awake as long as I could, but the alcohol was too strong and won. I throw the duvet off me before getting up, walking to the bathroom to release my full bladder.

When I am finished, I head back to the bedroom, throwing on some clothes and shoes. Once ready, I go to the door, opening it and head downstairs until I spot Soul and Wrath seated at the table.

I pause and look between them both as their eyes meet mine. "Where's Hell?" I ask, curiously.

Wrath's jaw is set tight as he looks away and Soul answers, "I think he's in the woods."

I eye him suspiciously before giving a small nod and then I leave the trailer.

HOLLOW HELLION

As I stride through the dense forest, it's early and foggy. The sky is a gloomy gray, and the air is cold. My thoughts drift to last night, to how Hell fucked me in a way that set my entire being ablaze. It was so passionate that I could hardly breathe. The memory of those soft strokes, how deeply he embedded himself inside me, the weight of his heavy body on top of mine, and those intoxicating neck kisses linger in my mind.

Fuck. I'm falling for him way too hard. He solidified it for me at that moment. I couldn't help but cry. I have never been fucked with love. It took me to a different universe when I came.

Once I reach close to Hell's underground chamber, I notice the doors are wide open. I trail along the field, eager to see him, but also curious about why he didn't come back last night. I stare down the dark hole in the ground before finally, slowly descending the steps. When I reach the bottom, I see right away that the door at the furthest end of the passageway is wide open—a room I haven't been inside before. I take cautious steps forward until I am walking past the threshold.

As soon as I enter the dimly lit space, there is a huge pinboard in front of me, full of photos of all different people that lure my attention. I continue with gradual steps until I stop, my eyes scanning over all the faces, none I recognize until suddenly I am drawn to one in the middle. My breath catches in my throat, staring at it with wide eyes.

My hand shakily reaches out until my fingers are softly brushing over it. Pinching it, I pull it away from the pinboard and gaze down at myself through blurred vision, confused.

"Do you know her?"

My body jumps so much that I almost leap off the ground at the sound of Hell's voice behind me. As I spin around to face him, I see that he is sitting in a chair in the corner of the room, shrouded in the darkness, only his menacing outline and spiral glowing orbs visible. Tears stream from my eyes, I can't help it and I swallow hard.

"No, who is she?" I try to say confidently, although my body is trembling, and my heart is pounding.

He gently stands, and I watch his every move as he stalks toward me, gradually emerging from the shadows until he is entirely in my space. His eyes scrutinize my features before he takes the photo from my hand.

"She killed my cousin," he responds in an eerily calm manner.

My eyes expand, and I shake my head once. "What?" I manage to whisper, feeling my anxiety peaking.

He walks around me, sizing me up, but I try to keep my cool around his threatening aura. "She killed my cousin, Haze, Noir."

My chest tightens like nothing I have ever felt before and my eyes close, more tears dripping down my cheeks.

"What happened?" I murmur, trying to do anything I can to delay what is about to transpire.

"Well, around one year ago, Kai was found lying dead on the kitchen floor of his dad's mansion," he explains sternly. "After his throat was sliced, his cock and balls were stuffed down his fucking throat."

My brows pinch with confusion, almost ready to confront him until suddenly a flashback enters my mind. I stand in Kyro's kitchen, staring down at Kai on the floor, blood soaking my white nightdress and hands.

I shake my head, squeezing my eyes shut when he mentions his name. "No," I whisper before another dream-like sequence rushes through my thoughts.

"We need to get you out of here..." Arabella pleads, her words ringing in my ears from behind me.

When my eyes ping open, reality hits me, and I spin around, running out the door. I bolt up the steep stairs, hearing Hell hot on my tail, and as I stumble over the wet grass, I weep, desperate to get away.

"HARLEY!" He shouts my real name, his angry voice booming through the open space, and I come to a sudden stop.

The name hits me like a sledgehammer, reverberating through my mind as soon as it rolled off his tongue.

Harley. The name now feels alien, like a ghost from the past. I struggle to breathe, images of the day we fled becoming clearer, the murder we left behind, and I whirl around to face Hell, my eyes broad with dread.

My body is rigid as he takes a few slow steps over the grass. "You're Harley?" he asks, his finger pointed in my direction.

I sob uncontrollably and shake my head. "I'm sorry, I didn't know. I can't remember. I don't..."

He unexpectedly storms toward me with murder in his eyes, and I spin around to run from him. He catches up with me so quickly that I let out a high-pitched scream when he picks me up and throws me over his shoulder as if I weigh nothing. As he carries me through the woods, all I can do is cry and beg for him not to kill me as I sag in defeat. I can feel the anger and hurt radiating from him with each step, but he doesn't let me go.

The name Harley echoes in my mind, a haunting reminder of a past I've tried to forget. What the fuck have I done? The questions swirl around me, suffocating me, as Hell's grip tightens. I realize that everything has finally caught up with me and in the worst possible way. The man I have fallen so deeply for is related to Kyro.

His uncle. He isn't going to forgive me for this.

HOLLOW HELLION

As we enter The Hollow's trailer, I catch a glimpse of Soul and Wrath behind my hair, still in the kitchen. Hell jogs with me up the stairs until we're in his bedroom, and he kicks the door shut behind us, locking it. Before I know it, I am being tossed onto the mattress, but I scramble back, kicking my feet over the bedding to get away from him. With no emotion in his eyes, he kneels on it, grabbing my leg and yanking me back down beneath him with force. I press on his chest with my palms, my body shivering, trying to create some distance.

"Tell me," he growls, but not in a way that would usually rumble to my core. This growl is vicious. I stay silent, my eyes wide, my chest expanding as I hyperventilate.

"TELL ME!" he shouts in my face, and my body tightens.

"I can't remember..." I whisper through a sob.

"Just like you're completely oblivious to the fact you called me a fucking abuser the other night when you slit your arms."

I shake my head. "What?"

"You said I was just like "them," he declares before his jaw tenses. "Just like you told me you will never be owned AGAIN!"

Tears streak down from my eyes, and I turn my face aside, but he snatches it, forcing me to look into his swirling, furious depths.

"Stop fucking lying to me. You have one chance to tell me why and what, or I won't ever hear you out again."

"What do you want to know?" I croak.

"Fucking everything."

"I... I don't even know where to start."

"Kyro." The name rolls off Hell's tongue like a venomous river, and I feel sick to my stomach.

"My stepfather," I whisper.

"What?" I sense the confusion and shock in his tone as he slowly releases my face.

"He was married to my mom before she died."

He stays silent, his face painted with bewilderment before he finally answers. "But I don't know you. Why the fuck wouldn't I know you?"

My teary eyes meet his. "Because no one knew I was alive. He kept me locked away. Everyone presumed I had died along with my mom in that car crash."

His lips part in almost surprise before he responds, "You're my fucking stepcousin?"

I shrug my stiff shoulders, searching his shocked orbs before he comes back to reality and his face falls expressionless again.

"So why the fuck would he lock you away?" he breathes out bitterly, almost as if he doesn't believe me, and I start to feel defensive.

"Why don't you ask your uncle?"

His jaw tenses before he lowers his face to mine. "I'm fucking asking you. Don't fuck with me, Noir, although we've established that ain't even your real fucking name. You killed my cousin."

I narrow my eyes, lifting my head, my lips touching his. "If I killed him then I think we've established I am not afraid to fucking kill anybody. Not even you." I grit out with anger, the threat mingling with our heavy breathing.

I see the anger flash across his eyes before he grabs my throat and I raise my chin. "I could snap this delicate little fucking neck like a popsicle. You can act like the badass girl all you want but remember who the fuck you're lying beneath."

I swallow hard against his hand, more tears cascading from the corners of my eyes.

"FUCKING TELL ME!" He shouts in my face again, his rage spilling forth and I can't help but flinch. I find it hard to get the words out. The words I have never said out loud.

"NOIR!"

"THEY RAPED ME!" I scream back at the top of my lungs, and his face falls. "OVER AND FUCKING OVER UNTIL I WAS NOTHING!"

The words vibrate through us both and the room. He scans my eyes to try to detect the lie, but he will never find one.

"Since I was twelve," I murmur, the pain clear in my voice. "I was chained and nothing but amusement to them, Hell."

His eyes drift close, a slight wave in his posture as he takes in my words, then lowers his head, gently releasing my throat.

"That night is only coming in small flash backs, but not fully. I don't know what happened" I sob, "He had my sister too, in the other room, but I don't know where she is. We escaped together."

He lifts his head, his gaze meeting mine, "Kyro never mentioned a sister." I close my soaked, sore eyes and I look aside as he continues, "He only mentioned you."

"Then he must still have her." I mutter, my heart hurting.

He gazes at my side-profile, "I'm ordered to kill you, Dolly. It's my duty since you killed one of the Shadow's Society, members. I took the fucking hit." My eyes don't meet his as he continues, "And if I don't do it, someone else will."

I gently blink, the reality seeping into my bones, but I know he's only being truthful. "So kill me. I am not running anymore. I should have been dead a long time ago. I'd rather you do it than him."

He suddenly pushes himself away from me with a growl, and I perch on my elbows as he heads for the door, "Hell? Where are you going?"

"To get some fucking answers." He grits out.

"But—" Before I can say anything else, he unlocks the door, walks through it, and slams it behind him.

CHAPTER THIRTY

After telling Soul to keep an eye on Noir, making sure she neither tries to kill herself nor run, I storm straight to Madame's chamber, my mind a whirlwind of confusion and rage. I draw back the curtain and when I enter, I see she is sitting behind her desk, her initial smile fading as she sees the wrath in my eyes.

She stands, concern lacing her tone. "What is it?"

I pace back and forth, pulling at my hair, fists clenching tightly. "Hell, speak to me," she urges softly.

I turn to face her. "Kyro says Noir is the girl who killed Kai, and he's known she's been with me the entire time."

Her face displays disbelief, her head shaking once. "What?"

I swiftly pull out a chair and sit down, resting my elbows on my shaking thighs. "Her name is Harley, and she killed Haze."

Her hand meets her open mouth, and she takes a slow seat. "It's not possible," she gasps out.

My brows pinch as I look at her. "What?"

"Did you just say, Harley?" I give a small nod, and her eyes gradually close. "Harley is dead, Hell. She died in a car accident with her mother. I don't know what he is saying, but..."

"She fucking isn't. Noir has told me she's Harley, but she claims Kyro had her locked up for all these years, raping her."

Her face pales before she stands slowly, pacing the room until she stops, her eyes searching mine. "Not long before they both 'died,' Kyro found out that Harley's mom, Hana, was having an affair," she says. "With your father."

My eyes widen, and I stand quickly. "What?" I shout.

"I didn't tell you, Hell, because they were both dead. It wasn't of importance," she tries to explain.

"But she isn't," I bite out. "She's right fucking here, and I am utterly obsessed with her."

Her eyes soften, and she circles the desk until she is standing in front of me. "You know what he is like. He is vile. Please don't hurt her," she shudders out, placing a shaky hand on my arm.

"But she killed him, Ma. I'm order to... She—"

She sighs, dropping her hand. "What I am about to say to you might make you hate me forever, but I'm going to say it anyway."

I draw a deep breath, strolling past her, and take another seat, willing to listen. "He's playing games, Hell. He knew you would fall for her, and strangely, it makes sense," she says, and I watch her every move as she sits behind her desk again.

"Your father and Harley's mother couldn't stay away from one another as well. From what I heard all those years ago anyway. He was besotted by her, and Kyro knew that."

I sit up again, ready to hear more. "There were rumours going around that he caused that crash, and there were whispers that he could have been involved with your father's death as well, but you know how much trash people talk in this world," she waves her hand while taking a swig of her wine, and my brain ticks with unanswered questions.

"You're saying this is a fucking revenge thing?"

She gently places her glass down while thinking, and then she looks at me, giving a nod. "Revenge can do crazy things to a man, Hell, especially a man like Kyro," she states. "As I said, he's playing games and it's now too obvious. He is not only punishing Noir, but he is also attempting to punish you as well, for something that is neither of your faults. He wanted you to fall for Noir the same way his brother fell for his wife. Then he wants you to kill her, ripping her away from you entirely. Think about it."

As I sit there silently, my head lowered, my brain mulls over everything. It makes perfect fucking sense, and my rage mounts, hating this motherfuck more than ever.

"Again, you might hate me for this, Hell." Madame's voice breaks through my thoughts, and I lift my eyes to look at her. "If they did keep her locked up and rape her for years, can you really blame her? There is only so much someone can take before they finally snap."

My jaw tenses, my soul aching as I dip my head again, knowing she's right. The thought that they hurt my Dolly like they did in such a horrific way, breaking her to what she has become, makes me want to kill him so much more than I could ever want to kill her.

When I looked into her tearful eyes as she screamed it at me, I could hear and see there wasn't a fucking lie. It was pure pain and truth that seemed to shatter through me. They hurt her, they hurt her so fucking bad. I know exactly what my uncle is, but I am more outraged that Kai would do it too. I didn't want to believe it, but I guess the apple doesn't fall far from the fucking tree.

A new thought arises in my mind, and I look sharply at Madame. "Does Harley have a sister named Arabella?"

She shakes her head slowly. "No, she was Hana's and her father's only child."

I try to piece it all together internally until she speaks again, her voice gentle but firm. "She came to me the other day, asking for anti-depressants. She said she has been hallucinating and seeing her sister here. Her mental state is so fragile, Hell."

Could Noir be seeing and hearing things and truly believing she has a sister? I guess there is only one way to find the fuck out.

HOLLOW HELLION

After speaking to Madame for some time, I sat on the carousel for a while, trying to clear my frantic mind and figure out where the fuck I go from here, but no matter which way I looked at it, the answer was always crystal clear and unmistakeable. It all makes sense now. Why she wanted control on Dark Night. How she knew what drug to use to knock me out. All the little slip ups that had no real meaning, but now they do.

As soon as I arrive back at the trailer, I jog upstairs, seeing Soul by his door and I give him a nod before entering my bedroom. I spot her right away, and she pushes herself back against the headboard, knees up, hugging mini dolly. Her eyes are puffy from all the crying, and she attempts to avoid looking at me. I hate seeing her scared of me like this. I know we play our fucked-up games, but this is an entirely different level of fear I am getting from her, and I don't fucking like it.

Once I've locked the door, I pull off my jacket while staring at her. When my hoodie is off as well, I kneel onto the bed and her red eyes flash to mine. I crawl toward her, and the nearer I get, the more she curls into herself.

When I reach out, I take her leg and tug it without breaking eye contact. She's tense at first, looking at me warily until she lets me extend it. My hand moves down the back of her calf until it reaches her ankle, my gaze following the movement. I examine the scars on her ankle, now understanding why she was so worried and compassionate toward M. She saw something in him that represented what she went through.

"This is from where you were chained?" I ask, still looking at the markings.

"Yes," she finally whispers.

I trace the blemishes with my thumb, my touch gentle, and I feel a surge of protectiveness. I lift my eyes to hers and I creep toward her again until I am taking her waist and dragging her down. She looks panicked and confused as she lays below me, still cradling her dolly.

"Are you going to kill me, Hell?" she asks, her words trembling.

"I have to."

She gives a nod, seemingly accepting her fate with watery eyes until I lower my face to hers, our lips almost touching. "But I'm not going to."

Her brows knit together in confusion. "What?"

I reach up, my fingertips brushing away her blonde hair, wanting to see her clearly. My eyes circle her face before finally locking onto hers.

"I choose you, Noir. I'll always choose you."

She shakes her head, tears welling up, threatening to spill. "How can you say that? After everything I've done?"

I sigh, laying my forehead against hers. "Because you're my Little Dolly, and no one fucking hurts my Dolly but me."

A sniffle crawls up her throat, and I continue, "There is nothing in this life I desire more than you. From the moment you stepped into my chaotic world, you've blown my fucking mind in more ways than one and ignited an obsession within me. There's no fucking way I'm letting you go. You're the only person who's ever filled the hollowness inside me with something... Good."

I pause, letting the words sink in before I continue, "My loyalty to Kyro is non-existent, even more now for doing this to you; I'll fucking kill him. As for Kai, he got exactly what he deserved. I can't change what happened, and I may not have been able to save you back then, but I'll save you now."

She searches my eyes, desperate for reassurance. "But what about the society?"

I lower my eyes, thinking it over. "I need to speak to them," I reply before I lift my gaze again. "Whatever happens, no matter what, I swear no one will ever hurt you like that again. With me, you'll always be fucking safe."

I see the guilt in her gaze, and I shake my head once. "Don't do fucking that. Don't think you've done something wrong. I don't like it."

"But you shouldn't have to go through all of this for me, Hell," she murmurs, tears falling.

I lift my head, taking in her facial features, "Don't ever feel guilt, because I'd let this entire place burn to the fucking ground just to cover you from the flames. You, my pretty girl, are worth every damn burn I would suffer. With me as your shield, you're untouchable."

"Do you mean that?" she asks, bringing her shaky palm to my cheek.

"Every. Damn. Word," I declare through tight teeth.

Her eyes soften as I wipe her tears away with the back of my fingers. "It's time to recover your strength, Dolly. I've seen how fucking tough you can be—don't let him break you now."

She inhales sharply before giving a small nod, defiance in her eyes and I smirk, "That's my girl."

I lower my lips to hers, our connection igniting my dark fucking soul, and as our tongues collide, I growl. I slide my arm around the small of her back, gripping her waist, and when I drop down onto the bed beside her, I swiftly yank her to roll with me.

As she lies on top of me, our kiss remains unbroken, a burning collision of need and hunger. My hands move over the curve of her soft ass, where I grab handfuls, feeling the warmth of her skin beneath my fingers. I push her long shirt up her back with one hand, exposing more of her to my touch, as the other wraps around the string of her panties, pulling them upward until they're wedged between her pussylips.

After a while of touching her, feeling her mind and body unwind, I suck on her bottom lip, dragging it back until I release. "The moment you let me touch you was the moment you fucked-up, pretty girl. You're not getting rid of me now." I declare, and she grins, "I had a feeling I wasn't getting rid of you anyway. I had little choice. Fucking stalker."

I growl, slapping my palm down on her ass, "Shut the fuck up and show me how good you suck your stalkers dick."

She smiles before gradually moving down my body. I watch her every move as she pulls me free and when she engulfs me, her warm mouth and tongue sliding down my length, I suck in a sharp breath, relishing the feeling as she clears both our minds.

CHAPTER THIRTY-ONE

It's early morning, and I am sitting in the middle of my bed with Noir wrapped around my waist, riding my cock. Her arms are suspended upward, shackled in chains, bound to the canopy. With my hands squeezing her ass, I feel the ripples of her flesh against my palms. Her head is thrown back, moaning, lost in the ecstasy. I move one hand up the front of her body until I am taking a handful of her bouncing tit.

She's building up to her third orgasm, and I am torturing her in the best way possible, making her stop and start, her leg muscles slowing down. Our shared moisture is like a fucking puddle over my thighs and balls, my throbbing cock soaked since I've came inside her juicy pussy once already. I couldn't help it; I tried to hold the fuck on, but her cunt is far too good to fight the sensation. As soon as I'm inside her, the tingle that shoots through my dick almost tips me over the edge within a second every damn time.

"Oh, god, I'm so fucking close," she groans breathlessly.

Her tanned skin beads with sweat, glistening like silk, her gasps coming out uneven. As I lift her heavy tit, I lower my head, taking her pierced nipple into my mouth, sucking hard. Her greedy cunt clenches around me, a loud moan escaping her lips, and she starts to ride me harder, more eager, the heavy chains clinking with her movements.

I give her ass a sharp smack causing her to screech,

Then another,

Then another,

And another. Making her asscheek burn as severely as the searing heat in my tightening balls.

"Harder, slutty little dolly. Give me the ride of my fucking life and fuck the dark soul out of me while you're nothing but my puppet in chains," I growl the demand against her skin, each syllable thick with need.

I raise my arm, slipping my finger between her lips, and she sucks on it, making my cock twitch inside her. As I pull it out with a wet pop, I reach around. With my other hand, I firmly grasp her cheek, pulling it to the side so her little asshole is exposed, and then I slip it inside. As I start to finger her ass in the same rhythm as her bounces, she tilts her head forward, her mouth agape and her eyes glazed over with lust.

The sight is fucking perfect.

In a surge of sexual aggression, I reach up with my free hand, grabbing her throat, my teeth grinding. I hold it so hard that her breathing is constricted, my fingers digging into her skin.

I use her neck to pound her down on me, her face flushed, gradually deepening to a purple shade and the sight of her life almost wilting away through suffocation starts to make my own climax build.

"You either make us both fucking cum, or you die by my hand, pretty girl," I warn, my words a low, dangerous rumble.

I observe her face as I flick my pierced tongue over her nipple before biting it, making her walls squeeze around my cock. I repeat the action, forcing her to pulse on my dick with every sharp bite. Her eyes start to roll, about to explode until finally I feel her coming. Her body convulses and I feel the rush of her release.

I wait a few seconds longer, finger-banging her asshole until she is on the edge of passing out, then I release her throat. Her movements stop, her head flopping forward and her body hangs lifeless. I grasp her hips, lifting and slamming her spasming, dripping cunt down onto me repeatedly until finally, I shoot my jizz inside her. A beastly growl escapes my throat as I press my head against hers, both of us breathing heavily.

After a moment of silence, I kiss the side of her cheek. Reaching up, I run my hand over the ladder of her cuts before freeing the shackle surrounding her wrist.

"Always a good fucking girl." I praise breathlessly.

She slumps against me as I release the other, her face tucking beneath my chin. I stroke her hair away from her sweaty face, feeling the warmth of her breath against my skin and she runs her palm over my pec.

"I am so glad you're not treating me like some fragile little toy," she murmurs, her voice soft but steady. I tilt my head down until her eyes meet mine. "I thought you might be different with me, treating me like a victim."

She lifts her head, her icy gaze searching mine, "I don't want to be a victim, Hell. I like how we are, even if it's fucked. I trust you. I trust in everything you say and do because you have never pretended to be anything other than what you are."

She wraps her arms around my shoulders, her tits pressed against me, and I glide my hands up the curve of her back.

"And I know if my life is in your hands, you'll save me every time," she murmurs, her voice filled with vulnerability.

I raise an eyebrow, my eyes darkening. "I've thought about fucking you while you're dead more times than I can count, so don't bet on it, pretty girl," I respond bluntly.

Her lips roll inward, trying not to laugh at my honesty. "You're insane," she says, a hint of amusement in her voice.

"Why do you think I've always watched you when you're asleep? Yeah, you're a beauty when you're lying there, but it does something to me. How peaceful you are, how fucking lifeless, how vulnerable, and how I could take full advantage of your body without you moving a muscle," I growl, my feral eyes moving down to her perky tits. "The only thing I would hear is my wet dick sinking into your cold, dead pussy, and my own ragged breathing. Fuck, I would fill every fucking hole you had until you were overflowing with my cum then bury you full of it."

She searches my swirling orbs, completely unaffected by how horrific I am, because maybe, she is just as fucking strange as I am after all.

"Also, you come ten times harder when you're teetering on the boundary of death. Your cunt grips me tighter. That's why I test you to your limit."

She inhales deeply, a small smirk on her lips. "I noticed," she breathes out. "Does that mean you're going to fucking kill me?"

My brows pinch, my lips curling. "No. I'd never actually act upon it because a one-time thing isn't worth me not having you here ever again. It's just a sick fucking fantasy that enters my mind now and then." I softly swipe a strand of her hair away from her face with my fingertips. "You don't have to worry, my Little Dolly. No one, not even me will kill you," Her eyes move over my features with curiosity before she gives a small nod.

"Madame said something to me last night about our parents," I admit, and her head tilts to the side. "Our parents? Like what?"

I give a small nod. "Did you know your mom was having an affair with my dad?"

Her eyes widen, her mouth dropping open, then she shakes her head. "No, it can't be..."

"It is, Noir," I state firmly. "Madame wouldn't lie. Her loyalty is to me and now you."

Her eyes well up as she stays silent, realization sinking in. "That's why he did this to me. His words now make sense," she whispers.

I slide my palms up her back as she looks aside, thinking. "It seems he wants revenge on me as well. That's why you're here." Her eyes flash to mine, confused, and I continue, "He hired Limp Dick. He has always known where you have been. He must've promised him something in return. Probably his freedom."

Pain is evident in her blue eyes as she just stares at me, silent. "He's been playing games. Hoping me and you would fall for one another, just like our parents did, then he expects me to kill you."

She sniffles before lowering her head. "Eli pushed for us to come here. It doesn't surprise me that Kyro would drive me into a paedophiles arms. That's how his fucked-up mind works." She lifts her eyes to mine and continues, "But I'm glad he did."

I raise my chin, noticing she is changing the negative into a positive. She places her hands on my tattooed neck. "The worst thing he could ever have done was allow me to meet you, Hell. And no matter what happens, that's not something I will ever fucking regret," she whispers over my lips, staring deeply into my eyes. "You, Oddity, and everything in between has and will continue to make me stronger."

I grip the nape of her neck without warning, about to kiss her for being so fucking courageous when suddenly the door swings open. We both look that way, Dolly pressing her front against mine to cover herself as Wrath stands there, blankly looking between both of us. I push on the top of Noir's ass with my palm, drawing her in closer.

"Wrath, I swear to fuck, if you keep being this rude fucking…" I shout with fury.

He gives a silent head gesture before turning around and walking away. My teeth grind together as mine and Dolly's eyes connect.

"Don't worry about him. He's seen more cunt and tits to last him a fucking lifetime, the satyriasis." I sneer.

She gives me a small grin before starting to get off me, but I grab her hair, tilting her head to the side. "Manners, my Little Dolly. Clean up the mess you made. Lick me fucking clean."

She smiles before dipping down and I gather her hair into a tight ponytail as she works her mouth and tongue on me, licking my cock and balls until there is nothing left but her saliva. When she shoves my semi-hard cock down her throat, I yank her hair back, pulling her down on the bed beside me. As I lean over her on my elbow, I aggressively push her thighs apart with my hand before giving her pussy a swift slap. She squeaks, squirming beneath me until I rub it better and lower my lips to hers. "Greedy Little Dolly," I bite out.

Once my fingers are coated with our cum, I force them into her mouth, pressing down on her tongue. As soon as her lips are parted enough, I spit sharply in her slutty throat, then withdraw my fingers. "Don't worry, Noir. If you're hungry, I'll feed you dick all night long."

I grab her face, pressing my lips hard against hers, and when we part, I can see the amusement in her eyes. I roll off the bed, slipping my pants up my legs. Once I am ready, I give her one last look, seeing she is still where I left her, then I walk out the door.

HOLLOW HELLION

When I get downstairs, I see Wrath seated, and he slides his phone to the edge of the table. I look down at it, seeing Kyro on the other end of the call. With annoyance I snatch the phone off the table, pressing it to my ear.

"What?"

"You still haven't brought her to me, Hell," he says, his voice almost agitated.

"And what?" I respond calmly.

"And you were fucking meant to."

I scoff. "Fuck you, Kyro. You honestly can't be this much of a dumb cunt?" He stays silent, but I can feel his frustration mounting through the phone. "You were stupid enough to push her into my arms for revenge, and now you face the fucking consequences. Harley is mine, and the only time she will ever be around you again is when she is pissing on your fucking grave."

"You have no choice but to bring her to me. You're…"

"I'm fucking what, motherfucker? A member of the Shadow's? I don't work for you, and I never have."

"Yet she killed my fucking son, Hell. You know she's dead either way, and if you don't comply, you're dead too."

I pull my head back. "Says who? Are you my fucking boss?" He's quiet as I continue. "You think abusing that poor innocent girl for years, and locking her the fuck away from the world, is something they won't consider?"

"I don't know what you're talking about. She's a fucking liar, just like her whore mother," he snaps back.

I raise my chin, my jaw tensing, now knowing more than ever that he did it. "I know everything, Kyro. I know my dad fucked your wife and if he was anything like me, there is no doubt he fucked her good."

I hear a rustle down the phone as if he is squeezing it too hard and I smirk before my face falls. "You're a nasty, old, vengeful fucking nonce, and I am going to kill you brutally. I'm going to tear that ugly fucking head off your shoulders with my bare hands," I promise in a sinister manner.

"Yeah, and what's stopping you?"

I sneer, an evil grin spreading across my lips. "Absolutely nothing. I'll see you very soon."

"Don't bother, I'll be coming for her. She's mine," he shouts angrily, and it makes my blood boil.

"Yours?" I snicker.

"You're choosing a liar over your family? Over Kai?"

I roll my eyes. "Cry me a fucking river. But if you need the reassurance, yeah, yeah I am. You need to be put to sleep, Kyro, just like your son. Your plan just backfired, you're a foolish little man for giving her to me, because now, there is absolutely nothing or anyone on this damn earth that can take her from me."

I hang up before handing Wrath the phone. "Get Soul to call them and arrange for me to go there."

CHAPTER THIRTY-TWO

It's been a few days since everything came to light and, despite the mess, I feel a weight lifting off my shoulders. Hell knowing the truth has quieted my loud mind significantly. My meds seem to be working, and I feel calmer. Yet, beneath all the reassurance Hell gives me, and the numbness of the pills, a nagging feeling persists that so much more is to come. The guilt gnaws at me, making me feel responsible for all the chaos.

Sometimes, I have the urge to run again. It's an impulse, a natural instinct born from the fear of Kyro knowing where I am. The thought terrifies me when I dwell on it for too long, but I trust Hell. I know he won't let anything happen to me. I'm beginning to see him for who he truly is. He isn't just some guy working at Oddity Carnival; he is a ruthless killer with some authority in the underworld, even over Kyro, which I never expected.

When he said he chose me, I almost dissolved into the bed. He chose me, little old me, over his family and maybe even his morals. He understands that I must have lost my sanity when I did what I did, and he gets it. He is exactly what I've needed. He has set my soul free in ways he might never fully understand.

The night I left is still hazy. I'm trying to piece it all together and figure out if Kyro might still have Arabella. I don't want to burden Hell with too much, so I haven't mentioned it yet, but it's something I need to think about soon.

To find out Kyro has not only taken revenge on me, but his own nephew as well is insane, but in a strange way, I am grateful for the answers. They are answers I have needed since the day he first put his hands on me and took my innocence. He gave me no time to grieve my mother's death; it was so constant that I never truly mourned her. When Hell told me that his father had an affair with my mom, I was shocked, but it made sense to me. It also made sense to me that she would do that. Kyro is an evil fucking bastard, and if he treated my mom like that behind closed doors, then I don't blame her for falling for someone better. If Hell's father is like him, then I know that pull would have been irresistible, and that's the truth.

It's just a shame it has all gone this way. My mom is dead as a result of possibly falling in love. I knew her, and I know she must have felt trapped, just as I did, and in her desperation, she found solace in Hell's father. It's a tragic irony that the very thing that brought her a small moment of happiness also led to her demise.

Knowing all of this doesn't ease the pain, it probably never will, that's down to me, but it does provide some understanding.

My mother's death and the suffering I went through were both orchestrated by Kyro's spite. But in Hell, I've finally found my dark guardian, someone who wants me to regain my strength that was once stolen from me and although the past is filled with darkness, maybe, just maybe, the future holds a glimmer of light after all.

As I stroll across the trailer park in the early morning, I am holding my mini dolly tight to my chest, eager to get out of the Hollow's trailer for a while to hopefully see Blush. It's been a few days and I need some breathing space, some girl time. When I am at the front door, I knock, but I don't get the answer I was hoping for. I let out a heavy sigh and look around briefly.

I start to think about going to my old trailer to pick up the rest of my things that I left behind. When I have made the decision, I finally head in that direction until I am there. Fuck, I haven't got the key. I'm sure Madame said Eli dropped it off to her. Out of curiosity, I press the handle down and to my surprise it is unlocked after all. He must have not locked up before leaving.

After swinging the door open, I enter and glance around, noticing how cold it is in here now. Everything is exactly how I left it, and I make my way straight to the bedroom, so I don't have to be here long. Walking past the bed, I gently place mini dolly down on it, then go toward the wardrobe where I grab a bag and start to stuff my clothes inside. Suddenly, I hear a noise behind me, and I freeze, my gut dropping. I spin around to see Eli standing there, giving me an evil look.

My jaw sets tight as I turn to face him fully. The sight of him disgusts me. "I suggest you get out of here before I kill you," I bite out, rage filling every inch of me, making my body shake.

A grin twitches across his lips. "Not without you, Noir. Someone wants to see you."

I remain expressionless as he takes a calm step forward, and I point at him. "Stay. The. Fuck. Away."

"No can do. You're coming with me. You're my lifeline to get out of this."

"Get out of what? Abusing kids?" I snap back, tears blurring my vision. He stops, his eyes wide, and I continue. "I fucking knew you were a dirty fucking paedo. I should have killed you as soon as I sensed it."

"Yet you didn't. You trusted me like a silly little girl," he says calmly.

"Get the fuck out of here, Eli, before I scream. Me and Hell will gladly chop you into tiny little pieces and feed you to the pigs. This is your last fucking warning!"

Anger flashes through his eyes, and he suddenly darts toward my mini dolly, snatching her off the bed and I instinctively take a step forward in panic.

"He made this for you? This shit little thing? How sweet."

"Give me her, E, or I swear to fuck."

"You'll do what? Kill me? Do it."

He grabs dolly's head and rips it off.

"NO!" My breath hitches, tears streaming down my cheeks, and I feel my sanity slip entirely. When he goes to tear off one of her arms, I lose it, storming toward him, anger searing inside me.

I swing at him, my punches landing as he moves backwards, blocking them with his forearms. He suddenly grabs the side of my hair, yanking it, but I am so used to pain and roughness, that I am unbothered. I lift my arm, striking him in the balls and he groans, releasing me. As he clutches them, knees bowed, I spit in his eyes and then run toward the door. Hearing him get to his feet, I try to push the handle down on the front door, but it's somehow locked.

"You're not escaping him again, Noir!" he shouts before darting toward me.

I dash to the kitchen, desperate for a weapon of some kind. As I open a kitchen drawer, he snatches my hair, dragging me back before I can reach for a knife. I lift my hand without warning, poking his eyes and then stamping hard on his foot, causing him to release me again. I reach for the nearest weapon, and as soon as I have a huge, sharp knife, I swing my arm while turning my body rapidly. It connects with his stomach, a huge slice slashed across his abdomen.

His eyes widen as his intestines almost spill out and he grasps them, but I don't stop there. I raise the knife again with a scream, anger seeping out of me like an inferno, and I slash him across the throat, blood spraying across my face and body before he hits the ground with a loud thump. I breathe heavily with gritted teeth, my eyes pouring with tears.

As he gasps for air, trying to stop the blood squirting from his neck, gushing all over the floor, I become insane. Reaching down, I stand over him and shove my hands into his stomach, grabbing handfuls of his guts. I start to pull and pull, ripping his intestines out like I'm tugging on a fucking rope.

I watch as his life gradually leaves his convulsing body. "Dirty fucking cunt!" I scream before sobbing, "You will NEVER touch a child again!"

Suddenly, the front door crashes open, a jumbled blur in my peripheral vision, but I keep pulling, lost in my frenzy. Hell rounds the corner with Wrath right behind him, but I don't look at them. I just cry and yank until Eli's body finally goes limp, his eyes glazing over in death. I slip on the blood and collapse on my ass, leaning against the counter, my knees pulled up to my chest as I stare at Eli's lifeless form.

"Dolly?" Hell's voice is serene, a total opposite of my delirium. He steps toward me before crouching to block my view of Eli. My blurred gaze meets his as he reaches out, stroking my hair away from my eyes.

"What happened?"

"He tore mini dolly's head off, and I lost it," I weep.

His eyes ease. "Don't worry, I'll fix her," he calms me.

"He was trying to take me to Kyro."

Hell's eyes flash with irritation before he looks back at Wrath over his shoulder. "Lock this place the fuck down," he orders.

I hear Wrath walk away, then Hell turns back to me. "Come on, let's get you home," he says, gesturing with a small nod.

He takes my hands, helping me stand on wobbly legs. As we pass Eli's body, I glance down one last time, a shiver running through me.

HOLLOW HELLION

After having a shower, I feel like I've calmed down a lot, becoming used to the insanity that my life now brings. I stroll into Hell's bedroom, wrapping a black towel around my damp body. I spot him shirtless, resting against the headboard, stitching mini dolly's head back on. In awe, I crawl onto the bed before climbing over him and straddling him crotch. His dark gaze wanders down me briefly before he continues to stitch, and I watch in fascination.

"How did you learn to do this?" I ask, curiosity in my tone.

"In training I learned all kinds of things, including crafts." He answers, his eyes flashing to mine. "Mainly stitching corpses."

My gaze expands, and a grin twitches on Hell's lips before he looks down again. "How can you be shocked, my pretty girl? You just tore a man's intestines out of his fucking body."

I stay silent, knowing he is right.

"You surprised me you know?" he says, his eyes meeting mine, "You're a little fucking savage."

I lift a brow, "Well, he deserved it." I assert firmly.

He gives a slight nod, "Yeah, he fucking did."

When he finishes, he passes me my mini dolly. I gently take her with a small smile, gazing down at her and she is as good as new. Hell reaches over to the bedside, placing his sewing kit aside. As his focus returns to me, he observes me, sliding his warm hands up my bare thighs, under the towel, until he's gripping my hips bruisingly. I can't help but buck my hips and gasp, my eyes darting to his.

"I'm going to see the society tomorrow," he says, and I lift my head fully.

"Can I come?"

He shakes his head once, and I whisper, "Why?"

"Because I said so, Dolly."

"But wouldn't it be better if they didn't see me as some scared little girl on the run?" I protest.

He sighs, looking aside. "I can't risk it."

"Please." I plead.

"Dolly…" He gives me a warning tone.

"Please, Hell. Just take me, and if they want to speak to me, they can hear it all from me. They will respect me more for walking in there and facing what I've done."

He searches my eyes, thinking carefully with reluctance until finally, he gives the faintest of nods. He knows that in this system, they will prefer to hear this from me instead of hiding and not facing them.

"I am going to ask for mercy on you, but they will undoubtedly want me to give them something in return."

"Like what?" I question, tilting my head to the side.

He shrugs his shoulders, unbothered. "It could be absolutely anything that the cards draw."

"Cards?"

He nods. "Yes, the cards of skulls. You'll see tomorrow."

While scanning his painted face, I become lost in my thoughts for a while until I speak again.

"When are you ever going to let me see you without the paints? I ask, but he doesn't answer.

Leaning in close, I reach up and delicately slide two fingers down his cheek, smudging the black paints that conceal his handsome features.

"I want to see the real you, Hell."

As I gaze at him curiously, studying his reaction, he stays motionless, his whirling contacts peering deep into my eyes. Softly swiping my thumb over his bottom lip, I smear more paint, feeling the oily texture cling to my fingertips.

"Beneath the façade and the persona you play for everyone else. Give me a part of you that nobody else has seen."

He stays mute until finally, he gestures toward the bedside table. With confusion, I reach over, pull the drawer open and find some makeup wipes. A smile creeps on my lips as I lift them out.

Settling back, I tug a couple free and look at him. I raise the wipe to his face, gently removing the blackness that always masks him.

As I finish wiping away the last of the paint, he lowers his head, pinching his contacts and removing them one by one. I wait in breathless anticipation, my heart thumping in my chest. Finally, he lifts his eyes to mine, and I suck in a sharp breath involuntarily.

I stare at him, my gaze widening as I take in every detail. His sharp, chiselled features. Tanned skin with a shade of stubble. The way his loose curled, black hair cascades over his forehead. His dark, thick eyebrows. His ice-blue eyes, almost grey, piercing, and beautiful, framed by black lashes. His bottom right lip piercing is more noticeable and his soft lips. When he smirks ever so slightly, a small dimple appears at the corner of his mouth, making him look both dangerous and undeniably captivating.

"You look so different," I manage to murmur.

He lifts a brow, clearly unsure of what my words mean, and I quickly reassure him. "In a good way, of course. I just didn't expect…" I shudder, trailing off before continuing, my tone laced with awe and desire. "Fuck, you're so hot. I didn't expect your eyes to be that colour."

Now his face is bare, I can clearly see his jaw flex as he grinds his teeth, his enigmatic eyes sweeping down my front, igniting a burning need to spread through my core. "God, you have to ruin me like this, without your paints and contacts. Take it all. I don't care. Screw my ass until it's nothing if you want and do it deep."

His gaze lifts to mine swiftly, stunned by my filthy mouth, but I'm serious. I need to feel this man all over me, I am fucking feral for it.

Without warning, he grabs my throat harshly before slamming me down onto the soft mattress. With him between my legs, his hips grind against mine, his hard length sliding vertically against my bare pussy as he steals my lips, devouring my mouth with an animalistic hunger. I writhe beneath him, dragging my nails down his back, feeling the tension in his muscles. He rips the towel away from my body with a growl of frustration and we both become lost in the intensity of the moment.

CHAPTER THIRTY-THREE

It's late evening and I slip my cropped leather jacket up my arms, preparing to face the society with Hell. Nervous doesn't even begin to describe how I feel, but I know I need to ready myself for absolutely anything. I pull my tight black high-waist jeans further up, then turn and head for the front door.

Outside, it's dark and I spot Wrath and Soul already on their bikes while Hell waits for me to join him. I can hear the carnival buzzing with life in background, open again to the public under Madame's orders. Stopping in front of Hell, he slides a black, matte helmet over my head, then grabs my waist, lifting me onto the back of his bike. As he mounts the front, I wrap my arms tightly around him. He revs the engine with a booming roar, then speeds forward, leaving the carnival grounds behind us.

The cold night breeze whips around us as we ride, and I hold on tighter, feeling Hell's muscles beneath my hand on his abs. The tension of what's to come tightens in my chest with every passing minute.

HOLLOW HELLION

After some time, we ride through massive iron, spiked gates, and I peer over Hell's shoulder until I see a huge black mansion looming in sight, resembling a castle with bright lights from below illuminating it. When we pull up, Hell kicks out the stand and dismounts. I lift the helmet off my head, taking in the surroundings and noticing armed men guarding every corner. Hell takes the helmet, drawing my attention to him, then slides his arm around the middle of my back, lifting me off the bike.

When I'm standing, he brings his face close to mine. "Listen to me very carefully, Dolly," he murmurs seriously, and I give a tiny nod, swallowing hard. "Only speak when you're spoken to. Don't say more than you need to and don't ever fucking object to what they ask me to do, no matter what it is."

I stare into his eyes, my pulse racing. He gives me a firm kiss on the lips before taking my hand and pulling me toward the unknown. The huge doors open, and Soul and Wrath trail behind us. I look around the dark, castle-like décor, noticing only candles are providing light. It seems Hell knows exactly where he is going, his aura radiating confidence. We finally reach a large door, and Hell pauses, glancing back at me with a final, reassuring squeeze of my hand before pushing it.

When the door creaks open, I immediately notice the vast expanse of the room, pillars standing throughout. At the far end, a long, extended wooden table dominates the space, with three men seated behind it, side by side.

As we come to a stop, Hell releases my hand, his warmth dissipating, leaving me feeling exposed and vulnerable, but I try not to show my fear, though inside, I am screaming.

Hell takes a few steps forward before stopping in front of the men, all three of them intimidating, powerful, and dressed in black suits. Their presence is overwhelming, and I can feel their eyes boring into me, assessing, judging.

"I am here to ask for mercy on someone," Hell says, his deep voice echoing through the cavernous space.

The men lean in, whispering to one another until the middle one speaks, "Proceed."

Hell looks back at me, his gaze steady. "This is the girl who killed Hollow Haze last year."

"You want mercy for a girl who killed not only a member of the Shadow's but your family?" The man on the right asks, his dark eyes piercing through me.

Hell meets his gaze. "Yes," he answers, his voice unwavering.

"Reasons?"

"She was held captive by Kyro..."

"Not from you, Hell, from her." The man on the right gestures for me to step forward, and I do, my legs feeling like lead as I move to stand beside Hell.

"Name?" The middle man asks.

"Harley Miller."

Suddenly, the man on the right slowly stands, pushing his chair back with a deliberate motion. He keeps his eyes on mine as he circles the table, and we all watch his movements. He stops in front of me, leaning against the table, his hands clasped in front of him.

"Harley Miller?" he questions, and I give a small nod. "You're supposed to be dead aren't you?" he says, raising a brow in suspicion, and I straighten up, trying to project confidence.

"I was, but Kyro hid me."

"And why would he do that?"

I throw a glance at Hell above me and then look back at the man. "My mom was having an affair before she died. He revenge raped me from the age of twelve. I was being conditioned to be sold. Kai was heavily involved too," I murmur.

The other two men whisper to each other, their expressions unreadable. The man in front of me stares without a flicker of emotion, as if that is all normal to him.

"Your mother was a very dear friend of my wife's," he admits.

My brows pinch in confusion. "She was?"

He gives a small nod and I start to wonder if my mom knew all about this society; if she was more involved in the underworld than I initially thought.

"You killed Hollow Haze?" His voice is calm, almost too calm, and it sends a shiver down my spine. I nod again, trying to keep my composure.

"Speak," he demands, his tone turning cold, and I try not to jolt as his powerful voice booms through the room. "Why should we grant you mercy?"

I swallow hard, my mouth dry as I muster the courage to answer. "I had lost my sanity by that point, and I was desperate to escape after everything I had endured."

His eyes flash to Hell's beside me. "Why the sudden change? You were adamant to take this hit," he asks sternly.

I side-eye and when Hell speaks, I look at him. "Because I don't believe it's right what my cousin or uncle did. Kyro lured Harley to Oddity when she escaped by using a fucking paedophile to befriend her. He allowed me to have an intimate relationship with Harley when I didn't know who the fuck she was. He did this out of revenge because the affair Harley's mother was having was with my father. I will not kill an innocent woman for Kyro. I have no fucking loyalty toward him."

I look at the man, and he is eyeing Hell suspiciously. "But your loyalty lies with us, and she did kill a Shadow's member."

"She did," Hell answers truthfully, and I lower my eyes.

The man walks around the table again until he is seated beside the other two, and Hell steps forward until he is beside me. While they whisper into each other's ears, I wait nervously, my pulse hammering in my ears, wondering what is going to happen next.

When they're done, the middle one speaks, "Mercy will be granted to Harley Miller if Hell is to pull three cards. Since he is the one who is asking, he will need to pay the price." I glance up at Hell, but without hesitation, he nods in agreement, and my gut twists. Something dreadful settles within me, and I can't seem to shake it off.

The man on the right starts to shuffle cards before he spreads them across the table in a curve. "Step forward, Hell. Take three cards and lay them face down in front of you."

I watch his every move as he walks toward them confidently, and without a second thought, he picks out three cards, placing each face down. After gathering the stack of cards, the middle man leans over, flipping the first card, and I see it's a gold skull, shining against the light.

"A part of your loyalty – You are in debt to the Shadow's Society until the day you die. There will be no retrials."

I notice Hell stands straighter, as if that is something he didn't want, and I feel awful instantly.

He flips the second card, revealing a skull with a black cross over the right eye.

"A part of your strength – Mutilation of your right eye."

I suck in a quick breath, unable to help it. Tears start to blur my vision, and my fists clench. Hell stays completely silent, now giving nothing away.

The third card is finally flipped, showing two big skulls and one small one in the middle, surrounded by red roses.

"A part of your legacy – Your right to have children. A permanent vasectomy."

I step forward because this is utterly fucking crazy, but Hell looks at me sharply, and I stop. I give a small headshake, tears now tumbling down my cheeks, but he ignores my silent plea before looking at the men. "Let's get this done."

"No," I speak, my voice cracking.

"Harley…" Hell uses my real name to warn me.

"Please," I whisper, knowing it is so unfair that he has to lose so many good things in his life just to save mine.

"Enough!" He shouts at me, and my body tenses. "Get her out of here."

Suddenly, Soul wraps his arm around my midsection from behind, guiding me out. "He's made his mind up, Noir. Leave it," he murmurs in my ear, and I weep.

As we exit the room, my heart feels like it's being torn apart, and I can't help but feel an overwhelming sense of responsibility and sorrow. The door closes behind us, and I hear the muffled sounds of the men preparing to carry out the punishments.

HOLLOW HELLION

After what feels like an eternity of being in the foyer with Soul and Wrath, I pace up and down, fiddling with my fingers, hating every second of this agonizing wait. The tension is unbearable, and my mind races with worst-case scenarios. Suddenly, the doors open, and I freeze, watching Hell slowly come into view. He has one eye covered with a bloodied rag, and he is limping.

My heart clenches at the sight. I rush toward him, and as soon as I am close enough, he keeps his head bowed, wrapping his arm around my shoulder. I can't shake the horrible feeling in my stomach with every step we take toward the exit.

"We've got a truck waiting," Soul says. "They've loaded your bike on the trailer at the back, so you don't have to ride."

Hell stays silent, his head still lowered until we get outside and climb into the truck. As I sit in the back, Hell groans, lying across the seat with his head on my lap.

"Fuck, my nuts hurt," he mutters, his voice strained. I run my fingers through his hair, trying to soothe him, and I sniffle, which causes him to look at me with his good eye.

"What the fuck did I say to you about crying, Little Dolly?" he asserts sternly.

My eyes soften, tears fogging my vision. "I'm sorry, I can't help it." He takes in my features as I continue. "I wish…"

"You wish what? That I wouldn't have done that? Then they would have made me kill you there and then."

"I know," I weep, my voice breaking unable to control my emotions. "You now can't have children, you can't have a life, and it's all my fault."

He reaches up, sliding his hand around the back of my neck, his touch both comforting and grounding. "They didn't take my fucking life. You're still here," he says, his swirling eye boring into mine, and his words breathe warmth inside of me.

"I never fucking wanted kids. I am grown up enough to know not to bring a child into this madness, Noir. I could never be a father."

As he reassures me, although it doesn't make me feel any better, I rest my forehead against his, trying to compose myself. "This is so messed-up," I whisper, my voice trembling.

"This is my reality, pretty girl. Nothing is normal."

I lift my head, looking down at him. "And now it's my normal."

He gives a small nod. "Now I take Kyro out. They told me in there that he isn't officially part of the Shadow's; he's just an associate." I tilt my head to the side, trying to process his words and understand what he is trying to say. "You have mercy for your murder, Noir, but they will not stop Kyro from possibly killing or taking you again because you're not under their protection and you will never be."

I take a deep inhale, anger and frustration bubbling up inside me until he continues. "But you're under my protection. You always will be. Kyro can't kill me, or he will receive punishment for killing on Shadow's member. So, for now, you stay at Oddity until I find him." I nod in agreement, my heart feeling heavy because of all of his sacrifices.

CHAPTER THIRTY-FOUR

It's been a week since my eye was cut, and my balls were snipped. I'm standing in front of the mirror, staring at my reflection. The deep cut criss-crosses over my right eye, a reminder of the price I paid. I am still yet to see if I am blind or not.

The stitching was poorly done by Wrath; I swear he decided to make me look even more like a fucking monster than I already am on purpose. M will be impressed at least. The rough, uneven lines give my face a more menacing appearance, as if I needed any more fucking help in that department.

I've been wearing a black eye patch, but as soon as it is healed enough, I will just paint over it. Dolly is feeling guilt, and it's eating her alive, but she will come to understand that this all means nothing to me if it means she lives. My eye will heal, my pride will heal, but I would never have fucking healed if I had to kill her. This is nothing compared to the depths I would go for her.

I hear her enter the bathroom behind me, and I side-eye over my shoulder. She wraps her arms around my mid, placing a kiss to my back. I grab her wrist, pulling her around in front of me. She gazes up at me, her focus fixed on my eye, and I lean down.

"I'm going to pull it open, and you tell me what you see."

She holds her breath before giving a sharp nod in agreement.

As I pull from my cheek and eyebrow, I pry my eye open, gritting my teeth from the pain. Light strikes it straight away and then I see Noir's silhouette in a very blurred haze which is always a good sign.

"It's bloody and has a small line across it, but it's not as deep as I thought. It could heal, Hell," she murmurs. "Can you see out of it?"

I release it slowly, a hiss escaping my lips. "Kind of."

A big smile paints across her face, "I'm so happy to hear that."

Then, she looks at me seriously, "Look, I've been thinking about a plan…"

Suddenly Soul shouts from my bedroom, "HELL?"

I turn around swiftly, and he comes to the bathroom door, "Oddity is under attack. They're shooting the carnival to fucking pieces."

I look down at her quickly, "We need to get you out of here." I take her wrist and drag her behind me.

HOLLOW HELLION

When we're outside, the rain pelts down on us and I lift her, dumping her onto the front of the bike as I get on the back.

"What… What are you doing?" she stutters out.

"You're riding."

"What? I don't know how to ride a fucking bike!" she gasps.

"You will now. It makes sense if I'm on the back; they can't shoot me." I growl, making her place her hands on the handlebars. "Now fucking ride."

"Hell, I'm not sure…"

Gunfire erupts behind the circus, screams following suit and I glance back to see bikes rounding the corner, heading in our direction.

I place my hands over Dolly's, revving the engine. "You've fucking got this, Noir. Trust me on this one."

I make her turn the throttle and she screams as we bolt forward, with Soul and Wrath in tow.

I guide her through the woods as the boys shoot at Kyro's men. I need to get her somewhere he doesn't know until I kill him. I cannot believe this motherfucker has been stupid enough to allow his men to raid Oddity. If I don't kill him, The Shadow's will now.

I look back again, noticing they're gaining, many of them. I look at Soul and Wrath before I yell, "Split!"

They nod before they take separate routes, hoping to guide some of Kyro's men off course. We speed through the trees, the only light in the dark forest coming from the bike's headlight, illuminating our path. The muddy ground is uneven, but the bike handles it. I release one of Dolly's hands, retrieve my gun from the back of my pants, aim, and shoot until a bullet hits a rider that is close, sending him off his bike. But there are at least six more not too far away.

I seethe, looking forward, and make Dolly take a sharp left, causing her to let out a loud scream followed by laugh. As we ride, she seems to get more excited by the danger, and I can't help but grin.

Soon we're on an open pathway that leads near the ocean, and I look back to see them still following. I open fire, taking a few more out.

"Hell, if I was dead, it wouldn't be this way; you could kill him caught off guard." Her yelled words make me look down at her side profile.

"What?" I ask, shouting over the engine.

She shrugs her shoulders. "He won't stop until he has me."

"You're not fucking dying, Noir!"

"No, I didn't mean…"

I lift my head to see a dead end, a cliff edge coming up.

"Noir, squeeze the right break," I order because my gun is still in my hand. She does as I ask, and we come to an abrupt stop, jolting forward. I hear Soul's and Wrath's bikes close by somewhere in the woods.

"I can take these fuckers out," I state as I look back to see them closing in, readying myself with my gun aimed, until I feel Noir's hand reach back, her touch finding my cheek. With her head tilted, I gaze down at her. As I scan her pretty, wet features, I release the left handle, bringing my palm to the side of her neck, my thumb gliding down her jaw.

"I know we don't express any fluffy feelings or speak the words boring couples would use to bare their souls. But I want you to know that I have always liked it our way, on our terms. I need you to know I'm obsessed with you too, Hell," she murmurs. Despite the danger coming up behind us, I can't help but listen because of the sincerity in her blue gaze. "We might not be normal, but our broken pieces fit. Every injury, every stain, every chase, and every frightening whispered word in the night has brought us together. You taught me to accept my flaws, to see them not as imperfections but as parts of my story that you have always cherished. And I can't thank you enough for all you have done for me. For how you've made me feel."

I search her eyes which are filled with tears, "Promise me something?" She croaks and my brows knit with confusion, but I give a slight nod. "Promise me you'll take every single last one of them out and make them pay for what they have done."

"Dolly…" I whisper, about to shove my tongue down her throat until a gunshot goes off, whizzing past my head and I look back sharply, anger spiking in me.

The bike suddenly darts forward, and I glance down at Noir quickly. "What the fuck are you doing??" I yell.

She stays completely silent, determination in her eyes.

"Noir! No!"

She aims straight for the cliff's edge, and I feel a rise of anxiety. I drop my gun as she full throttles it, and I reach for the front brake. As soon as I squeeze it, we're already at the cliff's edge, both of us flung over the handlebars and we descend from the cliff, my bike following.

I hear Noir's scream until I submerge into the black, stormy sea below. The current smashes over me, filling my lungs with water as I try to swim to the surface, desperately wanting to find Noir, but it's near impossible with one eye. When I finally push my body upward to the surface, I take a huge gasp of air. I frantically look around, scanning the turbulent waves that continue to crash over me.

"NOIR?!" I roar, my voice hoarse with panic.

I can't see or hear anything as I float. The water is a dark, churning abyss, swallowing every sound, every sign of life. The currents toss me around like a fucking ragdoll, and my heart pounds in my chest. I start swimming around, desperate to find her, dipping my head underwater to see if I can spot her silhouette in the murky depths.

"DOLLY!" I continue to shout, the saltwater burning my throat and eyes. The worry in my voice echoes back at me and my muscles ache from the force of fighting the relentless sea, but I refuse to stop. I can't stop.

Each second feels like an eternity, her slipping away from me with each passing minute and the cold seeps into my bones, but the adrenaline keeps me going. I push through the discomfort, the exhaustion, the dread. I hear Kyro's men far above on the cliff edge, and they shine torches down, but my mind races with thoughts of her, of losing her, of the emptiness her absence would create in my life.

CHAPTER THIRTY-FIVE

I sit on the edge of the cliff, staring into the darkness below. The air is still, the stars twinkle brightly, beautiful and calm, the complete opposite to the tornado that rages within me. I gaze down at her mini-dolly in my palms, a tiny thing that feels like a cruel reminder of what I've lost. It's been a week since we rode off this cliff, and there is still no sign of my Little Dolly's existence. The dull ache inside me is almost un-fucking-bearable, her last words haunting me every moment of the day, tormenting me.

"Promise me you'll take every single last one of them out."

I will do it. I have to. I fucking want to. I have already found where Kyro is, and it's only a matter of time before I get my hands on him. I'm just waiting for the perfect opportunity. He thinks Dolly is dead, so he's living his fucking life as if there are no repercussions for what he has done, as if he is untouchable, as if this is now over, but he is so fucking wrong.

His focus has slipped, but if he thinks I am not going to make him pay for this, he is gravely mistaken. He clearly does not have a fucking clue how much Dolly meant to me. How obsessed I was with her. I just wish she had trusted me; trusted in the words and actions I showed to her. I wish she didn't do something so fucking stupid. Now it feels like it was all for nothing. I'm hoping, somewhere, she is still here, and she actually survived. I'm hoping she is lying low, but I can't keep my hopes up for much longer; it's fucking killing me.

The waves crash against the rocks below, a constant memory of that fateful night and I clench my fists, the mini dolly digging into my palms. I have to channel this pain, this fucking rage, into something meaningful. I have to make Kyro pay for everything he's done. For every scar he left on her body and soul. For every moment of fear and torture she suffered. For stealing the future we could have had together.

I close my eyes, the memory of her voice, her touch, her smell, her smile temporarily filling the void within me, but it's not enough. It will never be e-fucking-nough. I won't let her sacrifice be in vain. I'll take every single last one of them out and when I finally stand over Kyro's bloodied body, he'll know the true meaning of vengeance.

When my phone vibrates in my pocket, I pull it out and gaze down at the lit-up screen to see it's a private caller. I answer and stay silent, pressing it to my ear.

"Hell, we have made a decision and before we go ahead, we would like to offer you the opportunity first," a voice says, calm and confident.

I lie back on the cold grass, staring up at the stars. "What?"

"Since Kyro gave the go-ahead to rain terror on Oddity when it was open to the public, we have made the decision to put a hit on his head. As you know, having even our own associates go against us or wreak havoc on our grounds is not something we can tolerate or take lightly."

I sit up quickly, listening carefully as he continues. "Oddity is one of the best cleaners we have in the society, and he could have uncovered us by being so fucking reckless. He must be killed before he exposes Oddity for what it is."

"I agree," I say, gazing over at the sea.

"We're giving you the chance to carry out the hit, or we can hand it to someone else," he offers.

"Fuck no. I'll take it," I declare, knowing Kyro was already dead anyway, but I don't want the society to do it before I do.

"Seeing as he knows what he has done is wrong, he has contacted us in hopes to plead for mercy tomorrow night."

I straighten up, my interest piqued. "And?"

"And we have permitted it under false pretences."

"You've set him up?" I ask, a dark satisfaction creeping into my voice.

"Exactly. While he is on the way here, it would be a good time for you..." he trails off.

"No problem. I'll be ready," I respond.

"He also believes we have told you to hold off until his mercy plea, so he will not see it coming."

My natural suspicion raises. "All this for a man who has been your associate for years and years?"

"Yes. He has been around for so long, Hell, that he should know better than to be so fucking stupid," he retorts calmly.

I nod, although he can't see me. "I'll be in touch," he says before hanging up.

I wait a few seconds longer, staring down at my phone. I can finally end this, but it means nothing if my Little Dolly isn't here with me to witness his downfall and demise. I stand up, brushing the grass off my clothes, and take a deep breath. I slip my phone back into my pocket and make my way back to my bike, my mind racing and conducting my wicked plans.

HOLLOW HELLION

I ride across the field, the wind whipping past me, almost at my underground chamber. When I am close enough, I cut the engine and jump off, my boots hitting the ground with a thud. I walk to the doors, pull them open, and descend the steps. Once inside, I head straight for my empty torture room, intent on grabbing a gasoline can.

I stop in my tracks as soon as I notice something lying delicately on the surgeon's table. A single black, thorned rose. My heart rate picks up, pounding against my ribs like a fucking drum. I rush forward, my breath quickening with each step. I reach out for it, allowing the thorns to prick my fingertips, and a small grin stretches across my lips.

"She's a-fucking-live," I whisper, relief and confusion rushing through me. The rose is a message, a sign that she's out there. The dark petals and sharp thorns have always been a perfect symbol of her—dark, dangerous, and fucking beautiful.

CHAPTER THIRTY-SIX

It's been a week since I hurled me and Hell off that cliff in a moment of madness and desperation. I know he must think I am dead. I know he must be furious at me, and I don't fucking blame him. Although it might make no sense to him, in that second and still now, it made perfect sense. Hell was ready to risk it all for me, but he wasn't considering the fact that this will not stop as long as I am still alive or with Kyro. So, I took risks too. It's only fair. Kyro will keep getting his men to hunt me down, killing innocents in his wake. It's something my heart cannot handle or carry.

This has gone way too far already. I will never truly be free. But if Kyro thinks I am dead, there is every possibility that man will think he can live his life as normal again, begging the society for forgiveness and getting away with it. He will be stupid enough to let his guard down somewhere, and as soon as that guard slips, I know Hell can make his move. I guess I started to feel like a burden.

From a distance, I stand in the dark woods at the back of Kyro's mansion and stare at the gloomy structure. The lights have been off for three days now, with no sign of life, which tells me he has upped and left his home for a while to try to win the Shadow's over or maybe plot to take Hell out in some way to stop his evident murder.

I'm here because I need answers. I need to know if Arabella is still here. If she ever were here, and if she were, where the fuck she could be. I know I am taking a big risk, but that is why I have stalked this place for three days. Before I came here, I slipped into Hell's underground chamber, leaving him a black thorned rose, giving him a hint that I am still here yet lurking in the shadows waiting for the perfect time to be beside him again. It was eating me a live at the thought that he might think I'm dead when I'm not.

After a moment of reflection, staring at my old bedroom window, I jump up without any more hesitations, catching the metal fence and pulling myself up and over it. I land on my feet with a light thud before striding through the yard, my footsteps soft as I creep around the pool's edge until I am by the back doors. I pull on the handle to find it's locked, so I continue to see if any windows are open. When I finally find one that leads into the kitchen, I climb through and enter.

HOLLOW HELLION

The room is dark and eerily silent. Haunting memories flood back as I look around, but I push them aside, focusing on why I am here in the first place. I move sneakily, my senses on high alert, listening for any sign of life.

Making my way into the huge foyer, it is bathed in darkness, so dim that I cannot see anything other than the windows shining in the moonlight and the outline of furniture. When I come to a halt, I turn, ascending the grand staircase to the second floor. As soon as I reach the top, I notice all the doors, scanning them one by one until I spot the one where I was held captive at a far distance.

Suddenly, I hear a noise coming from down below and I duck, hiding behind the banister. My breathing picks up, my chest heaving before I place my hand over my mouth, trying to remain silent and calm my racing heart. With a shaky hand, I reach into my leather jacket's pocket and grasp the pocket knife hidden within.

As I peer through the wooden rail, I quietly flip out the blade and a light comes on in the living room. I see shadows moving around, and a few men murmuring, but neither sound like Kyro. Without warning, I hear one of them shout and all kinds of banging follow, sounds of what seems like metal swiping through the cold air, and liquid falling to the ground. Then, all goes quiet, and the light switches off. My eyes widen when I see a figure slowly emerging, and the silhouette stands still at the threshold. I try not to move until they unexpectedly decide to stroll toward the stairs, in my direction.

I gently stand, backing myself against the wall, and move along it, searching for an open door. My fingers finally grasp a doorknob and I twist it slowly, pushing it open just enough to slip inside. I close it behind me as quietly as possible and lean against it, listening intently. The sound of the heavy footsteps grows louder, each step echoing in the eerie silence of the mansion and anxiety tightens in my chest.

My heartbeat rings in my ears as I clasp my knife tighter, ready for whatever might come through the door. The footsteps stop right outside, and I hold my breath, every muscle in my body tense. The doorknob begins to turn, and I brace myself. But then, they retreat, shifting away from my hiding spot. I let out a slow, silent breath of relief and rest my head back against the door, closing my eyes for a moment.

I pull my hood over my head and wait for what feels like forever. When I finally gather the courage to get out of here and possibly come back another time, I gradually open the door, peering around the threshold from left to right. When I don't see or hear anything, I begin to creep into the hallway until I suddenly hear a soft noise behind me, and I freeze. I look back to see the same silhouette at the other end of the landing, but this time, they are looking right at me.

Shit.

They suddenly rush forward, and I run for my fucking life. I try to hold onto the scream that is threatening to rip from my throat, my legs feeling like they might give away as their footsteps get louder and closer behind me.

With nowhere else to go, I dash into a room, attempting to slam it closed behind me, but a foot blocks me from doing so. I jump back, raising the knife in my hand and as soon as the door is swung open, I swing my arm, releasing the knife. It embeds in their arm with a thud, and they groan, but the groan is all too familiar.

My eyes widen and he rips the knife out of his arm with a grunt, blood spurting and landing onto the wood floor below. Hell, storms toward me, anger raging through him, and I back myself against a wall, my eyes squeezed shut until he stops in front of me, grabbing my throat with both of his gloved hands.

He lifts me, slamming me against the wall in an act of frustration before his lips collide with mine. Although he is strangling the fucking life out of me, I allow his tongue to enter my mouth, wrapping my legs around his waist.

He presses his big body against mine, releasing my neck and lifting me higher by my ass. I place my hands on the side of his neck, my head tilted to the side, our kiss frantic and heated. I feel the loss between us pouring from our souls and the time lost pulls us tighter together. When we break apart, our breathing is frantic and the back of his fingers slide over my cheek, his forehead resting against mine.

"I might never forgive you for doing something so fucking stupid," he growls.

"Yes, you will," I whisper in response.

"Why, Noir, why the fuck did you do that? I thought…"

Tears well in my eyes as he lowers his gaze, and his vulnerability hurts me. "I'm sorry, I just wanted to give you breathing space. If he thought I was dead, I knew he would be careless."

His hand slips to the back of my neck, where he pushes on it, tilting my head back. He breathes heavily over my lips, "You could have fucking died, silly little fucking Dolly."

I try not to smile as I lift my hand to his face. "I wasn't going out like that, Hell. I was always coming back to you, and I always will." He presses his forehead against mine again, and I continue. "Have you found him?"

His one eye lifts to mine and I notice he hasn't got his contacts in, probably to be less detectable. After a brief silence and him sliding his thumb down my jaw, he gives a small nod.

"So what are you doing here?" I ask, and he arches his brow. "The question is, what the fuck are you doing here?"

I take a deep breath, my voice steady despite the pounding of my heart. "I'm here to find Arabella. I need answers, and I need to know if she's still alive."

"Dolly…" He says before lowering me to my feet and he shows his back to me, rubbing his mouth with his hand.

"What is it, Hell?"

He pauses at my question before he turns to face me, "I'm not sure if she is real." He says with honesty and my brows pinch, "What?"

He steps toward me. "I've tried to find anything I can about her, and no one knows who the fuck she is, Noir. She is non-existent." I shake my head once and he continues, lowering himself to my height. "Are you sure you weren't just imagining things because you were so fucking traumatized? There's always that possibility…"

"No." I declare through tight teeth with tears brimming. "I know she is real."

He sighs, stroking my hair, "Did you actually ever see her? Touch her?"

I just stare at him blankly as I think about it. How I only heard her voice close to my ear or far away, only ever seeing her fully when it's in a blur of madness or in the mirror. But it felt so real, she felt so real. She got me out of there, I am sure she did. I might not have touched her, but it felt like she was there to me. The only thing that makes me doubt it is when I saw her in the death rooms, and she almost got me killed with a trap.

"I was thinking maybe you have an altar, or you were hallucinating, but…"

"Like you?" I question.

He shakes his head once, "Hellion is merely my character, Dolly. He isn't inside my head, and I cannot hear him. He is just a part of me that I let loose on Dark Night. Parts of myself that I suppress. He is not a disorder, and he cannot control me in anyway. It's not the fucking same." He admits honestly. I continue silence as he carries on. "I'm no fucking doctor though."

I nod and lower my head. "Which room, pretty girl?" he asks while standing upright.

With a sniffle, I wipe the tears off my face and pass him, taking his warm gloved hand in mine. Leading Hell through the dimly lit mansion, his words and doubts linger in my mind. Every creak of the floorboards and every whisper of the wind outside seem to boom the uncertainty churning within me.

We reach the door to the room where I heard Arabella, where I believed she was. Beside mine. I take a glance at my door, a shiver running through me as each memory floods through my mind until I feel Hell's hands on my shoulders and his kiss on the top of my head. When I am ready, I turn the door knob and we enter.

I glance around the dark empty space, noticing there is absolutely nothing in here but a fireplace. There's no bed. No window. No anything. My gaze roams around the walls, trying to see if there are any chains or brackets where they would have been attached like mine were, but again, there is nothing.

Sadness washes over me, the reality hitting me like a ton of bricks. Is it true? Could she really be only an altar or a figure of my imagination? Do I officially have no family at all?

Hell's big arms wrap around my midsection from behind as tears fall from my eyes and he draws me in closer. We stay in silence for a while, until I move forward, and he releases me. I stroll around his tall frame, heading for the door and once I am outside of mine, I rest my head against it, trying to breathe through the anxiety until finally, I turn the knob.

As soon as I walk in, my watery, wide eyes dart around, noticing the makeshift bed in the corner, the bucket, the boarded-up window, and in the corner, the bracket to my chain lying on the floor. I slap my hands over my face, all of it becoming too much and I weep. When Hell enters, I hear him place something down onto the floor before he cloaks his arm around my shoulders, drawing me into his chest.

"Is this where he kept you?" He asks while looking around.

I sniff and nod, then I feel him move away from me. When I hear a liquid being poured all over the floor from a distance, I lift my head, slowly removing my hands from my face. Hell has a gasoline can in his hand, dousing absolutely everything in fuel, and the toxic fumes assault my senses.

"What are you…" I trail off as he drops the can onto the hard floor with an echoing thud.

I observe his every move until he stops behind me again and he withdraws something from his pocket. He pulls out a box of matches and when he ignites one, the light is bright in the dark room, making my breath catch.

"Let it go, my Little Dolly. Light it the fuck up and let it all burn."

With a shaky hand, I take the match from him, and he places his lips on the side of my head. Without hesitation, I toss the match onto the ground.

The flames climb into an inferno, a wave of fury, destroying all the horrific memories that happened here and I feel a sense of satisfaction. We wait for a few seconds longer before he guides me toward the door. I take one last look back at my childhood, my old life, burning away just as it should, then with a release of a tense breath, I follow him, leaving it all behind me.

HOLLOW HELLION

While standing by the fence at the back of the mansion, we watch as it disintegrates into nothing but ash and haunting goodbyes. The flames roar and the ember of the blaze fills the air. With my arms and legs wrapped around Hell, I lay my face on his shoulder, feeling the heat from the fire warming our skin.

"Thank you," I whisper, my voice full of raw emotion.

He glances down at me, his eye easing. "You don't have to fucking thank me, Dolly. Just don't ever leave me like that again, or I'll be forced to chain you the fuck up myself," he responds, his tone serious yet amused.

I gently smile and sigh, the weight of the past few weeks lifting slightly. "Don't worry, I won't," I promise.

He gazes over at the burning mansion again, the flames consuming everything in their path. The adrenaline fades, replaced by a strange calmness, and the crackling of the fire drifts into the background. I look up at Hell, his painted face illuminated by the distant glow of the flames.

"Will he know that I am at Oddity? I don't want all of that to be for nothing," I murmur.

He strokes my back soothingly with his gloved hand, then presses his lips against my head. "I'll sneak you in. It'll be fucking fine." he reassures me, "No one will know you're there until I finally kill this motherfuck tomorrow night."

I lift my head fully in shock, "Tomorrow night?" I gasp out.

"Yeah, tomorrow night. The Shadow's have helped me set him up since he raided Oddity."

A big smile spreads across my lips as he carries me away to his bike, I feel a small sense of closure.

"As I said, my pretty girl, this will all be over soon, and I fucking meant it," he reassures as I lay my face on his shoulder.

CHAPTER THIRTY-SEVEN

Early in the morning, I make myself a glass of water in the dimly lit kitchen, adding a few ice cubes. The first light of dawn barely pierces through the windows as Soul strolls in, slumping into a chair behind me with a big yawn.

"Where the fuck were you last night?" he asks, his voice gruff with tiredness.

I side-eye him, taking a sip of my water before turning around to face him. "I was with Noir," I finally answer.

His arms freeze midair, disbelief etched across his face. "What the fuck are you talking about, Hell?"

"She's upstairs asleep."

He shakes his head once, almost shocked. "No fucking way."

I nod, my expression deadly serious. "I'm not lying."

"How the fuck?"

I shrug, leaning back against the counter. "She thought it would be easier if Kyro believed she was dead."

He raises an eyebrow, sitting back in his chair, trying to process the information. "And what do you believe?"

"I guess it has. He's been acting more careless with his locations, thinking he's gotten away with shit," I reply, my words laced with agitation. He nods, and I continue, "The Shadows want him dead for raiding Oddity, and they are setting him up tonight."

"How?" he asks, his tone now full of intrigue.

I lean forward, my eyes locking onto his. "He's going to see them tonight to ask for mercy, but on the way there, we will fucking ambush him. Get the Dark Night crew together with all their ruthless weapons. We war at eight pm."

Soul's green eyes glint with murder, a devilish smile spreading across his face as he absorbs my words. I start to think about when I told my brothers that Noir killed Haze and how I chose her. Their reaction was exactly what I expected. Nothing. We always have each other's backs, no matter what. Our bond is unbreakable. Me, Soul, and Wrath—the true Hollow's—have proven our power time and time again. I trust their loyalty and decisions without question, just as they trust mine. No one comes between us. No one ever will. Together, we're a force.

I stand, keeping my gaze fixed on Soul's. "Tonight, Kyro fucking dies in the most inhumane way possible," I promise. I lift my glass of water off the table, the ice clinking softly against it, and head back upstairs.

HOLLOW HELLION

When I step into my bedroom, I pause to take in the sight of Dolly, still peacefully asleep on her back, one of her arms draped above her head, her face turned slightly to the side. I gently close the door, trying not to wake her, because she's so fucking pretty when she sleeps. I stand at the end of the bed, taking a sip of water, my eyes trailing over her, the outline of her naked body visible beneath the silk sheet.

My brow raises, my mind stirring with wicked thoughts as it always does when she is this fucking vulnerable. The urge to crush her lifeless body beneath me enters my crazed mind. I slowly walk around the bed before placing the glass of iced water down, then move back to where I was and reach down, taking a handful of the sheet, feeling the soft texture against my palm. I start to drag it down her body gradually, each slow tug revealing her perfect shape to me.

The satin material glides smoothly over the mounds of her breasts until her pierced nipples and stomach come into view. I devour her with wild eyes when her cunt is exposed, her leg turned outward, giving me a beautiful view.

My dick grows firm and painfully heavy in my boxers, a throb pulsing through it. I slip my hand inside, getting a good grip, my precum coating my skin. When I gently release the sheet and stand upright, she stirs with a soft moan, turning her head to the other side, but her position doesn't shift. I ease my boxers down my legs, then stroke myself, the hunger mounting inside me to fuck her while she's asleep.

I carefully kneel on the bed, dipping my head, and ghosting my mouth over her flesh as I trail up her inner thigh. Her skin breaks out in goosebumps the higher I get until my lips are hovering above her pussy. I inhale her sweet, intoxicating scent, my grip strengthening on my shaft, and my eyes roll back. I lower my head further, my breath hot against her skin, and I press a soft kiss to the scars on her thigh, but she doesn't wake, clearly in a deep sleep.

My hand moves faster on my dick, the need to be inside her now overwhelming. I position myself between her legs, one hand beside her head, and reach over to scoop out an ice cube. I place it on my fingertips before sliding them and the ice inside her pussy without warning. As soon as she takes a sharp inhale, her legs tensing, I force my cock straight in after with one smooth stroke. I feel her clenched walls along my piercings, and she releases a big gasp.

The sensation of her cold cunt enveloping my length instantly fills me with the twisted illusion that she could be dead beneath me, and my eyes slowly close, relishing the feeling.

When I gaze down at her once more, she is now breathing heavily, her eyelids fluttering, trying to make sense of what is happening while still dazed and half asleep. As I lower my mouth to her ear, I draw back to the tip and thrust back inside her with a groan, my balls tightening.

"Play dead for me, Dolly," I demand breathlessly, my arousal evident in my strained tone.

I notice she bites her bottom lip before she falls limp, giving me exactly what I desire, like the deranged good girl she is. I take her arms and lie them down beside her, positioning her as I see fit. With her face turned to the side, I lick my tongue up her cheek with a growl before staring down at her, starting to fuck her. I bury my shaft as far as I can get myself and I know I am not going to last fucking long, I can already feel that pathetic tingle shooting through me, a wave of pleasure building with each thrust. Her lifeless form beneath me, her tits bouncing with every movement, drives me fucking wild.

I lose myself in the rhythm, brutally screwing her cunt, my hips slamming against hers as she lays ridged. The room fills with the sounds of our bodies colliding, the iced water slurping up and down my rock-hard length, and my own ragged breaths.

As I sink my teeth into her neck, I feel the climax approaching and when it strikes, the sensation rocks my entire body, my eyes rolling back as I let out a loud growl. I cum deep inside her, my warm juice mixing with the ice-cold liquid in her pussy.

Losing my mind, I pull out swiftly, flipping her onto her front, and she rolls like a rag doll. I grab the back of her hair, lifting it and pressing her face down into the pillow. With my hand on the back of her head, pushing, I use my knees to spread her legs high and wide beside her. When I'm satisfied, I reach over again, scooping out another ice cube and slide it into her asshole.

I force it all the way in with my finger, then creep down her body. As soon as I'm low enough, I spread her ass wide with my hands, admiring her little pink ring, then dip down and start eating her out. I devour her violently, sucking the cold water out of her and viciously use my teeth to gnaw, madly wanting to be buried deep inside, to live inside. The stillness of her body, how she remains motionless and doesn't make a sound while I violate her, pushes me to the verge of madness and I grip her ass cheeks tighter, my fingers digging into her flesh as I feast. My tongue plunges inside, swirling and exploring, tasting, and sliding against her walls. I growl against her skin as her muscles yield, allowing me to lick deeper with each thrust.

I pull back, giving a sharp spit before driving my tongue in deep one last time, then rise. I move up her body, taking a handful of her hair and yanking her head back. As I gaze down at her face, her eyes are closed, her lips parted, and I take my solid cock, guiding it into her asshole.

I force my cock inside her with one hard thrust, noticing her brows pinch ever so slightly, a breath escaping her lips, but she continues to play the dead game for me, heightening my disturbed arousal. I gather her hair into a ponytail, wrapping it around my fist, pulling and pressing it against her back. My other hand finds the headboard above us, gripping tightly as I start to fuck her cold hole with deep, slow thrusts. My eyes don't leave her face, picturing her dead beneath me, and I am doing unholy things to her body.

My thrusts grow rapidly over time, and soon I am slamming into her so fucking deep that her cheeks slap against my hips. When I finally cum, I growl against her lips, before panting against them.

"Good dead, Little Dolly," I whisper breathlessly.

I don't stop, knowing she must be close, and she's held on for my own sick enjoyment.

"Open your eyes," I order.

They fly open, and she looks straight into mine. I smile which she returns before I plunge my tongue into her mouth, and she moans while sucking on it. I fuck her cum-filled asshole ruthlessly until she explodes, a scream tearing from her throat. I slow down as she pulses around me, then, unable to hold myself up any longer, I collapse on top of her, the force of my weight knocking the wind out of her lungs.

I pull her with me as I roll onto the bed beside her, and she cuddles into my side.

"Tonight's the night, Noir." I state, still trying to gather my breath.

She lifts her head with a smile, and I can see the happiness in her eyes. She's finally feeling free of her past and seeing her like this makes me want to do everything I can to fucking keep it that way. She'll only ever feel the cold metal of chains again when it's under my control, knowing she's safe and can be freed whenever she needs to be. After I give her pussy a good fucking beforehand, of course.

CHAPTER THIRTY-EIGHT

It's finally the early evening of the day that will change my entire life forever. No more will I be bound to his wickedness. No longer will I feel trapped in this world. I'm so close. So close to ended it all so I can finally be free. Knowing he will no longer be on this earth, breathing the same air as me, fills me with a feeling I can't describe. I am finally looking forward to my future. Kyro may have stolen a huge part of my past, but he cannot steal anything else from me anymore and I only have one person to truly thank for that. Hell. I owe him fucking everything and I will give him everything.

"I think it might be best you stay here, my little dolly. I'll have someone here with you."

My gut drops and I whirl around as he places his eyepatch over his eye. "No," I say sternly, "Hell, I need to be there."

Lifting his hood over his head, he looks at me and we both stand in a silent stare off until he speaks, "Let me handle it, Noir."

He begins to walk away, and I become irritated. "How many times do I need to show you that I am not some innocent little dolly, Hell." I grit out.

He stops, his tattooed hand on the door handle and I continue, "The shit you've seen me do. How I've handled you, Oddity, and everything else this whole fucking time and you think what? That I am going to crumble to the sight of my abuser?"

He lowers he head, "It's not that, pretty girl."

"Then what the fuck is it?"

He finally turns to face me, "This could go so many fucking ways and I don't want a single hair on your head hurt."

I stand straighter, "And I am ready for anything. Please just trust me."

I can see the reluctance on his face, he is worried about losing me, but I need this. I need to fucking end this with him.

"For me, just put how you feel aside and look at it from my point of view, wouldn't you want to see your abuser die?"

He just stares at me in a way that I've never seen before, and I am confused by it. "Wait…" I step forward and he looks away, "Just don't, Noir." His eyes flash to mine as he shakes his head once.

I suck in a sharp breath, reality hitting me. "Why didn't you tell me."

"Because it's fucking irrelevant."

"Irrelevant?" I pull my head back with confusion. "Do you think what I went through is irrelevant then?"

"Of course not!" he snaps back sharply.

I stay silent just staring at him through wide eyes, hardly believing this.

"It was totally different circumstances; we all went through it and I'm over it."

He walks toward me and when he stops, I have to tilt my head back to look up at his tall frame.

"I'm not saying it's not fucking wrong, Dolly. I am not saying that what you went through doesn't matter either," he grips my chin, lowering his lips to mine. "I dealt with it differently, I let my anger out over the years. One day, you will hopefully get there too."

I scan his features, "Did you ever kill them?" I whisper.

He shakes his head once, "I don't know who the fuck they were, no one does. It was years ago when I was young. It's happened to most of us in this system."

My face scrunches up, "What?"

"Noir, leave it."

"Leave it?" I repeat, searching his eyes.

He stands upright, releasing my chin. "This is reality, pretty girl. You should understand that."

"It doesn't make it fucking right!" I yell, my voice trembling.

He lowers himself to my eye level. "I know," he asserts firmly.

I take a deep breath, trying to steady myself, feeling his gaze pierce through me as he assesses my reaction.

"You're right," he continues. "I would want revenge, but I don't have that fucking option. I never have."

He nods toward the door. "Stay in the back of the truck at all times."

My eyes soften, the anger slowly ebbing away. "Thank you."

He leans in, pressing a firm, reassuring kiss to my lips before turning and walking out the door. I stand there, staring blankly for a second, the weight of his confession baring down on me, then I follow behind him.

HOLLOW HELLION

After Hell rounds up the Dark Night crew, they all mount their bikes or climb into their vehicles. Hell gives me a kiss on the head, before seating me in the back of a blacked-out truck. With only the driver for company, I watch through the tinted windows as we speed toward the location where Kyro will be. I fiddle with my hands in my lap, nerves, anticipation, and a strange excitement all bubble within me.

The truck rumbles along a dark, empty road and I peer through the windows, catching glimpses of Hell on his bike behind us, flanked by other Dark Night members. Facing forward, I notice the headlights of other cars, and a sense of unease settles in my gut. Suddenly, the crack of gunshots shatters through the night. I whip my head around to see more cars closing in from behind, clearly not from Oddity.

"Fuck, has he been tipped off?" I mutter, my heart racing.

Everything happens so fast and the car I am in slows down as Kyro's men attempt to block the path ahead. Soul and Wrath speed past us, heading straight for the blockade. My driver, drenched in sweat and wide-eyed, suddenly presses the accelerator to the floor. A gunshot rings out, exploding the back window. I scream, ducking as glass rains down around me. The driver panics, keeping his foot on the gas, swerving wildly around the cars in front.

"What the fuck are you doing?" I yell.

He ignores me, his focus solely on the road ahead. We speed past the roadblock, and I turn my head swiftly to see Hell trying to gain on us, but he is still too far behind. The truck's tires screech, and I hold on for dear life.

"Slow the fuck down!" I demand.

Every jolt and swerve sends my heart pounding against my ribs. I catch a glimpse of Hell in the side mirror, but my relief is short-lived as a car I don't recognize matches his speed beside him, its windows rolling down. Hell unleashes a round of bullets, his aim steady until one strikes his shoulder and his bike swerves violently.

"NO!" I scream, panic clawing at my throat.

The enemy car tries to knock Hell off his bike and as soon as Hell slows down slightly, they seize the opportunity, speeding ahead and heading straight for my truck. My eyes widen as they close the distance until they hit the rear. The impact is brutal, sending our truck into a dizzying whirl until we flip over and over again, my screams drowned out with the sounds of shattering glass and screeching metal. The world spins in a chaotic blur when I hit my head on something hard, drifting in and out of consciousness.

Before I can gather my senses, rough hands drag me from the wreckage and my body aches all over as I'm lifted and thrown over a shoulder. Realizing it's not Hell carrying me, I start to fight back, thrashing and kicking.

"Let me go, motherfucker!"

I lift my head and through a haze, I hear the roar of The Hollow's bikes growing louder, the sound slicing through the madness.

"Hell!" I scream as I'm tossed into the back of another car, my body hitting the seat hard.

The car door slams shut, and I scramble to the window, pressing my face against the glass, trying to tug the handle frantically, but it's locked. The enemy car lurches forward, speeding away from the wreckage and my heart races as I pound on the window.

The driver glances back at me with a sneer, and I feel a surge of fury. I start looking around frantically until an idea enters my mind, an idea that might get me killed, but an idea, nonetheless. I unbuckle the belt on my jeans, ripping it from the loops, and without hesitation,

I wrap it around the guy's throat before pulling down, attempting to strangle the life out of him. I use all my body weight to pull as hard as I can, feeling the car swerve violently. He reaches back, grabbing and ripping out chunks of my hair in a desperate attempt to stop me, but I don't relent, focusing all my strength on the belt.

When his movements slow down, his grip weakening, the car speeds up uncontrollably, until suddenly, there's another massive crash, and I smash into the back of his seat, my entire body crunching from the force. I groan, letting go of the belt, my eyes closing as I struggle to catch my breath.

The sharp smell of gasoline fills the air, and I feel an intense heat from a nearby fire. Panic surges through me, but before I can react, the window beside me shatters. I flinch, covering my face as shards of glass cover me. Strong arms reach inside, grabbing hold of me and pulling me out of the window. I stand on wobbly legs, an arm wrapped around the bottom of my back, until Hell grabs my face, his eyes intense and filled with concern. "Dolly?"

When I hear his voice, my eyes open, and I see his face, although in double form. I take a moment to gather my focus, blinking rapidly until my vision clears and when I am ready, I give a small nod, pressing my brow against his strong chest.

He strokes the back of my hair. "You good to get on my bike with me? I know where he is."

I nod a few times before he walks me to his bike and lifts me onto the back. As we ride, I take the opportunity to snuggle into his back, letting the steady rumble of the engine help me regain my bearings. Soon enough, my vision straightens out and we're entering a woodland area, Soul, and Wrath on their bikes behind us.

I hear commotion up ahead and peek over Hell's shoulder to see the Dark Night crew attacking a moving car with all kinds of weapons as they surround it. Hell picks up speed, his rage spilling out of him. As soon as he is close enough, he whips out his knife, lifting it and swings his arm, the blade embedding into the car's back wheel.

The car swerves out of control on the muddy ground and we all slow down, watching as it slams into a tree with a huge crash. Hell doesn't waste a second, and we both dismount swiftly.

Dark Night members close in on the car, their weapons drawn, ready for whatever comes next. Hell grabs my hand as we move together towards the wreckage and when I can see movement inside the car, my pulse quickens.

Hell reaches the car first, yanking the door open. Inside, Kyro is bloodied and dazed, his driver slumped dead beside him. Kyro suddenly draws his gun, but Wrath is faster, shooting from behind us and taking Kyro's fingers off. He lets out a loud roar of pain followed by a whimper, dropping the gun.

I watch with wide eyes as the crew drags him out of the car. Hell keeps a tight hold on my hand, leading me around to where Kyro has been dumped on the ground. As soon as he comes into view, Hell releases me and storms toward him, fury seeping from every pore. He mounts Kyro's chest and unleashes blow after blow to his face, each punch more powerful than the last, letting all of his anger out. I watch, stiff and unmoving, as Kyro's face is bloodied and caved in until he is unrecognizable.

When Hell is finished, he looks back at me, breathing heavily. He gestures for me to step forward and slowly, I move toward him, each step heavy. I slip my hand into his and stand over Kyro, whose eyes meet mine with a hollow, yet almost desperate gaze.

"I always told you; you'd get what you deserve, Kyro," I say emotionlessly.

Before he can even attempt to respond, Hell shoves his thumbs into Kyro's eyes. I tense as he pushes inward, Kyro's shriek filling the forest around us.

"That's the last time you ever look at her, you cunt." Hell grits out.

The sound Kyro makes is unlike anything I've heard before, but it gives me immense satisfaction. He's in agony, and it's being delivered by the man who drives me crazy. Gore squirts everywhere, gushing from his eyes, and Hell's face is a picture of revenge and hatred.

When Hell pulls his thumbs out of Kyro's almost empty eye sockets, blood trails down Kyro's face and Soul steps forward handing Hell a machete. I swallow hard, my throat dry, as Hell grips the handle tightly, his knuckles white.

Hell grabs Kyro's sweaty, bloodied hair tightly, then lifts the machete, the blade gleaming in the light before delivering a hack to the side of his neck. Each strike makes my body tense, but I keep my eyes glued on the action, wanting to see every second of his death because he deserves it. He starts to gurgle on his own blood, his body convulsing until Hell drops the machete halfway through, leaving him suffering and suffocating.

He stands, taking my hand and pulling me behind Kyro's almost lifeless body and as stands behind me, his breath is hot against my ear. "Shove your fingers into his fucking eye sockets and rip his ugly head off his shoulders," he murmurs chillingly.

Without hesitation, I bend over, sticking my fingers in Kyro's sockets, the warmth of his blood coating them. I tuck them beneath the bone to get a good grip, and I start to pull with all my strength, each tug ripping more of the muscles in his throat. Hell leans over, his hands finding mine, and he assists me. With some powerful pulling, his head finally comes completely off, sending me and Hell falling onto our asses into the mud.

As Kyro's head rolls onto the floor, his dead features face me, and I collapse against Hell's chest, the weight of it all taking it out of me. In a blur, tears stream down my cheeks, the faint noise of the Dark Night members cheering in triumph over the brutal murder. Soul and

Wrath suddenly pass us, kicking Kyro's head around like a fucking soccer ball, Soul chuckling like a menace.

Hell wraps his big arms around me, placing a kiss on my cheek. "It's fucking over, my pretty girl," he whispers into my ear. His deep voice is soothing in the mayhem around us, and the adrenaline begins to fade, replaced by a strange merge of relief and exhaustion. *It's finally over. I am finally free of him.*

CHAPTER THIRTY-NINE

It's been a week since we killed Kyro, and Hell and I are walking through the bustling carnival, playing games, and spending the night together with everyone. With his arm around my shoulders, I slip my hand into his and tilt my head back. He glances down at me as I smile widely, and he grins ever so slightly before bringing his mouth to mine. "It's good to see you smiling, my pretty girl," he murmurs, his voice a low rumble.

He gives me a firm kiss and as we part, I lift my head, looking forward at the bustling crowd as we walk through, everyone moving out of our way. The vibrant lights and sounds of the carnival surround us, creating a surreal atmosphere that sets my soul alive.

Suddenly, I notice someone in the far distance, and I come to an abrupt stop, causing Hell to do the same. My wide eyes stay fixed on her, her back to me and I take in her dark hair cascading down her back. I feel Hell's hand slip under my blonde locks, gently grabbing the nape of my neck.

He lowers his mouth to my ear as he dips down from behind. "You're not as insane as I thought you were, Dolly," he whispers.

My eyes water, my pulse pounding, and when she turns around to face me fully, my breath hitches. Her blue eyes find mine instantly, and the world seems to stop.

"Are you seeing what I'm seeing, Hell?" I ask, my voice trembling, wondering if I am losing my sanity again.

"I do," he finally answers. "I found her in one of his properties in another city." He turns his head, gazing at my side-profile. "Arabella isn't a figure of your imagination after all. I shouldn't have fucking doubted you."

A sob escapes my lips, and he releases me as I rush forward, eager to get to her. I become frantic, pushing people out of my way, and as soon as I am close enough, I crash into her, wrapping my arms around her neck. She hugs me back just as tightly as I weep. I stroke the back of her soft black hair, my voice breaking. "I'm so sorry, Ara," I whisper.

She pulls back, cupping my cheeks, her icy eyes searching mine, a reflection of my own. "Don't apologize. You've done nothing wrong."

I take in every feature of her face now that she is close, noticing how much she looks like me in certain ways. I place my hand on her cheek, my fingers trembling.

"What the fuck happened?" I sniffle, my voice choked with emotion.

Arabella's eyes soften, and she takes a deep breath. "It's a long story, but I'm here now. We're together, and that's all that matters."

I nod, tears falling down my cheeks. "I thought I lost you forever. I even started to think you weren't real and I was imagining things."

She smiles softly before wrapping her arm around my shoulders, guiding me to a bench nearby. I throw a glance at Hell, who is standing beside Soul and Wrath in the distance, and he gives me a wink before looking away.

When we sit down, we face one another. "When we fled, we split, but I was caught and taken somewhere else," she explains, and my eyes close, guilt gnawing at me before I dip my head.

"Don't worry, Harley." She assures me.

"I shouldn't have left you."

"Why? You deserved freedom. I had to listen every fucking day for a year to what those monsters were doing to you. I hated it and was determined to get you out of there."

"Did he hurt you?" I ask softly.

She shrugs her shoulders before lowering her eyes. "Nothing he wouldn't usually do. He roughed me up a bit, but it wasn't like what he was doing to you."

I give a small nod in response. "Did he ever…"

She shakes her head. "No. I don't understand why I was there, in all honesty. Maybe to give you some false hope? He was fucked in the head."

I inhale deeply. "Well, he's dead now."

She smiles gently before looking over at Hell in the distance, who is watching us both. "I know, your boyfriend told me."

"He's so much more than a boyfriend, he's my fucking everything" I admit in a daze as mine and Hell's gazes stay locked.

"It's good to see you so happy, Harley."

I break eye contact with Hell and look at her. "Why didn't I ever know about you? I didn't really know my dad before he died, but my mom never mentioned you."

"I was placed in foster care the moment I was born. Kyro found me living in a shelter when I was twenty-one and took me," she explains.

My brows pinch. "You're younger than me?"

"Don't you remember we had this conversation through the wall? I'm only eleven months younger," she says with her head tilted to the side.

I shake my head slowly. "I don't remember much in the last two years of me being there. Everything was becoming a blur."

She nods in understanding, and I ask her something that I have always wanted to know. "Who killed Kai?"

Her eyes fix on mine as she answers truthfully. "After I freed my chain, I came for you. I got you out of there, but you were extremely weak. He caught us trying to sneak out and he hit me. That's when you..." She trails off before continuing. " But I suppose we both went a bit too far with the mutilation."

I take a sharp breath, knowing my sister is somehow as messed up in the head as I am, and we have a lot to catch up on. She suddenly stands, and on instinct, I stand too, grabbing her wrist. She glances down at it before her gaze reaches mine.

"Please don't go," I plead, my voice desperate. "I can't lose you again. Stay here, with us."

She looks around the carnival. "Here?"

"I mean, it's a pretty fucked-up place once you live here, and it may not be normal to the outside world, but it's actually very comforting. The people here stick together and look after one another."

She swallows hard, appearing reluctant, but I continue to tempt her. "Even if it's just for a while, until I find you somewhere to settle if that's what you choose to do. I can't let my little sister go and live how she has her entire life again, can I? I now have responsibilities, and we're family. Actually, you're the only family I have left."

I raise a brow, and she grins. "Okay," she accepts quietly, and I feel my shoulders relax.

I link my arm around hers. "Let me introduce you to some people."

When we're standing by The Hollow's, who are playing a game at one of the amusement booths, they pause, looking back at us.

"This is my little sister, Arabella," I announce to Soul and Wrath.

Soul raises his chin to her in acknowledgment before continuing to play his game, but I notice her and Wrath locked in a silent staring battle, something dark and sinister sparking between them. My eyes flash to Hell, and he grins, sensing what I sense. *Fuck.*

CHAPTER FORTY

It's Dark Night, and I'm wrapped around Hell on the front of his bike. With my arm securely around his shoulder, he speeds through the carnival, dodging frantic people running for their lives. As we pass them, I laugh and shoot a nail gun with my free hand. Each hit sends a jolt of exhilaration through me, their blood-curdling screams filling the air, and I relish the sensation of it.

I rock my hips against Hellion's cock with no panties, smothering his neck with my tongue and lips, pulling a growl from him. He slows the bike down, one of his hands slipping to my ass where he rips a hole in my tights with frustration.

"Finger my pussy; let's see how many people I can kill until I am coming on your bike and hand," I murmur seductively in his ear, the thrill of horror making me feel aroused.

He suddenly hits the brakes, and I tighten my legs around him, so I don't fly off. He wastes no time, dipping his hand between my thighs. He snatches the front of my throat, pushing me back over the handlebars and tugs my corset down until one of my breasts pops free, neither of us giving a shit who could be watching.

The mayhem surrounding us seems to blur as he slides his fingers into my wet pussy and immediately starts to bang them into me. He grabs my tit, viciously attacking it with his mouth, and I try to glance around to make sure no one tries to kill us.

"Fuck yes, harder, baby," I moan out loudly, my back arching.

He continuously hits the right spot, my eyes rolling back, and I start to hyperventilate. The sensation of fear, arousal, and his delicious movements make me build rapidly.

When I open my heavy eyes, I notice more people, and I shoot with my head upside down, hitting them.

"One."

"Two.."

"Three…"

"Oh, fuck. Oh, fuck. Oh, fuckkkk…" I scream out, mingling with their shrieks of agony as they fall to the ground.

I lift my head in a daze, hearing someone approaching behind Hell. When I see a woman attempting a sneak attack, a surge of frustration courses through me. With rapid movements, I raise the nail gun and unleash a flurry of nails, plowing them into her face.

"FOUR!" I throw my head back over the handlebars, my pussy dripping all over his seat, and he yanks the other side of my corset down, moving on to destroy my other pierced nipple.

I lace my hand through his hair, taking a handful, and his fingers become ruthless. I let out an embarrassingly untamed moan that echoes through the carnival. I feel him grab the nail gun, and as he continues to plunge his fingers into me to push me over the edge, he lets off some rounds.

"Five, six, seven, eight, nine, ten, eleven…" he says rapidly with each shot.

The chaos around us intensifies, the sounds of screams and weapons being unleashed blend into a symphony of destruction. My climax crashes over me, waves of pleasure merging with the adrenaline coursing through my veins. Hell's fingers drive deeper and deeper until I'm a quivering mess.

As soon as I am finished, he rips his fingers out of me, grabbing my throat and forcing me to sit up. In my orgasmic state, I try to focus on his swirling eyes, dark with desire and intensity.

"Now run, my slutty Dolly. Run as fast as you can, because when I get my hands on you, I won't stop screwing every hole you have," he growls his menacing rhyme.

I bite my bottom lip, the thrill of his words sending a shiver down my spine. Hopping off the bike, I feel his gaze burning into me, watching my every move. I take off running, my heart pounding with a mix of fear and excitement. I glance back, a big smile on my face, and hear him rev his engine, darkness stirring in his spiral eyes before speeding toward me.

EPILOGUE

It's nighttime, and a group of us are sitting around a fire in the trailer park. The evening sky sparkles with fireworks over Oddity, glittering bursts illuminating the atmosphere. I rest against Hell's chest, nestled between his legs on the grass, feeling his warmth seep into me. Glancing down, I notice he has something in his hand. He lifts it, revealing a silver piece of jewelry with a charm that glints in the light.

Gently, he pulls my leg upward, and I lift it, draping it across my thigh. He pushes my skinny jeans up and starts to wrap the jewelry around my ankle.

"What's this, Hell?" I ask, my tone tinged with confusion.

"It's a sign of freedom," he replies.

I glance up at him, staring at his painted side-profile in awe. When he finishes, I look down at the delicate piece. He places the small charm on his fingertip—a silver dove with a black diamond set in it and I notice he has placed it on my scarred ankle.

"This is the only chain that will ever be on your fucking ankle again, Dolly. Freedom; the freedom you have always deserved and will always have here, with me." he declares.

My eyes well up as I touch the charm, feeling the importance of its meaning, my soul filling with his dark form of love. I turn my head, and he looks down at me. I take in his painted features, his healed eye, then press my lips to his.

"Thank you, I love it," I whisper, my tone thick with emotion.

He pulls me closer, placing a tender kiss on my head as we continue to watch the fireworks. My eyes wander around the group, each person engaged with someone else, until they land on M, who is also watching the spectacle, chain-free. We trained him together and he now lives amongst the rest of us, just as I knew he could with some understanding and care. My eye's move to Arabella, Blush, and everyone else here.

I reflect on everything that has happened since I arrived here, how far I've come with Hell by my side. We've found something in each other that's rare to find. When I first stepped into Oddity, I never thought it would become a home. And when I met Hell, I didn't think it would turn into love. Yet here I am—happy, content, free and I am slowly getting myself off the meds. Embracing who I am in a place where insanity is accepted.

I snuggle deeper into Hell's arms, feeling his heartbeat against my back. The fireworks light up the night, mirroring the spark within me. This place, these people, and especially Hell, have changed everything. I never imagined finding peace in madness, but I have. Right here, at Oddity Carnival & Cirque.

THE END OF HOLLOW HELLION

Acknowledgements

I just want to take this opportunity to thank my little family for their continuous support and love. My readers for keeping faith in me as your author. And of course my friend and PA, Fiona Mohan for continuously putting up with my crazy ass.

Love you all! – Jodie

Hollow Wrath and Hollow Soul's books will be released in 2025!

Made in the USA
Monee, IL
07 December 2024

72889331R00223